TOR BOOKS BY CLAIRE DELACROIX

Fallen
Guardian
Rebel

Rebel

CLAIRE DELACROIX

TOR®
paranormal romance

A TOM DOHERTY ASSOCIATES BOOK
NEW YORK

This is a work of fiction. All of the characters, organizations, and events
portrayed in this novel are either products of the author's imagination or
are used fictitiously.

REBEL

Copyright © 2010 by Claire Delacroix, Inc.

All rights reserved.

A Tor Book
Published by Tom Doherty Associates, LLC
175 Fifth Avenue
New York, NY 10010

www.tor-forge.com

Tor® is a registered trademark of Tom Doherty Associates, LLC.

ISBN 978-0-7653-5951-3

First Edition: September 2010

Printed in the United States of America

0 9 8 7 6 5 4 3 2 1

For Kon, as always

PROLOGUE

New Gotham—March 15, 2100

"We were tricked." The former angel Armaros folded his arms across his chest and leaned against the wall, not troubling to hide his irritation from his two companions.

His oldest friend, now known as Baruch Harding, barely smiled in acknowledgement of his complaint, so focused was he on his work.

That, at least, hadn't changed.

"Tricked?" Tupperman asked quietly, his expression revealing his doubts. Although Armand had not known their earthly contact long, he already found the mortal man irritating. Tupperman seemed smug to him, confident in some knowledge he would not share.

That Tupperman was at ease in this sphere, with its dirt and deception, was no endorsement of his character. For Armand, there was nothing of merit in the physical realm. He heartily regretted the choice to sacrifice his wings—which he had only made because he had been deceived was like salt in the wound.

He didn't care who knew it.

The three were in a hidden room adjacent to Tupperman's living unit, secreted from the watchful eyes of the Republic as the former angels planned the fulfillment of their mission.

"It's a sin to kill," Armand said, focusing on just one element of his displeasure. "There has to be another way."

"Don't you trust in the divine plan?" Tupperman challenged. "Don't you believe in the greater good?"

Armand stepped away from the wall to challenge the mortal. "Have you forgotten that murder is wicked?"

"Is it wrong to kill someone who is evil himself?" Tupperman retorted. "What about the greater good? The safety of others?"

"Justifications and rationalizations!" Armand paced the width of the hidden room, annoyed again by its close confines. Baruch worked steadily at the desktop in the middle of the space, but Armand knew he had to be listening. "It is not the right of any of us to choose the duration of a life. That decision lies in the hands of the divine alone."

"And who do you think dictated your quest?" Tupperman asked.

Armand glared at the man. "I don't know. I didn't hear the order being given. Neither, I suspect, did you." He arched a brow. "Don't tell me that you hear the secret word of God yourself."

Tupperman's lips tightened. "Look," he began.

"Fulfilling the mission is our only way back," Baruch interrupted softly. "That's the simple truth. Our wings are forfeit forever if we don't complete the assignment."

"Not forever," Tupperman corrected. "You're mortal now."

They could die in this hell.

Armand's heart clenched at the prospect. He paced, well aware that Tupperman watched him closely. Armand had a suspicion that this ready justification of wickedness might be the root of all earthly troubles. He couldn't say as much before their host and supposed ally, Tupperman, though.

So he paced and he seethed.

The only souvenirs of Armand's celestial existence were the two diagonal scars upon his back. The loss of his wings was key to his transformation to the mortal man known as Armand McKinley.

Actually, his scars weren't the only memento—he had memories of what he had been, memories that made the extent of his sacrifice clear, memories that made him impatient to return to that existence.

He had been prepared for the pain, expected the sudden burden of flesh. Armand hadn't realized he'd lose his intellectual connection to the angels, to the flow of thought in the universe.

But the angelic surgeon's finger had severed that connection as surely as it cut the wings from Armand's back. Had Armand known this price, he might never have volunteered.

He hated the solitude.

The silence.

If he'd known the truth, he would *not* have volunteered.

But what was done was done. Now he and Baruch were mortal men, devoid of their angelic capabilities, unable to even look upon the brilliance of angelic splendor. Now they were burdened with flesh, and desire, and tempted by pleasure. And the only way back to what they had known, to what they both yearned to recover, was the successful completion of their mission.

To kill Maximilian Blackstone, front-running candidate for the presidency of the Republic.

And this mortal, this Tupperman with his slippery moral code, was their aide.

Tupperman worked for the New Gotham Police, and secretly guided the efforts of some number of fallen angels. He wore the black pseudoskin favored by law enforcement officials, a heavy-gauge layer of polymer embedded with lead that protected the Republic's finest from radiation poisoning. It also showed every muscle to advantage on a physique so finely honed as Tupperman's. His hair was shaved to nothing, his expression impassive, his eyes bright with intelligence.

Armand particularly disliked that he couldn't read Tupperman's thoughts. Once Armand had been confident in the motivation of others. Now that power was gone, gone with his wings, and its lack left him uncertain.

Filled with unfamiliar doubts.

Would Tupperman betray them? That would add insult to injury. Armand watched Baruch work and was irritated that he couldn't share his friend's thoughts anymore either.

"You knew you would take flesh and become mortal," Tupperman said finally.

"But it was never made clear how compromised our abilities would be," Armand replied.

Tupperman shook his head. "You must have guessed. You spent nearly a year in the Nouveau Mont Royal Circus, able to observe mortal men. You had to know that they lacked your powers."

"But I could hear their thoughts then," Armand complained. He gestured to Baruch, his dark head bent over the desktop. "I could share Baruch's every observation. I had no idea that power would be lost to us. We should have been told!"

Tupperman's smile broadened. "The angels reserve the right to explain only so much as suits them."

"It's not right," Armand growled. That angels should be deceptive in promoting their own agenda was a dangerous notion.

Baruch spoke softly. "But it explains so much, doesn't it?"

Armand's heart sank. Baruch had come to the same conclusion. Creation was slipping into immorality, or had lost its compass, and they two would be caught up in its course. He stared at Tupperman, his every conviction about goodness in the celestial realm drawn into question. Tupperman held his gaze, evidently at ease with the same conclusions.

It was wrong.

Unless the assassination of Blackstone would make that much of a difference. Armand had to hope.

"Perhaps there are other compensations," Baruch interrupted, his tone playful. Even without their old bond, he clearly sensed Armand's dark mood. "What of that pair of women last night in the pleasure fringe?"

Armand made a dismissive gesture. Unlike his partner, he wasn't enamored of the pleasures of the flesh. They were a novel experience for one who had been made only of light and thought, but Armand had wearied quickly of the physical possibilities. He would readily trade sensation for knowledge.

"Distractions," he said. "There has to be more than physical pleasure to justify this existence."

Tupperman snorted, evidence that he had never been one of them. Any former angel would understand what Armand meant. Any fallen angel would understand that Armand's complaint was about more than physical limitations.

"Always the blunt one," Baruch teased. "Perhaps the

problem is simply that you're incapable of hiding your thoughts from anyone."

"I will not kill."

"Then you will be trapped in the realm you so despise," Tupperman concluded. "Your choice."

Armand heaved a sigh and tried to have faith. "We were deceived," he murmured, hoping there was a point to it.

"Maybe not," Baruch said, then gestured to the display. "There. It's done." He spoke with such satisfaction that both Tupperman and Armand leaned close.

Baruch had cast a horoscope to choose the most auspicious day for their task. His decision to consult the stars to aid in their strategy was a characteristic choice, for as the angel Baraqiel he had once taught men how to interpret the stars above. It was his conviction that the universe reflected the truth of divine will.

"What does it mean?" Tupperman asked.

Armand resented that he knew no more than this wretched mortal.

Baruch touched the desktop with his long fingertips, thoughtfully assembling the details he needed. He was handsome, Armand's oldest friend, tall and slender with dark hair and dark eyes. A mere month in this realm had proven that he could beckon a woman with the merest glance. Baruch was intent upon exploring all of the possibilities of sensation, even as Armand was impatient to be done and gone.

Baruch had taken great interest in clothing and texture, and had persuaded Armand to humor him in also dressing as a man of advantage. On this night, Baruch wore his favorite waistcoat of crimson velvet, cut to show his physique to advantage, a froth of ivory lace at his wrists and neck. He and Armand both wore the dark breeches favored by the fashionable gentlemen, and tall dark faux-leather boots. Armand's jacket, also Baruch's choice, was similar to that of his friend but cut of velvet of so dark an emerald green that it was nearly black.

Baruch said it highlighted Armand's eyes.

Armand didn't care.

"It must be September eighteenth." Baruch's eyes were lit with a familiar joy, the one he found in doing what he did so well.

"Why?" Tupperman demanded. "It's so late. Too late."

"No," Baruch argued. "It's the only date that will do."

"Why?" Armand leaned closer. The pair of charts glittered gold on the display, all lines and curves and planetary symbols. They were beautiful, medieval in their elegance, but incomprehensible to Armand. Even knowing the symbols and their rough meanings, he could never interpret transits and nuances as Baruch could.

"You see here, the second of November?" Baruch said and both men nodded.

"Election Day," Armand said.

"There's a new moon, a sign of a fresh start."

"But Van Buren is the incumbent," Tupperman argued. "A fresh start would mean that he won't win, that Blackstone must win in order for there to be a change." He rubbed his chin. "On the other hand, Van Buren's popularity rankings have taken a nosedive."

Baruch smiled with familiar confidence. "No. It means that someone other than Van Buren will win."

Tupperman blinked. "But there are only two candidates, Van Buren and Blackstone. If Van Buren loses, Blackstone wins."

Baruch shook his head. "Not necessarily."

"Unless Blackstone is unable to complete his campaign," Armand said, recalling their mission. "A dead man can't win the presidency."

"Then his running mate could win instead," Tupperman mused, frowning with impatience. "But what do we really know of Thomas O'Donohue? He might be no better a choice. If nothing else, Blackstone chose him. That's no endorsement!"

"This chart shows the confluence of variables." Baruch's eyes gleamed as he leaned over the desktop, touching the display with his fingertips to indicate points of reference. Each point he touched, each planetary symbol, was magnified momentarily as he referred to it. "On September eighteenth, we have a conjunction of Saturn and Jupiter in Libra. It happens roughly every twenty years and is a sign of social, economic, and/or political change. Jupiter rules kings and presidents, leaders of men. Saturn indicates a change, perhaps one gained in chaos. Unpredictability. In summary, there's a cusp here, when matters could go either way."

"Meaning?" Tupperman prompted.

Baruch leaned back. "Either the culmination of everything that has gone before or its destruction." He smiled. "That's all."

"A new era or the Apocalypse," Armand guessed, his mouth dry. The stakes were higher than he'd anticipated. Could Blackstone's survival truly make earthly life that much worse?

Tupperman inhaled sharply. "*If* the chart is true."

Armand straightened, his faith in Baruch's abilities complete.

Baruch eyed their contact, his opinion of that man's doubt clear. "Have you heard of Tecumseh's Curse?"

Tupperman leaned one hip on the desktop and folded his arms across his chest. "That every twenty years a president of the Republic will die in office? Superstition! There's no evidence that Tecumseh ever made such a curse."

Baruch smiled. "Tecumseh died in 1813. Remember what I said about this conjunction occurring every twenty years?" He touched a sidebar and a list of presidents of the Republic was displayed. "It occurred during William Henry Harrison's term as president—he died in office of pneumonia in 1841. The second conjunction occurred during Lincoln's term and he was assassinated. The third conjunction occurred while Garfield was president—he, too, was assassinated. The fourth during McKinley's presidency—"

"And he was assassinated," Armand guessed, eying the list.

"The fifth occurred while Harding was president, and he died in office. The sixth during Roosevelt's term as president."

"And he died in office," Tupperman said with dissatisfaction. "The seventh?"

"Kennedy," Baruch said. "The eighth was in Reagan's term and he was shot."

"But not killed," Tupperman noted.

Baruch nodded. "That one was a triple conjunction, as well. That was probably the deciding variable." Again, Armand had the sense that his friend was omitting a detail.

"The ninth incident?" Tupperman prompted.

"2040," Baruch said.

"Not sooner?" Tupperman arched a brow.

"Bush got lucky in 2000, particularly as it was in an

earth sign that time." Baruch tapped the display. "In December 2020, the president had a seizure, but didn't die. He had already lost the election anyway, so it's less important in a way."

"Two curse breakers?" Armand asked.

Baruch shook his head. "Lopez wasn't so lucky in 2040."

Tupperman frowned. "He was shot but survived, at least until he had a heart attack two weeks later."

Armand noted two more presidents who did not finish their terms on Baruch's list, then considered his friend's expectant manner. "So?"

"So, Saturday September 18, 2100." Baruch's satisfaction was clear as he tapped the display. "It's the best possible time to undertake our mission, the moment most auspicious for success. It's not only the date of the full conjunction but there's a full moon that day. Jupiter in Libra favors justice. Saturn in Libra is exalted, which means in its most powerful position—it too favors justice and clear thinking. Mercury and Mars are close to the conjunction, too. A potent date."

Armand studied the chart, wishing he could understand it better. Despite his own uncertainties, Baruch's conviction was infectious. He dared to hope they might succeed and regain all they'd lost.

Tupperman frowned at the display. "Let's see where Blackstone will be on that date." He tapped the desktop, pulling up the itinerary for Maximilian Blackstone's campaign stops, then caught his breath. For once, his thoughts were easily read. "You can't go there." He straightened and stepped back. "It would be insane. We need an alternative date."

"Where?" Baruch asked.

"Blackstone will be at the opening reception of the annual meeting of the Society of Nuclear Darwinists," Armand read. "At the Institute for Radiation Studies in Chicago."

Baruch met his gaze for a heartbeat, then looked away.

Armand wondered what his old friend was hiding from him, then dismissed the thought. This sphere was even making him suspicious of those he knew to trust.

"The most treacherous place for you to be," Tupperman said, his tone stern. "I forbid you to do this. Choose another date."

"But it's perfect," Baruch said, leaning back in his seat as he tapped his chin with one finger. He smiled with a confidence that Armand trusted, even though he didn't fully understand the reasons for it. "Isn't he promoting a plan to eliminate the Society?"

"He won't be among friends," Armand said, his excitement rising as he felt a vestige of that old intellectual connection with his friend.

"Every person in the hall will be a suspect," Baruch agreed.

"And we'll easily be able to escape in the confusion of such a crowd." Armand frowned. "Except . . ."

Baruch grinned. "Except that you won't kill. Trust me to be partnered with a rebel angel."

"You know the commandments as well as I do."

"Maybe that's why we're a team," Baruch said lightly, lifting his hand to silence Armand. "Fair enough, old friend. Trust me. It will all come right."

Armand understood that Baruch *did* know something more.

And that made all the difference. His faith multiplied in

that instant. Baruch's smile warmed, his gaze flicking quickly to Tupperman and back. Even without their old connection, Armand understood his implication.

"I'll do the deed," Baruch said. "We've worked together too long to split now, Armaros." That he used Armand's old name was as reassuring as his steady gaze. "I cannot imagine eternity without your friendship and this, to me, is a small price to pay."

"Then we will succeed." The pair smiled at each other.

"No!" Tupperman interrupted, his agitation clear. "No! It's not that simple. You can't go to the Society! If they see your scars, you'll be harvested and, at best, dissected for study. It's absolute madness . . ."

"They'll never expect it," Armand said.

"Right into the heart of darkness," Baruch agreed. "Perfect."

"No!" Tupperman said. "Besides, Blackstone will be surrounded by bodyguards . . ."

"He always mingles with the electorate after a speech," Baruch said, his fingers tapping busily on the desktop. In seconds, he had the layout of Convocation Hall displayed, all its exits and entrances and passageways.

Armand indicated the stage. "He'll come forward to meet them here, just as he did last night in New Seattle."

"I'll come from one side of the stage and you from the other," Baruch agreed. "Look at how close this door is to the right of the stage."

"Divine providence?" Armand suggested and Baruch laughed.

"Must be!"

Tupperman sputtered outrage but the pair ignored him.

"How will you do it?" Armand asked.

Baruch drummed his fingers on the desktop. "A knife will be the easiest to smuggle in. I'll stab him, then we'll flee together for the door . . ."

"No!" Tupperman argued. "This is reckless. What if you're caught? There won't be time for anyone to intervene."

"Maybe we should invite Lilia to go with us," Baruch suggested, then rolled his eyes in appreciation.

Armand chuckled with his friend. Lilia Desjardins, the shade hunter who had purportedly discovered them, had fought hard to keep them from being shipped to the Institute for study. She had even been expelled from the Society for her choice.

"You're not taking this risk seriously!" Tupperman complained, but Armand met his gaze steadily.

"You don't understand," he said, his tone both soft and forceful. He knew his eyes were shining with conviction. "As soon as the deed is done, the angels will collect us. We will regain our wings and be returned to the celestial sphere. No mortal man can intervene then."

"But—"

"At this point," Armand continued, "we have very little left to lose."

Tupperman's lips tightened and he averted his gaze. "Even if you are right, how are you going to get into the Institute? That hall will be secured for weeks in advance and only members of the Society will be allowed admission."

"Oh, that's the easiest part of all," Armand said, liking that he was thinking more quickly than their contact. He gestured to a small notice on the desktop display of the reception. "The Institute for Nuclear Studies is accepting applications for new students. We'll enroll in the program to become Nuclear Darwinists."

"What?" Tupperman said in shock.

Baruch laughed, his eyes dancing at the cleverness of Armand's plan. "We'll be of them, and guaranteed seats for the reception."

"Above suspicion even," Armand agreed.

"Perfect!" Baruch said with a laugh.

"Not perfect—insane!" Tupperman corrected. "You *are* crazy."

"No," Armand said, sobering as he held the mortal man's gaze. "We are *motivated*. By Election Day, we'll be long gone." He put his hand on Baruch's shoulder, grateful that his old friend had found a solution. "Together."

"Only if all goes well," Tupperman argued. "And chances of that are diminished, because I'll have to remove a lot of the software on your palms." He looked between the pair with displeasure. "They'll do complete checks on applicants at registration, and any nonconformist applications will make you targets." He sighed and ran a hand over his shaved head. "Never mind the illegal ones."

"Does it matter?" Baruch asked.

Tupperman's lips tightened. "I don't like that you'll have fewer tools at your discretion, and I like even less that you'll be off my network. What if you need help?"

The former angels exchanged a glance and Armand knew they were in perfect agreement.

"We won't," Armand said with conviction.

"Remove the apps," Baruch said, extending his left hand with the installed electronic palm.

"We'll do this our way," Armand agreed, offering his as well.

"I think this is a bad idea," Tupperman growled. "It's against my better judgment." The two former angels smiled at him, serene in their conviction, until he pulled the probe from his desktop and inserted it into the port on Baruch's palm.

For the first time since their arrival, Armand was optimistic. He and Baruch were thinking as one once more, despite the loss of their powers.

It was a pale shadow of what they'd retrieve in mere months.

He couldn't wait.

from *The Republican Record*
February 24, 2100
download v. 1.4—archived

Angels Disappear ·

NOUVEAU MONT ROYAL—The most popular attraction at the Nouveau Mont Royal Circus, the angels Armaros and Baraqiel, appear to have vanished along with the other circus performers this past weekend. Although theories abound as to the location of the former occupants of all the circuses in the Republic, citizens are nearly unanimous in their conclusions about Armaros and Baraqiel.

"They've gone back to heaven," declared Suzie Cuthbertson of New D.C. "It's because of the Oracle," concurred her companion, who declined to name herself. "God's will has been done and the angels are leaving us to ourselves." Both women wore the red temporary tattoos on their foreheads, which mimic the mark of the angel's kiss on the brow of the newly appointed Oracle, Delilah. The Reverend Billie Joe Estevez referred to the disappearance of Armaros and Baraqiel in her vidcast sermon today, calling upon the faithful to "awaken the angel within," by which she insisted citizens can create a future in the Republic that is a finer echo of the heavenly ideal.

Armaros and Baraqiel first came to the attention of citizens throughout the Republic last year, when the assertion of shade hunter Lilia Desjardins that she had found genuine angels provoked a controversy within the Society of Nuclear Darwinists. Ms. Desjardins's refusal to surrender the two individuals to the Society, in order that their nature might be fully explored and verified at the labs run by the

Institute for Radiation Studies, subsequently led to a lawsuit initiated by the Society against both Ms. Desjardins and the Nouveau Mont Royal Circus. (It is a matter of protocol for shade hunters, who are all members of the Society of Nuclear Darwinists and graduates of the Institute for Radiation Studies, that all unusual specimens harvested will be surrendered to the Society for further study.) Ms. Desjardins's standing in the Society as a Nuclear Darwinist Third Degree was also revoked in October 2099 as a result of her actions. That suit is still progressing through the courts.

A member for the Society who requested anonymity suggested that there was nothing otherworldly about the disappearance of the two subjects and that Ms. Desjardins herself might be responsible for it, given her "wanton disregard for the law in the past."

Ms. Desjardins could not be reached for comment.

Associated links:

- <u>Angels Among Us?</u>—archive from April 6, 2099
- <u>Armaros and Baraqiel</u>—archive images from the Nouveau Mont Royal Circus
- <u>Vidcast of the Oracle's Appearance</u>—archive from February 19, 2100
- <u>Awaken the Angel Within</u>—today's vidcast by Reverend Billie Joe Estevez

* AN INVITATION *
to all members of the Society of Nuclear Darwinists
and all students enrolled in the Institute for
Radiation Studies
to attend the opening session of the
76th Annual Convention
of the Society of Nuclear Darwinists
to be held
Saturday September 18, 2100
8:00 P.M.
in Convocation Hall at the Institute for Radiation Studies

Please join past president Ernestine Sinclair and the Board of Governors of the Society of Nuclear Darwinists in welcoming Blake Patterson, newly elected president of the Society. This year's A.G.M. will focus upon the question of the Society's future role. Our new president will elaborate upon his vision for the direction of the Society.

Three special guests will be in attendance to contribute their perspectives to the evolving role of the Society and its mandate, including Maximilian Blackstone, candidate for president of the Republic and author of *A New Plan for the S.H.A.D.E.*, and Delilah, the Oracle of the Republic, who attends at our new president's express invitation. Dr. Paul Cosmopoulos will also present his perspective on options for the Institute's labs in these changing times.

Note that four important proxies will be voted upon by the membership at this year's conference and members are urged to inform themselves in advance at <u>AGM Proxies for 2100</u>.

The presentation will be followed by the serving of light refreshments.

• • •

R.S.V.P. <u>Sonja Anseldotter</u> before August 20, 2100.

I

Chicago—September 18, 2100

SOLITUDE WAS the key to success.

At least to the wraith Theodora.

Relying upon others always introduced the possibility of betrayal.

That there were others who relied upon her was a detail.

Perhaps that isolation was the reason for Theodora's success. She was reputed to be cold, even unfeeling, which was an accomplishment within the ranks of the wraiths, themselves notorious for their lack of emotion or ethics.

Wraiths lived outside of the system, frequenting the perimeters and the shadows of the Republic. Their identities were recorded in no databanks, and their actions invisible to the many eyes of the Republic. They were the lost souls of the world. They should not exist. Technically, they did not exist.

But they were everywhere, their numbers untallied.

Amongst themselves, the wraiths commented upon Theodora's clean motivation, her commitment to cred and cred alone. Highest bidder always claimed Theodora's services, and everything had a price. That made her reliable, more reliable even than most wraiths.

Which was how she had gotten this job.

Theodora waited in the best vantage point within the Convocation Hall at the Institute for Radiation Studies. The contract was for assassination, and the price was high.

Very high.

The target was none other than the recently revealed Oracle of the Republic. Theodora wasn't particularly interested in the buyer's motivation, only in the proof he supplied to the wraiths of his ability to pay.

The location Theodora had selected for the deed was perfect.

Even if it did terrify her. It was no small thing to enter any corner of the Institute for Radiation Studies without official authorization or documentation. It was said that no barrier in the Republic could stop a wraith, but the Society routinely—and secretly—sucked wraiths into its maw, never to release them from the confines of the affiliated Institute's research labs.

Theodora would never have risked it if the location hadn't been ideal and the reward so very rich.

But then, perhaps all the world was gambling with Fate. The Oracle herself took such a chance in accepting this invitation that her decision was the talk of the Republic. Theodora did not believe that there could be any goodwill between the Society and a former shade condemned by that Society's edicts, but perhaps she had become cynical. No one would be surprised if the Oracle's choice ended in disaster—and every soul in this hall would be a suspect. The image-snatching crews were here to document whatever happened.

But they'd get a surprise. The entire Republic would know immediately of Theodora's deed. The money would be paid—or collected—without delay.

Theodora had prepared with the thoroughness that was key to her success. She had investigated the hall while the Institute had believed it empty and locked. She had chosen her location and secreted her weapon inside, long before the security protocols had been initiated. She had chosen a narrow room above the mezzanine, once used for spotlights for the stage. Those lights had been replaced by brighter smaller lights mounted on the ceiling, and this abandoned space left for the mice. Theodora found the thick layer of dust in the room reassuring.

She had arrived very early the day before, long before the first janitors and stagehands came to prepare the stage. She had slipped into her targeted space as quietly as, well, a wraith. She had disguised her passage and settled down to wait in silence.

An eternity later, the hall began to fill with excited spectators. Theodora rose and moved to watch. She remained in the darkness, at one with the shadows, as she surveyed the auditorium.

She was not surprised that there were no shades in the audience. She hadn't expected any to willingly enter this place—and any who had tried would have been turned away by the Institute.

Shades only entered the Institute in shackles.

She could see some in the shadows, sedated and working in the employ of the Institute slaves.

Shades were those human children who had failed the Sub Human Atomic Deficiency Evaluation, abbreviated as S.H.A.D.E., which gave rise to the colloquial term of "shade." They were children who had been assessed as defective as a result of exposure to radiation, typically in utero, often mentally challenged and thus condemned to labor for the good of the Republic. Traditionally, they had remained in underground netherzones, generating power or performing services fit for no citizen.

The Society of Nuclear Darwinists, being at the forefront of research into the biological impact of the detonation of nuclear warheads—an oft-repeated incident in the Republic in the early twenty-first century—had defined the S.H.A.D.E. and worked actively to harvest shades from the population.

That had been the practice, until the Oracle's selection. Delilah, the current Oracle of the Republic, had been condemned as a shade at birth and had spent her life in labor until her gift for prophecy had been revealed. She had risen from obscurity the previous February, with the aid of the charismatic vid-evangelist Billie Joe Estevez, and her story had seized the public's imagination.

In that month, President Van Buren had locked down the netherzones throughout the Republic. The Oracle had unlocked the netherzones of Chicago and released the shades from their captivity. In so doing, she had compelled the Republic to remember those who might have been forgotten and compelled a reexamination of the Republic's moral climate.

In Chicago, the shades remained at large. The city had been plagued by mobs of shades each night, as those shades foraged for food. There was no public will in the windy city to confine these shades, because of their lack of violence, perhaps because of the Oracle's explicit role in their release.

The Oracle's popularity remained high, while Van Buren's had plummeted. It was clear that the populace blamed the administration for the problem.

It was clear that public opinion was with the Chicago shades.

Theodora suspected that the public's adoration of the Oracle was behind this contract for assassination. There were always people who disliked change and were prepared to pay to stop it. She could have guessed who was funding the bounty she intended to collect, but it was not her business to speculate.

Theodora was not without her own connection to the Oracle, for she had aided Delilah in her escape from the authorities the previous February. It had not been a sentimental choice—the credit had been in the Oracle's favor, then.

But no longer. And Theodora ensured that everyone knew that cred was the only thing of importance in her world.

Even if it wasn't.

As the hours passed, she waited and watched from her vantage point. The noise of the audience grew greater with every passing moment, their excitement rising in anticipation. Finally, she heard a distinctive sound and touched the amplifier on her ear.

Theodora smiled. A helicopter was landing on the roof of the building.

The Oracle was arriving.

Theodora checked her palm. Her prey was right on time.

IT WAS time.

Finally.

Their ordeal would be ended shortly. Armand could barely contain his anticipation. He let himself be pushed into Convocation Hall by the other students. He had befriended a group of other first-year students in his first weeks at the Institute. They were young and impetuous, so focused on the material world that he found his thoughts wandering in their company.

Armand was restless. Ready to leave this sphere.

Ready to do what had to be done, and regain his old powers.

He and Baruch had separated months before, at Tupperman's suggestion, so no one would guess the connection between them. The eyes of the Republic were everywhere, after all. They had even feigned dislike of each other after arrival at the Institute, and had no communication with each other. It had been necessary, but the isolation had nearly destroyed Armand.

But, finally, the end was in sight.

Armand pretended to scan the hall, acting indifferent even when his heart leapt at the sight of Baruch's crimson jacket in the opposite aisle. That crushed velvet coat was a bit the worse for wear after Baruch's earthly adventures, but it was distinctive in its brilliant color. Baruch was laughing, accompanying a pretty girl, making the most of his last moment.

Armand stifled an affectionate smile.

Baruch chose a seat in the orchestra close to the stage. Armand knew that Baruch would join the students who thronged before the stage to talk to Blackstone themselves, that he had a knife hidden on his person, if not two. Baruch would approach Blackstone immediately with a question and Armand would hang back in the same group. His role was to ensure that Baruch wasn't interrupted in his quest, to keep their path clear to that door backstage and to the right.

To that end, this very day, Armand had stolen three loaded vials of Ivanofor from the labs. He had to have some means of doing his part, but didn't want to do permanent injury to any human. As soon as he had learned about Ivanofor in his first week at the Institute, he'd known it was the perfect solution.

This sedative, so favored by the shade hunters of the Society, was actually a muscle relaxant. It eliminated the subject's ability to control his or her body by rendering a temporary paralysis, and it worked quickly.

Armand could sedate three adults with the syringes secreted in the pocket of his jacket. Ivanofor didn't even need to be injected into a vein, simply pushed into a muscle.

Armand hoped he had enough.

His heart was pounding in anticipation as he eased closer to a seat. He was barely aware of Philippa chattering at him, fluttering her lashes and touching his arm. His indifference seemed only to encourage her, but it was easy to ignore her.

Armand took one glance to confirm Baruch's position as the lights dimmed, but saw his old friend striding up the aisle toward the mezzanine.

Baruch wasn't following the plan.

What was wrong?

Armand abandoned his seat and his new friends without a word. He strode in rapid pursuit of Baruch.

What had changed?

As the opening music began, Theodora quickly fitted together her high-powered laze. It was ferociously accurate and illegal for anyone except those elite members of the Republic's S.W.A.T. teams. She respected its capabilities, which came courtesy of the sighting mechanism with its artificial intelligence subroutine.

The ritual composed her, focused her, drove all other details from her mind. There was only the weapon and the mission.

The lure of the cred.

When her laze was ready, Theodora watched, as still and emotionless as a machine. She might have been watching a vid, not live people. On the stage below, the guests were introduced. The Board of Governors for the Institute for Radiation Studies were first, followed by the Board of Directors of the Society of Nuclear Darwinists, Professors Emeriti, then past president of the Society, Ernestine Sinclair. The new president Blake Patterson. The applause was steady and polite, the names so much nonsense to Theodora.

Until the Oracle Delilah and her Consort, Raphael, were announced.

The hall fell into uneasy silence. The lights from the vidcams brightened and more than one attendee raised a hand above the crowd to create a personal vidcast with his or her palm.

How interesting that even within the Society and Institute, the Oracle had fans.

Without musical fanfare, the Oracle herself strode onto the stage. Theodora took a good look at her intended victim. Delilah had changed since last their paths had crossed. The Oracle stood taller and moved with a confidence she hadn't possessed just months ago.

It didn't hurt that she was dressed in flowing white, with the shining star of the Oracle bound to her brow. Her dark hair hung loose to her shoulders and her eyes were so brilliant a blue that they might have been cut from sapphires. That red kiss on her forehead, the mark of the angelic endorsement, was almost burgundy.

A port wine stain of favor. She seemed a creature apart, a gleam of angelic radiance, a woman who was more than most.

The hall fell silent.

Perhaps it was the power of the Oracle's presence. Perhaps it was the challenge in her stance. Perhaps it was her words.

"I come, as invited," she informed the audience, her tone resonant with conviction. "I come with the confidence of the angels that my person shall be safeguarded." She surveyed the audience, her eyes glittering. "And I thank the Society for the opportunity to contribute to the creation of a bright new future for the Republic."

The new president, Blake Patterson, a tanned blond man sleekly dressed in black and white, was the first to applaud. "I thank you for accepting my invitation and gracing us with your presence," he said, apparently sincere.

The Oracle smiled at him, then blew him a kiss.

Blake's smile broadened as he crossed the stage to shake her hand.

A tentative applause began and at first Theodora couldn't place the source. Then she realized that the shades working in the hall were applauding the Oracle, stepping out of the shadows to honor her. The response was cautious, as one would expect from those silenced for most of their lives, then gained in volume. Ernestine Sinclair's expression turned sour as she glared at the shades.

Her look didn't stop them.

A few students joined the applause, then the sound grew louder, the ripple of approval passing through the ranks of the hall. Some older individuals, possibly shade hunters, folded their arms across their chests and looked grim. The journalists moved through the hall like bees, capturing the array of responses on vid.

Things would only get more interesting, Theodora knew. She looked through the sight of the laze, wondering whether the red kiss on the Oracle's brow was as fake as the temporary tattoos worn by her many fans. No matter how she increased the magnification, the Oracle appeared to be the genuine article. Delilah was radiant.

Lit by angelfire.

But Theodora knew that nothing was genuine. The world was tainted and twisted, a trap in which there was no truth.

Only greed. Selfishness. Ego. Illusion and manipulation. There was no angelfire and Theodora believed any divine force had long ago abandoned the unfortunates of the Republic.

If it had ever existed.

Survivors were those who took care of themselves, those who had enough cred to ensure their safety and that of those they loved.

She focused on the prize.

Theodora surveyed the Oracle's official consort, the only true obstacle to her success. In contrast to his partner, Raphael Gerritson had changed little since the previous winter. He was still tall and tanned and muscled, his broad shoulders and determined expression making Theodora's heart skip.

Theodora accepted the lack of intimacy in her life, although there were moments when she regretted the necessity of denial.

She treated herself to another look. Rafe was more than handsome, a fine specimen of masculinity, even though she was not attracted to fair men. His blond hair and his golden skin made him look otherworldly.

The story was that he had been part of the angelic host, but Theodora knew good PR when she heard it. He was a man, a mere man, albeit one in better shape than most. It was cred that made his good health possible, nothing more than cred. She told herself that it was only his vigor that attracted her—she saw so many sick and weakened humans that it was easy to forget how powerful and attractive the human body could be.

She peered through the sight of the laze. Raphael, to her surprise, was armed even on the stage. Had this been a term of the Oracle's appearance? Theodora felt a new respect for the Oracle's—or her Consort's—understanding of this weary world.

Unless Theodora was mistaken, both lazes Rafe carried—one on each hip—were the same as the one she aimed at his partner. He'd replaced the laze she'd confiscated from him, replaced it with better hardware.

Twice. Cred spoke again.

Theodora already knew Rafe was a crack shot. Her heart skipped a beat in trepidation.

At least she would have the benefit of surprise.

The Oracle moved to her position at one side of the stage, waving to her supporters as the applause echoed through the hall. Theodora let the display slide over the Oracle's body, her concentration complete as she chose the best target. Three shots, she'd decided, three programmed for rapid succession. That would leave no opportunity for resuscitation.

Theodora sighted the laze once in the middle of that angel kiss.

She sighted the laze the second time between the Oracle's breasts.

She made to sight it the third time, just above the Oracle's pubis, but froze when the Oracle turned slightly to the left. With the magnification of the sight, Theodora could see the Oracle's rounded belly through the white fabric.

Delilah was pregnant.

Of course, that had been in the news. How had she forgotten?

The reminder unsettled her, though, made her hands shake. A child! A child was innocent and should stand—however briefly—outside the world's chaos.

Theodora glanced again at Rafe. He would intervene after the first shot—he would shelter the Oracle and his unborn child with his own body as he fired back. She'd witnessed his selflessness, his commitment to his partner. Its rarity made his tendency impossible to forget.

The second and third programmed shots would hit him.

But she didn't want to kill Rafe. She told herself that her hesitation was because he wasn't named in the contract—there was no cred in it—but recognized the lie.

He was another survivor, kin of a kind.

She didn't want to kill his unborn child either.

It seemed that Theodora had boundaries after all.

But the cred, the cred, she needed that cred.

Ferris needed that cred and what it could buy.

The child would likely die if the Oracle died, but Theodora chose not to think about that. She had to complete her mission. She had to think of the greater good, of the others relying upon her, of the surgeries this bounty would allow her to buy. She had to think about the future of those she was determined to protect.

What would Ferris think of her eliminating the Oracle? Theodora refused to consider it, refused to have doubts at this late point. She hadn't told him where she was going, and clung to the belief that she'd never have to confess her deed to him.

The death of Delilah might break his heart.

The retrieval of his voice would make it possible for him to live as a norm.

Choices. This world was about choices.

And only cred permitted choices to be made.

Theodora cleared the laze programming and resighted it, setting it for one shot, the shot that would shatter the mark of the angel's kiss. Her hands trembled ever so slightly, but she attributed it to a last-minute change of plan.

She knew what had to be done.

She knew the greater good that had to be served.

Theodora took a deep breath, peered through the sight and set the laze. The Oracle smiled at Rafe, eyes shining, and Theodora's finger slipped to the trigger.

She hesitated for an instant.

And it was too long.

IN THAT instant, Theodora heard the door open behind her. She knew she'd been discovered, and that only she or the assailant could live to tell of this encounter. She pivoted, braced the laze with her left hand, cleared the setting with her thumb and fired at the man silhouetted in the doorway.

The laze was fast and hot, quiet in its efficiency.

But not quite silent.

The man gasped and dropped to one knee, grabbing his shoulder and turning away from her in his pain. There was blood, a lot of blood, and he looked up, his expression frightened as the blood ran through his fingers.

"Why?" he whispered, as if confused.

Theodora had no answer to such a foolish question.

Then she saw that he carried no weapon, that she had fired at someone who could not have injured her.

Who was he? Why was he interfering?

There was no time to think, no time to ask. The audience was stirring at the sound of the laze shot. Security guards were running for her sanctuary and Theodora knew she had seconds to escape. The intruder knelt in the doorway. He was still looking at her, still able to interrupt her flight. He wasn't small either, but a muscular man.

There was only one choice. She had to abort the mission, save her skin, destroy any evidence that could condemn her.

And she had to do it quickly.

Theodora fired at the man again, her heart pounding, and he spun from the impact. She held the burn as he crumpled and rolled. The shot left a burning trail across his shoulders. His crimson velvet jacket was razed from his back and he bared his teeth in pain.

He fell to the floor and didn't move again, a red stain spreading across the tile beneath his body. If he wasn't dead, he would be. She didn't have time to shoot again, wasn't callous enough to shoot him in the head.

Would she pay for that? Theodora hoped not.

She ran, all the while wondering who he was, what he had wanted. When Theodora made to leap over his fallen body, she saw the two diagonal scars on his bared back. They startled her.

What would cause such marks? She stared down at his fallen body in confusion. How could he have scars? How could he be a shade in norm's clothing? What had caused such scars? Who was he?

It was only a heartbeat, but Theodora was distracted at precisely the wrong moment. A man suddenly seized her by the shoulders and lifted her from the ground. She hadn't even heard his approach.

Theodora struggled instinctively. No! It was all going wrong! She couldn't fail in this mission, couldn't be captured, couldn't be trapped in the Institute. No!

Who was this man?

Her captor was tall and handsome, certainly the finest specimen of masculinity she'd ever seen. He was strong, with remarkable power in his hands. She looked up to find that his hair was auburn and his eyes a brilliant green. He was livid, his eyes flashing and his lips drawn taut, his face only inches from hers as he easily held her above the ground.

"What have you done?" he muttered.

Theodora supposed that he must know the man she had shot, but she owed him no explanation and she would accept no interference. His strength frightened her, made her fight harder. She heard the boots of the guards on the stairs and panicked. She wouldn't die in this inferno. She couldn't raise her laze high enough to shoot him, so she resorted to old-fashioned methods.

She bit his hand in the same instant that she drove her knee up toward his crotch.

He grunted in pain.

Even better, his grip loosened. Theodora drove her elbow into his ribs and he dropped her. She took advantage of the moment, knowing he'd recover quickly. She ducked under his arm and sprinted toward the hidden portal to the netherzones.

She only hoped she was faster than he was.

II

ARMAND HAD been on the stairs when he'd heard the laze
shot. He'd bounded through the mezzanine lobby in terror,
following the sound. He'd been scanning the empty space,
uncertain where to find his friend, when the second shot
had fired.

He'd seen the unmarked door then, slightly ajar, at the
other end of the lobby and had raced toward it. A figure
had erupted from it in the same instant and he had instinctively snatched at that individual.

He'd assumed it was a young boy, lithe and strong.

But it was a woman, a slight woman dressed in a patched
pseudoskin. There could be no mistaking her gender when
he caught her by the shoulders and saw the curves of her
breasts.

Armand's heart stopped cold when he saw Baruch on
the floor behind her. Blood ran from Baruch's body like
a river, pooling beneath him, making his crimson jacket
even more red.

But the woman wasn't trying to help Baruch.

She'd killed Baruch!

She fought his grip like a feral cat. Obviously, she was
intent upon escaping the scene of her crime.

What kind of woman would kill Baruch—or anyone
else, for that matter? Armand stared down at her. She was

gloved and booted, only her face uncovered. A tightly fitted hood covered whatever hair she had. Her skin was fair, her features delicately curved and her lips full. He saw that she carried a potent laze and its recharge light was blinking, proof positive that she was responsible.

"What have you done?" he demanded.

She struggled against his grip instead of answering him, then looked up at him with open hostility.

Her eyes glowed orange, with vertical slits for pupils.

She had to be wearing filters, he realized that, but Armand was shaken. Those amber eyes made her look primitive and untrustworthy.

Like an animal.

She twisted and writhed, taking advantage of his astonishment. She was as slippery as a fish in his grasp. She suddenly drove her knee high and he anticipated the move, ensuring that she didn't connect. But in the same instant, she sank her teeth into the exposed skin between his glove and cuff.

Armand swore at the pain. Her teeth could have been knives, for she cut him deeply and his hand began to bleed. His grip loosened in his shock, and she wriggled free.

She was fast.

In a heartbeat, she had crossed the mezzanine. She kicked a panel on the far wall and a narrow passageway opened into darkness. She leapt through it, disappearing in the shadows, and would have pulled the panel closed behind her.

But Armand was right behind her, jamming his fingers into the space to halt the door.

He couldn't let Baruch's killer escape.

He knew he'd never find her again if he lost her now.

Armand lunged through the doorway, closing the panel

behind him and freezing in the darkness. He was sealed into a passageway with a killer, and he suspected she already knew the layout of the space. He cursed the limitations of flesh as his eyes took time to adjust. She was getting away! He heard the sound of the guards entering the mezzanine, his impatience growing, then discerned stairs extending downward on the right.

It was a long staircase by the look of it, one that made a quarter turn every dozen steps but had no visible bottom. When he stepped closer, he heard the soft sound of boots on the stairs. He took the stairs four at a time, not caring about their destination. He saw the silhouette of his prey a beat later, his height giving him a speed advantage over her.

The pale oval of her face shone in the darkness as she glanced back over her shoulder. She halted, then he saw the red blinking light of the laze.

She fired just as Armand dropped to the floor. The shot slipped through his hair, leaving a line of heat.

She meant to kill him, as well.

Barbarian!

Armand's fury raged that this woman should dare to attack angels, that she could ensure that he and Baruch never regained their wings, that their decision to volunteer to aid humanity should be so poorly rewarded. Anger gave him strength, and he bounded down the stairs, snatching her off the ground from behind. He had to struggle to hold her captive, for she was strong and determined.

She also had enticing curves. The way she fought in his grip distracted Armand in a surprising way. He forced her to the wall, trapping her against the concrete with his body. He had one arm wrapped around her body, keeping her arms against her torso. She gritted her teeth and wriggled, and Armand leaned his pelvis against hers to keep her from kicking him again.

She lifted her gaze and glared at him. This time, he wasn't surprised by her filters.

"Who are you? Why did you kill him?" he demanded, not troubling to hide his anger.

She was, to his surprise, unafraid of him. "I only did what needed doing," she snarled.

Her voice was odd, reverberating in a way that made it sound computer generated. He saw then that there was a voice-box modifier on the side of her throat, held beneath the pseudoskin. Her defiance and her crime made it tempting to do her injury, but Armand was determined to not descend to some pitiable moral code.

"Perhaps I disagree with your choices," he said softly, and her eyes narrowed with wariness. He smiled, knowing precisely what would infuriate her and guessing what she would do.

He snatched her weapon from her hand, and flung it down into the abyss below, liking how it clattered on the metal stairs as it fell. He hoped it was damaged beyond repair, unable to do injury to anyone ever again.

He doubted that it was so fragile.

She made a cry of pain. Armand released her as if she had fought her way free, anticipating what she would do. She lunged after the weapon, showing her priorities and her nature clearly.

In that same instant, Armand pulled a loaded syringe from his pocket. In three steps, he caught her around the waist, tipping her upside down. She hissed with frustration, kicking violently as she struck at him.

Armand stabbed the needle into her buttock, forcing it through the pseudoskin, and began to empty the Ivanofor from the syringe. He marveled that a woman could be so vicious just when she gave a violent jerk.

The needle snapped, the syringe still partly full.

She fell to the metal stairs, panting. She sprawled there and glared up at him, hatred in those strange eyes as she felt for the broken needle.

"What was it?" she demanded.

"Ivanofor." Armand shrugged. "What else?"

Her eyes narrowed. "How much?"

He considered the syringe and guessed. "About eighty milligrams."

She punched something into her palm, moving so quickly that he couldn't stop her. Then she glared at him. "Still a loading dose!"

So, she had been doing the calculation for the drug, based on her weight. Armand, who clearly knew less about the drug than she did, wished he knew all of the answer she had gotten. It would have been handy to know how long she'd be out.

But he had no chance to ask. She leapt for him, her gloved hands outstretched. Evidently she was going to make her last moments of power count.

The drug didn't fail Armand. She stumbled even before she reached him, her arms dropping as her lips slackened. He saw then that she could have been beautiful, if her expression hadn't been vicious. He watched the passion fade from her expression and knew he'd had no choice.

She would have gladly killed him.

This was the better option, even if it was inconvenient.

He'd have an answer from her before they parted, that was for certain.

He caught her up in his arms before she fell, feeling her whole body go slack. She trembled, her displeasure with the situation more than clear.

"You . . ." she managed to murmur and then no more.

He didn't doubt that she feared his intention, given that her own actions were so reprehensible. But he'd never hurt her. He'd never hurt anyone.

He was in no rush to explain as much to her.

"Say good night," Armand murmured and her eyes flashed fury one last time.

Her last action was to spit at him. By the time he had wiped the spittle from his cheek, the sedative had claimed her completely. He slung her limp weight over his shoulder and climbed the stairs with purpose, determined to claim Baruch's corpse.

But when Armand nudged open the door to the mezzanine, that space was filled with guards. A crowd of students was jammed into the space as well, whispering as they watched. The vidcams were running, the lights blinding in their intensity.

He supposed that was inevitable, then caught his breath.

"His blood pressure is stable," declared a paramedic. "His pulse is still erratic, but we can move him now. Make way!"

Baruch wasn't dead.

Armand felt his lips part in shock.

Shadow.net Bounty Notice

WRAITH DOWN

Issued September 18, 2100, 20:05

*Automatically Generated from Preset Parameters and
Palm Alarm*

The following wraith has been injured or harvested:
Theodora 7639

The following reward bounty has been prearranged by said
wraith:
10,000 Republican units

Said wraith was last verified in this position:
*Upper mezzanine, Convocation Hall, Institute for Radiation
Studies, Chicago*
<u>*Longitude and Latitude*</u>

Restrictions placed by said wraith on bounty pay out:
Must be retrieved alive, all intellectual capabilities intact

This bounty alert has been sent to all wraiths logged into
Shadow.net, at 18:09:00, 20:05 CST. Shadow.net is not liable
for interrupted or intercepted messages, for failure to receive
requested messages or for any actions, legal or illegal, resulting
from any recipients' attempts to retrieve said bounty. This
message serves as an information update only.

Theodora was livid. She had been taken captive by the most gorgeous man she had ever seen, one who also happened to be an idiot.

Had he run from the scene of the crime?

No.

Had he hidden from the authorities?

No.

Had he ensured the survival of both of them?

No. He had stayed right in the Institute, putting her life in jeopardy. He hadn't run to the exit to Chicago's netherzones, oh no—he'd gone straight back to the scene of the crime, staying within the walls of the Institute. It was the worst predicament possible.

It seemed that she had made a tactical error. Even worse, she'd hit the alarm on her palm in panic, triggering the bounty notice with 10,000 units of cred on it before she'd realized that she might be able to save herself.

At least she'd lied to her captor about the loading dose.

The Ivanofor was tingling in her fingers and toes, but it hadn't immobilized her. She'd deceived him deliberately and at least, she still had the element of surprise on her side.

The trick would be not revealing herself when her captor was so unpredictable.

What on earth was he planning to do?

He must be allied with the man she'd shot. Why else return to the mezzanine?

But what was he going to do with her? Was he going to surrender her to the authorities? That wouldn't work out well. They had to have a file on her that was megagigs in size. But if she escaped, how would she get out of this crowded hall unscathed?

Odds were long, longer than Theodora liked.

He'd already relieved her of her laze, a loss that annoyed Theodora as nothing else could have done. She reminded herself to remain impassive and limp, and wait for her moment.

Then she'd get even.

Her captor stood in the shadows at the top of the stairs, watching the hive of activity in the mezzanine. Theodora took advantage of his distraction to look, even though she witnessed the scene upside down and past the muscled strength of his thigh. She could feel the rhythm of his breathing and the heat of his skin, the subtle musk of cologne and his own scent mingled together. She felt the power of him, the solid grip of his hands on the back of her legs, and felt an entirely untimely and inappropriate reaction.

It was, unfortunately, russet-haired men with green eyes whom Theodora found most attractive. And there was something alluring about a robustly healthy man, independent of his coloring.

Not that it mattered.

The man she'd shot wasn't dead, but Theodora had guessed as much. If she'd wanted him dead, she should have shot his brains out. She knew it, but hadn't been able to do it. That she hadn't been able to complete that basic act of self-preservation meant that he would offer testimony against her.

If he ever woke up.

She had a very bad feeling that her luck had finally turned against her.

The injured man was being loaded upon a stretcher beneath the paramedic's watchful care, even as one guard barked into his palm. Two custodians cleaned the floor of blood as Theodora's captor remained motionless in the shadowed portal.

She truly hoped he wasn't stupid enough to reveal himself. Or her. Her heart pounded with the uncertainty, and she became aware of his thumb tracing little circles on the back of her calf. The gesture, which surely was unconscious, sent little tingles through Theodora.

What was he thinking?

What did he want?

From the other side of the mezzanine, a man approached the victim, his features filled with concern. He was fair and tall, trim and well dressed. Theodora recognized Blake Patterson, the new president of the Society.

"What's going on here?" Patterson demanded, and the crowd parted to make way for him. "Get those image-snatchers out of here. No vidcast from this space." Guards moved to usher the media out of the mezzanine, confiscating vidcams over the journalists' protests.

"Mr. Patterson, sir! He was armed with a knife," one guard said. "No telling what he had planned. Somebody intervened, thank goodness. The police have been summoned."

A knife? Theodora was surprised. Who carried such a crude weapon in these times? And why? Were these two trying to kill the Oracle themselves? It wouldn't have surprised Theodora to have competition—the wraiths routinely double- or triple-booked assignments, to ensure their completion.

She heard the distant chop of a helicopter and grimaced with the conviction that the Oracle was gone from the building.

If not from Chicago.

Theodora bit back a curse.

Patterson bent down toward the fallen man, then touched his crimson jacket. "This is a laze burn. Who's armed in the building?"

"Everyone was scanned upon entry, sir."

"Then it must have been a security person."

"No, sir. I have no report of Security firing a weapon."

Patterson frowned and paled. "Then security measures must have been breached. Search the building immediately." Theodora guessed that Patterson knew it wasn't the burn of an ordinary laze, because his gaze flicked over the crowd, assessment in his eyes.

She closed her eyes and prayed her captor wouldn't be seen.

"He has scars," Patterson said quietly. His manner was thoughtful and Theodora wondered whether he knew what could cause diagonal scars like the ones she'd glimpsed. She had no idea.

Did her captor know about his partner's scars? The assembled people pushed forward, and one held his left hand high for his palm to record the scene.

Patterson pointed and a guard wrestled the offender's arm down.

"Hey! I have the right . . ."

"You have no such right. This is a private facility and a secured function," the guard said.

"This is a free country," the man who had been recording the scene continued to argue. Theodora almost laughed aloud at that bit of lunacy.

The guard said no more, simply pinned the man's hands behind his back and locked them there with a securoband. There was all the proof a thinking person needed of the true state of the Republic. The man was marched away, protesting loudly all the while. Theodora wasn't surprised that the other people pretended not to notice. It was a useful survival technique in this place.

"If he has scars, then he's a shade," the guard beside Patterson said.

"It doesn't matter," the paramedic argued. "He's injured and needs care. We'll take him to the hospital immediately . . ."

A pair of police officers pushed their way through the crowd. They held their lazes at the ready and seemed to be prepared to take command of the situation. The students backed away, whispering.

Things were getting worse by the moment. Theodora wished again that her captor had just run. What did he expect to accomplish?

How could he stand so still? It was as if he'd been turned to stone—except for that circling thumb.

Patterson held up a hand to stop the police. "The Institute claims jurisdiction. The victim is a shade and the injury was incurred on our property." He straightened and faced the police officers, who hesitated. "He'll be one of ours."

"He needs medical care," the paramedic insisted.

Patterson smiled thinly. "I remind you that the Institute is a medical research facility. I think we can handle treatment of a laze wound."

"But," the paramedic tried to intervene one more time.

Patterson gestured to the guards. "Take the victim downstairs to the labs. When he revives, we'll question him."

One of the guards smirked, his expression in perfect agreement with Theodora's assessment. Question him?

That wasn't how the Institute operated. The man she'd shot would never see daylight again. He was a shade, which was why Patterson had claimed him.

It was also why the police didn't argue jurisdiction.

By shooting the man in the red jacket and letting him live, she'd condemned him.

That slice of reality caught at her heart.

"And see that these individuals are similarly escorted to the doors," Patterson said. The guards nodded, then the group headed directly toward the pair in the shadows, bearing the stretcher with the injured man sprawled upon it.

They would use this staircase to reach the labs.

Theodora knew she jerked. She couldn't help it. Her captor, having waited far longer than was wise, pivoted and retreated.

At least he was tall. He raced down the dark stairs far more quickly than she could have done. All the same, Theodora willed him to move faster yet. He was quiet too, as quiet as a wraith.

That gave more credence to her suspicion that he and his friend were her competition.

She supposed he'd kept her alive so that they could make a deal. Well, the terms might not be quite the ones he envisioned.

Theodora was ready for her captor to take the exit to the public netherzones, but once again, he surprised her.

She had a feeling she was going to need to get used to that.

BARUCH WAS alive.

Armand was both relieved and terrified.

They'd never surrender Baruch to his care, not when he was injured. Could he spirit him away from the Institute while he was injured? Was it possible that Baruch could be treated and released, that their plan could continue after a delay? Armand didn't know, but he was profoundly glad that his friend was alive.

The pair still had a chance to retrieve their wings. Even with the odds stacked against them, the situation was infinitely preferable to Baruch's death.

In fact, the best way to save Baruch from the Institute might be to incite the angels' intervention. The angelic host could spirit Baruch out of this place, as no locked door provided an obstacle to their passage.

But Baruch was injured and likely unable to kill Blackstone.

Somehow, Armand needed to fulfill their mission alone.

The prospect terrified him until he realized one key detail. His captive had no issues in doing injury to others.

She might prove to be very useful indeed.

He felt a flicker of faith in divine providence.

The stairs ended at the primary level of the Institute's underground research labs. There were said to be two more levels beneath this one, then the Institute's offices towering above, accessible to the public at ground level.

Armand recognized the level by the decor. The walls were tiled in white and the floors were poured concrete. Fluorescent lights hung at regular intervals, casting the whole area into a blinding white light. Stainless steel doors lined this corridor, leading to laboratories and surgeries, and he could smell the formaldehyde. Even two weeks into his coursework, Armand knew this space well. The service level below this one was more austere, and provided access to the underground train station of the Institute. The third and lowest level was but a rumor, in Armand's experience.

There was a gurney parked under the stairs, and he instantly knew how he could disguise the woman.

He dumped her body onto the gurney, listening to the approaching party. They were coming down the stairs much more slowly, probably because of their burden. He could use every second to his benefit. He glanced down at the woman and recalled his sense that she had twitched at the top of the stairs.

She shouldn't have been able to do that. Had it been involuntary? Was she really sedated?

Or was she lying to him?

The evidence so far didn't indicate that she was the most honest of individuals. And truly, he didn't know how much Ivanofor would be required to affect her.

He needed to be vigilant.

And to ensure that he had something she wanted, in order to negotiate. He spied the woman's laze on the floor under the stairs. Its red light blinked as it recharged.

Perfect. He retrieved it, shoving it into the back of his belt, under his jacket.

Armand pushed the gurney into the darkened surgery, breathing a sigh of relief to find it empty. The woman was watching him, her eyes open and unblinking.

Even if she was under the effect of the Ivanofor, she would still be able to hear and understand him.

He showed her the laze and her eyes flashed.

Then she blinked, pretending to be drugged again.

Aha.

"So, now I have something you want," he murmured,

bending toward her so that she could hear him. "Here are my terms—save my friend and you'll get your laze back."

Did she inhale?

Armand was sure she did.

It was time to end her ruse.

"First things first, though," he continued easily. "You'll need a new disguise." He reached quickly for the front fastening of her pseudoskin, opening it to the waist so that her pale skin was laid bare.

Armand wasn't surprised when she leapt up to fight him. He caught her by the wrists and forced her back down on the gurney. With a quick gesture, he locked the strap across her torso so that her arms were fastened at her sides. She swore and kicked, but he did the same with the other strap, binding her knees to the gurney.

She hissed and spat, struggling in her fury.

He wagged a finger at her and whispered, "It's not nice to lie."

"How dare you restrain me," she whispered, eyes flashing. "Release me immediately! You have no right . . ."

Armand leaned closer, keeping his voice low. "I have every right. You shot my friend."

She stilled and glared at him. "He interrupted me."

"From what?"

She clamped her mouth shut and averted her gaze.

"Keep your secrets, then," he said, not missing her quick sidelong glance. "Before we negotiate, we'll level the field."

Terror flashed in her eyes, but Armand had no intention of doing her injury.

Of course, she didn't know that. He doubted he could say anything to convince her of his intentions. The blood on his wrist was a telling reminder of how viciously she could fight.

And maybe a clue as to a tool she had.

Armand caught her jaw in one hand and forced her mouth open. She fought against him, but he was ready and she was bound to the gurney. Holding her jaw open, he removed the metal appliance that was locked to the back of her upper teeth. It had a blade that retracted slightly and a trigger she could clearly operate with her tongue.

"Nasty piece of work," he murmured, then snapped it in half before her very eyes.

"But necessary," she argued.

"Perhaps in your trade."

"You know nothing about my trade."

"I can guess." He gave her an assessing glance. "A disguise, a hiding place, a fear of capture, and a potent laze. You must be an assassin."

She glared at him. "I admit nothing."

Armand leaned closer, bracing his hands on either side of her shoulders. "Who was your target?"

"I don't have to tell you anything."

"No, you don't," he admitted easily and smiled. His smile surprised her, and he was relieved to catch a glimpse of her thoughts. "I could push you out into the hall right now, present you as Baruch's attacker and let justice have its way."

"There is no such thing as justice." Her bitterness surprised him, as did the speed with which she negotiated. "But if you do that, I won't be able to help your friend."

"He doesn't need more of the kind of help you gave him."

"I could help you free him."

Armand leaned against a counter, folding his arms across his chest. "Maybe I'm skeptical." He watched her avidly, unable to dismiss his sense that her cold manner was in opposition to something. Her nature? Her inclination? Had she learned this coldness? He didn't have a hard time believing that life in this realm might leave a person cynical.

That was a long way from earning a living as an assassin, though. She was probably trying to manipulate him.

"Maybe you don't have any other options," she challenged.

He smiled again, liking how his amusement troubled her. "You might be surprised."

She shook her head. "No. I can get your friend out of here."

"Alive?"

Her eyes narrowed. "If it's worth it."

He arched a brow, inviting her terms.

"Cred," she said tightly. "Everything is about cred."

She couldn't have said anything more distasteful to Armand. "Maybe the time to set a precedent for justice is now."

"Don't be naive!"

"Bad time to be uncooperative." Armand leaned closer, dropping his voice to a conspiratorial whisper. "Don't you hear them coming? The moment to make a deal is now."

"Even though you missed the chance to get away," she countered, even her whispered words scathing. "I'm not sure it's smart to bargain with a man who doesn't anticipate trouble."

"Why assume that I don't?"

Her skeptical expression said it all. "We're here, in the worst possible place . . ."

"But I have a plan."

"Why would I make a deal with you? There doesn't appear to be any cred in it."

"No cred, no. Just your life. That must have some value to you."

"Cred talks," she insisted. "Only cred."

"I have no cred." Armand shrugged, not believing her words for a minute. On the other hand, he recognized that it might be useful that she couldn't read his thoughts. He could provoke her. "So, I might as well just give you to them. Easy, and it's your choice. Do you think they'll call me a hero?" He unlocked the wheels of the gurney and made to push her toward the door.

"No!" she said, struggling with real fear. "You wouldn't. You couldn't!"

Armand kept moving. "I offered you a deal. You declined." He shrugged. "Makes no difference to me."

She swore with an eloquence that made him blink. "It's not easy to get someone out of this place," she muttered, her fury clear. "Especially a shade being watched. There has to be motivation . . ."

"Funny, I thought your own survival would be motivating enough."

"It has to be planned. It takes time."

"We have no time." He looked down at her and smiled. "Would it change your mind to know that you don't actually have to ensure his release?"

Her eyes narrowed with suspicion. "What do you mean?"

"All you have to do is kill Maximilian Blackstone, and the rest will take care of itself."

She stared at him, then blinked.

Armand nudged her a little further. She was clearly thinking about his suggestion. "Maybe Blackstone was your intended victim anyway."

"No, not him."

"Then who?"

"What's Blackstone got to do with anything?"

"We all have our secrets."

She frowned. "I'd need my laze."

Armand chuckled. "*After* Blackstone is dead."

"Be serious. How else will I take him down?"

"I'm thinking that you're a very creative individual, particularly when it comes to violence for your own benefit." Armand could see how furiously she was assessing options and discarding them. She could make this work.

"I'll do it," she said and he liked that she was decisive.

"Then we have a deal," he said, stopping the gurney. "And now you have to get naked."

"What?"

"Corpses don't wear pseudoskins." He flicked a glance toward the double doors and the sound of the approaching party, aware of her astonishment. "Better be quick."

III

⟡

HER CAPTOR was either brilliant or insane. Theodora couldn't decide and didn't have time to think about it.

How could killing Maximilian Blackstone free his friend?

She didn't know, but there was something about her captor that persuaded her to trust him. That might have been a big mistake, so she wouldn't go that far. She would, though, make the best deal she could while she could.

Somehow she'd finish Blackstone without her laze.

It wasn't as if she hadn't considered doing as much in the past. This could be the perfect opportunity to pursue her personal vendetta, under the guise of making a bargain.

And the Oracle was out of range for the short term anyway. What was key was to survive.

He made to unfasten her pseudoskin, but Theodora twisted and protested. "I can do it faster myself," she said, feeling her blush rise. To his credit, he got a sheet and put it on the end of the gurney.

He gave her a steady glance, as if in warning, then unfastened the straps. The party on the stairs became louder as they drew closer. There wasn't much time.

Theodora tugged off her boots and unfastened her belt, then wriggled out of the snug pseudoskin. He had the grace to avert his gaze, purportedly to fetch a laundry sack while she removed the heavy polymer suit. By the time he turned back, she had pulled the sheet over her bare skin.

She didn't doubt that he knew he could catch her. Also the only obvious place to run was out into the corridor, which was filling with Nuclear Darwinists and students of the Institute.

She had very few choices, at this point.

He shoved her gear into the bag, moving with brisk efficiency. He hauled the hood from her head and the long golden braid of her hair fell loose, startling them both for a precious moment. Theodora felt even more naked with her hair revealed, especially when she saw the admiration in his eyes. She wasn't used to men looking at her like that.

She felt a blush begin at her breasts, a warmth of self-awareness that wasn't unpleasant.

Just unwelcome.

And inappropriate.

The group on the stairs was close enough that their conversations became clear. Her captor abruptly rolled Theodora over, casting aside the sheet as he held her down with his gloved hand on the back of her waist. She had time to brace to fight before he spoke.

"You're not making this easier," he murmured and she felt the prick of that broken needle. To her astonishment, he used a pair of tweezers to remove it from her buttock.

His act of kindness completely confused Theodora.

When had anyone last shown a measure of consideration for her, or for her comfort? Theodora couldn't remember.

Who was this man?

Where was he from?

What had made him so unpredictable?

When he rolled her back over, his expression was determined. He plucked the voice-box modifier from the side of her throat. It didn't break the skin, simply had a plasma layer on one side of it that extended over the front of her throat. The amplifier in the skinny box that had been concealed beneath her pseudoskin ensured that the reverberation was heard instead of her real voice. The device went into the bag as well, then he strapped her legs down to the gurney.

"Hey!" Theodora protested, but he pushed her shoulder down hard.

"You might think I don't trust you," he murmured, then tightened the second strap around her midriff, trapping her arms against her waist. His eyes twinkled, looking even more vibrantly green. Theodora caught her breath. He looked mischievous and even more attractive. "And the truth is that I don't."

"You—"

His gloved finger landed heavily across her lips, then he bent so close that their noses were almost touching. "Corpses don't talk, either," he murmured, then winked.

Winked. As if he was flirting with her.

Theodora's heart skipped and galloped. She opened her mouth to argue with him, closed it again, caught a glimpse of his amusement and felt herself blush. He smiled, obviously aware of his effect upon her, which only made it worse.

It was a strange situation, even for a woman well accustomed to strange situations. With another man, she would have feared for her safety, but she was oddly confident of his intentions.

Was there truly an honorable man left in the Republic?

"I doubt corpses blush," she muttered and his grin flashed.

Then he grabbed a sterile swab from the supplies in the room.

"Don't move," he muttered, sobering as he carefully removed first one eye filter and then the other. He straightened and stared at her, and Theodora tried not to fidget.

She was completely naked.

"How does it feel for a woman so protective of her secrets to be laid bare to view?" he mused, then flashed that smile again. That admiration was in his eyes again and she felt her cheeks burn.

"Don't gloat." She struggled against the bonds but froze when his fingertip fell upon her arm.

"Corpses don't struggle."

"No one will know . . ."

"You're abrading the skin, and they will notice that."

There was no argument Theodora could make in reply to that. She stilled, letting him see that she wasn't happy about it. He raised a finger to his lips, looking reckless and sexy, and her heart leapt for her throat.

The party had reached the base of the stairs, their conversation becoming louder. He glanced over his shoulder, then lashed the laundry bag to the underside of the gurney, hiding it from sight. At least he wasn't discarding her gear. He tugged the sheet over Theodora's face.

"Best behavior," he whispered and she heard anticipation in his tone. Was he looking forward to his scheme, whatever it was? "It's the only way you'll have any chance to deliver."

His choice of words made her heart skip. What did he really have planned? Was she a fool to trust him? What if her instincts were wrong?

Theodora didn't like that playing along was the only way to find out the truth.

* * *

THE WOMAN was strikingly beautiful, her hair like spun gold and her eyes the same silvery blue as a winter sky. Armand couldn't entirely suppress his surprise—or his body's reaction to her beauty.

She had a strange effect upon him, and Armand marveled at it. Why was it that this mercenary woman, the one who had injured his best friend, made him feel so aware of his physical body? In addition to the pulse of desire—an irrational desire, given her nature—his senses were heightened. He felt alive, as he hadn't yet, aware of the danger and welcoming it. He felt more keenly engaged in the moment, in this place.

Which was precisely where he did not want to be.

By rights, he and Baruch should have been collected by the angels by now.

Maybe she was right to not believe in justice.

His thoughts flew as he pushed the gurney toward the door.

Was she truly as harsh as she seemed?

Or was her attitude just another deceit?

Armand remembered his stolen glimpse of her nudity well enough and could see her dimensions beneath the sheet. She was slender and young, slightly curved at breast and hip but all muscle. He liked the length of her, and the lean power of her body, and found her more alluring than any of the mortal women he had seen.

Why would she disguise such beauty? He realized the answer even before he fully formed the question. She didn't want to be remembered or even noticed—no assassin ever did. It was a symptom of her trade that she hid her features.

And it was human nature to remember beauty.

She had to hide hers to survive in the trade she'd chosen. On the other hand, hers might well be a treacherous beauty, one that hid a malicious nature with a pretty face, one that incited trust where none was due.

There *was* something attractive about her passion. He liked that she was spirited, and appreciated the contrast with the many citizens of the Republic who simply went through the motions of daily living. This woman would never stand by passively, waiting for others to shape her situation.

Even if she chose wrongly, he doubted she would ever express regret over a choice.

Was that the root of his fascination with her? There had to be a point to a mortal life. There had to be a reward, and Armand could appreciate that it might be found in passion and risk. He was curious as to what could turn a woman to crime, especially one who seemed so clever. What was her history?

Was he a fool to wonder?

Armand was sure that he was. He shouldn't wonder. He should simply be glad that a quick-thinking assassin was in his captivity precisely when he had need of such an individual.

She would help him, perhaps against her will but motivated to regain her weapon, and he would leave with Baruch.

She would undoubtedly continue her harsh life.

The prospect saddened Armand unexpectedly, then he caught himself.

It wasn't as if this woman desired or would welcome his compassion.

Impatient with himself, he gave the gurney a hard push through the doors in exactly the same moment that the group pooled at the base of the stairs. He didn't look at Baruch, tried to hide that he had even noticed his friend. Instead, he excused himself, trying to work the gurney through the group as if he was focused on getting it to the right destination.

"Armand!" Philippa said, slipping her hand through his elbow and pressing her breast against his arm.

Armand felt a twinge of irritation. His classmate had been focused on him from their first meeting, even though Armand had tried to avoid her. It was clear that she was amorously interested in him, and the less encouragement he gave, the more determined she became.

He glanced down at her, wishing she hadn't spotted him, and made a polite comment.

But with that glance, he realized how he could get his assassin out of the labs.

Or at least off the gurney.

All incoming corpses were assessed in the mornings for autopsies and investigative surgeries. His captive had to be out of the labs before that, or she might become a corpse herself.

And she wouldn't be of any use to him then.

But Philippa shared the same slight build as his captive. The assassin couldn't slip unnoticed out of the Institute either nude or in her pseudoskin. She needed a change of clothing and Philippa's would be perfect. The first-year student was more curvaceous, it was true, but her determination to become involved with Armand seemed like a gift in this moment.

He still had two syringes loaded with Ivanofor, after all.

Armand looked down at Philippa with a warm smile, not surprised when she eased even closer to him.

He wasn't insane, just loyal.

He stayed in the Institute to help his friend. Theodora had to admit a grudging admiration of that objective. It wasn't very common for people to be selfless, to put the welfare of others before their own. Maybe he didn't understand the risk.

Maybe he was foolish instead of crazy.

Theodora found that she didn't much care. She respected his choice and she understood it. How many risks had she taken over the years—including this one—for the sake of those who relied upon her? It was strange to think that they had anything in common.

She'd never tell him as much, of course. No. They'd made a deal and he'd believe she was compliant because of it. He didn't need to know that Theodora secretly respected his choice.

He wasn't so foolish as to leave her tools behind and she appreciated that. He had retrieved her laze and carefully stowed her pseudoskin. She had a better chance of getting it back from him than from the Institute's arsenal.

He was smarter than she'd originally thought. Or more cunning. His plan to disguise her as a corpse wasn't a bad one. No one truly looked at corpses, especially in this place.

And he had assessed her own motivation well enough. The offer of the return of her laze in exchange for seeing his friend released had been tempting.

But the weapon hadn't been the only thing she'd wanted

of him. Theodora was surprised to realize that she would have made a much more basic exchange. She'd gotten lucky in that he hadn't offered that—or guessed that she would have been amenable.

Maybe her luck was back.

Her heart skipped as he pushed the gurney into the corridor, as she heard the hum and felt the heat of others around them. Why would he reveal himself so clearly? She panicked, then heard the rustle of skirts.

"Armand!" a woman exclaimed with pleasure.

Theodora had a second to like his name, to decide that it suited him, before she realized the truth.

Armand was known here, in the bowels of the Institute for Radiation Studies.

Which meant that he was one of them. He could walk the corridor, mingling with this company, because he belonged here. Was he a Nuclear Darwinist or still a student of the Institute?

It didn't matter. Anyone associated with this place was evil, right to the core.

Theodora judged as one who had a passing acquaintance with evil herself. Was she making a deal with one of the devils?

If he belonged to the Institute, he had to be lying to her about his plan. It had to be a trick. No one associated with this place would try to free a shade from the labs, whether that shade was a friend or not. If she helped him, she shouldn't imagine that he'd truly return her laze. That was an expensive piece of equipment, and as far as she could discern, he carried no weapon.

He must be lying to her. He was toying with her. He must have another agenda.

Unfortunately, there wasn't much Theodora could do to save herself or escape him in this precise moment.

"Philippa!" Armand exclaimed, glancing over the chattering group. "What are you doing down here tonight? What's going on?"

Theodora wished Armand hadn't had such a beautifully rich voice. It was patently unfair for a deceptive man to both look good and sound good.

"Didn't you hear?" the woman chirped. Theodora halfway wished she could see the other woman. The warmth in Armand's voice indicated that he was fond of this Philippa, and that made Theodora curious.

What kind of woman would catch his eye?

Philippa continued breathlessly. "Baruch was shot and then it was revealed that he has scars."

"No." Armand managed to sound surprised.

"Yes! He's a *shade*. I mean, it's a shade. Can you believe it?" The woman chattered, as excitable and stupid women were inclined to do. Theodora disliked her for that. What kind of moron was excited to see anyone harvested by the Society?

"It was ever so exciting," the woman gushed. "The whole ceremony was cancelled and the hall was all confusion . . . but where did you go? Why did you leave? You could have seen the whole thing yourself."

"But I'd promised Dr. Anderson that I'd move this corpse into his surgery, and I forgot." Armand's voice was melodic, low and rhythmic, and the slow cadence of his speech seemed almost decadent to Theodora. She'd never forget his voice, that was for certain.

"Oh, you don't want Anderson mad at you! He's terrifying!"

Armand chuckled, a rich sound fit to make Theodora shiver. "I know. I just remembered when we were sitting there. I was hoping to get back in time for the ceremony."

"Oh, but it's all cancelled."

"What about Blackstone?" Something changed in Armand's voice. Theodora heard the shift, and recognized it as a sign of interest. Had he and Baruch been planning to kill Blackstone tonight? They had said that Baruch had a knife. What a disgusting idea. It was better, far better, to do what had to be done from a distance.

She thought of Baruch's blood flowing between his fingers and felt a bit sick.

"I wanted to hear him speak," Armand said and Theodora knew that killing Blackstone tonight *had* been the plan.

But wait. Why had Baruch come looking for her? He couldn't have used a knife from the mezzanine.

"I know, I know!" Theodora wanted to roll her eyes at the woman's honeyed tones. "They said they'd reschedule and would ping us all with the alternate date. Maybe it'll be Monday and they'll cancel our classes. I don't want to take Dissection and Vivisection." Her voice rose an increment. "Will you be my lab partner, Armand, and do all the lab work?"

"It might not be up to us," he said mildly.

"But still, would you try, please?"

"Well . . ."

"Armand, please! I'm begging you. Why, I'll do anything!" Her voice dropped to a purr. "You have only to ask."

"I suppose there's no harm in trying, is there?"

Theodora wondered whether she imagined the smile in his tone.

The woman giggled. "Oh Armand, I knew you would help me!"

The pair walked in silence for a moment, the wheels of the gurney squeaking slightly. Theodora could hear that the larger party had gone on ahead.

"So, what's going to happen to him?" Armand asked.

"Not him, Armand. *It*," the woman scolded. "It's a shade. You have to remember that, especially if you're going to be a Nuclear Darwinist."

It was true, then. Armand was a student at the Institute. He was one of them.

But his friend had been a student, as well, from what the woman had said. Was it possible that they had enrolled as a cover? Theodora was fascinated by the possibility.

It was the kind of advance planning she would have done.

"Of course," Armand said without conviction. "But what's the plan for the shade?"

"Patterson said it'd be treated." The woman's voice dropped. "But I heard that it might get claimed for a research project."

Theodora's heart stopped cold. Could there be any worse fate? She felt badly for her part in the harvesting of Armand's friend.

Even so, it might be a fool's mission to try to retrieve any shade from the Institute's labs. Even wraiths didn't escape unscathed—if they escaped at all—from these corridors. It was one thing to help those shades who had evaded the Society, quite another to steal shades in the possession of the Institute and Society.

Theodora reminded herself to ensure her own safety first.

There were victims and there were victimizers in the Republic. She'd long ago decided which team was hers.

"You know all the stories, Philippa," Armand murmured. "I seem to miss everything."

"Oh, Armand, you don't miss anything important. Just gossip." She giggled and Theodora kept silent with an effort. "Besides, I'm happy to share *everything* with you."

He made some murmur of appreciation, even that low sound prompting a response from Theodora's traitorous heart.

"Oh, Armand," the woman cooed. "I've never seen a dead body." Her fingers brushed the sheet and she gasped. "Is it awful?"

Theodora froze in horror, eyes wide open.

"Not so bad," Armand said, amusement underlying his tone. "Come into Anderson's lab with me and I'll show you."

What? Shock rolled through Theodora.

"Oh, but you'll have to hold my hand," Philippa whispered.

Armand chuckled. "I'll do more than that, Philippa. You can count on it."

Theodora's mouth went dry. Was he going to seduce this foolish woman right before her eyes? The prospect was strangely titillating, which just proved that she was losing her reason.

"Oh, you sound so dangerous!" the woman trilled. Her voice dropped to a whisper. "And so sexy."

"In here." Armand's smile was audible, which only worried Theodora more.

The gurney was driven into a pair of doors, and they swung open on impact. It was dark in the lab Armand had chosen, until a light switch clicked and the room was suddenly illuminated. Theodora braced herself for the worst, then Armand tugged away the sheet.

She had one glimpse of the small brunette with wide eyes, then Armand's broad shoulders filled her frame of vision. He smiled down at her, his eyes sparkling with unexpected mischief, and she feared his intention. Was he warning her? Or scheming?

Unpredictability was the worst possible trait, in Theodora's opinion, but Armand was both hard to read and tough to anticipate.

Somehow she had to remain completely still.

ANDERSON'S LAB was all stainless steel surfaces and white tiles. Philippa smiled coyly at Armand, her smile broadening when he locked the doors from the inside. She wasn't a bad person and he felt a twinge of guilt at his intended deception.

On the other hand, she had applied to become a Nuclear Darwinist, which wasn't the most harmless of professions.

He flicked the sheet from the gurney and was startled again by the pale beauty of the assassin.

"Oh, it's not horrible at all," Philippa said. She stood beside Armand, and he knew she deliberately let her shoulder nudge against his side. Her hip bumped his, and she reached for his hand. "She looks like she's sleeping, with her eyes open."

"She hasn't been dead long," Armand said. He lifted the assassin's hand, showing that it was limp.

Philippa caught her breath and clutched his arm. "I couldn't do that!"

"You don't have to." Armand smiled and laid the assassin's hand back by her side, unable to resist sliding his gloved finger over her flesh. Maybe she'd take it as a warning to play along.

He thought he heard her catch her breath.

Philippa's tone hardened. "Perhaps I should be glad she's dead," she said. "I might have to be jealous of her, otherwise. She was pretty, wasn't she?"

"But beauty is as beauty does."

This time, he knew that the assassin inhaled sharply.

He spun Philippa away from the gurney, sliding his arm around her waist. He turned down the lights, so that there was illumination enough to see but not sufficient for surgery.

"Oh, but I wanted to touch, since you're right beside me."

"No need to frighten yourself." Armand didn't want her to realize that the assassin's skin was still warm.

She nestled closer to him, gazing up with wide eyes. "You said beauty is as beauty does. Did she have some awful history?"

"I don't know," Armand lied. "I only meant that you can't judge people by appearances."

Philippa laughed, rapping her fingers on his chest. "You're right, of course. But I'll judge you by appearances." She slid her hand up his arm to his shoulder, her eyes gleaming. Armand held his ground. "I think you look like a perfect gentleman," she whispered, lowering her voice to a purr.

"Do you?" Armand guided her farther away from the gurney.

"One who would kiss very well," she said with a coy smile.

"Really?"

"One who would reassure a lady who was unsettled."

"How unfortunate that I know of no unsettled ladies."

"Me!" Philippa shivered elaborately. "Seeing a corpse unsettles me," she whispered, her grip tightening on his elbow. "It frightens me." She looked up at him, her lashes fluttering as her lips parted in invitation. "It makes me glad to be alive." Her gaze dropped to his lips and she slid her tongue across her own.

Armand didn't need his old gifts to read her thoughts. He smiled, then ran a fingertip down her cheek. Philippa's eyes darkened with pleasure. "We never know when our time will come," he said.

"Never!" she whispered and slid her hands across his chest. "And here we are, all alone. Both in need of proving that we're alive." Then she smiled seductively.

It was obvious what she expected. Armand bent and touched his lips to hers.

Philippa responded with unexpected enthusiasm, winding her hands around his neck and pulling him closer. He was keenly aware of the assassin's gaze fixed upon them and felt self-conscious.

He did not feel particularly aroused by Philippa's interest.

Perhaps sensing as much, Philippa pushed her tongue between his teeth and arched against his chest. He caught her closer and lifted her against him, deepening his kiss as she made a soft moan of pleasure.

Then she spun away from him, flirtatious and flushed. "So quick!" she said, her voice breathless and eyes sparkling. She fanned herself with one hand, looking pleased with herself. "I knew you'd know how to kiss."

Philippa's clothing adhered to the Sumptuary & Decency Code, every increment of her skin except her face covered from public view. She swayed her hips as she crossed the lab, glancing coquettishly over her shoulder back at Armand.

He smiled encouragement.

"It's so hot in here!" She removed her lace gloves deliberately as she pivoted to face him, her appreciative gaze fixed on him. She laid the gloves on the counter to one side, her cheeks pinkening that he could see her bare skin.

Armand realized this was an artful game, that he was not the first to have seen Philippa's charms. He was reassured that they might be using each other, and his smile seemed to feed her confidence.

She arched her back provocatively as she pulled the pins from her hat, casting them beside the gloves so that they clattered on the steel, then dropping her hat there, as well.

"I wonder what has happened to the air-conditioning." She eyed Armand as she took a step back and unfastened her jacket. It joined the pile of garments and she licked her lips as she surveyed him. "Don't you find it warm?"

He shrugged, noncommittal.

Her blouse was sheer lace, her cleavage even more visible when she unfastened the top button and fanned her face. She moved closer to him again, those hips swinging. "You must be too hot, as well," she murmured, reaching up to run her hands over his shoulders. "All this velvet and faux-leather." She exhaled with delight. "So very masculine. Let me help you."

When Armand only smiled, she unfastened his jacket and slid her hands beneath the heavy velvet. "You *are* too warm," she declared, then closed the last step between them. Her breasts were against his chest and he could see directly down her cleavage.

Philippa smiled when she saw him looking.

"Perhaps the heat has nothing to do with the jacket," Armand murmured.

Philippa chuckled. "Perhaps not," she agreed, then stretched to lock her arms around his neck.

Armand bent his head and kissed her slowly, bracketing her waist with his hands and pulling her closer. He needed to get Philippa out of her clothing, but it didn't appear that would be a problem.

Perhaps he should take Baruch's advice and try to enjoy the moment.

from *The Republican Record*
June 11, 2100
download v. 2.3

Chaos Continues in Chicago

CHICAGO—Citizens residing in Chicago continue to be plagued by nocturnal bands of freed shades and are becoming impatient with the State of Emergency. Although the netherzones of Chicago were unlocked by the Oracle in February of this year, the Republic has not thus far managed to contain the shades and restore order to the beleaguered city. President Van Buren declared a State of Emergency in February, but despite the deployment of additional troops, the city remains chaotic each night.

Chicago resident Bernardine Rodriguez blames the mixed feelings of local citizens. "At first, the troops shot to kill, but it seemed so unfair. The shades are unarmed and innocent. Many of them are naked." She is philosophical. "They're just hungry, not violent. I think there should be some kind of care for them, not death sentences. It's not as if they made the choice to be what they are."

Mrs. Rodriguez insists that she can conduct her business in daylight, and that the surrender of the streets to the shades each night does not interfere with her life. In fact, she leaves food on her back steps for them and notes that it is gone every morning. "It's an act of mercy," she says, when reminded that her act is against the law. "I'm answering to a higher law, that of God himself. What have we become if we can't have compassion for the weak?"

Although few are as outspoken as Mrs. Rodriguez, a

quick survey of the city at night revealed foodstuffs left on more than half of the stoops and porches.

"It's a big problem," admits Mike McGuire, mayor of Chicago. "The police have been attacked by citizens for trying to clear the streets of shades. They're not authorized to use force against unarmed shades, but the shades are not cooperative in our requests that they return to their rightful place. They will die rather than be secured in the netherzones again, but if we use force, citizens are outraged. The president needs to make a choice. We need a new directive to see this situation resolved before it worsens."

President Van Buren was not available for comment; however, his office insisted that the situation in Chicago is under control. Chicago remains in a State of Emergency, but has been downgraded to a Code Orange, attributed to the shades' passivity.

The Oracle released a formal statement that she remains unapologetic for her decision to unshackle the shades of Chicago.

Related Articles:
- The Oracle Revealed—February 14, 2100
- "The Meek Shall Inherit"—Vidlink to today's sermon by Reverend Billie Joe Estevez
- A History of Chicago's Netherzones

IV

DISGUSTING!

Armand was making her watch his seduction of this stupid woman. What was he trying to prove? Theodora resented her position more with every passing second. The last thing she wanted to watch was these two becoming intimate—in a surgery, of all places—although she did admit that she was curious about seeing Armand nude.

His steady seduction was also infuriating because it excited Theodora. Theodora didn't consider herself a voyeur, but it was too easy to imagine herself in the idiot Philippa's place. It was easy to guess how those slow kisses would feel, how they would heat her blood and melt her knees. Theodora was intrigued by Armand's leisurely gestures, by the strength he held in check as he caressed the girl, by how gentle he was. He was no more a stranger to amorous involvements than Theodora was.

But he seemed to enjoy himself more.

Theodora didn't live in a world of much tenderness. That must have been the root of her fascination. His consideration surprised Theodora, just as his removal of the needle had seemed both unnecessary and kind. She wondered for the first time whether she had been living too long in the company of mercenaries.

But to be trusting and gentle in the Republic only made one a victim.

Armand, on the other hand, didn't seem to be a victim.

Who was he? Maybe the puzzle of his identity was what fascinated Theodora.

Or maybe that was just an excuse to ogle him.

"I feel like she's watching," Philippa whispered, her gaze flicking repeatedly to Theodora. "Can we go somewhere else?"

"I can't wait," Armand said, his words low and rough. "I want you now." Something rang false in his tone, something hinted that his words weren't entirely honest, but only Theodora noticed.

Philippa, in contrast, glowed with pleasure.

"I have a better idea," he promised, unfastening the belt of Philippa's blouse and spinning her in place. "What if you can't see the corpse?" He blindfolded the young woman with quick gestures and she gasped in delight.

"What a naughty game!" she breathed and he laughed.

His laugh was wonderful, so wonderful that hearing it ought to be taxed. The Republic would figure out a way, Theodora was sure of it.

"You like it?" he murmured.

"Just don't let go of me," Philippa begged, clutching at his arm. "I don't want to touch anything. Or anyone."

There was a glint of determination in Armand's eyes, one that seemed more predatory than amorous to Theodora. "Not even me?" he whispered, then kissed her deeply again.

Philippa sighed with pleasure. If she had possessed any inhibitions, the blindfold eliminated them. She dissolved against him, ready to surrender anything to him.

She was Armand's toy.

He glanced toward Theodora then, the sudden flick of his gaze making Theodora's pulse leap.

It skipped again when he winked.

As if they were complicit in this seduction.

Theodora was shocked, then even more aroused. What was his real plan?

Philippa's blouse was the first to be discarded, and she moaned when Armand brushed his fingertips across her breasts. In contrast, he seemed to be more of an observer than a participant. Philippa was more curvaceous than Theodora, her breasts ripe and so pale that the nipples seemed very red.

Armand didn't even remove his gloves to touch her. He watched Philippa with care, gauging her reaction, but apparently not feeling much of one himself. Philippa's skirt and petticoat were pooled on the floor shortly afterward, then Armand removed her boots and stockings with singular persistence.

Even Philippa appeared to be somewhat startled by his apparent determination to have her naked, while he remained fully dressed. She tugged at his jacket, but he spun her in place and easily evaded her touch. She pulled at his gloves and pouted when he wouldn't remove them.

She complained and reached for the knot of the blindfold, but he caught her wrists in his hands and kissed her to silence her protest. The glint in his eyes grew more steely with every passing moment, although, of course, Philippa couldn't see that.

Theodora's curiosity grew.

Philippa was clearly prepared to cede whatever was necessary to Armand, though, and met his every kiss with an answering hunger. When Philippa was bereft of everything except her blindfold, Armand caught her up in his arms and carried her to the surgical bay itself. She giggled with delight, rubbing her nakedness against him and whispering his name.

As he put her down, Theodora saw Armand's hand slide into the pocket of his jacket. She wondered why, then saw the glint of glass and steel. She knew she should have anticipated his plan when she saw him slide the needle into the buttock of his intended lover.

Philippa gasped, then arched her back. Armand steadily emptied the syringe. She started to ask a question, then sighed as the relaxant slid into her body.

By the time Armand had straightened, Philippa had collapsed into limp femininity. He immediately turned away, not taking the time to peruse her charms, purpose in his every gesture. He cast a sheet over Philippa, then gathered her clothing from the floor. He returned to Theodora and touched his fingertip to her lips.

Theodora was impressed by his plan. The clothing would fit her well enough, and it would be easier for her to escape the Institute dressed as a citizen.

There was more to her captor than met the eye.

She struggled a bit against her bonds, but he didn't release her. Instead, he smiled and leaned over her, his green eyes gleaming. His gaze dropped to her lips and she saw that glint of mischief in his eyes.

Theodora knew what he was going to do a heartbeat before he did so. She had time to gasp, to consider the merit of protesting, to yearn . . .

Then Armand brushed his lips across hers. It was a caress so light that it might have not happened at all. A kiss one would give a sister, maybe. She saw the hues of green in his eyes, the firm outline of his lips, felt the impress of his mouth on hers. She smelled his cologne and yearned to feel the thick wave of his hair, or run her hands over his shoulders. His fleeting touch set her body to tingling.

She wanted everything Philippa had had of him.

And more.

Their gazes locked and held, the green of his eyes electric and alluring. Theodora was certain he was going to kiss her again, *really* kiss her, and she had time to yearn for his touch.

Then there was a ruckus in the corridor. Men's voices raised in argument, vehement argument, and Armand dropped Philippa's clothes beside the gurney.

He moved quickly toward the door. The lab was plunged into darkness and Theodora saw his silhouette briefly in the opened doorway before he disappeared.

She wondered where he'd gone, when he'd be back, *if* he would be back, before she realized she was better off without a man who confused her so completely.

In Armand's absence it was easy to remember that her own objectives were the only things of importance, that cred ruled, that his objectives—however admirable—were not her own, that she had an assignment to complete.

Even if she wanted more of a kiss than she'd had.

But the decision was out of her hands. No sooner was Armand gone than Theodora saw the wraith slip out of the darkness. There must be a netherzone access in the wall of the lab.

The wraith was responding to her bounty call.

She recognized Big Ted.

Of course. He'd been employed as a cook by the Society

for years, and was one of the wraiths' best sources of inside information. It made perfect sense that he'd be the
closest and quickest to respond.

She recalled Armand's wink and knew it was better to
be gone.

"IT'S MINE," a man argued. His voice was low, as if he
didn't want to be overheard, but his determination was
clear.

"No," another man insisted. "We are obligated to treat
him, question him, and release him."

The voices carried from around a bend in the corridor
and Armand crept closer. They were talking about Baruch,
he knew it, although it had been the anger of their suppressed voices that had caught at his ear.

At least his assassin couldn't go anywhere. She was still
tied down and the bonds on the gurney were secure. He
could take a minute to investigate.

And maybe he would learn something more about the
plans for Baruch.

"It's a shade," the first man hissed. "And it has been harvested. That puts it into the pool of the Institute, and that
means I can select it for my experiment."

"Not without my authorization," the second man insisted.
"I made a public declaration of what will happen to this
victim, and I have to stand by it. The Society has already
been damaged in the public view, and the only way to ensure our future is to show that we are adapting to changing
times . . ."

Armand peeked around the corner. Blake Patterson argued with a shorter, older, and stouter man. The contrast

between them was striking, Patterson so handsome and young while the other man was balding and bespectacled, so pale and soft that he might never have left the hidden corridors of the Institute.

"You are an idiot," he sneered at Patterson. "The only way forward is to defend our interests and our rights. Ernest Sinclair knew that, but you've forgotten the basics."

"With respect, Dr. Cosmopoulos, the world has changed from Ernest Sinclair's day and it continues to change. Public perceptions are turning against us, and we have to adapt."

"We don't have to do any such thing."

"Don't you think it's more important for the Institute and Society to retain autonomy than to be subsumed by the government?"

"We are a research institute," Cosmopoulos said with hauteur. "Committed to improving the future of the Republic and sufficiently well funded to defend ourselves."

"Haven't you read Blackstone's proposal? If elected, he intends to seize our drug patents. The federal government will police the patents and collect the licensing revenue."

"He'll never manage it."

"You're wrong. His proposal is popular, maybe the key to his rising popularity. Since the Oracle was revealed, we have been demonized in the popular media. We cannot continue as we have, if we mean to survive."

"So, what's your plan?" Cosmopoulos sneered. "Open the doors and let everyone in to see? Abandon the research that characterizes our work? Release the shades to drool in public?"

"I propose to be more open and more accommodating—"

"The ugly work still has to be done," Cosmopoulos interjected. "Are you going to license drugs for public use without being absolutely sure of their effects? What other human subjects will you use for your tests? Shades don't know the difference. They are barely functional intellectually—but their bodies are precisely the same as ours. That's the point, Patterson. This is their main usefulness. It might even be the reason for their existence."

"There is an opportunity here to build opinion in our favor," Patterson insisted. "You cannot take Baruch into the labs."

Cosmopoulos smiled. "He's already there. You can't take him back."

"I insist that you surrender him to me . . ."

Cosmopoulos laughed. "I'll lock the doors against you. Didn't they tell you that the president of the Society doesn't get keys to every single corner of the Institute?"

Patterson's shock was clear.

"We always knew it was only a matter of time before those of you who sit at desks in the tower turned against true research." Cosmopoulos poked a finger at Patterson's chest. "You'd better get out of here, while you can."

"Don't you threaten me," Patterson muttered.

"I'm stating a fact." Cosmopoulos held his ground. "Giving you a little advice."

"Surrender Baruch and I'll forget this conversation."

"You can't make me comply."

"This is outrageous!" Patterson stormed. "The Institute answers to the Society, and you have no right to defy me in this."

"The Institute *funds* the Society," Cosmopoulos said coldly. "And you're talking about facilitating a plan that would eliminate our revenue stream. Those drug patents are our source of revenue. You're not the only one concerned with public appearances, Patterson. What I need is a triumph for the labs and this shade might just hold the key to that."

"What do you mean?"

"The Oracle is said to be allied with the angels, and this shade has two diagonal scars on his back. I've seen them before, but never had the chance to analyze the bodies of those who had them. There's no logical human reason for such scars."

"I don't understand."

Cosmopoulos became more animated. "I have a hypothesis, one that I need to prove. Lilia Desjardins claimed that she found a pair of angels, but refused to surrender them for study. Do you remember their wings? What would the scars be like if those wings were removed?"

"That's speculation."

Armand watched and listened, horrified.

"Is it possible that this shade was an angel?" Cosmopoulos challenged. "Is it possible that his physiology is different, that something in his body will reveal a benefit for humans? Angels are said to be transcendent, made of light, immortal, ageless—there are a dozen possibilities of impact upon humans." He shrugged. "Or maybe they are just frauds, charlatans whose tricks are due to be revealed."

"He's not an angel. He's just a shade in hiding."

Cosmopoulos smiled. "That would be consistent with his decision to apply to the Institute as a student. That's a stupid place for a shade to hide, but a shade might be too stupid to realize that. On the other hand, those who believe in angels might argue that there's a divine plan about to be revealed."

"You're evading the point . . ."

"No. You are. You must be smarter than this."

"Smarter than a shade, you mean?"

"Exactly!" Cosmopoulos wagged a finger at Patterson, who seemed to have been struck to stone in his indignation, and dropped his voice. "If I can prove that angels don't exist, that they're a trick, what will that do to the Oracle's claims? Her popularity? Her power over the minds of the Republic's citizens?" He paused to consider Patterson. "More importantly, what will it do to the future prospects of both Society and Institute?"

"One shade can't make a proof . . ."

"Who says there's only one?" Cosmopoulos challenged.

"This is ridiculous," Patterson objected. "It's not wrong for the Society to adapt and to compromise."

"It is if you have to surrender everything for the prospect of nothing at all. There are no guarantees in your game, Patterson. You're going to lose it all, drop by drop. I'm going to secure the present for the future."

"If you're right."

"Don't tell me that you believe in angels?" Cosmopoulos taunted.

"You're going to use Baruch for your agenda, independent of what results you find." Patterson's disgust was a shadow of Armand's own. "His scars condemned him in more ways than one."

Cosmopolous was dismissive. "Ethics aren't so important when you fight for survival. Even Blackstone is manipulating the facts and sustaining illusions. He's turning popular opinion against us, maybe even in league with the Oracle, and I'm just going to provide the evidence to stop him." Cosmopoulos leaned closer, his passion clear. "Don't you, as president of the Society, owe it to all of us to support my effort to save everything we know?"

"I owe it to members of the Society to pursue truth—"

Cosmopoulos interrupted Patterson sharply. "You can fight me, but you'll lose. Wouldn't it look better to provide a united front?"

"That's what I'm trying to do!"

Cosmopolous sneered. "Ernest Sinclair would have known his responsibility to all of us. Do you? What will you be president of, if Blackstone has his way?"

The two men glared at each other, Baruch's future hanging in the balance. Armand held his breath.

Patterson shoved a hand through his hair. He pivoted and paced, then turned back to the older scientist. "Send me the protocol within the hour."

Cosmopoulos smiled. "I knew I could make you see sense."

Patterson spun without answering and headed back toward the stairs, his expression troubled. Armand pulled back into the shadows so that the other man didn't see him as he passed.

What would the experiment protocol be? Armand didn't want to think about it. He had to get Baruch out of the labs as soon as possible.

He raced back to Dr. Anderson's lab where he'd left his assassin tied down. He was newly determined to motivate her to accept his deal, whatever the price. He flung open the door to the darkened lab, reached for the lights and froze.

The gurney was empty.

She had vanished, as surely as if she had never been.

But how?

* * *

"NOTHING FANCY, but here it is," Big Ted grumbled as he locked the door of his unit behind them. He'd freed Theodora silently and led her into the netherzones below the laboratories with the familiarity of one who had lived years in this vicinity.

"Thanks." Theodora had tossed on Philippa's long chemise, then grabbed her bag of gear. She opened the bag now and began to assure herself that everything except the laze was there.

Big Ted was, if anything, more heavyset than she recalled. He still dressed in black, still wore a tank top that left his heavily tattooed arms and shoulders bare. His skin was the color of mahogany, his tattoos midnight blue, and the gold caps on his teeth shone as brilliantly as ever. He kept his head shaved and his thoughts hidden. He was as trustworthy as wraiths came, and Theodora was glad that he had been the one to retrieve her.

She was surprised to find his unit so empty that it might have been unoccupied. He'd been planted in the Society for years, after all. There was a stainless steel crate on the floor against one wall, a hammock and nothing else in the room.

Maybe it wasn't his unit.

"Always said you were the luckiest wraith ever," he muttered.

"I'm not feeling very lucky right now," Theodora replied, her tone wry. She'd lost her laze, failed to secure the bounty on the Oracle, and now needed to pay Big Ted for saving her.

He considered her for a moment, then shrugged and

turned away. "You'd probably say it's not luck to get injected with Ivanofor in the middle of a hit."

She glanced up in surprise. "Did you see?"

"No, but I've got eyes in my head."

"It wasn't a loading dose."

"But it still messed with your game. You're pale, too pale, and your pupils are too small. Don't imagine I don't know the signs of that shit. They got some kind of site license for it around here, go through buckets of it." He cocked a finger at her. "Just don't puke on my floor when it wears off completely. I'm never cleaning this unit again."

He was right. Theodora's stomach was already churning. "I'll be out of here by then." Then she considered him, realizing what he'd implied. "That sounds final, like you're leaving."

Ted grinned. "I am, kid. I'm out of this hole tonight. Just took one last job out of the goodness of my heart. Hadn't been you, I woulda passed. Old times' sake and all that."

Theodora raised her eyebrows. "Then we don't need to worry about the cred?"

Ted laughed. "My heart isn't nearly that good." He strode toward her, removing the probe from his palm. "Not to be overly familiar, but you know it has to be done."

Theodora grimaced, then extended her palm. She averted her face from the transaction, feeling herself blush for the second time in short order.

Datasharing was considered a feat of remarkable intimacy in the Republic, more intimate even than sex. To insert the probe of one's palm into the port of another individual's palm was to be privy to every one of that person's secrets. In theory, there could be firewalls. In reality, most people's passwords were so pedestrian that they could be overridden automatically. And there was bootleg software to press deeper than that.

It was possible to catch a worm or a virus from another person's palm, a digital souvenir that could blight the operation of one's own palm for good or even destroy it.

Sex was far simpler. There were a limited array of secrets that could be learned through sexual union, and the entire array of biological souvenirs could be treated legally and effectively. One could keep one's secrets, or at least the secrets one's partner might find offensive. Cures could be found discreetly.

In contrast, the Republic was harsh with those who infected their palms and required replacements—such carelessness was considered to be a violation of the Republic's trust, and the willful destruction of federal property.

A person with a damaged palm could be charged, fined, and/or imprisoned for his or her cavalier disregard. That wasn't such a deterrent for wraiths like Theodora.

It was the intimacy.

But there was no other way to confirm her status for the bounty call. Big Ted had the right to request her verification. She'd known that when she'd preset the bounty parameters.

Even so, she winced as Ted slid the probe of his palm into the receptacle on hers. Theodora hated the sound of how it snicked home. She knew his palm would interrogate hers, confirming her survival for Shadow.net so that the bounty could be paid out of the escrow account.

"No unauthorized peeking," she said. The palm beeped and she confirmed both her own status and his save.

Ted laughed. "A girl's got to have some secrets, huh?" He whistled to himself, well satisfied with what he'd accomplished.

Theodora wasn't feeling nearly so celebratory. Ten thousand units was a lot of cred. As glad as she was to be free, she wished she hadn't had to pay it.

Especially as she hadn't earned the cred for the hit.

"Pretty much," she agreed, wishing she'd set the reward lower. It hadn't been that hard to break her free. On the other hand, he'd come because of the lure of the amount.

The palms illuminated simultaneously, retrieving the confirmation message as one, then Theodora pulled hers free.

"Especially if that girl's going to mess around with angels," Ted mused. Theodora stared at him. He nonchalantly tapped his palm, transferring his cred to some secure place, then grinned at her so quickly that she knew he was testing her.

She frowned at him. "What are you talking about? What angels?"

"Angels," Ted said, with a conspiratorial nod. He leaned closer and dropped his voice to a whisper. "You weren't going to take out the Oracle, were you? She's the real goods, that kid, and her Consort, he's a fallen angel."

Theodora laughed. "Oh, come on, Ted. Be serious!"

"I am. Didn't you see the ceremony?"

"Ted, you can't be that credulous. It's just PR, good PR, and showmanship. There are no angels, even if the Republic wants you to believe as much."

"Sure there are." Big Ted nodded and held up his hands. "They came out of the sky that night, dozens of them, all blinding white light. I would never have believed it myself but they were here. They knew her. They kissed her! And they took the scars from his back, right before our eyes."

"Ted, you have to know better." Theodora pulled her pseudoskin out of the bag and gave it a shake, impatient with his unexpected whimsy. "It was a trick . . ."

"Nah. It was no trick. I know tricks and I know truth. This was the real thing." He opened the stainless steel case, which was full of kitchen implements, and withdrew a folded shirt with care. "I would have believed she was a force for change, just because she unlocked the netherzones." He pulled on the shirt, then cocked a finger at Theodora. "That kid's going to stir things up, I guarantee it. That's why I'm out of here. She needs more than Rafe at her back."

"Where *are* you going?"

"I'm going to work for her, somehow. I'll do anything. Never mind these bastards. They'd sell anyone for a price—which is some kind of accusation coming from a wraith, I know." He leaned closer again, his eyes gleaming. "The thing is, what if there is more to life than what we see? What if there is a higher purpose? What if we can make the world a better place? Seductive shit there. I kind of like the sound of it. And I'm ready for a change."

"I don't believe that either," Theodora said, folding her arms across her chest. "You're wraith through and through, Ted, just like me. You're putting me on or you've gone soft."

He laughed. "You're such a cynic! Like I said, I didn't believe it either, not until I saw the angels. Not until I felt the burn of angelfire. Now I believe." He tapped his heart. "Now I know what's the truth, and I'm going to change my life."

Theodora stared at him. Was it possible?

No! He had to be lying to her.

Ted shut the case and locked it. He pulled something out of his pocket and Theodora saw that it was one of the temporary tattoos they sold in the streets, replicas of the Oracle's own tattoo. Before her eyes, he peeled off the backing and applied the mark to his forehead, then faced her proudly. "You'll believe if you ever see one."

"I won't hold my breath," Theodora murmured.

Ted shrugged and turned to leave. He picked up the handles of his case and tugged it toward the threshold, revealing that it was on casters. He suddenly snapped his fingers. "Oh wait. You did see one."

Theodora glanced up, caught his cunning smile.

"That kid they took down to the labs, the one with the diagonal scars on his back. You hit him, didn't you?"

"They said his name was Baruch. A student here at the Institute."

"No. An *angel*. That's what makes those scars. They get their wings sliced off."

Theodora was horrified. "By the Society?"

"No! They volunteer. They become mortal to help us out. And they sacrifice their wings to do it."

Theodora had never heard such a load of garbage in her life. "Come on, Ted. What have you been smoking tonight?"

"This is no joke. Don't you remember that pair of angels in Nouveau Mont Royal? They were in the daily download and everything."

"Ted, that was in the *circus*! Of course, they weren't real angels. You have to be more skeptical than that."

"I was, but no longer." He jabbed a heavy finger in her direction. "I saw the marks on the Consort's back and I saw the angels take them away. I know you think you did what needed doing, but you shot an angel, kid."

Theodora blinked. She thought about Baruch being captive in the Institute's labs. Angel or not, he didn't deserve whatever they were going to do to him.

Could Armand really save his friend?

Or would he end up on the adjacent gurney in a research lab? Her heart clenched with the conviction that she had to keep her promise to him.

And not just for the potential return of her laze.

Big Ted's gaze turned cold. "What if you have to answer for that one day? What if someone demands an accounting from you? You gonna tell them you shot an angel for cred?" He half-laughed. "Wait. You were going to shoot the Oracle for cred. If there's a hell, Theodora, you're going to have front-row seats."

"There is no heaven and there is no hell." Theodora was impatient with his comments. "You know that, Ted. It's all just superstitious nonsense, promoted to gullible people to keep them in line. You know that most people worry less about the present if they think there's a glorious future ahead of them. It serves the Republic to propagate this kind of—"

"Believe what you need to, kid. Thanks for the contribution to my retirement fund." Big Ted turned to leave. "You'll be all right here for half an hour or so," he said flatly. "They don't know I'm leaving and it might even be morning before they check. The door's not sealed from the inside, and you likely know your way out."

Big Ted glanced back, his gaze boring into hers. "By the way, just so we're clear—you come after the Oracle again, all bets are off. No past loyalties apply, no cred will change the outcome. I'll wring your fucking neck myself if you try to hurt her."

Theodora knew he meant it.

That he would defend the Oracle for no cred meant that he was serious about his change of course.

"Angels?" she whispered, trying to wrap her mind around his assertion. It defied logic that such beings should exist, let alone that they should mingle with men.

But what else would cause those scars?

Theodora felt the vibration of her palm receiving a message. Big Ted must have felt the same sensation, because they both glanced down simultaneously.

Ted let out a low whistle and Theodora sat down hard. Her worst expectation had come true.

"See what you got him into?" Ted muttered. "Unlucky bastard. There won't be enough left to incinerate when they're done."

As much as Theodora would have liked to argue, Big Ted was right.

Society of Nuclear Darwinists Internal Memo
Research Proposal 17243
submitted by Dr. Paul Cosmopoulos
September 18, 2100; 21:30

Seeking the Cause of Distinctive Dorsal Scars
Executive Summary

Distinctive dorsal scars have been observed in human subjects in the field numerous times over recent years, although individuals bearing those scars have proven to be elusive research subjects. None has yet been subjected to the investigative protocols of the Institute, thus the cause of these scars remains unknown. There is no plausible physiological reason for such a mark, the sole explanation being duplicate cancerous growths—few believe that they could or would develop in such a balanced fashion, particularly in multiple subjects.

The characteristic scars are similar to healed surgical wounds in appearance, remaining both reddish in hue and slightly indented even after healing has obviously occurred. These scars occur in pairs, one extending in a straight line from the left shoulder to just above the waist and slightly to the left of the spine. The second is a mirror image of the first. The wound does not appear to interfere with any other bodily functions nor does the general health of the subjects in question appear to be impaired—in fact, anecdotal evidence suggests that these shades are more vigorous and clever subjects than the population norm.

The best-documented example is the following dead shade, which was harvested and failed the S.H.A.D.E. At the time, the scars were not considered worthy of investigation, although subsequently the shade defected from assigned labor. Years later, this shade was killed—unfortunately the remains were incinerated before the Institute could intervene.

• <u>R786903</u> a.k.a. Rachel Gottlieb
<u>NGPD Cold Case File 99-87659-3A</u>

A second individual exhibiting such scars was the official Consort of the Oracle, who displayed identical scars on the debate between presidential candidates on February 19, 2100 in Chicago. They are clearly delineated in this <u>vidlink</u>, but disappear by the end of the event. It is possible that his scars were not genuine, though any reason for feigning them is unknown.

The fact remains that speculation has grown throughout the Republic, given the Oracle's reputed connection with angels, that these marks are from the removal of angelic wings.

The Institute has had the remarkable good fortune to harvest a live shade bearing scars in this pattern. We have the opportunity—if not the obligation—to disprove the rumored presence of angels in the Republic by investigating the precise physiological nature of this shade and determining the true cause of these scars. This study will include a complete investigation of all bodily functions and systems of the subject, including neurological, respiratory, digestive, muscular, nervous, and skeletal. Needless to say, any angelic origin should reveal itself in discrete differences from the human norm.

The investigation of the live subject will take approximately six weeks in total, following the attached protocol, and utilizing the drugs and supplies listed in Appendix A. Final analysis of the remains may take an additional six months, although results may justify an extended inquiry into specific areas of interest. See Appendix B for a full list of the scheduled experiments and Appendix C for a detailed budget request.

V

THEODORA READ the ping on her palm, her lips tightening. This had to be the man she'd shot, Armand's friend Baruch. Guilt shot through her that she'd been responsible for his situation.

If she hadn't injured him, his scars wouldn't have been revealed. Becoming the subject of an intensive Institute experiment was far, far worse than being harvested as a shade.

Which wasn't ideal, either. She should have been merciful and shot him dead when she'd had the chance.

Theodora averted her gaze, thinking furiously. Did Armand know about his friend's defect? Was he simply protective of the other man because of his flaw? What the heck were the two of them doing, enrolling as students of the Institute, with Baruch having those scars?

What *did* cause them?

Not that it mattered.

She knew what she had to do. There were times when cred wasn't everything—Theodora knew that in her heart, even though she would have denied it vehemently if challenged.

Sometimes, a person had to finish what she'd started.

"Surprised?" Ted granted her a wry glance. "Are you kidding? Cosmopoulos always ends his lab protocols with dissections. It even says as much. That guy will be chopped into ice cube trays in a matter of months."

"We don't need to review the details," she said, keeping her tone disinterested. "It's not like it matters to us."

"Not even if he's an angel?"

Theodora laughed. "Well, one thing he can't be is an angel," she said, her tone dismissive. "Although it's awful that they're going to kill him to make a political point."

"But if an angel sacrificed his wings, what kind of scars would he have?" Ted said softly.

"Assuming that there are angels and that they do sacrifice their wings. Sounds like a long shot to me, Ted."

"But Rafe's scars were like that. Didn't you see?" He tapped at his palm, replaying a vid of the Oracle's appearance in Chicago the previous winter. Theodora watched the performance, which he played without audio, recalling her own doubt that it was real. She saw the scars on the bare back of Rafe, then he was swallowed by brilliant light.

"Angels!" Ted breathed.

"You can't see the angels. It's just as I remembered. There's a lot of light, but that doesn't mean there are angels."

"Then who takes away his scars?" Ted asked.

When the light diminished, the scars were gone.

Theodora rolled her eyes. "Just because I can't explain the trick doesn't mean there wasn't one."

"People have been trying to explain the trick since February and nobody can." Ted shook his head. "Maybe the easy answer, that there *are* angels, is the right one."

There was something to be said for the fact that Big Ted, typically as skeptical as they came, was convinced.

Theodora decided that he was trying to fool her. She

didn't know what his game was, or why he'd lie about such a thing, but she wasn't going to be persuaded.

She wouldn't trust him or confide in him. He'd saved her life, but he'd been paid well for it.

"There can't be angels," she said, turning her back on him and stepping into her pseudoskin underneath the chemise. "You're crazy to believe all that propaganda. You have to know that someone somewhere is just trying to distract you."

She welcomed the familiar weight of the pseudoskin's protection, having felt naked without its burden. When it was over her shoulders, she discarded the chemise, then fastened the front. Her filters had broken and she didn't have time for the voice-modifier box. She pulled on her boots and locked her belt, painfully aware of how empty the holster was.

"Is that so?" Ted mused.

Theodora kept her tone skeptical, even allowing herself a little sneer. The last thing she wanted was for Big Ted to guess what she was doing. She didn't trust him any more than he deserved.

Which was not at all.

She scoffed. "Like those two angels you mentioned at the Nouveau Mont Royal Circus? They weren't real—you could tell because the circus owner wouldn't let any scientist near them."

"Maybe he was protecting them."

"Maybe you're seeing what you want to see, Ted." Theodora softened her words with a smile. "Maybe you're losing your edge."

He smiled back. "Guess we don't have to worry about you losing yours." He paused on the threshold to glance back, his expression sober. "Maybe you should have killed that shade when you had the chance. It would have been kinder and the world is a bit short of kindness these days."

Theodora frowned. "That's true enough," she ceded softly.

"Hope you like it hot, kid."

Ted grabbed his steel case, rolling it quietly out the door, then moved with surprising speed down the corridor.

When Theodora looked out a minute later, he had disappeared into the netherzones through some hidden access. She doubted she'd ever see him again.

Theodora oriented herself quickly, then cut a circuitous route back to Anderson's lab. No one was following her, but she wasn't leaving anything to chance.

THOUSANDS OF miles away, in a hidden room in New Gotham, Tupperman eyed the message on his desktop. He'd just worked a twelve-hour shift at NGPD, then another six coordinating the efforts of his hidden forces. He rubbed his face, feeling a day's growth on his chin, and considered this news.

It wasn't much consolation to know that he'd called it right.

He wondered where Armand was.

Tupperman had so few allies in Chicago, so few sources of information or assistance. The haven of both Society and Institute was a hole in Tupperman's network, which didn't surprise anyone. That, however, wasn't a very useful situation, particularly now. He considered the possible individuals he could reassign, but believed them all to be secure and critical where they were.

Whoever went after Baruch might fail, might be revealed, might be sacrificed. What was the greater good?

Tupperman tapped the desktop and pulled up the astrological charts, recalling what Baruch had said. He remembered the glimmer of angelfire in the eyes of the two newest recruits, their passion and optimism. Was it to come down to their loss?

When a new age could dawn, a new future for the Republic and all the souls within it? In just six weeks?

If the future could go either way, then this might be the start of a decline. It was possible that matters would only get worse from here, that there would be no recovery after Election Day.

Could he really delegate anything that needed to be done now?

Or was it time to finally risk his own safety and secrecy, to put everything on the line? Was it time to finally engage with this sphere, to risk it all?

One thing Tupperman knew for sure was that he had no desire to live in a Republic that was more repressive than it was currently. If they failed, there would be no point in earthly existence.

He pushed to his feet, decision made. With a tap of his fingertip, he forwarded the lab protocol to Montgomery, knowing exactly what would come of that. He sent one last message to his network.

Then he used his palm and the official network of the Republic to request a leave of absence, for personal reasons, from his superior in the New Gotham Police Department.

It was granted almost immediately, but by the time it pinged on his palm, Tupperman was already packed.

He didn't need much: his wits, his laze, and his connections. It seemed a meager tool kit to save the world, but it was all he had.

It would have to do.

Tupperman put street clothes over his heavy-gauge pseudoskin, then donned his thickest gloves. He destroyed the desktop in his hidden room by putting his fist through its display. He secured the room, then left his unit with purpose in his step, knowing he'd never see it again. He donned his helm, and started the police motorcycle that he routinely rode home.

Fortunately, he had filled the tank before leaving the station on this night. He had a full load of canola.

In his gloved hand was the tiny remote that he'd rigged years before, in anticipation that this moment would come. He'd secretly hoped it never would, but had known that was foolish.

Two blocks away, he stopped the bike and detonated the explosives. He heard the explosion and saw the plume of smoke. He waited, then detonated the second suite of explosives. He heard the building collapse, then smashed the remote beneath his heel and kicked the pieces into the sewer.

He revved the bike, made a U-turn, and headed straight for the ruined city of Gotham.

There was no turning back.

To all Students of the Institute for Radiation Studies
and all members of the Society of Nuclear Darwinists
September 19, 2100

URGENT
Notice of Rescheduled Event

Please be advised that the Opening Session of the 76th
Annual Convention of the Society of Nuclear Darwinists,
originally scheduled for September 18, has been rescheduled.
All registered attendees are requested to join our guests and
dignitaries, once again at Convocation Hall, on Wednesday,
September 22, 2100 at 20:00.

As participants have made arrangements to accommodate the
unanticipated change of schedule, it is hoped that members will
make similar sacrifices to attend this important meeting. Once
again, be reminded of the proxies at <u>AGM Proxies for 2100.</u>

As previously indicated, the presentation will be followed by the
serving of light refreshments.

R.S.V.P. immediately regarding this new date and time to <u>Sonja
Anseldotter</u>

Anderson's lab was just as she had left it. Theodora slid into the quiet room and touched the lights up slightly.

There was no sign of Armand. Had he come back for her? Theodora wasn't going to think about it.

The stainless steel and white tile gleamed on all sides, the soft breathing of Philippa telling her that the other woman wasn't dead.

She also wouldn't be very active until at least the next morning. The syringe had been full.

That meant that Theodora had twelve hours in which she could safely impersonate this student of the Institute for Radiation Studies.

It might just be long enough.

After confirming that the room was empty, Theodora locked the doors behind herself. She went to the gurney and quickly dressed, tugging Philippa's clothing over her pseudoskin. Because she was slimmer than Philippa, even the corset fit. She left the stockings and shoes, favoring her own sturdy boots. The skirts were long enough and full enough to hide them.

She tucked her heavy gloves into her belt and donned the lace gloves instead. Her hair was coiled beneath the hat, which she pinned securely in place, then she wrapped the veil over the hat. It would hide both the color of her hair and her face.

She considered her reflection in the steel backsplash and decided she could pass as the other woman. She'd have to keep the veil in place, keep silent, and work quickly, but she'd had worse disguises.

Theodora eased toward the sedated woman, tugging down the left lace glove. At least Philippa wouldn't have any evidence to offer, given that she was blindfolded. Theodora punched up a bootleg interrogation subroutine, removed the probe from her palm, then slid it into the receptacle on the other woman's palm.

It snicked home and began to suck information from the small computer embedded in Philippa's hand. There was something vaguely disgusting about datasharing with another woman, especially one she didn't like or admire, but Theodora didn't dwell on it. Theodora wasn't fond of the intimacy and seldom trusted that the other person's palm would be devoid of viruses and worms.

But Philippa, she guessed, would be the proverbial open book.

She was relieved, all the same, to find her suspicion proven correct. Philippa's software was all official and legal, rightly registered and protected only in the most superficial of ways. It took only instants for her interrogation software to break her passwords and firewalls.

With no reciprocal invasion.

Theodora watched the stream of data roll into her own palm with satisfaction. Philippa, it proved, was one nosy creature. She had gathered an impressive array of information about the Institute in her short time here, including a number of surreptitious palm shots of Armand.

It appeared that she had been prepared to stalk him.

She even had the security code to his room.

Nice. In seconds, Theodora had copies of electronic keys, floor plans, schedules, and more detail about Philippa's life than any other person could want.

The illicit software set to work, building a replica of Philippa's palm within Theodora's own. It would act as a façade for as long as Theodora commanded. She could send messages through the Republic's network that would appear as if they had come from Philippa. She could *be* Philippa, to all extents and purposes, until Philippa herself challenged the duplication.

Theodora estimated that she had twelve hours.

Tops.

When her palm had taken all that was useful, Theodora disengaged the probe. She used the police-grade scanner in her palm to read Philippa's identification bead, the one embedded in the back of her neck, finding all of the information recorded there to be as expected. She tapped in a suite of commands that she had found very useful over the years.

Then she clapped her left hand over the small bulge of her own embedded identification bead. One of her best investments had been swapping out the Republic's official I.D. bead for an illegal one with read/write capacity. She saved her own identity on her palm, behind that barrier, then recorded Philippa's on her bead.

No doors open to Philippa would be closed to Theodora.

Her impersonation complete, Theodora moved around the perimeter of the room. She wanted to leave Philippa locked within it, preventing the discovery of her sedated form as long as possible.

As anticipated, Theodora found an access to the netherzones on one long wall where Big Ted had appeared. It reassured her to find even this corner of the world to be so predictable. She locked the doors to the corridor from the inside of the lab, then returned to the netherzone access. She slid into the familiar embrace of darkness, then barricaded that door from the other side. She held up her palm, letting its faint blue light illuminate the passageway.

Just for the entertainment value, Theodora found her way

to the corridor, and bolted the doors to the surgery again from the outside. Philippa couldn't escape or be discovered alone. It gave Theodora the maximum amount of time she could buy, and it would have to do. She returned to the netherzones again, intent on making every moment count.

Theodora consulted the map of the Institute from Philippa's palm, charted her course, and set out in pursuit of Armand.

She hoped he was home.

She was ready to make a deal.

And not only because she wanted her laze back.

She was curious as to how killing Blackstone could possibly set Baruch free. Armand's assertion made little sense to her, but he had seemed to be a practical man. Clever, too. There had to be some detail he had omitted, something that made his plan sensible. Theodora respected his inclination to manage information—people generally didn't need to know much about whatever one chose to do. Details should be surrendered on an as-needed basis.

The prospect of solving a mystery must have been the reason why Theodora's heart was skipping in such an erratic way.

It had nothing to do with a deep voice and gleaming green eyes. She was sure of that.

THE SOCIETY OF NUCLEAR DARWINISTS
AND ERNEST SINCLAIR

excerpted from R. Fantino, *The Triumph of Science in the Post-Nuclear Age: A Commemoration of the Society of Nuclear Darwinists and Their Contribution to Society at Large on the Society's Seventy-fifth Anniversary*, Institute for Radiation Studies, Chicago, 2099.

The Society of Nuclear Darwinists, that familiar and prestigious scientific research organization, was founded by Ernest Sinclair in 2024 with the aim of studying the effects of radiation upon the human species.

After the devastating First Planetary War, the quantity of radioactive fallout and its effects upon the surviving population became an issue that could no longer be denied. The vast majority of children born in the decade after the war were born with physical defects, as itemized in Republican Law Code 201/8-349 Section IV (also known as the S.H.A.D.E.).

It was Dr. Sinclair's notion that a formal study of these children should be made, to better calculate the human cost of nuclear war. Because of the range of specialized information required to conduct this research, Dr. Sinclair established the Institute for Radiation Studies in Chicago in 2024. This academically demanding institution offered initially a four-year study plan—with a heavy focus upon biology, chemistry, radiation, and anatomy courses—to selected students, the successful completion of which resulted in a certification of a Nuclear Darwinist, Third Degree. Subsequently, advanced study options were made available to students.

The Society of Nuclear Darwinists, an affiliate organization also established in 2024 by Dr. Sinclair, originally comprised its membership of the faculty of the Institute and later included all graduates of the Institute. There is often common membership between the Board of Governors of each organization, and they often join for common purposes.

Shortly after the establishment of Institute and Society, it became clear that there were far more children affected with physical disabilities than even Ernest Sinclair had anticipated and that their numbers vastly exceeded the needs of any research program. Ernest Sinclair suggested a program to put those children to work for the good of society as a whole, and such was the extent of the relief of the populace and government at this solution, that all defective children were legally made wards of the Society and subject to its jurisdiction. The Sub Human Atomic Deviancy Evaluation (S.H.A.D.E.) itemized the standard against which all live births were measured.

There are seven degrees possible for a Nuclear Darwinist. First Degree is achieved by passing the examinations at the end of the first year of full-time study, and is also offered as a continuing studies program for mature students with an interest in Nuclear Darwinism. Second Degree is achieved by passing the examinations at the end of the third year of study, which focus upon laboratory technique. The fourth-year thesis and its oral defense before four faculty members ensures that the successful Third Degree graduate has a rounded understanding of the issues confronting a post-nuclear society.

Fourth through Sixth Degrees are contingent upon further years of study in an area of specialty, with a thesis presented and defended for each examination level. According to the literature of the Institute, the much-coveted Seventh Degree is awarded to those who have completed a "socially significant" research project. (More cynical observers have noted a remarkable concordance between the names of those Nuclear Darwinists whose laboratory research has resulted in new drug patents for the Society and those granted the Seventh Degree.)

Although the practice is not endorsed by the Society, it is not uncommon for Nuclear Darwinists to have tattoos. The tradition is by no means universal even among Nuclear Darwinists, but apparently, many graduates of the Institute for Radiation Studies obtain a tattoo upon earning each degree in their professional designation.

These tattoos are made over the chakras as follows: the First Degree at the base of the spine; the Second Degree around the navel; the Third Degree over the lower ribs or solar plexus; the Fourth Degree over the lungs; the Fifth Degree over the throat or Adam's apple; the Sixth Degree over the third eye or mid-brow; the Seventh Degree on the crown of the head.

Many different symbols are used in each position, although the logic behind each specific selection is either orally maintained or an arbitrary choice on the part of the individual. Ancient symbols of protection are common in all positions, but a comprehensive study of these tattoos is complicated by the comparative secrecy surrounding the tradition and the fact that the tattoos for the first four degrees are hidden from casual observance.

As of this writing, in the year 2099, the Society of Nuclear Darwinists holds no fewer than 320 drug patents, for drugs developed over their seventy-five year history as a direct result of research in their laboratories. As the Society is a privately held corporation, annual revenue from those patents cannot be declared decisively; however, the gross revenue must be significant. Of those drugs patented by the Society, many are in extensive use: for example, forty-seven are used in treating or curtailing mental ailments in the aged. Two drugs used to diminish the symptoms of the common conditions of Alzheimer's and Parkinson's diseases, respectively, are acknowledged to be the most frequently prescribed drugs among the Society's patents. Similarly, no less than ninety-two drugs and four treatment protocols developed by the Society are used in the treatment of cancer.

Lest one be left with the notion that the Society has few altruistic inclinations, much of the focus of their research has been upon developing drugs to minimize the effects of radiation exposure upon children in utero. This noble pursuit, originally spearheaded by Ernest Sinclair, has sadly not yet met with significant success.

from *The National News*
February 15, 2100
download v. 2.4

Valentine Scandal! Is <u>This</u> Maximilian Blackstone's Secret Baby?

"Maximilian Blackstone is my fiancé," sobbed Sarah Mac-Eachern from her bed at the New Arlington General Hospital yesterday. "But when our baby was born, the Society of Nuclear Darwinists harvested our son as a shade!"

Miss MacEachern collapsed in tears after her confession, so distraught that she was unable to say more.

Hospital officials confirm that Miss MacEachern did give birth to a son on February 14, and that the child did fail the S.H.A.D.E. The birth certificate, obtained by *The National News*, lists the father of Miss MacEachern's child as "Unknown."

"Max wanted it that way," Miss MacEachern confided when questioned. "He was so happy about the baby, but thought there was no time for a wedding during his campaign. He loves me! We're going to be married right after the election." When asked the whereabouts of her child, she took several moments to compose herself. "Those Nuclear Darwinists have taken my son away. You'll see. Max will intervene. Max will get our boy back."

"Oh yeah," confirmed Miss MacEachern's landlady, who declined to be named. "He was around all the time, at least once a week. Pulling up to the curb in that fancy black limo with eight shades in harnesses. You couldn't miss him."

The press secretary for Mr. Blackstone denied that Mr. Blackstone even knew Miss MacEachern and was skeptical of her claim that he had fathered her child. "It's an unfortunate malady of our times that a successful man like Mr. Blackstone will become the target of some portion of the population. Whether these claims are made out of malice or confusion, they are not to be given serious consideration. Mr. Blackstone, while a single gentleman, has always conducted himself in an appropriate manner. The record, which shows no incident of scandal over his long public career, makes this clear."

When presented with the evidence offered by Miss MacEachern's landlady, Mr. Blackstone's press secretary admitted that Mr. Blackstone does often use a black limo pulled by eight shades, but noted that it is a popular choice in New D.C. He questioned whether the landlady had ever seen Mr. Blackstone leave the vehicle, as well as the reliability of someone unwilling to attach her name to her testimony.

"It's a lie!" Miss MacEachern declared when told of this response. "Max has been my fiancé for over a year! He loves me! You'll see the truth when we're married!" Miss MacEachern was unable, however, to provide any image links of herself and Mr. Blackstone to support her assertion. She declared that her lover had always been vid-shy.

Mr. Blackstone himself was unavailable for comment.

Other Stories in Today's Download:
- <u>Ghosts in Our Old Cities?</u>—New Gotham witnesses share stories of "ghost lights at night"
- <u>Angels Armaros and Baraqiel Spotted in Kalamazoo, Michigan</u>
- <u>Mutant Leads Argentinean Rebels on Path of Destruction</u>

VI

ERNESTINE SINCLAIR, Nuclear Darwinist Seventh Degree and past president of the Society of Nuclear Darwinists, closed the door of her unit behind herself and let her shoulders sag.

It was all going wrong.

The Society founded by her father was being destroyed before her very eyes and there seemed to be nothing Ernestine could do to fix anything. Why did her term as president have to be over, just when the Society faced this crisis? Why had the membership elected Blake, so determined to placate everyone, just when they needed a tough leader?

What could she do?

Ernestine took a deep breath before glancing up at her father's image, illuminated on the opposite side of the foyer. Ernest Sinclair, founder of both the Society of Nuclear Darwinists and the Institute for Radiation Studies, had been photographed in the field, his favored locale. Even in his forties, at the height of his influence, he'd been athletic and his pseudoskin showed that to advantage. His helm was under his arm, devastation around and behind him, but Ernest stared into the distance with an optimistic smile. He gazed into a future of his own envisioning, one which was far, far better than the wasteland that surrounded him.

He'd never lost faith in the power of his plan.

Ernestine owed him better than doubt. As his sole surviving child and heir, she was obligated to protect his legacy, to ensure that future he envisioned.

She had to have faith that a way would become clear.

She touched the tattoo on her forehead, a commemoration of her Sixth Degree, with her fingertips, dropping her gaze before her father's majesty. Then she crossed the foyer and let her finger brush the items on the ancestral altar that was the focus of her home.

Here was his laze, laughably antique but seldom fired in his lifetime. Ernest had been convinced that words were the most effective weapon. With his persuasive charm, he'd needed no arsenal to get his way.

Here was his radiation monitor badge, long past glowing. Ernestine remembered as a child that her father had been fearless in entering hot zones, that his badge had always been radiant yellow when he returned home. Fearlessness had made him a good leader, though, one whom scientists and citizens had admired.

And here was the box containing his palm, removed upon his death so that none could violate his secrets. Ernestine brushed the plexi box lightly, running her fingertip around the framed dataport.

She'd never dared.

But hadn't fearlessness been her father's defining characteristic?

Would that lack of bravery on her part lead to the destruction of all he had built?

She wished that her older brother had survived, then she cursed herself for imagining that a man could have done anything better than she. She was her father's heir, and the future of the Society was hers to shape.

She murmured a prayer and lit the three flames on the altar, the three fires that burned all night long, every night. They symbolized Institute, Society, and Republic, the divine triumvirate that could lead mankind out of the darkness of nuclear war. Only science discerned the truth, only research could verify it, and only government could ensure its steadfast application.

There had to be a way.

Ernestine heard the approach of her domestic shade, Anthony, before he spoke.

"My lady, welcome home."

Her slave was a beautiful man, so handsome that the sight of him made Ernestine's heart skip even after years of having him in her household. Fair haired and blue eyed, he was a good foot taller than she and as finely toned as a man could be. Anthony spent—at her dictate and with her cred—every moment exercising his body that he was not in service to her pleasure. If anything, he looked better with each passing year.

There was no fear of his betrayal or indiscretion, for there was so little going on between his ears. He was perfect for Ernestine in that, if challenged to recall her favorite pleasures. Ernestine was inclined to be indulgent of his poor memory, given his other advantages.

"Good evening, Anthony."

At her gesture, he came to take her wrap, lifting it from her shoulders and pressing a kiss to the base of her neck. Ernestine closed her eyes and shivered with delight. She tapped her finger on the side of her neck and he kissed her again as commanded.

"I trust all was as usual," she said, beginning to turn into his embrace. A few hours with Anthony would restore her good humor. Maybe even her optimism.

"No," Anthony said, stilling as he frowned.

"No?" Ernestine surveyed him. He was perfect even in confusion.

"No, all was not as usual."

"How so?"

As Anthony frowned more deeply and fell silent, Ernestine suppressed her irritation. Anger only distressed Anthony and made him more forgetful. "How so, Anthony?" She ran her hand over his shoulder, then up to his chin. She smiled encouragingly when he faltered to recall. "What was different tonight? Think of what you did and when routine was changed."

His eyes lit. "A message came!"

Now Ernestine was confused. She glanced down at her palm, but the display showed that no new message had been received.

"On paper!" Anthony breathed in awe.

Ernestine was surprised, then thought he might be mistaken.

Anthony ran to the main room of the unit and returned bearing a flat square of ivory hue. He held it on his palms and presented it to Ernestine, his amazement clear.

And to be sure, she shared his wonder. It *was* paper.

Against all odds. Ernestine had only touched paper once, when she was a small child, and she halfway expected this square to disintegrate on contact as that one had. She lifted it from Anthony's hands with care, thrilled to see that her own name was written across the front in a bold hand.

"Handwriting, too," Anthony whispered, biting his lip to contain his excitement as he watched her.

Ernestine turned the square over. She saw now that it was folded, as if the corners of a sheet had been drawn together to enclose a message inside. Those corners were sealed together with a blob of red, which had an insignia pressed into it.

How curious.

Why would someone contact her this way?

She knew the answer immediately. Clearly, because he or she desired to leave no datatrail in the Republic's networks. Ernestine's heart began to pound more loudly. Had opportunity come knocking?

"Who brought this?" she asked Anthony.

He shook his head.

"You must know," she insisted, keeping her tone calm with an effort. "How did it arrive, Anthony? When did you first see it?"

"Someone came to the service entrance." He bit his lip, then nodded. "There was a knock. I went to the door and there was no one there." He touched the missive. "*It* was there."

Security controlled access to the service entrances. Ernestine knew she could find a vid record of who had used the dark passages. "Where was it, exactly?"

"On the floor. It fell toward me when the door slid back." He swallowed, his gaze filling with concern. "Didn't I do the right thing, my lady? Isn't that your name? The first letter looks right."

"It is my name, Anthony."

"Should I have left it there? But if it's for you and I left it, another shade from the building could have taken it . . ." His fears escalated and Ernestine put a hand on his shoulder to silence him.

"You did well, Anthony," she said calmly. "I simply wondered how it arrived. Thank you."

His mouth worked in silence for a moment, his gaze dropping to the missive and back to her. He had the most attractive mouth of any man Ernestine had ever met. His lips were both full and firm, tinged a luscious rose color but masculine all the same. She particularly liked that nothing of much import ever crossed those lips.

She reached up and kissed him lingeringly, feeling the tension ease from his body beneath her caress. When he shuddered slightly in his relief, she broke the kiss and smiled at him.

She tousled his hair, not needing to feign her affection. He looked boyish and attractive, eager to please. "Will you run a bath for me, Anthony? With scent number seven?" She let her hand slide down his jawline, then eased her thumb across that mouth in a proprietary gesture. "I have need of some intimacy tonight."

"Yes, my lady." He bowed his head crisply, just as Ernestine preferred, then strode away to do her bidding.

Ernestine watched him go, appreciating the view. Keeping her sex slave nude had been one of her more inspired choices. He was gorgeous, the sight of those rippling muscles filling her with anticipation.

She sighed when he had disappeared, then broke the seal on the message. She held it toward the light of the burning candles so that she could read the script.

"Then I saw another great beast that rose out of the earth; it had two horns like a lamb and it spoke like a dragon . . . it performs great signs, even making fire come down from heaven to earth in the sight of all . . . it deceives the inhabitants of the earth, telling them to

*make an image for the beast that had been wounded by
the sword and yet lived."*

*Our objectives are as one, and we can accomplish
more in alliance. Meet me at midnight tonight, suite
1865 of the Intercontinental.*
—M. B.

The quote sounded biblical, something about the end
of the world. After it was affixed one of the temporary tattoos that replicated the mark of the angels' kiss on the
brow of the Oracle.

The message itself was intriguing. The sender clearly
thought that the Oracle was a fraud, and the words suggested
that the supposed appearance of the angels was trickery.

M.B.? Ernestine had to think for only a moment to sur-
mise that it was Maximilian Blackstone who had sent the
missive.

He was in town, after all, had been in town for the meeting that had been interrupted earlier tonight. How interesting that he thought they should ally, when the plan he had
presented to the media called for the Society to become
part of the Republican government. Was it possible that
Blackstone hadn't revealed his entire scheme?

Ernestine interrogated the security system for her unit,
frowning when it showed no record of anyone accessing
the service corridor.

Except Anthony.

She reviewed the vid with narrowed eyes, slowing down
the replay. One instant there was no paper by the access
door, then it appeared. Ernestine replayed the segment,

enlarging the image. The missive simply appeared, seemingly out of thin air. That was when she noticed a skip in the timestamp. The record had been edited, undoubtedly to remove the vid of whoever had left the missive.

The hair prickled on the back of her neck. Did Blackstone have the power to interfere with the Society's security records?

Or had he simply bought the services of someone in the building?

Either way, her decision was made. He would know that she had received his missive. Ernestine would meet him, as suggested.

This could, after all, be the chance she sought. If nothing else, she was curious. There could be little threat to her person, given that she had no official power any longer. She wasn't afraid of Blackstone.

Not much, anyway.

But no one must know. If there was to be an alliance, it must be a secret one.

She simply had to get through the streets of Chicago, without being recognized as a Nuclear Darwinist. The only violence expressed by the mobs of released shades was against anyone they believed to be associated with the Society or Institute.

Fortunately, Ernestine was not without her own resources.

She smiled up at her father's image, then removed his radiation badge from the shallow bowl on the altar in which it was displayed. She dropped the paper into the emptied dish, then touched its rim with the flame of one of the candles.

Blackstone's message burned with enthusiasm, the fire's orange light dancing high. In moments, there was no evidence of its existence other than a little bit of ash. Ernestine appreciated the method of communication for its discretion, even if it had been tempting to keep the paper as a souvenir of history. She crumbled the residue with her fingers to fine dust, then blew it toward the intake of the air filter.

She was replacing her father's radiation badge in its rightful place when Anthony reappeared.

"But where is the paper, my lady?" he asked, his gaze darting around the unit. The oddity of it had clearly caught at his imagination.

Such as it was.

Ernestine would fix that. She smiled. "What paper, Anthony?"

"The message," he said, but she pretended to not understand. "The paper that came to the service entrance . . ."

"There was no paper, darling."

"But, but . . ." Doubt filled his blue eyes and his brow puckered in a frown again. "But I *saw* it."

"No, Anthony. You imagined it." She pushed a hand through his hair in a slow caress. "Or maybe it was on the vid."

He glanced across the unit to the vid on the wall, his consternation clear.

"Is the bath drawn?"

"Yes, my lady." He nodded, visibly relieved at the change of topic. "With scent number seven, just as you said."

"And are you ready to pleasure me?" Ernestine reached down to caress him, finding him as hard as she'd anticipated. Anthony seemed to find scent number seven particularly arousing.

Just as she did. She smiled at him as she caressed him.

"Yes, my lady," he said, catching his breath as she slid her nail across him. "My lady!"

"There was no paper, Anthony," Ernestine whispered, then kissed his earlobe. She closed her hand around his strength, coaxing his arousal. "No paper at all."

"No paper," Anthony repeated, wrapping his arms around her as he bent his head. "It must have been on the vid, my lady." Then he kissed her with that beautiful mouth, the one that Ernestine loved more with every passing night.

She had three hours to have her way with Anthony and guarantee he was too sleepy to notice her departure. Ernestine didn't think that ensuring the secrecy of her mission would be too onerous a task.

ARMAND SAT in his unit and eyed the assassin's laze.

He didn't even want to touch it, let alone end someone's life with it. It rested on the bed, as black as the sheet was white, exuding menace. Armand perched on a chair on the opposite side of the room, summoning his resolve. Blackstone was staying at the Intercontinental Hotel, a fact that had been easy to discover. It was after ten, too early to stage a covert attack.

At least that was what Armand told himself.

Maybe it would have been closer to the truth to say that it was too early for him to do what needed to be done.

He'd been issued a pseudoskin as a new student and it was on the bed beside the laze. His was one of the midweight models, not the heavy-gauge ones used by police and shade hunters who were more likely to enter hot zones. Even so, it had been fitted by a body scan. Armand liked the clean lines of it better than the street clothes Baruch favored, and he welcomed the burden of its weight. The pseudoskin made him more keenly aware of his body, its power and its limitations.

Its mortality.

If Baruch died in the Institute's labs, he'd be lost to the angels forever.

And that was the crux of it.

Given that fact, Armand's reservations were irrelevant.

Armand pushed to his feet, shed his clothes, and pulled on the pseudoskin. He moved quickly, his every gesture filled with annoyance. He hauled on the high sturdy boots that had been issued with the pseudoskin, abandoning his elegant faux-leather ones. These had thicker soles and were more robust. He preferred that they were so utilitarian. He was impatient with appearances, especially those that were deceptive. He donned his long gloves, then picked up the laze.

It was heavy. Portentous of what it could do.

It was also easily understood, clean in its functionality and design. Armand checked it with grim determination, putting his faith in the greater good. He had no holster, but he loosened the belt and shoved the laze into the gap. Its hard power was pressed against his side.

He'd probably need it even before he got to Blackstone. Armand wasn't looking forward to the journey to the Intercontinental Hotel, given the chaos that reigned in Chicago's streets at night. In one way, the Institute was a haven—in another it was a target for the restless mobs.

At least, in the pseudoskin, with his helm hiding his face, he would be anonymous and unidentifiable. If he was wounded, he had only to finish his task to summon his angelic allies. Once his wings were regained, any physical injury would be irrelevant.

It all sounded so simple and straightforward. Armand told himself it was.

In the corridors of the student residence, however, a pseudoskin would attract unnecessary attention.

He pulled his long emerald velvet frock coat over the pseudoskin, not bothering with trousers. If he was lucky, no one would catch more than a glimpse of him anyway. He took his top hat as well.

He had just tipped the hat at the jaunty angle Baruch has insisted was proper when the locked door of his unit suddenly opened behind him.

Armand pivoted, his hand on the laze.

And stared at Philippa, standing on the threshold. What was she doing here? How had she unlocked the door? What did she want? Nothing good after what he'd done to her.

But how could she be moving after that dose of Ivanofor?

He let go of the laze, letting his jacket conceal the weapon as she stepped into the room, uninvited, and shut the door behind herself. She leaned her back against the door panel, her veil disguising her expression.

There was something different about her. She seemed more assessing, more quiet, more intent.

Then she tore off the veil and revealed the reason why.

The woman wearing Philippa's clothes was the assassin.

That made a kind of sense, but her presence made none. What did *she* want with him? Her laze back? Why had she run from him and then pursued him?

She held up her left hand. "Tools of the trade," she said

in an undertone. "Sorry for the surprise, but I thought it was better to enter silently."

"With no concern for my privacy."

Her smile was quick. "Haven't you heard? The eyes of the Republic are everywhere. No one has any privacy."

It was a sobering thought. Armand had been careful to keep his back hidden, on Tupperman's advice, but her confidence made him wonder whether he had been careful enough.

Did she know his secret? Had she come to harvest him? Was there a bounty behind this surprise appearance?

The fact that she was even here was a concern. That she looked feminine and alluring in Philippa's clothing was even more troubling. He was keenly aware that there was a woman in his rooms, a woman whom he found more attractive than was smart. She was callous and unpredictable, he reminded himself, an assassin who worked only for cred.

His body responded to her presence all the same. He noticed the blond spill of her hair, the soft curve of her cheek, the neat indent of her waist. She was delicately built for all her attitude, her hands and feet tiny.

Her smile fired his blood the most, a hint of secrecy about that ripe curve, the red fullness of her bottom lip, the intelligence that shone in her eyes.

Maybe he should have accompanied Baruch to the pleasure fringes more often.

Maybe more of the truth would eliminate his unhealthy interest. "What are you doing here?"

That smile broadened, taking a knowing twist. Armand had the strange sense that she could guess his thoughts. "You don't expect women to come after you when you abandon them?"

"You were the one who disappeared. You were gone when I came back."

She grimaced, the smile banished. "And a pretty bit of cred that cost me," she murmured, her words making no sense to Armand. A challenge lit her eyes as she looked up at him. "What if I said I was keeping our deal?"

"I wouldn't believe you. You've come back for a different reason." He wanted her to deny that, knowing that the expectation was unreasonable, but she proved his assessment to be correct.

"What did you do with my laze?"

"It's safe."

"Prove it."

Armand knew so little about this woman, and didn't imagine that she'd confess much more to him. Maybe it was better that way. He did know, though, one thing that motivated her. Perhaps revealing that he'd kept his promise would earn some loyalty from her. He lifted the side of his jacket, unsurprised when her eyes shone at the sight. "Is that why you're keeping the deal? To get your laze back?"

"That's part of it." She took a step closer. The room seemed very small to him, full of him and a dangerous woman and his bed. "You have a pseudoskin," she murmured, her gaze dancing over him.

"Standard issue for students."

"Doesn't look very standard to me," she breathed. She flicked an appreciative glance over him and Armand caught his breath that they were both feeling the same attraction.

She'd probably put a price on its fulfillment.

Or was she feigning that, as well?

"Why did you really come here?" he asked.

"Did you see the protocol?"

"What protocol?"

"Right." She frowned, speaking quietly as if to herself as she tapped her palm. "You're not on Shadow.net so you wouldn't have seen it. It's not public knowledge."

"What's Shadow.net?"

"A network that doesn't officially exist. It's the information highway of the wraiths."

That made perfect sense to Armand, given that Tupperman ran a similar network for the fallen angels and their allies. He'd heard rumors of the wraiths, and this woman's connection with them also made sense. He appreciated now why Tupperman had been so reluctant to remove those links from his palm.

But then, the mission was for him and Baruch alone. They weren't supposed to need anyone's help.

She stepped closer then, raising her palm so he could see the displayed protocol. "Cosmopoulos is going to do Dissection and Vivisection with your friend," she said. "He starts in the morning. The time to get him out is now."

Armand was horrified but still cautious. "Why do you want to help him?"

She averted her gaze, hiding something from him. "Trust me."

Armand nearly laughed aloud. "How could I? I don't even know your name. I do know that you put cred above everything else, and I don't see any cred in this for you." He stepped closer. "What aren't you telling me?"

She bit her lip and hesitated. Her indecision intrigued him, made him wonder about her secrets.

When her words came, they were charged with heat. "Okay, I don't work just for the cred. It's for what it buys."

"And what does it buy?"

She licked her lips. Her agitation made her confession more credible, and Armand reminded himself to be on his guard. "There are those who rely upon me," she said heavily, the words seemingly drawn from her. "I make my choices for the greater good." She looked up at him then, her gaze clear and Armand, despite his better judgment, was inclined to believe her.

Still he forced himself to sound skeptical. "Who would rely upon you? Those with enough cred to ensure your dedication?"

She held his gaze in challenge. "Those who don't have a choice." That smile flashed, making his heart leap. "Like you."

"That's not a very compelling argument," Armand said, turning away from her. "I'm not sure I want your help."

Theodora caught his elbow and forced him to look at her. Her own eyes burned with conviction. "I fix my mistakes," she said with persuasive heat. "I might break rules on the way, but I stand by those who count on me, and I even the score. It's my fault your friend was harvested, and I'm going to get him out of the labs before it's too late." Her voice hardened. "Cosmopoulos is going to lose this round to me. It's a matter of principle, and that's all you really need to know."

The passion of her conviction carried the resonance of truth. Armand was intrigued. "What's your name?"

"Theodora."

"Is that really your name?"

Her lips tightened. "It is now."

Armand could have found it reassuring that she'd chosen a name that meant 'gift of God,' but he wasn't sure whether it wasn't just another deception.

He was standing close enough to Theodora to see the

wary glitter of her eyes, to smell her skin, to see how petite she was in contrast to himself. She seemed suddenly fragile to him, delicate and mortal.

Maybe that was the fault of the feminine clothes. She looked like a woman now, not like a young boy or a genderless criminal.

Maybe that was why his body was responding so keenly to her again. He could see the curve of her breasts, and unlike the glimpse of Philippa's ripe breasts, the sight of this assassin's slim curves sent a surge of heat through him.

He wanted to touch her.

Why her? Why did she of all women catch his interest? Why not Philippa? Armand wanted to know more.

That must be why he wanted to kiss Theodora. He couldn't dismiss his sense that she meant to trick him, that she wasn't trustworthy, that he was a fool to bargain with her.

He might not be prepared to shoot someone, but he still had one way to ensure her cooperation.

He still had one syringe of Ivanofor, after all.

And he knew she hated it.

Armand smiled as if convinced and saw her quickly inhale at the sight. "Maybe we should seal our bargain, then." He dropped his voice to a low murmur, watching how her eyes brightened in anticipation. He wasn't alone in experiencing this attraction, and that sense of common purpose only excited him more.

Perhaps she found it just as unexpected, and inconvenient.

But Armand would use it to his own convenience.

Her gaze flicked to his lips, then back to his eyes. "Armand," she whispered.

"Theodora," he whispered, then caught the back of her nape in his hand and tugged her closer. She fell against his chest with a soft gasp, but before she could protest—and he wasn't certain that she would—he closed his mouth over hers.

It was a most satisfactory kiss, long and slow and hot. Unlike kissing other women, Armand couldn't get enough of this kiss. He wanted it to go on and on. His reaction was completely different with Theodora but Armand didn't trouble to wonder why.

He simply deepened his kiss, savoring how she responded in kind. He could now see the appeal of this pleasure of the flesh, could see how people could drown themselves in sensation. He enjoyed her response so much so that he nearly forgot the syringe in his pocket.

But not quite.

It could wait a few minutes, for this.

VII

ARMAND WAS dangerous.

Any man who could kiss as if he was discovering intimacy for the first time, any man who could coax a slow burn of a response from Theodora, any man who could make her forget her reservations when she had so many of them, should be locked away for the safety of all women in the Republic.

Preferably in Theodora's own refuge.

She'd known that Armand meant to kiss her, and had been excited by the possibility. She'd expected to be disappointed by the embrace, as was generally the case, and had been certain that she would be able to resist even his considerable allure. She'd been sure that her reaction to his quick embrace in the labs had been amplified by the Ivanofor. She'd held her ground, curious about his touch.

It would be healthy to have her illusions shattered.

But she'd been completely wrong. Armand's kiss melted her convictions along with her knees. It dissolved her determination and made her forget her own plans. It pushed every thought from her mind that had nothing to do with sex—sex with Armand—and launched a series of fantasies that shocked Theodora with their detail.

And their appeal.

There was nothing but Armand, prime in his pseudoskin, and his potent kiss. Theodora found her hands on his shoulders with no clear idea of how they had gotten there, and was excited by the luxurious crush of velvet beneath her fingers.

No, she was excited by the muscled strength of the shoulders that filled that jacket, the breadth of his chest, the strength of his thighs. She liked his height, how he towered over her yet was fiercely gentle. She loved the slow massage of his fingers in her hair, the way he loosened her braid, the way he tasted and teased her. Her breasts were against his chest, the constriction of the corset only seeming to heighten her arousal. She couldn't breathe, her heart was hammering, and she hated the barrier of clothing between them.

She liked his proprietary grip, the hard demand of him in contrast to those firm yet tender lips. She touched her tongue to his, liking how he locked his other hand around her waist and lifted her closer to deepen his embrace.

His kiss was a taste of heaven, a pleasure destined to drive all other concerns from her thoughts.

Armand lifted his head all too soon and smiled as he looked down at her. Theodora caught her breath, fearful that her arousal showed and that he knew his power over her.

"Blackstone is at the Intercontinental," he whispered. "Let's go." His hand dropped, and she assumed he was holding fast to her laze. "All we have to do is assassinate him to save Baruch."

Theodora planted her hands on his chest and pushed him away. She had her back to the door, but every increment of space was good.

Maybe it would clear her thoughts.

Maybe it would diminish Armand's effect upon her. "First I need to know the details. How exactly is killing Blackstone going to free your friend?"

Armand folded his arms across his chest and surveyed her, looking more masculine, confident, and beguiling than Theodora would have believed possible. "Completing our assignment will guarantee Baruch's release. That's all you need to know."

Theodora eyed him, her confusion unabated. "Wouldn't it be easier to just get Baruch out of the labs?"

Armand hesitated, then spoke with care. Theodora had the sense that he was choosing his words and she wondered what he wasn't telling her. "When Blackstone is dead, our assignment will be done. The others will come to get us."

Theodora couldn't hide her skepticism. "Even from the labs? Even if you're separated?"

"No matter where we are."

She could have believed this if it was a wraith project, but she hadn't heard a whiff about the elimination of Blackstone. In all honesty, she would have leapt at the opportunity to take that assignment. "But who are these others?"

"The others," Armand repeated stubbornly. He reached for the door, gesturing for her to go ahead of him, clearly done with the conversation.

Theodora needed more information. She caught his hand in hers, and despite the barriers of lace and polymer between them, the contact made her pulse leap. "Who are the others? Wraiths?"

"No," he murmured, easing closer. His gaze fell to her lips again and Theodora's heart began to race at the prospect of another kiss. Armand smiled as if in anticipation of the same pleasure.

"No," she whispered, releasing her grip on his hand. "No, if they were wraiths, I'd know about it. Who else could they be? You have to tell me, so I can create a plan."

"The only plan we need is how to kill Blackstone. He's at the Intercontinental, so going there is the first step." Armand reached out to touch her chin with his fingertip, turning her face to his. Theodora had a heartbeat to think that he was deliberately distracting her, then he let his hand slide down her throat and she forgot everything but his caress.

Her eyes closed.

Was it the remnant of Ivanofor messing with her reactions?

Solitude for too long?

Or Armand himself?

"But it's dangerous," she insisted, striving to remain coherent. "I like to plan for every contingency. I need to know that your plan will work."

"It cannot fail."

"Be serious! This place is locked up tight, more secure than any other location in the Republic. I think you could steal a nuke more easily than you could steal anything out of here. How will the others get Baruch out?"

"They can," he said with resolve. "The angels can do anything."

That one word cleared Theodora's mind. "The *angels*?"

Armand nodded, utterly convinced of his words, then gestured to the door. "Shall we?"

The angels.

Armand *was* crazy. Just like Big Ted. What was it with people and angels? Even Dr. Cosmopoulos's protocol was intended to disprove the presence of angels.

Theodora supposed that she should have expected that Armand was too good to be true.

There was always something.

He was unpredictable, then, because he was insane. But that simply meant that she had to get away from him. Maybe surrendering the laze to him was worth the cost. Maybe she could trick him and get it back, then go on her way.

Leaving him to the angels.

Angels!

"Sure, Armand," she said cheerfully, hiding her thoughts. "That's a good plan. Let's go summon the angels."

Theodora spun crisply, evading even the possibility of another distracting kiss, and missed the flash of suspicion in Armand's eyes. She shoved open the door. She felt Armand move quickly behind her, too quickly, and glanced back.

Instead of him intent on another kiss, she spied a syringe in his hand and knew what he had planned.

The sight sent fury through her.

"Liar!" She kicked the syringe out of his hand, then leapt for the access to the netherzones.

Her blood was pumping, anger at having been deceived giving her speed. She heard the syringe shatter and smiled.

Then Armand caught her around the waist, scooping her off her feet. He swung her into his arms, held her captive against his chest, and kissed her to silence. It was a fierce kiss this time, possessive and demanding, and no less thrilling. When he lifted his head, Theodora was gasping for breath and his eyes were blazing.

"Quiet or we're both dead," he muttered.

She ceded because she knew he was right.

Theodora struggled but he kicked open the door to the

netherzones. He strode into the hidden stairwell, then they were enveloped in velvety darkness.

She was his captive again, but the situation wouldn't last long.

Theodora was betting her laze on that.

THEODORA FOUGHT like a demon once they were behind the door to the netherzones. Armand had no patience for it, this time.

Perhaps it was better to be without the Ivanofor. He didn't want to carry her around, either, and she could be useful, if she chose to be.

He wouldn't be so stupid as to trust her, though.

He cast her aside, then pulled her own laze, training it upon her. He touched the trigger to sight it and it beeped, its red light illuminating the darkness.

She froze instantly, then raised her hands.

"This will never work," he said sternly. "Either we have a deal or we don't."

"We can't have a deal if you lie to me," she said, her words hot.

"I haven't . . ."

"If you try to drug me!"

"You were going to betray me."

"You lied to me."

"I did not."

"There are no angels!" she said angrily. "I concede that you don't have to tell me who you're working with, even though it would be polite to do so, given that my butt is on the line, too." She glared at him. "Just don't *lie* to me."

Armand blinked. He had never considered the possibility

that a mortal wouldn't believe in what he was. "There are angels."

She rolled her eyes. "Please. Give me some credit. I'm not crazy."

"Neither am I."

She rolled her eyes. "Even though you believe the angels are going to save your friend from the labs?"

"Can we not believe different things?"

"Not if I'm going to get killed over it!"

"Blackstone for the laze," Armand repeated the terms.

"You have to know how dangerous it will be to get to the hotel. You have to know that it's long odds against our even arriving there safely, never mind whether we can get through the hotel's security, never mind Blackstone's personal security. Without good prep, it's a serious long shot."

He considered her. She must have an alternate plan, although he was wary that it might be one that served his purposes as well. "So, what do you advise?"

"Incredible as it seems, I think it'll be easier to get Baruch out of the labs." She winced. "Easier being a relative term."

"You're wrong."

"Well, you're wrong about the angels, so fair's fair." She unexpectedly smiled at him. Her hair was loose and her eyes twinkling and Armand was disconcerted.

She must have noticed his surprise, because she sobered and lowered her voice. "Look. Your main goal is to free your friend, right?" Armand nodded. "And that's mine, too. So, let's check on his situation before we leave the Institute. Maybe we can break him out of here without divine intervention."

"But Blackstone . . ."

"If I get your friend free, will you surrender my laze?" she asked.

"What about Blackstone?"

"Okay, I've agreed to that, but I need my laze. Your friend for the laze, then Blackstone."

Armand considered her with suspicion. "Why are you suddenly committed to both?"

She made a gesture of futility with one hand. "Blackstone is separate from my obligation to fix my mistake. Call it personal."

Her words resonated with conviction, yet her tone didn't invite further inquiry. Armand knew he'd have to take her word on faith. Despite the apparent folly of that, he believed he had seen a truth of her nature and chose to trust her.

The real truth was that he had little choice.

"Maybe the angels will change your mind about their existence," he said, lowering the laze slightly.

She laughed then, a sound all the more attractive for being unanticipated. "Anything is possible." She pointed to the laze. "Promise not to shoot me?"

"Only if you don't betray me."

"And no more drugs," Theodora insisted. Armand thought it was amusing that she was trying to dictate the terms, given that he was the one holding the laze.

On the other hand, he needed her expertise and he expected that Theodora had a pretty accurate view of her importance to the endeavor. She knew the netherzones and the Republic far better than he did.

She might also have guessed that he was unlikely to actually fire the laze to injure someone.

Could they save Baruch without shedding Blackstone's

blood? Armand admitted the possibility had appeal. He and Baruch would still have to complete their assignment to regain their wings, but if Baruch was killed, he'd be lost for all eternity.

"Anything else?" he asked, pretending to be tolerant of her requests.

"No more kisses."

Just the fact that she mentioned it persuaded Armand that his touch had troubled her. He liked their having something in common, even if it was physical reaction, and chose to take a stand on this issue.

"No," he said flatly, savoring her surprise. "There has to be some benefit to our working together and we both enjoy that one."

"But . . ." she began to protest.

Armand lifted the laze. "No lies, remember. That applies to both of us."

She shut her mouth and eyed him for a moment. When he smiled, she caught her breath. She spun in place, then peeled off Philippa's clothing, keeping her back to him. Armand knew he shouldn't have been surprised to see that she was wearing her pseudoskin beneath the skirts and petticoats. She tugged the hood from her belt and pulled it over her head, concealing her hair.

"Cosmopoulos's lab," she murmured, purpose in every gesture. "It'll be on the lowest level, the hidden one." She flicked him a bright glance. "Been there yet?"

Armand shook his head.

"No, it's not on the official tour. If you don't know the business of this place now, you'll learn it soon."

Theodora nodded once, then glanced around herself with narrowed eyes. Armand guessed that she was orienting herself and wondered how much of the hidden networks she had memorized.

"There's an access to the third level beneath this residence, adjacent to the kitchens for the student cafeteria. It leads to the public netherzones of Chicago, but is also linked to the labs. They use it for deliveries, but it should be quiet at this time of night."

She hadn't even consulted her palm. He wondered how much else she remembered, and couldn't help comparing that habit with the inclination of most mortals in the Republic to let their palms do the work of recollection for them.

But then, if you lived by your wits, it was better to keep them sharp. Better to not leave any bits and bytes to betray you.

"We're only at the ground level," Armand said. "There's a staircase to the right that goes down at least one level—we've used it to access the netherzone passage to the research labs."

"It'll go lower," Theodora said with confidence. "But the door will be locked. It might be concealed." She flicked him a hard look. "There will only be shades down there and it won't be pretty. Better brace yourself for some bitter reality."

"I'm ready," Armand said.

But, of course, he wasn't prepared for what he saw.

THE INTERCONTINENTAL Hotel was an oasis of calm.

Despite the war zone that erupted nightly on the streets of Chicago, the hotel had a crack security team. The fences were high and electrified, patrolled by sharpshooters with dogs. There were three security gates, three examinations of identification, three opportunities to filter out the unwanted.

Ernestine had taken the guise of a whore, summoned to a passionate client, and wore the kind of feathered mask that had once been common in the pleasure fringes. Her cleavage was displayed, but her tattoos were all hidden beneath black lace and velvet. The mask hid most of her face, including the tattoo on her forehead that designated her accomplishment of the sixth degree. The swastika tattoo was striking and one feature that people remembered.

She didn't look like a Nuclear Darwinist, even though she came out of the residences behind the Institute's fences. Her disguise had fooled the milling shades bent on seeking vengeance.

They probably assumed she was one of them.

A pleasure shade, like Anthony.

Having run the gauntlet from the Institute in her rented taxi, Ernestine found the inquiries, the lazes, and the helms of the commandos with their dark filters reassuring. They left nothing to chance at the Intercontinental, and no explanation was necessary. Her identification bead was scanned at the first checkpoint, but Blackstone had evidently indicated that she was expected.

The security gave her a confidence she hadn't felt in months.

She loved the infrared scan of the vehicle, although the driver was shaken by the attention. Ernestine wondered what he did to earn spare cred on the side, what was hidden in the vehicle.

The security team must have found out, because the taxi was barred at the second checkpoint, the driver dispatched into Chicago's mean streets with the paid fare. Ernestine transferred to the hotel's armored shuttle for the last increment of her journey.

She found herself looking forward to her meeting.

The hotel was also as sleek as Ernestine recalled. She hadn't been in the building since the reception following her father's funeral, but it hadn't changed much. The lights were low, the lobby full of discreet shadows.

At this hour of the night, it was quiet. She kept her hood up as she strode across the lobby to the elevators and was unchallenged.

But then, who could tell how far the information from her scanned identification bead had already traveled? Blackstone was probably aware of her proximity, and the desk shade, too.

The eyes of the Republic were everywhere.

Still, she pushed the elevator buttons for two floors in addition to the eighteenth, even though no one in the lobby appeared to be watching her. She wore gloves, so left no fingerprints to mark her passage.

The elevator rose smoothly, a testament to the quality and quantity of shades employed by the hotel. How strange that Blackstone chose to stay in such a place when the plan he was busily presenting to voters called for the elimination of the netherzones, the Society, and the Institute. Was it a question of personal safety, or an inconsistency between the plan he promoted and his personal preferences?

Ernestine wondered.

She was struck again by his reliance upon shade labor when the elevator opened. It appeared that the suite composed the entire eighteenth floor. Four shades in livery with neutral expressions stood in the corners of the foyer, their physiques revealing that they were bodyguards. She stepped out of the elevator, assessing the situation with caution. Her name was already displayed in red lights on a panel on the opposite wall.

So, she had been announced.

The door closed behind her and she heard the elevator ascend, leaving her with no means of escape. For better or for worse, she was in Blackstone's lair.

An alarm sounded quietly, a subtle but persistent ping.

One shade presented himself before her, his hand outstretched. "Your weapon, please."

The alarm meant that denial was futile.

Ernestine chose to argue instead. "I am licensed to carry a laze."

"Our mandate does not permit any armed person to proceed." The shade's eyes were cold, flat, his expression impassive. Ernestine recognized the signs of mercenary programming. This shade had had his memory wiped and any trace of compassion or morality erased. He would do precisely as he was told, even kill, with no regrets.

Perhaps without any recollection.

Mercenary programming brought shades as close as possible to machines. Their predictability was impressive, their lack of mercy frightening. Their presence here seemed an excessive safeguard for a political candidate.

Ernestine pulled her laze from its holster, checked the safety, and surrendered it to the shade.

The alarm didn't cease.

"The other weapon, please."

Ernestine removed the knife hidden in the side of her boot and surrendered it. The tone continued until her brass knuckles, penknife, and stun gun had all been surrendered.

Even though she was still masked and hooded, she felt naked by the time she was permitted to continue.

All she had left were her protective tattoos, and Ernestine feared they wouldn't be enough.

Two of the shades gestured to the double doors opposite the elevator door. The obsidian doors swung in silence at the sweep of their fingertips.

"Ernestine Sinclair, past president of the Society of Nuclear Darwinists," one murmured, even though her presence wasn't precisely a surprise.

Ernestine surveyed the lavish room, the velvet upholstered furniture and leather stools, the fire crackling on the stone hearth, the thick exotic rug on the floor. She'd just concluded it was empty when a silhouette rose in the periphery of her vision. She was sure it was a winged figure in black, cast in silhouette by the firelight, but no sooner had she looked directly at it, than it disappeared.

Faded to nothing, as if it had never been.

In the same moment, Blackstone himself rose from one leather chair, the one turned to the fire. He smiled warmly.

He was more handsome than Ernestine had realized, possessed of that same masculine assurance that had characterized her father. He was dressed casually, the first time that she'd ever seen him in anything other than a suit. The mock-suede shirt made him look adventurous and active, predatory even, the caramel hue making his eyes look golden. He held a snifter of amber liquid in his left hand and crossed the room to shake her hand. Every dark hair was in place, every tooth as white as fresh snow.

She had a striking sense of him as a lion, a predator.

A well-fed predator.

"Welcome, Ernestine!" he said as the warmth of his hand

closed over hers. He was even more charismatic in close proximity and Ernestine was startled by her body's reaction. "Lovely as always," he murmured, eyes glinting with appreciation as he scanned her outfit. He smiled slightly. "I'm so glad you chose to come."

Ernestine's mouth went dry. "I was curious, Mr. Blackstone. Our objectives seem to be at odds . . ."

He laughed. "Surely you of all women know that appearances can be deceiving." He leaned closer, eyes sparkling, and his grip tightened slightly. Ernestine smiled, keeping her smile prim as she extricated her hand from his grasp.

Blackstone was undeterred. His voice dropped to an intimate tone that made her heart skip. "Would you not remove your mask, now that we are among friends?"

Ernestine felt her lips part, but no sound came out. She was lost in the intensity of his gaze. His request wasn't unusual, but her sense that she was being laid bare to view persisted.

"We cannot be too cautious in these times," Blackstone continued smoothly. "I would prefer to have no artifice between us."

Ernestine removed the feather mask, sliding her fingers over it as she laid it aside.

His smile broadened. "I must insist that you call me Max."

"Max, then," Ernestine said, trying to remain business-like. "And you must call me Ernestine."

"Nessie," Max said in the same moment that Ernestine said her name. She knew her surprise showed, for no one had called her that in a long time. "Your father's nickname for you, I know," Max said with confidence, moving toward a sparkling decanter on the sideboard. "A drink, perhaps?"

He was slim and moved with an athletic grace that belied his age. How old was he? Ernestine had always thought him a contemporary of her father, maybe slightly younger, but he looked no more than thirty-five.

Maybe it was the light.

Maybe it was good surgery.

"Forgive my surprise," she said, moving into the room. "I didn't think anyone knew that my father had called me that."

"I doubt anyone else does. I remember him doing so, though." Max turned, giving her a sidelong glance that looked slightly sly.

She strolled the length of the room, running her hand along the back of the sofa. It was a luxurious room, decadent in its dedication to the senses. "You knew him?"

Max nodded. "We met, years ago." He gestured with his glass. "San Diego, 2051. In the fallout shelter." He shook his head as if recalling challenging times. "The West Coast was a mess after the Pacific Rim conflict. I was just a kid, a volunteer wanting to do my bit to save humanity and out of my depth. Ernest was not just in his element but in full command of the situation."

Ernestine did some quick math, assuming that Blackstone had been a teenager in 2051. He must have been born in the late 2030s, which would make him a good forty years younger than her father.

Which meant he would have to be in his sixties now. She wondered where he had had such good surgery done.

Never mind what it had cost him.

What was the source of his affluence? He'd been a politician for as long as she'd been aware of him, and while such men lived a comfortable life, this suite and the surgery would seem to be beyond such means.

Family money? She'd have to do some research.

Max was expansive. "I was in awe of Ernest, of his ability to delegate and be decisive, literally under fire. The man was a legend in his own time." He turned, a second snifter in his hand. "And when he sat with a bunch of us in the shelter one night, just to talk, I couldn't believe my luck."

Ernestine understood that. Her father had had an energy that wasn't common, that caught the eye, that persuaded men to take risks beyond reason. He'd been a leader and a warrior and she had idolized him from the day she'd been born. She'd been fourteen when he'd died, but had reviewed the vid images of him thousands of times. He was still the ideal man in her world.

And Max had known her father personally. It was an unexpected connection.

In fact, now that she thought about it, Max could have been deliberately trying to emulate her father. The shirt could have been one of his own, the room reminded her vaguely of her father's office suite at the Society.

That must have been why her heart skipped as Max handed her the glass. Their fingers brushed in the transaction and she was stuck again by the warmth of his skin, by his apparent youth and vitality. He had a charisma himself, perhaps as potent as that of her father.

"To Ernest," Max said solemnly, touching his glass to hers. "And the preservation of his legacy."

Ernestine paused in the act of taking a sip. "That would be the legacy you're planning to destroy."

"Not destroy, no," Max corrected, his voice rich with conviction. "Ernest's vision must adapt to ensure its survival into the Republic's future."

Ernestine put down the glass. "Usurping the autonomy of the Society and making it part of the federal government of the Republic cannot be reconciled with my father's vision for the Society's future." She picked up her mask, preparing to leave. "But why talk to me? I'm only a past president of the Society."

"Are you?" Max mused, his gaze knowing. "I doubt your influence is as meager as that, given the byzantine nature of the Society."

Ernestine bristled. "You know nothing of the Society and its inner workings, much less any *byzantine* nature of—"

"I know enough," Max interrupted softly, "to know of the Council of Three that secretly governs both Society and Institute."

Ernestine hid her surprise well, out of habit. "That is a rumor," she lied, her voice tight. "A conspiracy theory, perpetuated by those, like you, who would undermine my father's legacy."

Max continued, untroubled. "I know enough to know about the One, who secretly makes every decision of import for both Society and Institute."

When Ernestine would have interrupted, he raised a finger, his voice dropping even lower. "I know that Ernest was the One for years, courtesy of his complete inability to delegate. I do not hold that against him, having suffered from the same affliction myself."

Had her father confided this in Max? It seemed unlikely. But Max clearly had no doubt that he had hold of a truth. He paused to sip, then smiled that Ernestine had nothing to say. She fully anticipated his next words, but still it surprised her to hear them spoken aloud. "I know the One remains hidden and unnamed, masked as it were." His gaze dropped to her feathered mask and Ernestine's heart leapt. "But I understand enough of the Society's workings to guess that you are of the Council of Three now, if not the One. *That* is why I would talk to you, my dear Nessie. I believe in going directly to the top."

Ernestine folded her arms across her chest, prepared to concede nothing. "It is possible that I could deliver a message to those of authority. Since I am here, you might as well go on."

"Fine. Have your game." Max's smile broadened briefly before he spoke crisply again. "Here is my question for you, or for those mysterious individuals of authority. How does the current passivity of the Society reflect the initial vision of Ernest Sinclair, and what plans have you for its revitalization?"

"This discussion is inappropriate outside of the Society's governing council. I have nothing to discuss . . ."

"How does the Society's current failure to do anything to save itself honor Ernest's legacy?" Max challenged, his voice rising. That his question so closely echoed Ernestine's own doubts was uncanny. "Recall that Ernest was the One who organized the attack on Gotham in 2069, a scheme to ensure the Republic's supply of shades in a time of a diminished shade population. It was a bold play to launch a nuclear assault upon one of the largest cities in the Republic, and a scheme that was never ever linked to the Society. In fact, Ernest appeared as the hero of the subsequent disaster. Brilliant!"

Ernestine arched a brow. "There is no proof to support

such an accusation." As the One, she knew the truth of that assault, and others, but Max should not be aware of such secret ploys.

Max smiled, apparently confident in his information. "Just as there is no evidence to support the fact that the last Council of Three did try to replicate that feat by arranging for a nuclear assault on Chicago just a year ago, an attack that incidentally would have left the president of the Republic dead. Very bold." Max sipped. "If a failure."

"You speculate."

Max shook his head. "Yet such bold gamesmanship, such decisive leadership, in defense of the Society's ideals and objectives has no echo in these troubling times."

"There's no proof," Ernestine insisted.

"Do we need proof of everything we know to be true?" Max smiled amiably, his eyes glinting. "And perhaps there *is* proof, proof of which you are as yet unaware."

Ernestine could not hide her dismay at that possibility.

Max smiled. The proverbial cat who had swallowed a canary—or perhaps it was a lion and a gazelle. Either way, he had her undivided attention and he knew it.

"What do you want?" she demanded.

"I want to create a glorious future for the Republic. And that includes the Society founded by my dear friend, Ernest. Call me sentimental, but I feel obliged to respect the memory of another trailblazer."

Ernestine would never have called Maximilian Blackstone sentimental, especially after this discussion.

"How?" she asked, watching him warily.

"By ensuring that his organization survives." Max put down his glass and leaned forward, his expression intent.

"That is not your declared plan."

Max made a dismissive gesture. "The Republic cannot continue as it has. To eliminate the netherzones and free the shades is a popular issue, one we can cede because the supply of shades has dwindled to unacceptable levels. In the short term, the concession must be made to satisfy the demands of the Republic's citizens."

"And in the long?"

"The Republic needs fossil fuels and shades to continue with any semblance of prosperity. A nuclear war, intended to expand our borders beyond North America in conquest of those fuel supplies, will provide both."

Ernestine knew he wasn't joking. "That's not what you're telling the Republic."

"I'm telling them what they need to know. We free the shades, we subsume the Society into the government. Then war creates the need for the Society again, for the raw numbers of shades will be too great for the government to administer."

"Except that the new Society will operate under federal jurisdiction."

Max grimaced. "There must be a change in the optics, given the popular opinion of the moment, but I can use the Society's expertise to bring this plan to fruition."

"And the money from our drug patents."

"Every bargain demands a sacrifice. The alternative, dear Nessie, is that the Society will be wiped from the face of the earth, without regret." Max held her gaze. "I need a partner who shares my devotion to Ernest's ideals. I need a partner who understands the nuances of administering the Society's programs and the political necessity of not admitting everything to everyone. I need a partner who can deliver what I need to make a successful future for the Republic."

"And that would be me?"

"That would be you, Nessie." Max smiled. "All or nothing. It's that simple."

Ernestine considered his words for only a moment. Then she strode back toward the fireplace, picked up her glass, and sniffed of its contents. It was good brandy, but then she already knew that Max wasn't one to compromise. She held the glass toward Max.

"To my father's memory," she said, then drank of the potent golden liquid.

"To Ernest," Max said, then smiled with satisfaction before he drank her toast. "And to the future that you and I shall create."

There was something in his tone that made her cautious, even as the brandy sent heat through her veins. Ernestine settled before the fire to hear the details, convinced that Max had said everything he could that might surprise her.

She was very quickly proven to be wrong in that assumption.

The man's audacity was unrivalled. Ernestine Sinclair liked audacity in a man.

She liked it very, very much.

A Summary of Nuclear Events of the Twenty-first Century[1]

2014–First Planetary War–the Republic vs. the Emirate States
- triggered initially by conflict over control of remaining fossil fuel stores
- first use of hydrogen bomb in warfare, at Dubai, May 3, 2014
- nuclear bombs detonated in: Washington, D.C.; Whiting, IN; Philadelphia, PA; Pascagoula, MS; Houston; Port Arthur, TX; Baytown, TX; Baton Rouge, LA; Dubai; Medina; Baghdad; Riyadh; Cairo; Jerusalem; Algiers; Marrakech; Paris

2029–Post-Colonial Conflict–from which the Republic abstained
- triggered initially by conflict over removal of fossil fuels, race issues, and perceived abandonment of former colonies confronting profound health challenges
- nuclear bombs detonated in Cape Town (4), London, Paris, Brussels, Frankfurt, Geneva, Amsterdam, Cairo, Swaziland, Johannesburg, Harare, Kinshasa. Numerous other sites in continental Africa are suspected to have been bombed, but the incidents remain unreported and unconfirmed.

---

[1] excerpted with permission from Dr. Zenya Romanov, *A Nuclear Diary: the Twenty-First Century in War and Peace*, Institute for Radiation Studies Press, Chicago, 2075, pp. 215–216. Please note that for the sake of space considerations, only nuclear acts of warfare are cited here. Accidents and "incidents"—as, for example, the collapse of the sarcophagus enclosing the wreckage of Chernobyl in 2012—have been presented comprehensively in *Ibid.*, pp. 321–635.

2035—so-called "Second Planetary War"

- purportedly triggered by divergent religious beliefs, language and cultural changes; later recognized and acknowledged as an expansionist strategy of the Republic in pursuit of energy resources
- nuclear bombs detonated in Mexico City, Belize City, Sao Paulo, Caracas, Santiago, Buenos Aires, Rio de Janeiro

2051—Pacific Rim Conflict—the Republic vs. the Far East Economic Conglomerate

- a trade war escalated beyond all expectation, triggered by the refusal of the Republic to acknowledge the decision of the World Trade adjudicators over pricing of electronics components imports and food exports
- nuclear bombs detonated in Vancouver, Seattle, Portland (Oregon), San Francisco, Los Angeles, San Diego, Tokyo (2), Taipei, Shanghai, Hong Kong, Saigon, Manila[2]

2069—Attack on Gotham

- trigger unknown—never attributed with certainty to any one organization or individual
- nuclear detonations in and around Gotham leave the city a wasteland and hot zone

---

[2] For a concise if controversial summary of the evidence in favor of a correlation between these hostilities and the massive seismic shift that occured in 2052 (triggering, among others, the San Andreas fault line in California) please refer to J. Rabinovitch, *The Big One*, New View Publishing, Reno, 2055. Additionally, radiation leakage from Hanford, WA—the largest Republic containment of nuclear spent fuel—in the wake of the seismic shift and damage to the storage tanks was explored in the academically discredited work L. fitzHugh *Slipping Through the Cracks: Containment and Accountability*, Gaia Press, Spokane, 2065.

VIII

ARMAND HAD been in the netherzones of the Institute, of course, at least the primary levels used by students to move between buildings. The main labs were also on these levels. These spaces were characterized by their tiled surfaces, polished steel, and blindingly bright light.

He had heard that there was a lower level, used as a service passageway, but had never seen it.

Armand had also been in the netherzones of New Gotham, as well as various commuter passageways between Nouveau Mont Royal and New Gotham. These routes had been poorly illuminated, but functional in their design. Those who traveled within them had used moving sidewalks and kept to themselves. The few illicit tunnels that he and Baruch had been obliged to use for hiding on occasion en route to Tupperman had been dirty and rudimentary but deserted.

None of that had prepared him for the lowest level of the Institute's netherzones.

Theodora was clearly familiar with the Institute and its warren of hidden passageways. She cut a course through the shadows, slipping into the walls seemingly at will, always heading downward. Armand lost his bearings quickly, and focused on staying close to her instead of looking around himself.

She finally halted before a locked grate. A smell rose

through the grate, the scent of sewage and mold, although the darkness beyond was impenetrable. Dire warnings were posted above and beside the grate.

"You'll have to shoot off the lock," she said softly. When Armand hesitated, she smiled. "Or you can give me back my laze now."

Armand fired at the lock. It heated to glowing red under the laze, then suddenly shattered into fragments. A red light began to blink over the portal and Armand heard an alarm sound in the distance.

Theodora kicked the grate so that it opened, and darted into the darkness. "Hurry!" She lit a flashlight from her palm, moving with confidence into the netherzones.

Armand had no such light in his palm.

He spared a backward glance up the stairwell, heard the clatter of boots on the metal, and raced after her. She reached back and seized his hand, the pair of them running onward in the darkness. Theodora held out her left hand to light the way, while Armand kept the laze in his right, ready to shoot if necessary.

The light was poor, but he could see that the passageways were the same dimensions as the higher levels. The floor was level, although he couldn't be sure whether it was made of pounded dirt or stone. There was a pervasive wet smell, and standing puddles shone in some side corridors. He could also smell lubricant, a heavy oily scent that was only vaguely familiar. And there was the incessant whine of equipment. Theodora seemed to know her way, and charted an unerring course toward a destination.

He was glad to be holding her hand when he saw the shades. He might have faltered or stumbled, but Theodora guided him steadily onward.

Armand hadn't seen the shades at first, because the shadows were so deep and dark. He caught a glimpse of a pale arm though, and then a face, then realized that the nameless equipment churning on either side was operated by shades.

Humans. Laboring in the darkness. As soon as he noticed one, he became aware of many more. There must have been hundreds of them, walking treadmills, riding power generators like bicycles, moving trash, and hauling pulleys. They were naked in the netherzones, but their skin carried a patina of soot that made its true color uncertain.

He heard the soft whisper of their breathing and his scalp prickled.

They moved with a lethargy that caught at Armand's heart, a symptom perhaps of the knowledge that their entire lives would be spent providing captive labor. He couldn't see obvious defects in most of them—he glimpsed an extra thumb here or a lesion there—but the darkness hid many secrets. Some were hooded, others wore blinders, others yet were shackled to the equipment they operated.

The shades shook him.

Theodora spared him a glance. "Never been down, huh?" she asked lightly. "I suspected as much. It gets a whole lot worse, so don't say you weren't warned."

"We could free them," Armand said.

She shook her head. "They're drugged and dazed. They'd just keep doing what they're doing, or sit down and wait for someone to tell them what to do. The only thing you would do is get them into punishment—unless you could physically carry them all out of here."

There were hundreds of them, more everywhere Armand looked.

They had entered hell.

Footsteps grew louder behind them and Theodora tugged him abruptly into a side corridor. It quickly proved to be a dead end, terminating in a door with a security panel beside it. A light shone red above the panel.

It was incredible that she'd made a mistake. He had a moment to be fearful, to regret having trusted her.

Armand was certain they were trapped, but Theodora peered at the panel. She cast him a mischievous glance. "I know the model. Three tries, then it blows. Let's see how I do today at guessing combinations." He was astonished that she could be so cavalier, but then he saw her lips set. Before he could stop her, she punched in a sequence of numbers.

The red light shone steadily.

"One down." She glanced at her palm and pursed her lips. "I wonder how much that witch knew." She tapped at her palm busily. He braced his back against the wall, laze at the ready as the sounds of pursuit became steadily louder. He willed Theodora to hurry. Even here, he didn't want to injure anyone.

His heart pounded as it never had yet.

"The intruder came this way," cried a guard. "Fan out!"

Theodora wiggled her gloved fingers over the security panel, then rapidly tapped in another sequence.

Taking a chance.

Armand held his breath.

The light gleamed red, although it began to pulse.

Theodora swore. "Say your prayers," she whispered, then immediately tried again.

"You go left," said the guard at startling proximity. "I'll take this one."

Armand took the safety off the laze and eased closer to

the main corridor. Would he have to kill someone? Would he choose his own survival over that of another? His stomach churned.

He jumped when Theodora touched his elbow.

She pointed and he saw that the light over the security panel shone green. The door alongside it was sliding open. He darted after her, glimpsing the toe of the guard's boot just as they ducked into the doorway. They flattened themselves against the wall on either side of the portal as the door slid back into place. It moved so slowly.

The guard cried out, evidently seeing the movement, and raced down the short corridor beside it. Armand raised the laze, but the guard only got one hand into the door before it snicked shut.

The tips of his fingers were caught between the steel panel and the frame, his scream echoing through the door as they were sliced away.

"Lock it forever," Theodora whispered and pointed.

Armand shot the control panel and sparks flew as it shorted out. He felt sick.

Theodora gave him a nudge. "Them or us. It's that simple."

Armand supposed it was true, but he didn't have to like it.

"Let's see where we are," Theodora said, raising her hand as she stepped into the middle of the room. The blue light of her palm danced over rows and rows of jars, the glass reflecting the light.

The jars were large, each about two feet tall, and the reflection so bright that Armand didn't see their contents right away. They lined the room, placed on shelves and racked at least three jars deep. The jars extended all the way to the ceiling, which was high. There had to be eight rows of shelves.

And all those jars.

Armand realized that each jar held a baby, the child curled just as it would have been in its mother's womb. They were mutated, though, some with extra limbs, large heads, small heads, extra facial features, missing facial features. In such quantity, they were horrible and horrifying—the only mercy was that they were dead.

"Fetus Hall," Theodora murmured with satisfaction. "I always wondered whether it really existed. Needless to say, it's not on the Institute's official tour, or its maps." She cast him a wry glance. "I guess you're skipping ahead in the course plan."

Armand's throat tightened. A label on each jar provided a date, a locale, and a reference number. That someone had troubled to preserve them and catalogue them was even more horrific than the fact that they existed.

"These were the lucky ones," Theodora said. "They didn't survive to be harvested."

Armand knew he would be sick then.

Theodora watched him as he retched, her expression mingled compassion and curiosity. When she spoke, her voice had softened. "You really didn't know, did you?"

He shook his head, struggling to regain his composure. It was almost impossible, given these children on every side. What kind of creatures were the people who could do this, who could document this abomination, who could even stand in this hall of horrors? If this was humanity, what was the point of saving them? They were all lost souls already, these people who had made the world into their own hell.

He stared around himself, his gut churning, until Theodora touched his arm. "Come on, we've got to keep moving."

At the far end of the room, she paused, studying the wall with her hands on her hips. "If this is Fetus Hall, we're already off the map," she mused. "There should be a connection to Cosmopoulos's lab, though."

"You can get to the labs on the upper level . . ."

"I'm not looking for the labs where the endorsed research happens. No, there's another one, one rumored to be down here. Few people see it and live to tell the story, but we haven't got a whole lot to lose at this point." She ran her hands over the wall, making a sound of satisfaction as she slid her fingertip along a contour Armand couldn't see.

"Got it!" she whispered, then glanced back. Her eyes were dancing and he knew that she loved to take risks like this. Was this how humans compensated for their mortality? By pretending it didn't exist? By acting as if they were invulnerable? The show of spirit captivated him as little else could have done.

It also encouraged him.

It gave him hope.

Maybe Theodora's life was sweeter for the knowledge that it could end at any time. He wasn't sure, but he wanted to know more. He wanted to understand what drove her. He wanted to face danger with that same courage, even if it meant dying. There was something to be said for giving life one's best shot.

"How about a shortcut to graduate school?" she asked.

Armand moved to stand beside her. "Forget certification. Let's get to the lab. Just tell me what to do."

She looked down at the laze, flicked a glance back to the door they'd come in, then licked her lips. It was the first time he'd seen her nervous, but her gaze was steady. "First, I need you to promise that you won't let them take me."

"What do you mean?"

"If it comes to it, kill me." She looked him straight in the eye, her gaze unswerving. He knew she meant every word. "They can do what they want with the bits, but I don't want to be alive for the festivities."

"But how could you be?"

Her gaze hardened. "Promise me, Armand."

She was so determined. Armand wasn't sure how he would keep his word, but somehow he would. "I promise," he said softly and she smiled quickly.

"I knew there was a reason I liked you," she whispered, then rummaged in the small pouch at her belt. "Mint?" she asked, offering him a small hard disk wrapped in plastic. Armand accepted, refusing to look back, and she pressed the panel.

A door swung open and she strode fearlessly into the darkness before he could say more.

Did his promise give her that much confidence?

Armand could smell formaldehyde and a scent that made him think of roasted meat. It wasn't an encouraging combination, but Theodora didn't hesitate. She was familiar with this world and its horrors, comfortable in it in a way that he doubted he ever would be. She had armor he never wanted to have. He wished with sudden fervor that he was away from the earthly sphere, that he had never surrendered his wings, that he had understood fully what was at stake.

But who could have ever explained the thrill of Theodora's kiss? He would never regret that experience. And the only way back to his old life was in fulfilling his mission.

Onward was the only path.

Realizing that there was too much distance between

them, he quickly strode after her, the darkness and that scent feeding his doubts. The clean taste of mint was more welcome with every step.

Maybe he should ask Theodora for a similar promise, if words could be so fortifying.

ARMAND DIDN'T know.

He truly didn't understand the crimes of the Society of Nuclear Darwinists, or the Institute for Radiation Studies. He didn't fully realize the risk to his friend, didn't know what happened in the netherzones and hidden corners of the Republic. He couldn't have faked that reaction. He'd turned so white and she knew he was mortified that he'd been sick.

His innocence was a state of mind as different from her own as possible.

But maybe, it explained his ability to be gentle.

Theodora supposed there were many norms who had no idea of what was done in the darkness, purportedly for their benefit. She guessed that Armand wasn't the only new student at the Institute who didn't realize the full magnitude of what he would be trained to do. After all, they'd only enrolled to get to Blackstone.

She couldn't remember a time when she had been in ignorance of the fate of shades. She'd been brought to the wraiths as an infant, her mother desperate to save her from a shade's fate, and she had spent a lifetime appreciating what she'd avoided.

Exploring its full dimensions of possibility.

Armand's ignorance only increased her determination to tear the veil from his view of the world. He couldn't be blamed for not knowing the truth, the Republic hid that truth from casual perusal, but she wanted him to fully understand the peril his friend faced. She felt compelled to show him all of it.

Even though she feared its impact on him. It might be the jolt of reality he needed to dismiss this crazy idea about angels. It might drive him over the edge. Theodora didn't know, but she didn't believe that ignorance served anyone well.

She led him toward the hidden labs, heart in her throat, knowing that she might owe another person an act of atonement before the night was through.

MARRY ME.

Ernestine sat in Max's armored limousine, having accepted his offer of safe passage back to her unit, and marveled at his offer. She barely saw the wasteland that was Chicago, her thoughts spinning as she reviewed his proposal. She was dimly aware of fires burning in alleys, of smoke and milling hordes, but the limousine moved through the streets with purpose.

It was pulled by eight hooded and harnessed shades, and was the color of night itself. The four footmen and chauffeur were norms, and all five of them were armed. Ernestine felt as safe as was possible within the city that had so changed in these recent months.

The responsibility for that descent into anarchy could be laid squarely at the feet of the Oracle, with her ridiculous conviction that shades should be liberated and treated with compassion.

Only a former shade could be convinced of the merit of such a stupid and unworkable notion. Shades had merit only when they contributed to society as a whole, and they had to contribute at the level of their skills. For most, that was pathetically low.

Van Buren had called for lockdowns and punishment, in an attempt to restore order in the Republic's urban centers. His plans had only been partly successful, and his popularity—in contrast to that of the Oracle—had plummeted.

It was patently unfair.

Ernestine had been sure that Max had been complicit with the Oracle, for he appeared to be conciliatory to her notion in public. But his scheme was to outwardly appear compliant while moving the Society under the jurisdiction of the federal government, then secretly using the military to put shades back where they belonged.

He was avoiding Van Buren's misstep.

Officially, under Max's scheme, there would be an appearance of rehabilitation, one that Ernestine could design, but that would be short-lived under Max's plan. Once the influx of new shades began after the war and the fossil fuels won in battle were used up—and there were precious few of them left, anyway—the public would clamor for a better way of life. Ernest's ideas would be timely again, and Ernestine would be perfectly poised as First Lady to not only put them into action but give them the gloss of compassion.

Max had even suggested she might take the title First Mother.

His was an astonishing idea, one that made more sense with every passing moment. Max had not been unpersuasive himself, although what he proposed was a union of equals. A partnership, to make better use of their strengths. He needed Ernestine's knowledge and expertise to manage that sudden increase in the shade population. He needed the appearance of continuity with the Society to bring all Nuclear Darwinists into the fold of his vision for the future. He needed the power of the One to make his plan a reality.

Just as he needed the show of the government taking all authority out of the hands of the Society, an apparent punishment for an abuse of power. Max had made it clear that this was all a smoke screen, a response to the current situation of shades thronging the streets and the popular Oracle insisting upon their release from the netherzones.

Max intended for the Society to continue much as it had, but under the auspices of the federal government.

The guarantee came in the fact that he wanted Ernestine to run it all. As First Mother, she would be the honorary advocate for shades throughout the Republic, when in fact, she would be orchestrating their exploitation.

Ernestine loved the sound of that. She also liked that he had not immediately dismissed the notion of the revenue from the Society's drug patents being kept apart from the federal treasury, and Ernestine having control of those funds.

This might be a workable solution.

Never mind that Ernestine found power the most potent aphrodisiac of all. She could share Max's bed without any trouble at all, and he had hinted that their partnership would not be without its earthly pleasures.

He had given her until the rescheduled debate to give her agreement, as well as the assurance that she could bring the Society to heel. As the One, that would be readily done—once Ernestine herself was certain.

The trick to survival, Ernestine had learned long ago, was in choosing one's allies with care. Her only quibble with Max's offer was that it sounded almost too good to be true.

She'd expected him to argue about the drug patent money. Why would he cede so easily? Or at least negotiate? Was there something Ernestine didn't know?

That concern found root in the fact that she knew so little of Max. A quick survey from her palm turned up very little of interest—his official biography had been so polished that there was nothing distinctive remaining. An early history of volunteerism, popular admiration for his bravery, elected to mayor while young. An ever-ascending political path from there, one in which every issue he confronted was turned to his advantage. Governor of the fifty-first state for two terms. Senator for three, leader of various humanitarian missions, and now the front runner for the role of president.

This said little of the man himself, and left Ernestine dissatisfied.

But Max had been friends with her father, by his own admission.

What had her father known about Max?

Ernestine's heart rose to her throat at the one avenue left open to her. Her father's palm rested on his shrine, untouched since his death in 2076. Ernestine could datashare with him, even now.

The prospect filled her with dread and excitement.

Did Ernestine truly want to know all of her father's secrets? Did she truly want that intimate a union with him, especially so long after he was gone?

Such was the state of her agitation that she did.

The passage of the limousine was halted by a gang of militant shades just then. Evidently they had guessed the limousine's destination, and that its occupant was associated with the Society. They began to harass the eight shades pulling the carriage, casting taunts and fruit at the harnessed team. They saved the stones for the carriage itself. Ernestine watched through the tinted window with trepidation, knowing they would have been more violent if they had known precisely who rode within.

Max's shade team, though, were tranquilized and thus unable to respond to any insults or challenges hurled their way. Ernestine had always believed that a mild sedative vastly improved the focus and performance of shades, and had written both a research paper and an article for a popular magazine upon the issue. She approved of Max's choice and made a palm note to tell him so.

One of the rebel shades stepped forward, raising a club as if to make an assault upon one of the harnessed team. Surely they wouldn't hurt one of their own! The others jeered encouragement, the leader raised his club high, and Ernestine caught her breath.

She gasped when Max's driver shot the attacker dead.

The shade's body fell, smoking and twitching. Another stepped forward to aid the fallen leader, but the driver of Max's limousine took him down as well.

The other shades scattered then, disappearing like rats into the adjacent streets and alleys. Ernestine saw only the whites of their widened eyes before they fled. The bodies were abandoned, left for the vermin.

The shade team, despite being sedated, were skittish after the laze shot, but the driver cracked the whip repeatedly. Once they began to move, they fell into the rhythm familiar to them, moving toward the Institute with greater speed.

By the time the limousine had cleared the security gates and halted before Ernestine's building, she was closer to a decision. The Republic couldn't continue in this state. Shade populations had to be brought back under control, just as Max insisted, and the way to do that was with the force of the federal militia.

Nukes and crude oil and marriage.

But first, she wanted the final reassurance of her father's insight.

IT WAS too quiet.

Theodora had expected a bustle of activity in the lower netherzones, at least a buzz of excitement over Cosmopoulos's new experiment. She had feared to encounter the great man himself, busily launching himself into his new venture.

Instead, the low netherzone was as quiet as a tomb. There were no shades here, at least not outside of the labs.

Could she hear them breathing?

Theodora felt her pulse race. Maybe it was the smell of antiseptic. She stood listening, her finger to her lips. Armand watched and waited, his gaze locked upon her for some cue.

Theodora was afraid, as she was seldom afraid. Would she open the wrong door? Discover a dissection and vivisection in progress? Have to look in the eyes of a shade snared in some loathsome experiment—and need to turn her back for her own survival?

Armand reached out and took her hand; his firm grasp helped to settle her nerves. She glanced toward him and he smiled, serene in his confidence that all would be well. That his calm was born of blissful ignorance was something she could live with.

She was very glad to not be alone.

Which was interesting, given that she normally preferred solitude.

Theodora chose not to think about that.

They continued, hand in hand. Their footsteps, as quiet as they were, seemed to be magnified and echo far beyond their location. The darkness down the side corridors seemed Stygian, filled with menace and mystery. Even the quiet sound of machinery piping liquids was remote, the electronic beeps of monitors muted as if from another world.

There was very little that gave Theodora the creeps. This place did.

What was she missing?

Why was there no one here?

She glanced at Armand who appeared to be similarly wary. She supposed it was the middle of the night, and all right-thinking Nuclear Darwinists would be asleep.

Was Cosmopoulos right-thinking? Theodora had always suspected otherwise.

At the end of the corridor was a pair of stainless steel swing doors. They were closed, but a sliver of light gleamed from beneath them. Theodora was certain that the only sounds of activity came from that lab. There were no other doors in this corridor, and indeed, the main corridor seemed to lead directly to this pair of doors.

Theodora hoped it wasn't a final destination for her and Armand, although it was undoubtedly one for many unfortunates.

She paused to interrogate her palm, reviewing the files collected by Philippa, but found precisely what she'd expected. There was no other approach to this lab, which was probably just a confirmation that it was the place they sought. No netherzone access opened into it, no secret corridor encircled it. Dr. Cosmopoulos allowed for no accidents.

But if Baruch was in there, the only way to save him was to go in after him.

And the only way to know his situation was to look. They eased closer, at one in the intent to be silent, and Theodora considered the lit panel beside the doors.

Research Project 17243

She double-checked the number assigned to the experiment planned on Armand's friend, even though she knew the number.

This was it.

She took a deep breath and nodded minutely to Armand. His lips set and he gave her fingers one last squeeze before he released her hand and reached for the door. He held the laze high, looking as if he was ready for anything.

Theodora's instincts for self-preservation screamed as his gloved fingers touched the door.

She sensed the trap just before it was sprung.

IX

ERNESTINE DISMISSED Anthony and stood in the foyer of her unit, alone. The candles were burning lower on her father's altar, although they would last until morning. She liked the smell of them, the golden light they cast, the way her father looked like a conquering hero in his portrait.

She remembered him always seeming to be calm. Had he truly never been surprised? Or had he simply been better than most in hiding his emotions? Maybe that was why he had that aura of command.

Ernestine in contrast felt disheveled. Maybe it was the effect of the alcohol—she certainly wasn't accustomed to drinking any. There was a faint patina of perspiration on her skin and she could smell the evidence of the evening's uncertainties. She removed her mask and shook the pins out of her hair. She peeled off her dress and boots, standing in her lingerie before the altar.

She met the steely gaze of the man in the portrait and imagined that she saw approval in his eyes. She swallowed, eyed the boxed palm, then lowered her gaze. She felt as if her whole body was blushing, as if her skin was on fire.

But Ernestine had to know.

"Forgive me, Father," she whispered, then slid the probe of her palm into the port of his. She turned over her hand, watching the display on her palm.

Its blue light flickered, and she had the whimsical thought that her father's palm was sucking her dry.

Then her palm flashed and displayed a summary of the contents of her father's palm. It took her a minute to adjust to the ancient symbols, and a few taps to develop a sense of his organization.

Then she found the directory marked OUTSTANDING DETAILS.

It could have contained anything—a packing list for a trip he had yet to embark upon, a weekly To Do list—but Ernestine sensed otherwise. She opened the directory, surprised that it only contained one file.

A letter to her mother.

Strictly speaking, it wasn't what she was looking for, but Ernestine had crossed the line. Having chosen to pry into her father's secrets, she wanted to know them all.

She wanted to read this.

She hesitated only an instant over the fact that the message had never been meant for her eyes. Her mother had died before her father—Ernestine had only the barest recollection of Roberta.

This was a letter, she guessed, that he had never sent. She opened the file, dreading what she might find.

And rightly so. It was her father's confession, and reading it changed everything.

January 5, 2062
Chicago

My dearest Roberta,

Last night, I watched you sleep. You slept so deeply that you weren't aware of my restlessness, and I regret that this pregnancy has been so difficult for you. Miracles are like that, I suspect, wondrous but exhausting in their demands. It is almost time, though, and I know your thoughts are on the delivery.

Just as you think naturally of the future, so my thoughts have been inclined to turn to the past. I never thought to have another child, never thought to fall in love again, certainly never believed I would marry again. I never imagined that I deserved any of that.

Yet here we are, your stomach rounding more every day in defiance of all I believed.

My guilt seems to grow as quickly as our child. And that is the point of this letter.

You know, of course, about my first wife and my lost son, but what you know, what I have told you, is the official version. It is the one in which I am blameless, a helpless bystander caught in some cruel joke of fate.

You might have guessed that it is not my tendency to stand by and wait. Fate is made, and I made mine. As your delivery looms ever more near, I feel more and more compelled to tell you the truth, to reveal to you what kind of man you have married.

At the same time, I know that the truth will send you away. Why would you remain with a man who has done what I have done? Of what value is my word, given that I have deceived you about my past? No, I will never actually give this message to you and risk your rejection, but what I will do is record what I know, in case you have need of it. Perhaps committing the truth to some form will decrease its burden upon me.

If so, that is more mercy than I deserve.

Once upon a time, I loved a woman. At the time, I would have said that I loved Julia more than life itself, but that would prove to be a lie. When it came time to choose, I chose myself over Julia easily.

I made that choice not when Julia became pregnant with our first child, but when I was informed that she had been having an affair. All that love evaporated with the allegation that the child she carried was not mine. I have never felt such rage, nor such despair.

My so-called love was evidently a liar. The Republic was in the midst of the Second Planetary War, so I believed I could make change with my influence. Perhaps it was an illusion of potency. Perhaps it was an excuse to be away from home. I went to war zones and I gave speeches and I rallied troops and I consulted with politicians. I managed the Institute and presided over the Society. I worked tirelessly, but it made no difference—I could not face my wife. Julia seemed to have no guilt, and her easy charm, her comfort in my presence, ate at me.

I had a confidante in those days, a young man of considerable promise. He had been, in fact, the one to bring the evidence of Julia's indiscretion to me. He said he had lingered over it, dreading my learning of it. Ultimately, he decided that he could not mislead me or hide what he knew. I even thanked him for this horrible news, for his sense of honor in delivering it. And when despair nearly consumed me, I dared to turn to him for advice.

His counsel shocked me, but such was my rage that I followed it.

I did evil.

When next Julia complained of my absence, I suggested we meet in the field. I offered the destination of Mexico City, a place she had always wanted to visit. I sent her the tickets, made the arrangements, all the while knowing that the Republic was planning an attack. I "missed" my flight and was in the north when the bomb was dropped. Julia had only just arrived in the city, so she was not near the epicenter. Still, she was five months pregnant and caught in the maelstrom. Although she personally experienced only minor injuries, the child in her womb was exposed.

Too late, I feared the results of what I had done. I thought the child would be born dead, or have to be harvested as a shade. I played the concerned husband, but truly, the situation awakened some terror in me of what I had done. I knew that no crime merited my choice and I strove to be everything to her and the child.

It was not long until Julia learned that I had known in advance of the pending attack. The fight was terrible, especially as she insisted she had never been unfaithful, that she had never deserved my "punishment". Indeed, who could? My lack of faith in her vow destroyed our marriage completely. Was the child my son? Who lied? My wife or my confidante? The uncertainty gnawed at me, given my choice, until Julia insisted upon a DNA test of the child. If she thought it would ease my concern, she was wrong— the child she carried was my own. My so-called friend had lied to me, and I had responded in passion, without one shred of evidence to support his accusation. Our son, Ernest, was born apparently whole and healthy, and

Julia and I continued to live together under an unhappy truce.

Could I have saved the marriage? Was there some penance I could have paid to make everything right again? Probably not, but there was little opportunity. Ernest was diagnosed with thyroid cancer before he was three years old. It was from the radiation, we both knew it, and Julia blamed herself for not recognizing earlier that I was a monster. She committed suicide, unwilling to see her only child harvested as a shade by the Society her husband had founded. I was able to have the records changed to indicate that her death had been natural. Her family clung to the old faith and I tried to protect them from her choice. It was a small gesture to the woman who had been true to me.

It was too late to protect Ernest, though, the son that favored me in every way. There was no evading the fact that I had deliberately condemned him. I kept him from the Society. I kept him with me until the very end. I held him that last night when he died, and felt life slip away from him. I established "Sunshine Heals" in his honor, as a kind of penance.

Meanwhile my old confidante, the one who had lied to me and led me so far astray, became a politician. He began to work to undermine the Society and the Institute, using the knowledge he had gained in working beside me to ruin everything I had built. I recognized that his scheme all along had been to destroy the Society. And me. I am not without my resources and I am not so worthy an individual that I am above the need for vengeance.

So it is that I know that Maximilian Blackstone is not without his own dangerous secret, not without his debt to

my Society. Perhaps he has no idea that the records that
exist within the Institute differ from those of the Republic,
perhaps he is not sure, but I have searched the databanks
and I have compiled the evidence against him.

His suspicion that I have that file and that I have ensured
its survival is the only reason that I am alive to tell you about
this. We play a game, Max and I, our secrets keeping us
locked into a delicate balance. One day that balance will
shift, as such tenuous accords must do, and you will need
this file to guarantee your own safety and that of our child:

Revelation

You can guess the code word easily enough, Roberta.

I am sorry that I am not the man you believe me to be. I
love you enough to wish that I could have been worthy of
your esteem. And in my coward's heart, I hope that you will
never need to read this letter.

Yours,
Ernest

Armand pushed open the door to the lab. The light was muted, although it reflected off the tile and stainless steel.

The first thing he saw was Baruch, lying on his stomach on a gurney. The sight of his fallen friend caught at Armand, and he saw nothing else.

Baruch's clothing had been cut away, leaving his nudity exposed. The wound on his shoulder was dressed, but the scars on his back seemed vehement beneath the lights.

He was virtually harnessed, circles of plasma affixed to his body in a dozen places, wires connecting those points to monitors surrounding the gurney. His dark hair was tousled and his eyes were closed, as if he were asleep.

Armand wondered whether he had been sedated. Baruch looked frail, exhausted, as far from his robust self as Armand could imagine. The sight terrified Armand and he took a step closer to console his oldest friend.

Something cracked when he crossed the threshold.

Baruch's eyes flew open, panic in his gaze. He bared his teeth as one of the monitors began to emit a low screech. Then he began to scream in pain.

They were torturing him!

Armand shoved the laze into his belt and leapt to his friend's aid.

"No, no," Baruch murmured, so confused that he battled Armand with his hands. "No, no."

"It's a livewire!" Theodora hissed. She snatched at him, but Armand was already across the floor. He began to seize wires and pull them from the sensors on Baruch's body, desperate to stop his friend's suffering. He'd ripped a dozen loose when Theodora grabbed his hands.

"You're making it worse," she said.

"Can't you see that he's hurting?" Armand said and pushed her aside. "How can you stand by and watch?"

Theodora wasn't so easily pushed, despite her size.

"Because you'll kill him," she spat and Armand froze. "It's planned that way."

Armand was horrified. "What?" Baruch writhed as Theodora came to stand beside him.

"Yes," Baruch whispered even as a tear fell. "Yes."

Theodora was scanning the equipment, her lips tight. "A livewire is a trap. Our arrival triggered it. It's intended to lure you closer, to make you the one who makes him suffer." She flicked him a hot look. "They wired your friend as bait."

"No!" Armand stared at her, aghast that any living thing could devise such a scheme. She was so certain, though, that he knew it was true. "We have to help him. What do we do? How do we stop the pain? You must know."

But she didn't. Armand saw that. It was in her hesitation. He watched Baruch and shook his head.

Theodora's gaze was flying over the monitors in confusion. "They're all different," she said, and he heard her doubt. Baruch squeezed his eyes shut and moaned. "Choose the wrong one and he dies."

"Although that's not strictly necessary now," a man said from behind them.

Armand and Theodora spun as one. The short man Armand had seen talking to Blake Patterson earlier stood in the doorway, two helmeted guards behind him.

"Dr. Cosmopoulos," Theodora murmured.

"The very same," he said, pushing up his glasses. He tapped something into his palm and the high whine from the equipment stopped.

Baruch collapsed, a ripple dancing over his flesh. His eyes closed in relief and he panted slightly. Armand put a hand on his friend's shoulder, hating the occupants of this sphere more than ever.

At least Baruch's pain had stopped.

For now.

How could a man do this to another person? To another creature? Armand couldn't comprehend the malice at all.

Yet the Nuclear Darwinist was untroubled.

"A most resilient subject," Dr. Cosmopoulos said as he advanced into the lab. "And a most successful strategy, if I do say so myself."

"You knew we would come."

"I knew he would have friends. What kind of friend would not want to free him from this place?" Dr. Cosmopoulos smiled. "You probably don't even realize how easy I made it for you."

Theodora made a soft growl, one so low that only Armand heard it. At least they shared their dislike of this man and his methods.

Dr. Cosmopoulos considered the pair of them with a small smile. "There is nothing like a larger sample to lend credibility to laboratory results. Now, do you both share the same scars, or only one of you?"

"I don't know what you mean," Theodora said. She was on Armand's left and he could feel her fairly itching for her laze. He kept it slightly hidden behind his right thigh, uncertain that violence would truly help them escape.

He'd have to kill—or seriously injure—not one but three individuals, and Baruch was still on the livewire. He didn't doubt that Dr. Cosmopoulos could activate the torment again, simply from his palm.

Which told him what he had to target.

The doctor put his hands into the pockets of his lab coat and sauntered closer. "There's no need for games," he said. "I'm going to find out sooner or later, and it would be so much more civilized for you to just tell me."

"What do you know of what is civilized?" Theodora demanded.

Dr. Cosmopoulos caught his breath. "For a student of the Institute, Philippa, you have an unhealthy level of audacity."

Philippa? Armand tried to hide his surprise. Why did Dr. Cosmopoulos think that Theodora was Philippa?

But then, he had thought as much, as well. Had she stolen Philippa's identity as well as her clothing? He couldn't imagine how such a thing could be done, but he was sure that if it was possible, Theodora would know how to do it.

Dr. Cosmopoulos stepped closer. "I have a mind to volunteer you for a memory wipe. We have been wondering about the impact of such procedures upon norms and you might be the perfect candidate." He gestured to the guards, then indicated Theodora. "We can start tonight."

It all happened so quickly, although at the time, events seemed to unfold in slow motion for Armand.

"No!" Theodora screamed and launched herself at the older man. He should have guessed that she would go down fighting.

One guard raised his laze, targeting Theodora, and Armand shot at his hand. He closed his eyes against the man's cry of pain, heard the clatter of his laze on the floor.

When he looked, Theodora had changed course, leaping after the weapon.

Armand trained his weapon on the other guard, who

froze in place at the sound of the sight locking upon him. That guard dropped his weapon and raised his hands.

His finger on the trigger, Armand hesitated to kill an unarmed adversary. If he fired, he would be abandoning his own moral code. He would be rationalizing the same violence that everyone in this sphere condoned. The guard seemed to guess that Armand wasn't going to shoot because he leapt toward him.

Armand fired, but he aimed for the man's knee. The shot hit home in a blaze of light, the guard falling to the ground as he screamed. He rolled backward, holding his shattered leg against his chest.

At the same time, Theodora wrestled with the injured guard, kicking him hard and rolling beneath him. He seized her before she could escape, his blood running down the front of her pseudoskin. Theodora bit him and drove her heel into his crotch at the same moment.

His codpiece evidently offered insufficient protection, because he fell back in agony. Armand had a moment to be surprised, then he saw the blade flash and realized that Theodora had retractable blades in the heels of her boots. She was free of the guard in a flash, even snatching his laze from his hand.

She stood, sparing a glance for the other guard, and leveled the weapon at Dr. Cosmopoulos. She audibly sighted it and smiled. "Don't imagine I won't," she said and Dr. Cosmopoulos raised his hands slowly.

Armand seized the opportunity to make a difference. He fired at Dr. Cosmopoulos' palm, holding the shot long after the smell of burning flesh filled the lab. He was so intent on his task to save Baruch from pain, that he didn't keep track of the guard with the injured knee.

That man reached across the floor and grabbed his laze. He moved quickly, bracing himself on one elbow, and fired a shot at Armand.

Armand took a hit on the shoulder and fell backward at the onslaught of pain. It ran through his body like fire. It was excruciating and debilitating, as vehement as the pain when he had lost his wings.

No. It was worse. He hadn't been prepared for it. He fought for a grip on the lip of the steel counter, but his fingers were shaking too hard. His hand slipped, his knees gave out beneath him, and he collapsed to the tiled floor.

There was nothing in his universe but pain.

ARMAND WAS down!

Impossible!

But he fell in slow motion, crumpling to the floor. He didn't move again, his stillness—and the steady river of blood emanating from his pseudoskin—infuriating Theodora.

No! The most decent man she'd ever met couldn't just die.

It was outrageous that he could lose his life, just because he hadn't defended himself first, just because he hadn't claimed the guard's weapon or fried him to oblivion when he had the chance.

"I want them alive!" Dr. Cosmopoulos cried when the other guard might have cooked Armand to cinders.

Theodora wasn't going to miss the chance to intervene. She'd been enraged before, but this was different. Her anger gave her strength beyond expectation, made her vicious.

She shot the guard who had attacked Armand, showing

no such interest in his survival. She aimed directly for his heart, used full intensity, and finished him in one. He fell heavily but he didn't move any more. He never would. The other guard lifted his laze, targeting her, but Theodora spun crisply and treated him to the same fate.

Two down, no regrets.

Dr. Cosmopoulos, his left hand smoking, took advantage of her diversion to retreat across the lab. Theodora guessed that he wasn't retreating. He stretched his right hand toward a button on the wall, but he never reached it.

Theodora didn't know what it did, but it couldn't be good.

Her shot caught Dr. Cosmopoulos in the right elbow. She could have sworn she heard the joint crack.

He screamed and fell back. "My hands!"

"Are the least of your troubles," Theodora declared. She aimed right for his chest, but the laze only clicked.

It was out of charge.

She flung it across the lab, impatient with cheap tools. Dr. Cosmopoulos threw something after her, bracing his right hand, but Theodora rolled to evade it. The projectile was a small dark ball. It landed, rolled and fizzled, beginning to emit smoke.

Theodora knew that whatever that smoke was, it wouldn't be good for her health. She held her breath.

Her roll left her beside Armand and she seized her own laze from his limp grip. That he didn't fight her, that his whole body was lax, was no cause for celebration.

But when she looked for Cosmopoulos, he had disappeared.

So there *was* a netherzone access, after all.

Interesting.

Theodora spun, surveying the room, seeking other accesses that might allow other guards into the lab. Nothing. There was blood spattered all around the two guards. An alarm sounded dully in the distance, and she knew they would soon have company of the least desirable kind.

She should run.

But she couldn't leave Armand. He was down but not out, his hand still braced against his shoulder. His eyes were squeezed tightly shut. It was as if he had never experienced pain before, although Theodora knew that made no sense. He opened his eyes and considered her, disappointment dulling that magnificent green.

"You have your laze back then," he said quietly. Theodora knew he expected her to abandon him, now that she had what she wanted.

In normal circumstances, she would have done just that.

Incredibly, though, this wasn't about the cred.

It had become a matter of justice. Theodora wasn't leaving without Armand.

THEODORA KICKED the ball that was emanating a dark smoke, launching it into the corridor that led to the lab. Let the new arrivals deal with it. It just might slow them down.

Then she locked the doors to that same corridor, dragging the bodies of the sentries to barricade it even more. She checked them over, scored the laze that had been fired the least and was of the best quality.

"We're going out the back way," she said to Armand, handing him the pilfered laze. He nodded, wearily, and she worried about him. Fear made her move even faster.

Theodora found the netherzone access easily, once she knew it was there, and the levered panel that opened it. Darkness yawned through the other side of the portal.

Then she strode back to Armand, hiding her concern as well as she could.

"We're not done," she said. "But I can't carry you out of here."

His lips set stubbornly. "I won't leave Baruch."

"Don't you see?" She spoke quickly, her words low in case the lab was bugged. "It was a trap, set to broaden the size of the study group. We have to get out of here while we can. They're not going to just forget we were here."

Armand shook his head. "I won't leave Baruch, even if it is a trap."

Theodora sighed, aware of the passing time, yet not wanting to leave him even if he was being ridiculously noble. How would she persuade him to save himself?

She didn't have to.

Baruch's eyes opened, revealing a gleam of blue. That man reached out and touched Armand's shoulder, making Armand glance at his friend in surprise.

"Blackstone," Baruch said softly, his voice filled with exhaustion. "Get Blackstone and they will come."

Armand frowned. "But you aren't safe here."

Baruch winced. "So, quicker would be better." A glint of humor lit in his eyes and to Theodora's astonishment, he almost smiled.

Armand's grip visibly tightened on his friend's shoulder and it seemed that there was a silent bond between them. Theodora could have sworn she saw Baruch draw strength from Armand's grip, and similarly saw Armand's conviction grow.

Once more, she witnessed that tenderness in Armand, but this time it was an affection she had never seen between men. It wasn't sexual—she'd seen that lots of times—but the friends gave each other a charge they each needed. They had a common purpose, a connection greater than either of them, and they each drew on it.

She had a hard time believing that the need to see Blackstone dead accounted for all of it.

"Go," Baruch whispered. "For all of us." The men's gazes met and Theodora saw something she couldn't name pass between them. Affection? Admiration?

Was this friendship? She knew very little of that, either, but was intrigued.

Armand nodded once, then eyed her. "I can't do it alone," he said quietly. She swallowed when she saw the blood still running between his fingers. "Not like this."

He had a point.

Theodora moved to his side. "Open your pseudoskin so I can see the wound."

He did so, did it immediately and without hesitation, his trust still having the power to astonish her. His physique was just as good beneath the pseudoskin as she'd imagined. She was amazed that his skin was tanned to a healthy golden hue and that his muscles were so well developed. She felt herself flush as she leaned closer, keenly aware of the amusement in his gaze as he watched her.

"How bad is it?" His words were low and soft, resonant enough to make her shiver with desire.

"I've seen worse," she said, speaking crisply in contrast to her emotional response. She was thinking about the way he kissed, the way those firm lips fit to hers and coaxed her response, how welcome one of his intoxicating kisses would be when her whole body was trembling with their near miss. There was something about cheating death that made a person want to celebrate life, and celebrate it in the most basic way possible.

But there was no time.

Theodora frowned and pretended to be only concerned with Armand's injury. He had pulled back the pseudoskin enough to bare just the front of his left shoulder. She could smell his skin, the healthy clean scent of him. She could see the auburn hair on his chest, the curve of his pectoral muscle. She wanted to run her hands over him. His flesh was warm, his body strong. Theodora told herself that she was experiencing a normal human reaction, an adrenaline rush after a fight, and knew it was a lie.

This man had the power to undermine all of her convictions.

The wound was clean and not as deep as she'd feared. Theodora took advantage of the supplies in the lab to clean it and put a bandage on it. She would have bound his shoulder, but Armand pulled the pseudoskin back over his shoulder and fastened it again.

"That's fine," he said, pushing to his feet with an effort. Once again, he towered over her, looking hale and masculine despite his injury. He paled at the effort of standing, then his jaw set as if he would run on pure determination. At least the blood had stopped flowing. He straightened, meeting her gaze steadily.

"Can you move? Can you run?" Theodora asked, her questions falling quickly in her awareness of him.

Armand nodded. "I'll do what's necessary." She saw a new resolve in his eyes, one that she respected. He shoved the guard's laze into his belt.

"Okay," Theodora said, checking the charge on her laze. "Blackstone it is. But hold me back and I leave you behind."

Armand smiled, the warmth of his expression awakening a flutter in Theodora's gut. "Liar," he charged quietly.

"What do you mean?"

"You're not leaving me behind now," he noted. "You could have been long away by now."

He was right.

Theodora felt herself flush and couldn't avert her gaze. "That was different."

"Was it?" Baruch smiled in turn, his gaze almost as warm as Armand's.

Yet it didn't have the same effect upon Theodora.

She swallowed, then headed for the netherzone access Dr. Cosmopoulos had used. She was happier in the dark and would gladly face one wounded Nuclear Darwinist rather than an army of guards trained to kill. They had to be close—she and Armand had lingered too long.

The pair watched her, smiling slightly. Theodora had the sense that they could see her secrets, even the ones buried deepest. Their serenity was disarming.

It reminded her of something, an image that tantalized but remained just out of her grasp.

"Call it a weak moment," she said gruffly and pivoted, laze at the ready. "Let's go."

She didn't miss Armand's exhalation or the amusement carried in that slight sound. But she didn't look back either.

They had a mission to accomplish and the prospect of success diminished with every passing moment.

X

GOTHAM WAS dark and still.

Tupperman heard the wolves howl and knew his arrival had been noted by one species at least. It wouldn't have surprised him if other residents let the wolves be their sentinels.

He knew the way, he had charted it out a hundred times, and he followed it diligently. If he abandoned his usual caution, it was only reasonable under the circumstances.

He reached Grand Central Station and left the bike—with some regret—in the grand departure hall. He wasn't at all convinced that it would still be there when he returned.

On the other hand, he might never need it again.

Tupperman swallowed, feeling the perspiration gathering in his pseudoskin and knew he would have some fast talking to do, if he could find the outcasts hidden in the old city. For years, he had heard rumors that they met here in times of crisis. He hoped he wouldn't have to wait long for them to gather.

He didn't doubt that they, courtesy of the wolves, already knew that he had arrived. Still, they wouldn't likely confront him. Wraiths, exiles, runaway shades, circus performers, and survivors of the nuke on Gotham, these outcasts would have a healthy disrespect for the authority of the Republic.

As a uniformed member of the New Gotham Police Department, Tupperman only hoped he had the opportunity to do some fast talking.

There was no point in delay. His geiger was ticking merrily and the radiation badge on his sternum already had a healthy glow of exposure. He gave the bike one last pat, then headed for the stairs. He had only the light in his helm to guide him, but the stairs were broad and gracious, evocative of another time and place.

Tupperman went down, down into the heart of the old city.

Each flight took him deeper into darkness. Each step took him into lower and damper zones, and he felt the cold stone of the building close around him. He heard the scuttle of rats, and didn't doubt that his bike had been surrounded by wolves.

If not thieves.

He saw thick dust in the corridors that housed the train tracks, tracks that hadn't been used in decades. He smelled the ash and felt the cold, even though his filters and his heavy-gauge pseudoskin.

When he saw the flickering light of a torch, he was both relieved and fearful.

But he strode directly toward that golden light. Invitation or trap, there was no other way forward.

MONTGOMERY WAS at the window when Lilia returned to their unit. The unit was dark, despite the hour, only the light of the city and the stars slipping into the room. It wasn't like her partner to stare pensively out at the night, not when he could actively be making a difference instead, and she knew immediately that something was wrong.

Of course, she'd known that when he'd sent her a curt summons with no explanation.

It was even less like Montgomery to not wonder where she had been and what particular law she had been breaking. He didn't even look at her, but she saw that his hands were knotted together behind his back.

What had happened? A thousand dire possibilities flicked through her thoughts, every single one ending with Montgomery leaving her.

Could he still go back to the angelic host?

The bottom fell out of Lilia's gut. Less than a year into their committed relationship, she was only more afraid of losing him. She knew that Montgomery would choose duty or the greater good over himself, every single time.

That trait was part of what she loved about him. Her throat tightened and she couldn't say a word.

She just waited, as uncharacteristic as that was for her.

"Tupperman bailed," he said finally. His words were low and softly uttered, but filled with resolve.

That fact had import, import for them. Lilia heard it in his tone. She glanced over their unit, seeing that his desktop had been destroyed, as had the vid unit on the wall. Montgomery hadn't chosen to be in the dark so much as he had eliminated the potential sources of light.

"I don't understand. What does that mean?" she asked, keeping her tone carefully neutral with an effort.

Montgomery turned and she saw wariness in his eyes, a wariness that terrified her. "It means it's time."

Lilia didn't know what time he meant. She was momentarily astonished that Montgomery had any more secrets from her, but guessed from his gravity that this was the last one.

And it was a big one.

Well, she'd never been one to flinch from the truth.

Lilia took a deep breath and went to him, prepared to argue for her place in his life, prepared to beg for it, prepared to do anything necessary to keep this man she loved so much at her side.

"I have to go," he said. "It's time."

He caught her in his embrace before she could argue and held her close, pressing a kiss to her temple. "It's up to you whether you come along."

Lilia's knees went weak with relief. "Where the hell else would I be?" she demanded in mock annoyance and she saw the brief flicker of his smile.

"It's the end, Lil. You have to understand that it could go either way. It might be safer for you here."

She eased away from him, tilting her head to look at him. "What makes you imagine I'd want anything less than front-row seats for the end of the world? I thought you knew me."

He shrugged. "There's Delilah . . ."

"She has an angel of her own. I'm sticking with you."

He smiled then, the slow smile that heated her blood. "Good." He brushed his lips across hers, all too fleeting an embrace. "We have to go now, and we have to go bareback. Get your pseudoskin. The bike's tank is full and I've packed some provisions . . ."

"Bareback?" Lilia was shocked. Her palm held a thousand useful details—no, ten thousand—and to clear its memory would leave her without alliances, maps, or connections. It would leave her vulnerable, which was precisely how she didn't want to confront the end of the world.

Montgomery was adamant, though. His lips set in a tight line, one she knew brooked no negotiation, and he tapped his palm. "Clear it out, ASAP. No possible datatrail."

"But we'll need maps, won't we? And connections."

"No." Montgomery shook his head as he began his own data dump. He flicked her a hot glance. "We both know the way to Gotham already."

Gotham. Again. Lilia suppressed a shiver.

"And you might find some old friends there," he murmured.

Lilia eyed him, noted his conviction, appreciated that this was something she needed to take on trust. Well, she trusted Montgomery, had done so for a long time. The man knew all of her secrets and then some.

Maybe proving as much to him would make the difference, in the end. If he had to choose.

"Okay," she said, and saw his smile flash. She hesitated only a moment, her finger held over the keypad, then shook her head and initiated the commands to clear her own palm.

When both displays were dark, Montgomery pulled a swab from his belt. "To dull the pain," he said, then rubbed it over the back of her neck. Lilia's eyes widened, as much from the tingle on her skin as the knowledge of what he intended to do. As much of a rebel as she was, Montgomery was better.

He planned for every eventuality, instead of acting on impulse.

She closed her eyes against the sure slice of his knife against her nape. Montgomery murmured an apology as he worked the glass identification bead free from her skin. He then wiped the wound clean and bandaged it, putting the bloody bead on the desk.

Lilia immediately did the same for him. When the two beads were resting beside each other, she went to the closet to dress quickly. She put her pseudoskin on beneath her street clothes, chose her heavy boots, and took a cloak. Montgomery had the beads in his gloved hand when she returned.

A quick scan of the unit they had shared, and they were gone, running down the stairs hand in hand. In no time, they were on the bike, roaring toward Gotham, her legs wrapped around him and their helms stashed in the back.

Montgomery stopped the bike on the cusp of Nouveau Mont Royal's pleasure fringe. Lilia could see the illuminated cross over the old city, and the darkened silhouette of the abandoned circus where she had worked for so long.

Montgomery dropped the two beads to the pavement and crushed them under his heel, much to Lilia's delight. Then he took her left hand in his and reached for the fire hydrant. They smashed their palms against the metal nut securing the top of the hydrant.

And they were free.

Lost to the Republic's databanks.

Bareback.

Lilia found herself laughing, liberated from the Republic's tether for the first time in her life. They donned their helmets and checked their filters, securing themselves against the radiation of the old city. Lilia checked their geigers and radiation badges, then nodded and gave the thumbs-up.

Montgomery gunned the bike and they were leaving the new city and plunging into the old one. It was darker there, darker in the abandoned streets of the forbidden zones, and

Lilia loved its cobbled streets with new vigor. She had been here before, entered the old city illegally, but never like this. Never bareback. Never alone with Montgomery, with nothing much left to lose. Thousands of stars gleamed overhead as Montgomery drove south.

Heading for the end of the world.

If Lilia held on to Montgomery a little more tightly than usual, neither of them was going to tell.

"RISE UP!" came the cry from the room five layers beneath the streets of Gotham.

Tupperman eased to the bottom of the stairs. He stood in darkness, his laze at the ready, and pushed up the filter on his helm so that he could see better.

Ahead of him was a room filled with rusted pumps and engines, machinery that had been silent for years. Old pipes lined the ceiling, the valves thick with dust and cobwebs. Asbestos hung from some pipes, the wrapping having disintegrated over time so that it, too, resembled thick cobwebs. There were many sources of light, none of them bright, and he guessed that individuals were using their helms and palms to illuminate the scene. The torch, constructed of rags and dipped in oil, was a beacon.

The room was apparently crowded, although Tupperman couldn't see very many of them in their entirety because of the equipment. He saw legs and boots and arms, all covered with patched pseudoskins. He saw a startling mix of old helms, all from the rear, but this was no museum of abandoned armor.

He'd found the group he sought.

The people huddled together, their attention fixed on

someone Tupperman could not see. "The time has come to rise up and be counted!" declared that man, his cry perfectly echoing Tupperman's own plan.

Maybe this *would* end well.

Tupperman took a cautious step forward, practicing how he would declare himself.

He never had the chance.

He was jumped from behind by four men, all of them erupting from the shadows simultaneously. They moved with the silence of those accustomed to working without detection. He never saw their faces, disguised as they were behind old helms. He was seized and his head slammed against the wall. Even with the protection of his helm, the hit left him reeling and disoriented.

It was the only advantage they needed. Hands assailed him, so many busy fingers that Tupperman couldn't fight back.

His laze was confiscated, his helm ripped off, and he held his breath in fear of contaminants.

One of his assailants laughed. "Loser cop," he snarled. "Afraid to breathe what we're forced to inhale every stinking day."

When Tupperman made to argue in his own defense, he was punched in the mouth for his trouble. It loosened his teeth. He spun and struck at his attacker, but two others grabbed him from behind, holding his arms behind his back.

The assailant grinned, punched Tupperman in the face, then kicked him hard in the gut. There were hobnails on his boots.

All the air left Tupperman's lungs at the force of the blow and he fell to his knees when they released him. He didn't dare to inhale again. The four attacked him in unison then and, in a heartbeat, Tupperman was down hard. They struck him repeatedly until he fell into the dust on the floor, then kicked him. They spewed expletives as they beat him, venting their frustration about the Republic and its police forces.

Tupperman felt himself bleeding, felt his eye swelling shut, and knew that he had made a fatal mistake. When he collapsed, their hands were all over him, removing his belt, his boots, his gloves, and he could only close his eyes in defeat.

This would be it, then. He would die on earth, picked clean by the mortals he had volunteered to defend, then left to die of exposure. The disappointment—in humans, in himself—stole the last of Tupperman's will to fight. He was tired, exhausted from too many years of remaining optimistic in the face of wickedness, and he felt his spirit break.

He didn't have the will to fight back.

He felt his pseudoskin being unfastened, felt the rough gestures through a haze of pain. When there was so much sensation in the world, why did his last moments have to be filled with the anguish of pain? He appreciated that the pseudoskin would be valuable amongst this group, and hoped that it would save one of them.

Maybe even that was too much to ask.

They rolled him over roughly, swearing that the pseudoskin didn't easily come free and his battered cheek collided with the cold steel of the floor.

It took Tupperman a moment to realize that they had stopped, that no one was touching him.

There was only silence.

Had they abandoned him? If so, why?

He opened his eyes and saw the boots of his attackers, backed away from him in a watchful circle. He heard a light stride and felt someone bend down beside him.

A finger touched his back, touched his scar.

With wonder.

And Tupperman knew that he had been recognized for what he was. A tear slid from his eye and fell into the dust, then he opened his eyes at the slight sound of metal on metal.

A small wizened man with dark hair peered at him, his nose not a hand span away from Tupperman's own. He had removed his helm and his hair was standing on end, darker yet with perspiration. Tupperman thought at first that it was the proximity that made the man's features look odd, then he realized that the man was a dwarf.

"You're one of them," the dwarf said, his gaze flicking over Tupperman. "Do you know Armaros and Baraqiel? They told us it was time."

"It *is* time," Tupperman agreed softly, choosing his words with care. "I'm the one who sent the surgeon to them."

The dwarf's eyes widened with wonder. "I saw," he whispered, glancing again at Tupperman's back. He lifted his hand away, his discomfiture clear. He swallowed, then looked at Tupperman again. "I saw where those scars come from."

A dwarf who knew Armaros and Baraqiel. This man could be only one person.

"Joachim," Tupperman guessed. "Owner of the Nouveau Mont Royal Circus."

"That's me. At least it was." The little man reached for Tupperman's neck and ran a fingertip over the curve where his shoulder began. His grip worried a nub embedded beneath the skin. Tupperman knew Joachim was feeling the glass-encased identity bead embedded in Tupperman's nape.

Joachim leaned closer and whispered. "You gotta lose this if you're going to stay."

Tupperman closed his eyes in agreement and relief. "Do it," he murmured.

He grimaced as the knife cut into his skin. He felt Joachim work the bead free and heard the crunch of it being ground to oblivion beneath Joachim's boot.

He was in.

Still alive and still fighting.

"What about your palm?"

"I cleared it already, destroyed all the connections."

He felt rather than saw Joachim's approval.

Then the dwarf pushed to his feet and glared at Tupperman's attackers. "He's one of us. Give him back his gear and help him up." They hastened to do his bidding, even as Joachim exuded displeasure.

"I brought you from the circus," Joachim added with disdain. "You should know better than to assume that the surface always shows the truth."

"Nothing is as it seems," Tupperman managed to whisper after he sat up with assistance. He felt his gut and scowled, halfway certain the attacker had broken at least one rib.

"Ain't it the truth," Joachim agreed with false cheer. He surveyed Tupperman with concern and Tupperman then saw the others standing behind him. "You're not going to die on us, are you? 'Cause it would be rotten luck to kill an angel."

"Not yet," Tupperman said, gritting his teeth as he rose to his feet. "At least not if you have a plan."

"We're going to New D.C.," Joachim said with resolve. "It's time to be visible, time to demand a new order with a better place for us. We've got the trains and we've got the tracks." He gestured to the group, which had split into two groups. The larger group stood behind Joachim. "Or you can stay here with the ones who've decided to defend the fort."

"What about power? There's no juice in Gotham."

Joachim snorted. "Shades aren't afraid to work. It's all we know, and it's going to get us to New D.C. before Election Day. We're going to rise up, no matter what the consequences are."

"And you're going to get there under your own steam," Tupperman teased and his new ally grinned.

"Something like that." Joachim sobered. "So?"

"I'll go to New D.C. with you. I want to see."

Joachim leaned close to Tupperman. "Why do *you* think it's time?"

Tupperman held his gaze steadily. "Because they're going to dissect an angel at the Institute for Radiation Studies, just to prove that we don't exist. They've got Baraqiel and they mean to kill him slowly." He saw Joachim's horror, focusing on that man's reaction instead of the outrage that stirred his followers. "It doesn't get much more wicked than that."

"You're right," Joachim said quietly. "It's time."

XI

ARMAND WAS fascinated by the change in Theodora. He felt as if her façade was cracking, the truth of her nature becoming more clear with every exchange. He would have bet that her motivation wasn't really the cred, that there *was* something else driving her actions.

And he wanted very much to know what it was.

He was also grateful for her expertise and experience. She led the way through the netherzones, her laze in her right hand and the lit palm of her left held high. She was fearless in the dark, something that he admired greatly.

She would help him achieve his mission, as Baruch could not.

But what would be her reward? Armand had little cred and that question began to trouble him as they worked their way steadily through the darkened corridors. It was only right that he compensate Theodora for helping him, but he had no means to do so.

He watched her stride ahead of him, admiring more than her intellect. He thought again of the golden spill of her hair, of the way her gaze could soften when she was close to him, the sweet taste of her kiss, and found his codpiece suddenly restrictive.

In another time and place, he might have found it amusing that it had taken an assassin and a wraith, a woman

living outside the law, to awaken his interest in the pleasures of the flesh.

They found no obstacles to their passage, something that
clearly troubled Theodora. They didn't see Cosmopoulos
again, nor were they pursued by any guards.

"It's possible that this is an undocumented passageway,"
Theodora said when he asked, but Armand could hear her
doubt. "It's not even on the wraith map of the Institute." She
cast him a rueful smile. "It's also possible that they want to
see where we'll go."

"How do you know where we are, then?"

"Educated guesses. The GPS doesn't work this low. We
want to get into the city's netherzones, preferably on the
west side of the Institute." She showed him the display on
her palm, and he saw that she had pulled up the map of the
lowest level of the Institute's netherzones. "We should be
in this vicinity," she said, indicating the terminus of a corridor on her palm's display.

"The perimeter of the Institute should be ahead on the
right," Armand said. "Surely even a secret netherzone has
to be on their property?"

"I wouldn't make any such assumptions," Theodora said.
"Who would ever know the difference?" She lifted her palm
to light the way.

A cinder block wall terminated the passage twenty feet
ahead.

Theodora turned her light to the left, shining it upon the
wall. There was a short run of metal stairs, with a sealed
metal door at its summit. "Bingo," she murmured. "I'll bet
this accesses the documented corridor on the wraith map."

They climbed the stairs together, Theodora examining
the security panel. It wasn't lit, but had a keypad for a code.

She pursed her lips, then glanced at him. "I think they know where we are," she said quietly. "On the other hand, I don't think we've got a lot to lose at this point."

"Except time," Armand said.

Theodora's expression turned grim as she made her plan. "If we're where I think we are, the exit from the Institute will be through this door and on the right. Maybe ten feet away."

"Will they pursue us into the city's netherzones?"

"I don't think so." She narrowed her eyes, giving his question due consideration. He liked that. "Maybe once they would have, but with Chicago's shades rioting, I'd think that would be too dangerous for Nuclear Darwinists." She met his gaze. "If we can get through that portal, they'll let us go."

"Ten feet?" Armand heard her concern and respected it. "You think they're waiting for us on the other side of this door?"

"Let's just say it wouldn't surprise me." Theodora raised her laze and put her hand on Armand's chest to ease him backward. "Which means there's nothing to be gained by subterfuge. Let's fire and run."

Before he could reply, she shot at the access panel. Sparks flew, then there was an explosion and smoke filled the corridor.

The lock was destroyed.

Armand immediately shoved open the door. Theodora leapt through the smoke ahead of him, firing in all directions.

"Four!" she cried, clearly counting their opponents. "Two down. Go!"

Armand had learned to respect her judgment. He ran

past her. The door to the netherzones was indeed to the right. One security guard stood on either side, laze at the ready. They wore pseudoskins and helms, two men sheathed in black.

Armand bent and ran as the first one fired, driving his shoulder into that man's chest. The man exhaled sharply as his back collided with the metal doors. Armand twisted the laze out of the guard's grip, slammed his head into the wall, then fired in the direction of his partner.

Despite his helm, the guard he'd assaulted had been hit hard enough to fall bonelessly to the floor.

Armand's shot sparked off the other guard's helm. Armand fired again at that guard's hand, the shot making him drop the laze. Armand kicked it down the corridor, and it slid readily on the tiles, disappearing into the shadows.

The guard lunged at Armand. He went with the man's momentum, catching the guard around the waist. Armand slammed the guard into the wall beside the lock, then punched him in the back.

The guard went limp.

The steel portal to the city's netherzones was still closed. There was a narrow box beneath the blinking red light, one the shape of a left hand. There was a probe lurking in the shadow at the back of the box, and Armand guessed its purpose.

He shoved the guard's left hand into the space so that the probe snicked into the port of the palm, located between the second and third finger. Armand saw the light of the palm being interrogated, then there was a chime.

And the door to Chicago's netherzones opened.

The red light over the door began to pulse. Armand guessed that the opening was on a timer, and that the door would automatically close in some predetermined length of time.

He was sure it wouldn't be long.

He glanced back to see Theodora racing toward him. There were four guards fallen on the floor and smoke filling the corridor. An alarm droned as she leapt closer.

One fallen guard moved suddenly, snatching at her ankle.

Armand fired at his hand. Theodora jumped, spun, and shot him right between the eyes without slowing down.

The pair of steel doors began to close.

"Hurry!" Armand stepped through the space, blocking the doors' passage with his body. He didn't doubt that they would slice him in half if he failed to move away in time. Theodora ran for him. She shoved her laze in her belt and stretched out one hand.

The guard with his hand in the access panel grabbed at her wrist. He tightened his grip and pulled her back. Theodora twisted but Armand saw that the angle wasn't good, that she'd injure herself as well.

The door steadily closed.

Armand caught Theodora's other hand and pulled with all his might. He fired at the guard who held her wrist, frying that man's hand. The guard screamed and released her in the nick of time.

Armand hauled Theodora through the space.

She only made it because she was so tiny.

Her boot was barely through the gap when the doors nested together with a clang.

Armand held his laze high, certain the guard would open the door again. Theodora was panting as she backed away, her own laze at the ready.

"This portal will remain secured for ten minutes," declared a toneless female voice from the other side of the door. "Access is temporarily denied. Please try again later or use an alternative exit."

Theodora and Armand exchanged a grin as the guard pounded on the steel. They turned as one and ran into the darkness.

"Let the adventure begin," Theodora muttered.

"Begin?" Armand echoed in dismay.

She cast him a smile that made his heart leap. "Trust me. That place is paradise compared to what we'll see out here."

Armand marveled that this world could have any more surprises for him. He trusted Theodora, though, and was glad of both her assistance and her knowledge.

He was sure he'd need it even more once they reached the Intercontinental Hotel.

THE PLACE was locked up tighter than a missile silo.

Of course.

Theodora and Armand were hidden in the shadows, watching the sentries patrol the netherzone access to the Intercontinental Hotel. Of course, the hotel would have increased security, given the instability of the streets and their need to ensure that their clients felt safe.

Keeping those clients safe was the best way to guarantee their business, after all.

"Shooting our way in isn't going to work," she murmured, thinking out loud.

"Too many security guards," Armand agreed. "We won't get ten feet before we're shot down."

"If we're lucky," she said. "Plus, if the Society raised the alarm, they might not kill us. They might harvest us instead."

Armand grimaced, his gaze fixed on the access. "I'm guessing your laze won't make it past security either."

"Neither will the guard's laze, but I don't want to go in without them." Theodora winced. She hated this. That they could have come so far just to be foiled by plain old security measures was patently unfair. "They'll have metal detectors, so hiding them won't work either." She considered Armand as she had an idea. "Wait a minute. We don't have to hide the weapons if whoever is toting our arsenal is authorized to carry."

He blinked. "Are you?"

"I don't officially exist, which gets in the way of permit applications." Theodora smiled, noting how he watched her mouth. This man could give her ideas with just a glance. Dangerous, seductive ideas. Ideas they unfortunately didn't have time to pursue. She sighed without meaning to do so.

"Well, I don't have authorization," Armand said with some impatience. No surprise there, given his determination to not kill another being. "That won't work."

Theodora recalled that she had swiped the identity of that Philippa. She tapped her palm, daring to hope that the nosy student had the right to carry a concealed weapon.

No luck.

"Neither does Philippa," she said, thinking furiously.

Suddenly she knew how they could do it.

They could masquerade as a shade and a Nuclear Darwinist.

She knew who had to play which role. There was absolutely nothing defective about Armand. Theodora would have bet on that.

Although she would have liked to have seen him naked, just to make sure.

No one would ever believe that he had failed the S.H.A.D.E., which left the dirty work up to her. And he was a student of the Institute, so should be able to make it work.

Provided he could lie with any plausibility.

"Look, one of us could pretend to be a shade, and the other a Nuclear Darwinist making a delivery," she said. "They might not fully examine the Nuclear Darwinist or his credentials. People are a little spooked by Nuclear Darwinists."

"And if they do?"

"You'll have to get insulted and shoot." Theodora shrugged. "Actually, that could work out well, because you won't shoot to kill. The repercussions would be less." She scanned her palm for a map of the local netherzones. "We need to do some prep first. Get some rest and work out our story."

"But we should attack now."

"No. There's no substitute for preparation. There's a storeroom not too far away."

Theodora turned and walked in that direction, knowing he would follow.

He did.

"Me?" Armand demanded. "What do you mean, I'll have to shoot?"

"You're the best candidate. Your palm says that you're a student at the Institute." She spared him a look. "Plus nobody is going to believe that you've been a shade all your life, undernourished and working in the dark."

"You're going to pretend to be a shade?"

"It's not that hard. I'll keep my head down, pretend to be

drugged, and shuffle my feet. You'll do all the talking." She smiled at him. "Try to avoid my getting shackled to a crap job, would you?"

His eyes flashed. "It's too dangerous . . ."

"This whole scheme is dangerous!" Theodora hissed. "Remember that you're planning to assassinate a presidential candidate. This isn't the same as going to church on Sunday."

"But you could be injured."

Theodora might have been more touched by his concern if he hadn't shown a reluctance to injure or hurt anyone.

"If we manage this with no greater injury than the one you've had so far, I'll be amazed."

"Then why are you helping me?"

They had rounded a corner, entering a silent corridor. Armand was walking right beside her, and Theodora could practically feel the intensity of his gaze. The man seemed to have X-ray vision, vision that would let him read her thoughts and her deepest secrets.

Theodora didn't answer, hoping he'd abandon the question.

She wasn't truly surprised that he didn't.

"Why?"

"This is it," she said, ignoring him. She surveyed the metal door, liking the patina of dust near its opening edge.

Armand stepped into her path and caught her shoulders in his hands. "Why?" he asked again.

Theodora made the mistake of looking up and nearly lost herself in the vivid emerald of his eyes. With an effort, she shook off his grip and turned her attention to the door.

"Let's just say that eliminating Maximilian Blackstone sounds like a really prime idea to me."

"Why?"

"Too many questions, Armand. I'm helping you, not baring my soul to you."

His voice dropped low. "Are you sure?"

Theodora felt her face heat at that question, uttered in such an intimate tone. She couldn't look at him, she didn't dare. He was far too perceptive.

Instead, she fired the lock off the door.

ARMAND WASN'T startled when Theodora shot off the lock. He also suspected that she had resorted to action to avoid more conversation. It wasn't her way to exchange confidences, which made him appreciate how much she had already told him of herself.

They entered the space with care, only to find it in shadows.

"Nobody," she murmured and Armand heard her surprise.

Who did she expect?

Before he could ask, she turned away, exploring the space. The light of Theodora's palm revealed that the room was filled with sacks of dried corn kernels. The sacks were piled on metal palettes that kept them above the floor and potential flooding. There was a staircase leading from the storeroom to a floor above.

Armand climbed the stairs silently and peeked into the storeroom overhead. It looked like a shop, although it was dark. They were closed, but it had to be the wee hours of the morning by now so that wasn't unreasonable. He listened and there was no sound of breathing or sense of another presence.

Maybe it was one of the businesses that had ceased operations because of the disorder in Chicago. Armand took no chances. When he descended, he blocked the door at the top of the stairs from the basement side with several sacks of corn. The sacks could probably be dislodged with a firm shove from the other side, but that would make a noise to warn him.

Theodora, he saw, had locked the door to the netherzones with a drop latch on the inside. She sat down on the sacks of kernels and sighed, tugging off her hood and shaking out her hair. "It'll do," she said, her weariness showing. "And maybe we'll be able to find a pen in the shop."

"What for?"

"I'll need a shade number, and it's too late to get a tattoo." Theodora yawned and Armand halfway thought she was evading his questions. "Any chance you have a razor?"

"No, why?"

She laid down on a pile of sacks, her laze in her hand. "We'll worry about it tomorrow. We should go in the evening, so that gives us some time to sleep."

"Sleep? But . . ." Armand fell silent, realizing that his words were falling on deaf ears. Whether he liked it or not, Theodora wasn't going anywhere. She closed her eyes and diligently ignored him.

Her last gesture was to extinguish the light on her palm, plunging them into darkness.

Armand was restless and dissatisfied, not at all prepared to sleep. His shoulder hurt and his pulse was pounding. He sat with his back against a pile of corn sacks and thought about all that had happened. The darkness embraced him, only the sound of Theodora's steady breathing carrying to his ears.

To his surprise, he eventually slept.

THEODORA AWAKENED with a crick in her neck.

She opened her eyes cautiously, lighting her palm to its dimmest setting and scanning the storage room. Everything appeared to be as it had been the night before. Armand was sleeping, his arms folded across his chest and his lips still drawn to a tight line. That his disapproval could continue even in sleep amused Theodora.

It would be tough to live in the Republic with such a high moral code. She marveled that he'd managed to do it for so long. He had to be, what, thirty years old? Maybe thirty-five? That was a long time to evade being tainted by the reality of the Republic.

Maybe the angels had helped him with that.

She smiled and checked her palm without getting up. She noted that it was nearly noon, then scanned the messages that she had received.

One made the bottom fall out of her universe.

It was a bounty.

Upon Armand, complete with an imagelink of him that was deadly accurate. Theodora exhaled slowly, her pulse leaping as she read the notice.

The Society was offering a bounty on him of 50,000 units, and they had forwarded the message not just to their own shade hunters but to Shadow.net.

Theodora swallowed and rolled to her back. She stared at the ceiling, not even wanting to think about what risk someone would take for that much cred. Fifty thousand units would buy a lot.

Freedom.

Security.

Surgery for Ferris with lots of change left over.

Replacement of the bounty she'd had to pay Big Ted and then some. Fifty thousand cred would buy everything she had ever wanted, and leave her with change. Theodora's lips tightened. She glanced toward Armand, sleeping in her company, as sure a sign of his trust as was possible, and sat up abruptly.

She'd never do it.

Theodora deleted the message from her palm, not wanting anything to do with the Society and its dirty cred. She'd never turn in Armand for profit, never condemn him to whatever fate Dr. Cosmopoulos had planned for him.

It wasn't about the cred.

It wasn't even about the angels, if they existed.

It was about Armand and the way he made her feel.

She couldn't relax after reading that message, a new restlessness filling her body. She thought about their mission and reprogrammed her identification bead, impatient to do something more active. She got up and checked the door to the shop, quietly moving the sacks of grain away. A glance down the length of the shop revealed that there was a glimmer of light around the door to the street.

No traffic, though.

She ventured into the shop but couldn't find a writing instrument of any kind. She found a knife that was sharp enough, but no razor.

It would have to do.

She strode back to the storage room with purpose, unwilling to acknowledge the anxiety that had taken root within her. Would Armand be harvested by another bounty hunter? Would she be able to protect him?

Fifty thousand units. It was a lot of cred. She couldn't think of anyone who wouldn't compromise his or her morals for that kind of money.

Except, apparently, her.

Who would have guessed?

Armand was awake when she returned and he glanced toward her with concern. "I wondered what had happened to you," he said and she heard the fear in his voice.

She knew then that she couldn't tell him what she'd learned. She didn't want to be the one who disillusioned him. She didn't want to be the one who showed him that the world was an even more callous and disappointing place than she'd already shown him. She might have to witness his loss of innocence, as she had in Fetus Hall, but she didn't want to be responsible for it anymore.

So, she forced a smile. "Time to prep," she said. "Let's review who you are."

"Preparation is the key to success?" he said, his lips pulling into a teasing smile that made her heart leap.

"You're learning fast."

"Maybe you're teaching me well."

"Maybe there are some things I'd rather you never learned." She didn't wait to see his gaze turn somber, simply turned her back on him and reached for the fastening of her pseudoskin.

There was nothing for it. If she was going into the hotel as a shade, Armand was going to see her naked.

And technically, he already had.

Theodora peeled down, refusing to think about it any

more than that. She did keep her back to him, though, and did hear his sharp intake of breath.

"Are you sure?" he asked softly.

"It's the best plan I've got. Let's make it work." She piled her boots and pseudoskin together, making a neat package that she hoped no one would nick while they were gone. She was cold and felt even more naked than she was.

Then she pivoted and handed him the knife.

His confusion was clear.

Theodora swallowed. "Cut off my hair. No shade would have it. I can't find a razor to shave it bald, so you'll just have to hack it off."

"But it's so beautiful."

"It'll grow back. And it'll give us away."

Armand considered her, his hesitation making her feel keenly aware of her nudity. "Are there no barriers to what you will sacrifice, Theodora?"

She could have softened at his appeal, could have taken that last step and reached for his kiss. This was a time for resolve, though, a time to face what needed to be done. "Do you want to fulfill your mission or not?" she demanded, her tone more harsh than she had intended. "Time is wasting."

"Then why did we wait this long?"

Theodora didn't answer him, didn't want him to guess about the bounty. "No one can be effective when they're tired," she said instead. "How's your shoulder?"

"Better." He lifted the knife, its blade shining in the shadows. His gaze searched hers, though, his eyes piercing. She was getting tired of the sense that he was determined to figure her out, and doubted they'd have much time to know each other better than they did now.

She was determined to help him, though, maybe more so now that there was a bounty on his head.

When they completed his mission, they'd both be hunted.

She refused to think about that prospect.

"Cut it choppy and rough," she instructed, embarrassed to hear her voice turn thick. "Like it was hacked off by barbarians."

"Theodora . . ."

"Do it, Armand! Do it now." She snapped her fingers with impatience to have this job finished.

Even if it meant not seeing him ever again. Would the angels really come? She didn't believe that for a minute.

She did believe, though, that completing this quest would mean that their ways parted forever.

One way or another.

And she wished, as she had seldom wished for anything, that that wouldn't be the case. It wouldn't be so easy to be alone after this. Theodora sensed that truth.

Wishing, though, didn't change anything. Theodora had learned that a long time ago. The best gift she could give Armand was her aid in completing his assignment.

Whoever had really given it to him.

Theodora felt Armand's hesitation. She sensed his doubt, felt it replaced by an understanding of what had to be done.

He reached for her and she closed her eyes as the knife sheared through her hair. The blade pulled against her roots, the edge less sharp than would have been ideal. His second cut was faster, more decisive, and she felt the chill of the knife close to her scalp. He was doing exactly as she'd instructed and Theodora felt a tear slip through her lashes. She blinked it away quickly, before he could see it and ask even more questions.

It wasn't long before the weight of her hair was gone.

She felt Armand's hand on her jaw, felt the heat of him as he leaned closer. She was ashamed to be so naked as this, to look no better than the shade she would have become if her mother hadn't intervened, and she didn't want to see the horror in his eyes.

She couldn't look.

But he bent and kissed her, the warmth of his lips sliding over hers. It was a sweet kiss, a hot kiss, a kiss that warmed her from within and made her realize that he appreciated her choice.

"Thank you," he whispered, his breath against her lips when he broke his kiss. "Thank you."

When Theodora opened her eyes, her field of vision was filled with Armand and his gleaming eyes. She had to look away from the warmth of his smile, had to swallow and compose herself.

She was surprised to see no sign of her hair. It wasn't scattered over the floor of the netherzones, nor was it with her pseudoskin.

Armand smiled when she looked at him in confusion, and he patted the pouch on his belt. "Treasure shouldn't be thrown in the dirt," he whispered.

She was both astounded and touched that he had kept her hair. Didn't lovers keep locks of each other's hair? It seemed like an intimate gesture, one that hinted at an emotional connection between them that she would never have expected.

But one that she found herself yearning to have.

It also left her flustered, as she seldom was.

"Let's go," she said, her voice surprisingly hoarse.

Armand nodded once. He checked her laze, squared his shoulders, and eyed the access. He put one gloved hand on the back of her neck and Theodora drooped her head. The solidity of his grip was reassuring, the cool smooth leather centered her. She shuffled her feet as he guided her toward the door, trying to hide her agitation.

It was her worst nightmare come true.

And she had suggested it.

IT WAS ridiculously easy to get into the hotel under this guise. Theodora was brilliant.

Armand was shocked by how readily the guards believed that he was on legitimate business, that he was in fact one of them. He tossed around a few catchphrases from the Institute, which seemed enough to persuade them of his authenticity.

One pinched Theodora's buttock and made a joke about sex slaves—she managed not to flinch and he managed not to punch the man for his crudity. They were walking into the hotel when one guard called after them.

"Hey, why doesn't she have a tattoo on her arm?"

Theodora froze.

Armand froze.

He had to think fast. He turned casually and shrugged. "Special request," he said. He kept his eyes downcast, apparently preoccupied with keeping a grip on Theodora. He knew his eyes would reveal that he lied. "They don't mark all the ones to be used for pleasure, since some clients don't like the reminder."

The guard nodded, convinced. "No place to hide it when

they're naked." He leered at Theodora and Armand had to turn his back on the man. He wanted to shield Theodora from their gazes, but knew that to do so would reveal them.

Instead he swallowed his annoyance, and kept his pace steady.

They were in. There was a slight buzz as the security lock into the hotel netherzones proper was released. The corridor ahead was functional and unadorned. Bustling shades moving up and down its length, some in uniform and some naked. Most had glazed eyes and dull expressions.

At least there would be fewer questions from this point.

Armand strolled, his hand on Theodora's nape, as if he did this all the time. The shades, even in their sedated state, seemed to recognize him as a hunter—each and every one gave him lots of space in the passage. His heart was pounding and he was so outraged at the injustice humans showed each other that he couldn't believe his fury didn't show.

He feared it would betray them.

"Find the shade elevator," Theodora murmured after they were out of earshot of the guards. "There will be a service elevator to all floors, and it'll have less security."

"Maybe we should go with the sex slave idea," he murmured. "And deliver you right to Blackstone."

He heard Theodora catch her breath.

"It's simple," he explained. "And they might have programmed it into the hotel computer. I promise that I won't leave you there. No matter what."

It took only a second until he felt her minute nod. "Stay close," she whispered. "I'll need my laze."

She was right. There was a moment when Armand wished he could be as ferocious as Theodora, then he realized that would be a violation of his very nature.

He was what he was.

He hoped Theodora didn't pay the price for that. His heart was hammering as he sought the elevator and he didn't doubt that his grip had tightened on Theodora in his fear.

But then, if killing Blackstone had been an easy job, they wouldn't have dispatched angels to do it.

ERNESTINE COULDN'T put her father's confession out of her mind. She stared at the ceiling, an exhausted Anthony snoring on his cushion at the foot of the bed, caught in the maelstrom of her thoughts as the night ticked away.

Her older brother's illness had been inflicted by her father.

At Max's instigation.

Max wasn't just older than he appeared, he was far less benign than he appeared.

Ernestine had tried to decode the file Ernest had left for her mother, but hadn't managed it before she'd heard Anthony approaching. Now she thought furiously, seeking possibilities for the password. Her mother might have readily guessed it, but Ernestine hadn't figured it out.

Yet.

What was Max's secret? It was imperative that she learn it, and that she know the truth before giving him her answer.

Then she had an idea. The guilt which had prompted her father's confession was over the fate of her older brother, Ernest Jr. That same guilt had led her father to establish a program through the Society to deliver Vitamin C to children throughout the Republic. Ernest Jr. had been involved in this endeavor, his own drawing of Orv the Orange becoming the mascot for the program.

Ernestine rolled out of bed silently, hesitating to ensure that Anthony didn't awaken. His breathing remained in the same steady rhythm as Ernestine stood watching him.

Of course, he must be exhausted, given the number of times she'd had him since meeting with Max. She'd worn him out, trying to exhaust herself.

In trying to solve the puzzle of her father's palm.

She stared at Anthony, her chest tightening at his perfection. He was beautiful, the obedient golden boy.

Ernestine waited only a moment longer to ensure that Anthony slept deeply, then slipped from the bedroom. She headed straight for her father's shrine and pushed her probe into his old palm.

It was easier the second time.

She navigated her way to the locked file, the palm prompting her for the password. Ernestine took a deep breath, then tapped on the keypad.

sunshine_heals

It was the slogan for the program of delivering oranges to children throughout the Republic, the slogan that had been emblazoned on the trucks that had delivered the nuclear bombs into the heart of Gotham at Ernest's command.

There was a second while the display hung up, a second to fear that it had been wired to self-destruct at a failed password attempt, then data began to scroll rapidly across the display.

Ernestine was in!

XII

THEODORA'S RAGE grew with every passing moment. The opportunity for retribution, the one she'd never thought to have, was close at hand. The prospect of getting even with Max for everything that had happened to her in this life, all of which was his fault, was enough to make her dizzy.

But she couldn't make a mistake.

And she didn't want to let Armand down.

The elevator was slow, painfully slow, seeming to inch its way between floors. The eighteenth floor could have been an eternity away. There was another shade in the elevator, taking a room-service tray to floor sixteen, so they didn't talk.

The elevator was filled with the smell of steak—though surely it would be faux-flesh styled to look like beef—and she realized with a start that she hadn't eaten in more than a day.

Hunger kept her sharp, though.

If they lived through this, she'd eat then.

The shade nearly pressed himself against the wall in his determination to avoid any contact with Armand, which might have been funny in other circumstances.

To consider Armand a threat to a shade's existence was about as far from the truth as possible. But Theodora kept her head down and tried to control the racing of her heart.

The smell of the hot food made her stomach churn, but she had no time for biological concerns. The weight of Armand's gloved hand on the back of her neck was impossible to ignore. His grip felt possessive and it both steadied her nerves and aroused her.

Instead of thinking about how long it had been since she'd eaten or slept, she was thinking about how long it had been since a man had touched her.

Too long.

Theodora wished they had time for one last kiss. She had a feeling that this mission was going to end badly, and she would have liked one more of Armand's kisses.

No, she wanted to see Armand naked, to run her hands over him, to have wild unbridled sex. One night with Armand was what she wanted as her last request.

But she was out of luck.

With the other shade in the elevator and the eyes of the Republic everywhere, there couldn't even be a caress.

Finally, the elevator chimed for floor sixteen and the doors slid open. Theodora glimpsed plush red carpet and glittering lights, decor so at odds with the service areas of the hotel that she blinked in surprise. There was also a pearly light from the overcast sky coming through the windows, a light that showed every repair in the plaster walls and every stain on the carpet.

Then the doors were closed and the elevator began to move again. The bottom fell out of Theodora's stomach and she began to smell her own perspiration.

Anxiety.

The worst possible response for an assassin with a job to do.

"Be good in your new assignment," Armand said softly.

His low voice caught Theodora off guard, his words confusing her all the more. "I know it's a change for you, but it will work out well."

She realized with a start that he was remaining in his supposed character. He, too, was aware that they might be overheard.

But he knew that she was frightened.

"This is an important task you've been given," he continued and she was appalled at how much she'd taught him so quickly. His fingers began to massage the back of her neck, his caress sending little tingles through her body. Theodora felt herself shiver, but in the wake of that, she felt more settled and composed. "Though I know you don't fully understand, promise me that you'll be good."

Theodora nodded dully.

He touched his gloved fingertip to her chin, compelling her to look up at him. Theodora caught her breath at the brilliant light in his eyes, knowing she could lose herself forever in that shimmering green. He smiled ever so slightly and her heart clenched. "I'll miss you," he whispered, then winked.

Her breath hitched, then he bent and brushed his lips across hers.

It was a brief touch, all the sweeter for being so short. He meant to reassure her and Theodora knew it. He must have sensed her nervousness, and she appreciated his consideration.

With another man, she would have assumed that he only wanted to ensure that she completed the task she had taken on for him.

With Armand, she believed his concern was genuine.

That gave her strength.

He straightened almost immediately, his gaze on the lit floor numbers. He tightened his grip on the back of her neck and Theodora saw his right hand fall to her laze.

Then she looked down at her bare feet again and took a steadying breath. The elevator chimed slightly and she heard the doors slide open. She glimpsed that same deep red carpet, caught the glimmer of the light from chandeliers, then saw the toes of a man's boots.

"Who are you?" he demanded, his tone unfriendly.

She flicked a glance through her lashes and knew immediately that he was a mercenary shade. No other being could have such cold eyes.

He must be Blackstone's bodyguard.

Could Armand bluff his way past this one? Theodora feared not and her fingers itched for her laze.

ARMAND HAD anticipated an obstacle, although he hadn't anticipated one so formidable as this armed bodyguard. The man's hair was shaved to nothing, his features impassive, and his eyes cold. He wore boots and tights that revealed every hard line of his body. His reevlar codpiece shone, and his fitted sleeveless shirt left nothing to the imagination. He held his laze as if it was a toy, his hands large and powerful. He was all muscled strength and Armand had the thought that he was a killing machine.

The tattoo on the inside of his left arm was visible, which revealed his shade status.

What had condemned him? Armand looked into his eyes and guessed that his adversary didn't possess a powerful intellect.

He had to be able to fool this bodyguard.

At least long enough to get past him.

The elevator opened into a short corridor, one that ended at both the left and the right with closed doors. A quick look revealed the lit security locks on each door.

So, they would need this thug to open at least one of them.

"Delivery for Mr. Blackstone," Armand said so smoothly that it sounded like the truth.

The bodyguard's eyes narrowed. "We're expecting no deliveries."

"Are you certain?"

He gave his palm a cursory glance, then eyed Armand with suspicion.

"Who ever expects a gift?" Armand mused. He gave Theodora a slight shake. "This is a token of esteem, from the Society of Nuclear Darwinists, intended to entertain Mr. Blackstone during the unfortunate delay in his schedule. It's entirely possible that the donor hasn't yet sent a message to Mr. Blackstone about it." He smiled, feigning confidence. "We made good time so early in the day."

The bodyguard did not smile. In fact, he raised his laze. "From who at the Society?"

"An admirer who prefers to remain anonymous. I was assured that Mr. Blackstone would receive a private message."

The man hesitated, then the elevator chimed again.

"I can always return it to the donor," Armand said quietly, "but cannot answer for any repercussions over the rejection of such a generous gift."

"I need to know the source."

"I'm not at liberty to say." Armand took a step back and lifted his hand from Theodora to consider his palm. "What is your shade number, then? I'll just add that to the official rejection form so there can be no doubt as to who rejected the gift. Are you, in fact, authorized to make such decisions?"

He tapped, as if he had just such a form. Theodora stood, with her head down, the perfect abject shade.

Just as the elevator door began to slide closed, the bodyguard's foot shot forward. The door halted when it touched his boot, then opened again.

"All right," he said, gesturing with his laze. "You wait here and I'll ask Mr. Blackstone."

"Of course," Armand said, hiding his relief. "One can't be too careful in these times." He urged Theodora from the elevator. He heard the double chime of the reader in the lintel over the elevator door, as it scanned the identification beads in the back of his neck and Theodora's. His name and a shade number immediately appeared on the lit display beside the door to the left.

It was shocking to be so clearly declared.

Thank goodness Theodora had those bootleg applications. She must have anticipated the reader. Once again, he was grateful for her experience.

"I'll have your laze before you proceed," the bodyguard said.

Armand smiled, trying to look cold and mercenary. "You'll have it when it's clear I am going to proceed."

Their gazes locked and held for a moment.

Armand reached back and touched the call button for the elevator.

The bodyguard understood. "Don't move," he insisted, then went to the left door. He put his palm against the reader in the security panel and Armand felt Theodora tense.

Armand saw the glimmering eye in the wall when the bodyguard stepped away and knew that there was an image-snatcher embedded there. He squeezed her neck hard in warning.

Then the door to Blackstone's suite opened and everything happened very quickly.

ERNEST'S HIDDEN file was a list.

It appeared to be a list of live births and associated shade numbers.

Why would her father secretly track some group of shades? What did they have in common?

Ernestine had a moment in which she imagined that her father had sired all of these secret children. It wouldn't have been implausible, given his tendency to enter hot zones, for his children to have failed the S.H.A.D.E.

Then she recalled her father's comment in his confession that Max had had a secret to hide. She guessed then who the father of them all might be.

And they were shades.

What would this revelation do to Max's political aspirations?

Nothing good. Ernestine was sure of it.

She clicked through on the first on the list, and found an entire file on that child, with images of the mother, personal data that must have come from that woman's record in the Republic's databanks, and a tracking of Max's movements nine months before the child's birth. There were half a dozen hotel reservations, a record of Max giving a speech on the same dates in the town where the woman lived, and vid of the two of them arriving at the hotel. Even the hotel room number and invoice had been added to the file. It showed the connection without being entirely damning. It was an implication, not an indictment, given that there was no actual image of the pair having intercourse, or any DNA test proving that Max was the father.

The child, though, had failed the S.H.A.D.E. and died young in a labor facility.

Ernestine thought of all of Max's work in the field, his heroic volunteer efforts, his determination to arrive in a timely fashion to give solace to the troops. He gave good vid, and his bravery in entering hot zones made him popular.

But the man should have been shooting loaded bullets, genetically speaking. This wasn't as surprising as it could have been, although Max would have a hard time making light of it.

Ernestine went through each record, finding the compilation more compelling with each successive child, as her father evidently recognized the patterns and knew where to look. That he had snatched the information and embedded it here hinted at a conviction that it would be eliminated—"forgotten" by the Republic's and possibly even the Society's data banks, for a price—over time.

On impulse, Ernestine skipped down the list and opened one of the last entries, a child born in 2074. The mother was blond, quite pretty. Image-snatchers had captured a man who was unmistakably Max in the woman's company, entering her house, silhouetted in a vehicle that picked her up. There were hotel reservations, vid of the woman being collected and delivered to Max's location. Her pregnancy confirmation was included, along with the ultrasound image and the detail that the child would be a girl. Everything looked normal in the ultrasound image, but one never knew.

A grainy security vid from a hospital, time-stamped months later—within days of the anticipated delivery date—showed a man who might have been Max arriving at that hospital. He moved like Max, although his hat was pulled down and his collar turned up. The mother's hospital file was copied, and Ernestine saw the familiar stamp that the daughter had failed the S.H.A.D.E.

She had issued that stamp herself, any number of times. She scanned the evaluation, noting that the child had had a cleft palate.

Oddly enough, there was no image enclosed. That was protocol.

Ernestine looked again.

Ernest had included an evaluation time-stamped an hour earlier. Ernestine had assumed them to be near-duplicates, the first version missing some detail. She opened it, seeking the image.

The earlier evaluation declared that the child *passed* the S.H.A.D.E.

Ernestine frowned. There was no middle ground. Pass or fail. It was one choice or the other, and there was no wiggle room in the assessment. A cleft palate meant a failure. Period.

The first evaluation did have an image, similarly time-stamped.

The child had no cleft palate.

Ernestine was horrified by the implication. Were there shade hunters who lied?

Or who could be bought?

Ernestine didn't want to think about it, although it

appeared that Max had done so. Maybe, just maybe, a few
genuinely failed S.H.A.D.E. assessments had given him
the idea to buy the others.

Maybe illegitimate normal children weren't any better
publicity than illegitimate shade children.

Possibly her father had retrieved the initial form from the
shade hunter who had made the decision, because no record
of this earlier evaluation existed in the Republic's databanks.

Ernestine, though, couldn't see a shade number assigned
to the child. She went into her own palm, through her own
access to the Republic's databanks and cleared the firewalls to her access level.

She found the record for the mother, and her skin crept
when she saw that she had died in a street accident two
days after giving birth to a child.

A *dead* child, according to the Republic's databanks.

Ernestine flicked back to the image of the baby, who was
clearly born alive and healthy. What had happened to this
child?

And how many more of these children, fathered by Max,
had been consigned to the netherzones with a false
S.H.A.D.E. assessment?

Ernestine's heart was pounding and her palms were
damp. She knew instinctively that this was big, that Max
would not be amused, that even having this file put her at
risk. She clicked through the records even so, finding the
pattern repeated over and over again. Her father's access
level had allowed him to capture more information than
most investigators could have done. At least two-thirds of
Max's children were normal, but had been condemned with
a failed S.H.A.D.E. There were even receipts for payments

made to shade hunters for services rendered, the same shade hunters who had issued the assessments.

Ernest had built a blackmail file.

But Ernest had died in 2076 and Max was still alive. Had her father ever used the file?

Could Ernestine find more such children, if she could figure out the pattern?

Did she want to know that Max had continued on this path? Did she want to reveal him, or challenge him?

No, she just wanted to have something in her corner, information she could use to ensure that he didn't betray her. The past couldn't be changed. These children were effectively destroyed, whether they had survived or not.

The point was that this file could destroy Max.

And he, she was certain, would destroy her to ensure its secrecy.

Ernestine had to figure out who she would tell, who she would pass this information to in order to protect herself and her father's legacy. She had to make a plan for a last-ditch message, much like the ones dispatched automatically by the palms of the Council of Three if a council member's pulse stopped.

There was only one person she could think of, one person who was not afraid to defy convention, one person who wouldn't back down from destroying the Society of Nuclear Darwinists or even the Republic itself, if necessary, in her determination to out the truth.

Lilia Desjardins.

It didn't hurt that there were rumors within the Society that Max had fathered Lilia's daughter, Delilah, the new Oracle of the Republic.

But Lilia was unpredictable. She might have her palm programmed to block any message from Ernestine, given that the pair had been enemies for years. Ernestine tapped a fingernail, then knew who else she could rely upon.

Who other than Reverend Billie Joe Estevez had taken the cause of the shades as her own, and had argued for their release? If the videvangelist saw opportunity for herself in a cause, she would champion it.

Revealing Maximilian Blackstone as the vermin he was would certainly qualify. The reverend would be on every vidcast in the Republic.

THEODORA WATCHED through her lashes as the bodyguard used his palm to open the security lock. She felt Armand's grip tighten on her neck, knew he was advising her to be cautious, and didn't care what he thought. Years of experience had taught her to recognize a moment, and this was one.

The door to the suite opened.

The bodyguard stepped through it, keeping one hand on the frame. He bowed, which meant Blackstone was there.

"Sir," he had time to say and no more.

Theodora reached across Armand, grabbed her laze from his belt, and fired at the bodyguard. The elevator chimed softly behind her, responding to Armand's earlier summons.

Perfect.

She caught the bodyguard in the butt, aiming to cook his hip joint.

He fell, but twisted as he went down. He pulled his own laze, and fired back at her before he even hit the ground.

Theodora pushed Armand hard, and he fell against the wall with the image-snatcher. She ducked into the elevator, staying there until the blaze had ripped down the short corridor.

The elevator chimed and she leapt through the closing doors in the last instant. Armand had caught the security door, and was using its heavy metal as a shield. Theodora shot the bodyguard in the forehead, finishing him off. She didn't pause beside Armand, guessing that this wouldn't be Blackstone's only bodyguard.

She leapt into the room, knowing that she wouldn't have much time.

Blackstone stood by the fire, his expression shocked. He was wearing a dressing robe and held a whiskey glass in one hand. "Who are you?" he demanded.

He looked older than she'd expected, thinner, too, but Theodora wasn't interested in the manipulation of vid. She had less than seconds to do what she'd come to do. She raised her laze, locked in the sight, and looked Blackstone in the eye.

"This is for my mom," she said, saw his confusion, then squeezed the trigger.

It was even more despicable that he didn't remember.

Theodora held the burn as Blackstone fell, letting the smell of burning cloth and flesh and bone fill her nostrils. Her tears began to fall and her hands shook, but she ensured her own vengeance.

She was vaguely aware of Armand erupting into the room.

She knew that others arrived, as well.

She sensed the sighting of a laze, but she was determined to finish what she had started.

When she felt the burn strike her own temple, Theodora wasn't surprised.

But it was done. Blackstone was down. The final balance had been rendered.

She almost didn't care that they would take her now.

She knew it was Armand who reached her first, knew it couldn't be anyone else who would touch her hand so gently. The room was swirling all around her, darkness pressing into her field of vision. The dull throb of pain rose to a crescendo.

Theodora pushed her laze into his hand.

"You promised," she whispered, then everything faded to black.

ARMAND HAD been shocked at how quickly Theodora had moved, although her speed had been the reason for her success. The bodyguard had assumed that she was drugged, and that assumption had led to his downfall.

But what did her words mean? What did Theodora's mother have to do with Blackstone? Why had she thought that killing Blackstone was such a good idea? Why had she really helped him? It hadn't occurred to him before that she might have a motivation of her own.

There was no time to think it through.

When she leapt into the suite, Armand pulled the security guard's laze from his belt and fired at the additional bodyguard who appeared. That man was too late to save Blackstone, but in plenty of time to injure Theodora.

That man raised his laze to take aim at Theodora and Armand fired at his right elbow. The laze fell as the bodyguard grimaced in pain.

Armand had scanned the room for other attackers.

To his dismay, that bodyguard quickly picked up the fallen weapon in his left hand. He aimed and fired.

Directly at Theodora.

Armand thought the world stopped as she was hit. He saw the blaze strike her temple, leaving a red angry mark. Her collapse seemed to happen in slow motion, her body falling like a rag doll. He was horrified to see her blood flow and meld with the crimson hue of the carpet. He could smell blood and burning flesh, a scent that made his stomach churn.

And he was filled with a rage beyond anything he had ever known.

Armand pivoted and shot her assailant right in the chest, holding the blaze until the man's chest was incinerated.

The room was still then, and silent. It was just almost evening, the gray light of an overcast sky filling the suite. It was a harsh light, one that revealed every damning detail, and one that fostered no illusions.

Armand knew they had mere seconds before any reinforcements arrived.

Shaking at the carnage, he went to Theodora. His heart was in his mouth as he knelt beside her, but she was breathing.

Her eyes were closed and her face was pale, but she was alive.

She seemed to be aware that it was him, because she sighed. It seemed as if all the air was leaving her lungs, as if she'd never inhale again. Her lashes fluttered to her cheeks as she pushed her beloved laze into his hand.

"You promised," she whispered.

She didn't move again.

Armand was terrified. It was true that he had made that pledge, but he wasn't going to inflict more damage on her.

Yet he wasn't going to leave her behind. Somehow, he'd have to persuade the angels to bring her along. He wasn't sure how that might work, but didn't have time to consider the details. He picked up Theodora, casting her weight over his shoulder as he looked around the room expectantly.

But where *were* the angels? Their absence made no sense.

Blackstone was dead, there could be no doubt about that, but there was no radiance gathering in the morning sky. The clouds were as dull as usual. Armand couldn't hear the singing of the angelic host, couldn't feel the hum and vibration of their arrival.

Had he and Baruch been deceived in that, as well?

No. Armand refused to believe it. The angels would keep their pledge. There was another explanation. There had to be a reason for the delay.

As soon as he got Theodora out of this hotel, he'd figure it out. For the moment, he was on his own. He heard voices approaching from elsewhere in the suite and knew he couldn't linger.

Fortunately, Theodora was light—and in no condition to argue.

Armand raced back to the service elevator, only to realize that the elevator was gone. Did the other door lead to a staircase? How else would he escape the eighteenth floor? He couldn't jump from the suite and survive such a drop, even if the windows hadn't been too thick to readily shatter.

He shot out that image-snatcher on general principle, then destroyed the security lock on the other door in the corridor.

He kicked it open, holding fast to Theodora, and his heart leapt at the sight of metal stairs.

He took them four at a time, hoping that he could outrace any pursuit. He wouldn't bet on it, but he'd try. He ran as quickly as he could, leaping around the corners, racing down those stairs with lightning speed. He didn't care how much noise he made—he just had to get out of the hotel.

Armand was three flights from the ground floor when he realized where the angels were. They hadn't lied—his assignment was completed. They had come.

But they'd come for Baruch, not for him.

He'd been abandoned in this sphere.

Because in killing the guard, Armand had committed a murder. He'd defied the commandments. In so doing, he hadn't just sacrificed his wings, but his chance of redemption. He'd killed and that meant that he'd condemned himself to remain mortal for the duration.

He'd been right, right from the beginning.

The realization redoubled his determination. He didn't intend to die before he ensured Theodora's safety. He leapt down the last stairs, heard pursuit from above, and ran with all his might.

ONCE THE assailants were gone and the suite was secured, Maximilian Blackstone came out of his safe room. He considered the carcass of his fetch on the floor of his suite in silence. Even if the man had possessed a passing resemblance to Max, even if that had been surgically enhanced, it was clear the poor man had never had a comparable intellect.

Two bodyguards hovered behind Max, as well as a decidedly nervous secondary fetch.

There had been a reason why Max had put the deceased fetch in the front lines. The other, well, he wasn't optimistic about that one's survival if Max himself was being hunted.

He supposed that meant less guilt for him over the doomed mission he'd send his fetch to complete.

Ernestine, after all, was not a fool. He was sure she had sent the student from the Institute and the assassin disguised as a sex slave. He was sure that Ernestine had decided against his very generous offer.

There was no need to actually discuss her choice. She had made it, she had failed in her attempt to eliminate him, and he would retaliate in the brief interval in which she believed herself successful.

The news of his survival would come with his arrival at her unit.

Apparently desperate for her assistance.

That it would be his fetch who came to her door, and that that fetch would be assigned to kill Ernestine in her own unit, was something Ernestine would likely realize too late to make a difference to her own survival.

It was unfortunate that she had not seen the wisdom of his plan. They could have made a good team.

But Max had learned a long time ago that transgressions should never be forgiven—and an attempt to assassinate him was definitely a transgression.

Ernestine would die.

The mercenary shades had already removed the debris of the fallen comrade, their features as impassive as ever. They stood like identical statues, hands folded before themselves, heads bowed, awaiting his command. They were alien, these shades, their memories wiped and manipulated so that they were little better than robots.

The fetch, in contrast, was very human. He eyed Max and swallowed. Max smiled deliberately and that man's nostrils flared in terror.

"It seems that you have been promoted," Max said, keeping his voice low and silky.

The fetch almost twitched. "Yes, sir." His voice was pleasantly modulated, quite close really to Max's own.

Max was certain that his plan for Ernestine would work. He turned to the window, listening to the telltale signs of the fetch's anxiety.

The city was still at his feet, the rebellious shades still wherever they hid in the daytime. The streets were empty, except for security patrols. The lake was choppy, but Max was indifferent to the view—instead he watched the fetch's reflection in the glass.

"I can only hope that your predilection is similar to mine," he said, feigning a fascination with the city below.

The fetch looked at the indifferent bodyguards, then at Max, his confusion clear. "I'm sorry, sir?"

"Do you prefer women or men?"

The fetch smiled then, a wolfish smile that Max found reassuring. "Women, sir. I assure you that we have that affection in common."

"Excellent." Max paced the width of the room and back before he spoke. "Did you take notice of the lady who visited here earlier? In the night?"

"Yes, sir. A very attractive lady, sir."

"And of her name?"

The fetch's eyes gleamed. "Yes, sir."

"Well, then, feel free to enjoy her before you kill her." Max straightened and smiled. "You'll have to do the work of two men, seeing that I will have no opportunity to enjoy her delights."

The fetch was visibly encouraged. "Yes, sir!"

Max paced slowly and steadily, wanting to ensure that there was no doubt of what he wanted done. "You will go to the lady. You will admit, pretending to be me, that someone has tried to assassinate you. You will beg for her help and her protection. You will renew my pledges to marry her and make her First Mother—by all means, sweeten them if you so desire. I don't care what she believes when she dies."

He spun smartly to confront the fetch, who was looking markedly more confident. "You will gain admission to her unit however necessary, and once there, you will ensure that she does not leave it alive. You will complete this assignment by midnight tomorrow. That should give you enough time to satisfy your own desire."

"Yes, sir."

"Let me be completely clear. There will be no evidence of your presence, no transmissions, no records. She will send no messages. I believe she has a sex shade, a promising sign of her own appetites, so you'll need to eliminate him as well."

The fetch nodded crisply. "Will that be all, sir?"

"No. But it will be first." Max made a dismissive gesture. "Take the carriage. I'll see you tomorrow at midnight."

"If not before, sir."

As that man turned to leave, Max indicated the mercenary shade on the left. "You will go with him as a bodyguard."

"Yes, sir."

Max began to tap on his palm, sending a command to the escort shade even as he departed with the fetch. He eyed the remaining mercenary shade. "And you have unfinished business to resolve."

The shade clicked his heels and waited for instruction.

"The intruders. Hunt them down and eliminate them. The sooner the better."

The shade hesitated. "But you will be undefended, sir."

Max smiled. He removed a laze from the holster hidden beneath his jacket and checked that it was fully charged. "Only if you fail." He lifted the laze as if sighting it at the shade, then let his smile broaden. "I would suggest you hurry."

The shade had been in Max's employ long enough that he didn't need to be told twice.

When he was alone and the doors secured, Max poured himself a generous measure of single malt scotch.

XIII

WHEN THEODORA regained consciousness, she was enveloped in darkness. She could smell the damp earth of the netherzones and hear the distant sound of laze fire. She was cast over someone's shoulder, that individual striding quickly through the corridor with such purpose that she felt sick.

They were in the netherzones.

He held her left hand aloft, the light from her palm casting its blue glimmer into the darkness ahead.

It was Armand.

Relief flooded through Theodora, making her dizzy all over again. Against all expectation, Armand had gotten her out of Blackstone's suite, comparatively intact.

Theodora breathed a shaky sigh of relief.

Then she had to know the worst of it.

"Why?" she asked, and felt Armand start at the sound of her voice. It said something for her state of mind that her first question wasn't what he would want in exchange.

Armand glanced back one last time, then eased her weight from his shoulder, letting her slide down his chest. When she stood before him, he locked his hands around her waist, as if uncertain whether she could support her own weight. His eyes seemed bright in the darkness, his concern as he stared down at her palpable. He sheltered her from the corridor, barricading her against the wall.

"Are you all right?" he asked softly, the deep resonance of his voice touching Theodora in places she would have preferred to ignore.

She swallowed. "Well enough, I guess."

He touched her temple, frowning as he considered the laze wound. His fingertips were gentle, but Theodora still winced. "You bled a lot," he murmured and she heard how it had disturbed him.

Actually, he looked quite shaken. She remembered him retching in the labs. Was he troubled because there was blood, or because it was *her* blood?

Theodora knew what she wanted the answer to be.

"Flesh wounds do," she said, then smiled for him. "I'll be as good as new soon enough. Sooner if we had a tissue regenerator." She fixed him with a stern look, trying to hide the rapid beating of her heart. "You never answered me. Why did you bring me out?"

He was watching her closely, as if he could read her thoughts. "You sound surprised."

"It would have been easier to leave me there."

"Easier physically, perhaps, but not morally." His words were soft, his attention complete, and Theodora knew her discomfiture showed.

Did her awareness of him show? His hands were strong on her waist, his grip sure, his gaze knowing. He was close, very close, and she could feel the heat of his body, the power of him against her. It would have been so easy to lean against him, to rely upon him, to ask him for comfort.

But that wasn't her style.

Theodora tried to make light of his comment. "I told you already. Morals have nothing to do with my life."

He exhaled ever so slightly, glancing back. "Do you think they'll follow us?"

"I'd be surprised if they didn't. You still didn't answer me . . ."

"We have to get back to the storeroom. You'll need your pseudoskin." He bent and averted his gaze, all efficiency. Theodora had the sense he was hiding something from her.

"How did you get us out of there anyway?"

He frowned. "I ran, I lied, I shot when I had to." She saw how that troubled him and tried to make a joke.

"Guess I've taught you too well," she teased. "Who knew you'd be such a keen student?"

His scowl deepened, then he straightened and turned his back on her, watching the passage behind them with concern. He gave her a stern look, then scooped her up again.

Theodora was glad. She couldn't have matched his pace and she was still dizzy. Within moments, he eased open the door to the storeroom and closed it behind them with evident relief. He put Theodora down and she hastened to her pseudoskin.

"We've got to get out of here," he muttered. "They'll track us down."

Theodora dressed quickly, pulling the pseudoskin over her body. It felt good to be covered again, but every time she bent down, the world spun around her.

She was going to need a mirror to check that wound.

She considered Armand and spoke gruffly, wanting to know the worst of it as soon as possible. She felt vulnerable and that made her edgy. "We're not going anywhere together until you tell me what you want for bringing me out."

That surprised him, made him look at her. She was glad to have the pseudoskin fastened, even though he looked into her eyes. "What do you mean?"

"Everything's about the cred in this world. I've told you that. There was no cred in your saving me, so I'm asking why you did it." Theodora heard her own nervousness. She had a feeling what Armand might ask as reparation and she halfway thought it would be a good idea. "I'm not paying another bounty, I can't afford it."

He considered her, and then that mysterious smile touched his lips. "Liar," he charged quietly.

"It's no lie. I'm not paying . . ."

His smile broadened and his gaze warmed, the combination flustering Theodora. "But that's just it, isn't it? It's not always about the cred, not even for you."

Theodora tried to look away from his perceptive gaze but the focus of his attention was inescapable. She even turned her back on him, pretending to need to check the stairs and the shop. She could smell that no one had disturbed the space, though. "Don't pretend that I have your moral code. I take care of myself."

Armand pursued her, catching up easily, cupping her elbow with one hand. He seemed to realize that she was less steady on her feet than would be ideal. As much as Theodora would have liked to have been independent here, she recognized that she was in less than great shape. She didn't twist away from his grip, although she tried to ignore it.

"There was no cred in shooting Blackstone," he said. "Not one miserable unit."

It was true.

"But we had a deal," Theodora argued. "I did it for my laze."

"You already had your laze back. Wouldn't that have been finders keepers?"

Theodora regarded him warily. "You're seeing more than there is," she protested. "There's a code, even between wraiths. I promised to help you and I kept my promise."

Armand shook his head. "I don't believe it. After all, you said the shot was for your mother."

Theodora was shocked that she had spoken aloud. "You couldn't have heard that!"

"I did." He leaned closer, his expression intent. She fought against the urge to squirm. "So, it's not about the cred and don't try to tell me otherwise."

She opened her mouth to argue, but his voice hardened.

"Tell me the real reason." His gaze bored into hers. "That's the price for getting you out of there."

It was more than fair.

Theodora glanced across the storeroom, then tapped her palm, calling up a map of Chicago's netherzones. She found their location but didn't see any other good prospects for hiding out. She sat down heavily, not having the energy to examine each one.

"This place will do for a bit of time," Armand said, his gaze filling with concern. "We'll barricade the doors."

"There aren't many other options," she admitted, grimacing at the display.

"And you're in no shape to travel. We'll stay and make the best of it." He flicked her a potent look when she might have feigned sleep. "Don't imagine you'll evade my question."

"Don't imagine you'll love the answer," she replied, slanting a glance his way. "Because it *is* about the cred. Always has been and always will be. Just not in the way people assume."

Her pulse grew louder and she felt more dizzy when she tried to stand up again. Armand made her stay put, and he secured both doors once again, after checking the shop. Theodora enjoyed the sense that she wasn't alone, the conviction that there was someone defending her. It was new, and would be easy to get used to.

It might even be worth the surrender of her secret.

It was what he had asked for, after all.

No one ever got without giving, and Theodora was grateful that Armand hadn't left her behind. He was different from other men she had known, fully equipped with an enviable moral code and a determination to keep his word. He was kind, a quality Theodora had never seen before in any human.

She could trust him.

In fact, she realized to her astonishment, she already did. And that was good, because the backup she needed might be walking right beside her.

Except that the moral code she so admired might condemn her in Armand's eyes. That was another reason to tell him what he wanted to know. The truth might earn his support.

And the mercenary shades in the service of Maximilian Blackstone wouldn't abandon the trail. They'd come for her. They'd exact their vengeance, even with Blackstone dead. Her lost children were going to need a new champion.

She didn't have a lot of time to find out whether Armand was the man she could trust with the children.

She'd better start now.

Theodora exhaled shakily. For their sake, she would confide in Armand. For the sake of the future, she'd tell him the truth.

ARMAND WASN'T happy.

He didn't like the notion of staying in the same place two nights in a row, and didn't doubt that they would be pursued. On the other hand, Theodora seemed to wilt once they made the refuge. She seemed smaller and paler, more fragile, even lacking some of her former edge.

That she had softened told him she had no choice.

And that was terrifying. He was used to her being resilient and tough, not vulnerable—that she was vulnerable shook him to his core. She smiled when her gaze landed on him and he went to her side to examine her wound.

"Clean it out for me, would you?" she said, and he heard the strain in her voice.

She had some packaged hygienic wipes in her pouch, and winced when he cleaned the dried blood away. The wound was running clean and the flow of blood had slowed. She held the last wipe against her temple, keeping pressure on the wound, and closed her eyes. She looked tiny to him, delicate and insubstantial.

As if a stiff breeze could blow her away forever.

The prospect frightened him.

Armand knew that she was troubled when he was close to her, so he backed away and sat on the metal staircase. He also found her proximity enticing, but would keep his distance for the moment. He had his own concerns to worry about, his own fate and future without the angels retrieving him.

What would he do in this sphere, with no hope of ever escaping it?

He would die.

He hoped he didn't die soon.

Armand worried, he prayed for Baruch, and he waited for Theodora to gather her strength. The storage room was dimly lit by her palm's light. He noted the patches on her pseudoskin, and the fact that only her laze was new and expensive equipment. It was another inconsistency. An assassin bent on revenue would spend every unit on her equipment.

What did she do with the cred she earned?

He waited, then thought she might have fallen asleep.

"If it was only about the cred," he prompted quietly. "You'd have a new pseudoskin."

Theodora straightened and her eyes flew open. She plucked at one patch, then brushed her hand across her own knee. "It *is* about the cred, don't kid yourself. That's because cred is the closest thing I've ever found to believe in."

"A strange kind of faith," he said when she fell silent again.

"Not so strange." She frowned, then met his gaze as she tried to explain. "The Republic is filled with deceit, with people using words to mean something different than what you'd expect. It's filled with people who lie and use others to their advantage. It's filled with people who have power and abuse it."

Armand listened, surprised not only by her bitterness but by how her disgust echoed his own.

Theodora shrugged. "Cred, in contrast, is simple. It's clean. It is what it is and it's not anything else. It never pretends to be something else. It's just cred."

"And what is cred, exactly?" He didn't truly expect her to answer him, but she did.

"Opportunity." Theodora looked up at him, her gaze clear. "Cred gives choice. You can buy anything in the Republic, anything at all, *if* you can pay the price. As the wraiths say, everything has its price—the question is only whether you can pay it or not."

"And what do you buy?"

Theodora winced. She averted her gaze. "That's complicated."

Armand went to sit beside her. She didn't look at him, but she caught her breath. He let his leg rest against hers, let her be aware of his presence. He heard her breathing quicken and felt her shiver.

It was good to know that he wasn't alone in his desire.

Maybe being trapped in the Republic wouldn't be as lonely as he'd believed. Could he and Theodora make a partnership?

"It's probably less complicated than you think," he suggested.

When she didn't reply, he took her left hand in his right. He looked at her palm, the small flat computer embedded in her left hand. "Is the answer in here? Or just in your mind?"

She met his gaze steadily. Her eyes were bright, glittering with a shimmer of tears. "Both."

He thought she'd end the conversation then, maybe turn away, but she surprised him. She hesitated only a moment, then tapped a sequence of commands into her palm.

He was amazed by her trust.

And determined to never betray it.

Theodora's voice was hoarse when she continued. "Okay.

The Republic and the Society have a place for those children who fail the S.H.A.D.E., and Nuclear Darwinists actively hunt and harvest those who evade early detection. It's not a good place."

"I wouldn't expect it to be."

"It's not a place you'd choose to go, if you had a choice. So, there are people, citizens even, who do not want their children to live in this designated place. Some of them are prepared to pay for sanctuary."

"Is that where wraiths come from?" Armand was curious as to Theodora's own circumstance and how it came to be, but he sensed that he'd have more luck learning her truth by letting her talk in general terms.

"Some of them," she acknowledged, averting her gaze. "The parents usually aren't wraiths, but they know about the wraiths and they take the child to the wraiths."

"I'll guess that sanctuary has a price."

Theodora's smile was fleeting. "A high one. It's not easy to make someone disappear. Wraiths don't exist in the databases of the Republic. Some of them have slipped through the proverbial cracks, some have deliberately evaded detection. There are a lot of people documented as dead in the Republic's databanks who are alive and well, living in the shadows."

"So, the deaths of these children need to be fabricated."

"Sometimes. Sometimes the records can be modified. It's not easy and that's probably why there aren't many babies who come to the wraiths and survive."

"The eyes of the Republic are everywhere."

"And the Republic doesn't let anything go easily." She swallowed. "Most wraiths are those who chose to disappear after they became adults. They made the active choice to leave society, and maybe that gives them a bit more incentive for the subterfuge necessary." She squared her shoulders. "I'm not that concerned with wraiths, but with the children who fail the S.H.A.D.E."

"Who are condemned to live as shades, and harvested by the Society." Armand thought that her compassion for these unfortunates was laudable, although he still didn't understand her insistence.

"It's bad enough that the S.H.A.D.E. exists," she said with care. "It's bad enough that children born with birth defects are harvested. But I told you already that anything can be bought in the Republic. There are people, powerful people, who use the Society to rid their lives of inconveniences." She looked up at him and he knew he wouldn't like whatever she said next. "A failed S.H.A.D.E. evaluation can be bought."

Armand was horrified. "Everything has a price," he said with disappointment.

"And once the individual is harvested and sedated, he or she is effectively lost forever." Theodora held Armand's gaze, weariness in her own expression. "Independent of whether or not there was actually any reason for the child to fail the S.H.A.D.E."

"The Oracle was harvested as a child," Armand remembered.

"But she had a third eye. She genuinely failed the assessment." Theodora's voice turned hard. "Either way, it was sheer luck that she ever got free of the Society."

"Not destiny? What about the involvement of the angels?"

Theodora's smile was quick and rueful. "Believe what you need to."

"And what do you believe?"

"That those who wanted her liberated had more cred than those who wanted her to disappear." The notion seemed to sadden her, for it put a shadow in her eyes again.

Armand leaned closer. "Is that why you want cred? To be the highest bidder?"

"Not exactly."

"What do you buy with your cred, Theodora?"

"I buy opportunity," she admitted. He felt her agitation, sensed that she was poised to flee, then she tapped her palm again.

Armand watched as images began to scroll across the display.

They were children, children of all ages and colors.

No, they had numbers instead of names. They were shades.

"These are the lost children," Theodora murmured. "These are my sisters and brothers. What I do keeps them alive."

ARMAND REALIZED that Theodora had arranged the images in before and after shots, the first image of any child invariably showing him or her wary and distrustful, perhaps with eyes glazed from drugs. The second shot always showed the child laughing, eyes dancing with happiness.

This was what she did with her cred.

She saved lost children. Armand was overwhelmed that she made such a selfless choice, that she took such risks with her own survival to help others.

"Why?" he asked and she glanced up. "It has to be dangerous."

"Of course it is, but it's right." She bit her lip. "Someone helped me, once upon a time. I guess I'm just continuing the tradition."

"Why did you need help?"

Her smile turned bitter. "Because someone paid to have me disappear into the netherzones. I was only a baby. My mother took me to the wraiths rather than let the shade hunters harvest me. She risked everything to ensure my survival, and the wraiths raised me as one of their own."

"You were one of the few, then."

She nodded, her expression grim.

"And your mother?"

Her lips tightened. "Chose not to disappear, even though I was later told that she was advised to do so. She had a fatal accident within days of my disappearance. The wraiths told me later that they were worried she might have confessed my location, and they were vigilant for years, but she must not have told." She met his gaze, conviction in her own. "I don't exist. We've checked at every level we can access."

"And these children, the ones you protect, do they exist?"

"Not anymore." Her tone was fierce.

She looked at the changing display, the bluish light playing over her delicate features. It took Armand a moment to realize that Theodora was whispering their names, like a mantra.

"Daniel. Cosmetic surgery to separate his fused fingers. Nicola. An illegitimate and unwelcome arrival. Carroll. Ditto. Dina. Plastic surgery to remove a facial scar, deliberately inflicted. Ferris." She stopped and swallowed. There was only one image of Ferris, a lanky dark-haired boy with suspicion in his eyes and a scar on his throat.

When she didn't speak, Armand prompted her. "What about Ferris?"

Theodora clicked the image away. "He can't speak. He had a tumor removed when he was a child and his vocal cords were damaged during the surgery. I found a surgeon to do the repair, but he's expensive." She grimaced. "Actually, it's his silence that's expensive."

Armand said nothing, giving her the time she needed. He watched her closely, though, seeing the depth of her compassion for these children and her determination to help them.

It wasn't about the cred, even if she insisted otherwise. This was love.

And Armand realized that he could love this woman, with her ferocious defenses and soft heart. She was principled, though the principles she had been taught were more self-motivated than Armand believed to be ideal, her own twist upon the code of the wraiths was closer to his own notion of how beings should treat each other.

Theodora shook her head and he heard her frustration. "I don't have the cred. I thought I would, but I was wrong. Ferris is still lost."

Armand remembered how they had met. "How did you plan to get it?" He thought he knew the answer but he wanted her to say it aloud. He needed to hear that she undertook horrific tasks in order to pay for the treatment the children needed.

"You know already," she said, averting her gaze. "I was going to assassinate someone for the bounty."

Armand thought it was telling that she couldn't hold his gaze. Did Theodora have mixed feelings about her choices? Did she feel that she didn't have a choice, that it was her obligation to serve the greater good? He deliberately kept any condemnation from his tone. "Who? Blackstone?"

"No. The Oracle." She sighed and frowned. "There's an enormous bounty on her head."

"But you didn't claim it."

"I was interrupted." She lifted her head and considered him, her own expression wary once more.

"You had mixed feelings even before that," Armand guessed and she blinked with surprise.

"Well." She traced a line on her thigh with a fingertip, a more pensive gesture than was characteristic of her. He appreciated that she was trying to answer him honestly. Armand held his breath, not wanting to interrupt her confession. "There was a certain irony in targeting the Oracle in order to pay for Ferris's surgery."

"How so?"

"He became a wraith because he tried to defend her against a shade hunter." Her lips twisted. "I think he loves her. I took him into my care to keep him from being harvested."

Armand was appalled. "Theodora! How could you even consider collecting such a bounty? He'd hate you forever."

Her lips set. "Not once he was healed and had choices again. He'd call it the greater good."

"No," Armand insisted, knowing that this was a point he had to make clear. "No. Love is not like that. If he loves the Oracle, he'd willingly carry any burden to ensure that she survived. He'd choose to forgo any repairing surgery rather than see her killed. He'd stay a shade to protect her, and gladly so."

Theodora looked at him, then, her confusion clear.

"You're too idealistic. People don't think like that, Armand. Not in this world."

"No?" He knew his eyes were flashing. "You know that's true—that's why you had mixed feelings even then."

"I don't know any such thing," she argued. The way she shut him out of her thoughts, especially after they had had such an honest discussion, made Armand livid.

"Really?" he demanded. "What do you think your mother did for you? Don't you think she guessed what the repercussions would be? Don't you think she chose to ensure your life instead of her own?"

Theodora pushed to her feet, putting distance between them. Armand knew she was listening to him. "That was different."

"Was it? I don't think so." He pursued her across the storeroom, determined to change her perspective. "I think you see what you want to see. I think you make justifications for your choices, justifications that aren't necessarily deserved."

Theodora spun to face him. "I defend the lost children!"

"At what price, Theodora?" Armand flung out his hands. "At what price?"

She stared at him, then turned her back. "I don't know what you're talking about. I earn cred and spend it on them. There is no other price." A charged silence filled the space around them, and Armand tried to temper his response. He took a deep breath, noted that Theodora was almost quivering.

She wanted to hear what he had to say.

She wanted to be persuaded.

"The price is in your heart," he said softly. "The cost is

to your soul. Just because you can't count it in cred doesn't mean it isn't being paid."

"Is that right?" She glanced over her shoulder at him. "Despite all this talk, my talent was useful to you in doing the will of the so-called angels. You didn't have any problems enlisting me to complete your mission. Wasn't that for the greater good?"

Her accusation stung, because it was true. "Fair enough," Armand acknowledged. "But a mission from the angels is different."

"What angels?" Theodora demanded, her tone harsh.

Armand blinked. "The angels. They are part of the heavenly host . . ."

"There are no angels," she said flatly, to his shock. "If we're dealing in truth, let's get that bit straight. Angels don't exist."

"Of course they exist!"

"Didn't you notice, Armand?" Theodora asked, her voice a soft whisper. "The angels didn't come for you. Blackstone is dead, but they didn't come. They don't exist."

He confronted her without flinching, unable to argue with her conclusion, but determined to be honest. Her expression was world-weary, devoid of the surprise he'd felt at the same realization.

"They do exist," he insisted, keeping the tumult of his emotion from his voice. "I know it."

"Then maybe they lied to you." Theodora shook her head, reaching for her hood. "It wouldn't be the first time a client lied. Maybe they're no different from everybody else."

Her defeated tone caught at his heart, made him want to give her something real to cling to. He could appreciate that she had seen a great deal, that what she had witnessed in this world had disheartened her. But he wanted to give her hope. He wanted to prove to her that there was goodness and merit.

Maybe that was the point of his existence on this earth.

"No," Armand said, his words low and hot. "That's not it."

There was urgency in his tone, and maybe that was what made Theodora turn to face him. Her gaze danced over his features. "Why do you think they didn't come, then?"

He understood that she was humoring him, that she still didn't believe, and that knowledge irritated him more than anything else could have. "It makes perfect sense. I killed that shade, the one that hurt you." He finished, determined that she understand the truth. "They came for Baruch, but they left me behind because I sinned."

To his surprise, his assertion made Theodora furious. "You think you're a failure because you defended yourself?" she demanded, her voice rising. She marched across the floor, jabbing her finger into his chest to punctuate her argument. "Because you're alive? Because you killed some bastard who would have killed you first, if he'd been fast enough? Because you *won*?"

Armand folded his arms across his chest. "It is not our place to choose when anyone lives or dies. That's what I'm trying to tell you. That decision lies in the hands of the divine."

"Who told you that?"

"The angels."

"No. No, no, no." Theodora was dismissive. "You've got to lose this idea. There are no angels! You can't believe in something that doesn't exist, especially if it's going to get you killed! You can't stand by and wait for the gods to intervene . . ."

"There is only one God."

Her eyes flashed. "Then clearly He's stretched a bit thin, because there've been a whole lot of times I could have used some divine intervention. Where the hell is goodness in this place?"

Theodora's refusal to believe what he knew to be true made Armand angry. "So, I should discard everything I believe? Is that your advice? I should become focused on the physical at the expense of the spiritual? That I should become as damned as all of you, and think only of myself? Don't you think that's the problem with this sphere?" He knew his own eyes were flashing, and heard his voice rise. "You suggest that I should believe in something as insubstantial, worthless, and ridiculous as *cred*?"

"You should believe in doing whatever you can to make a difference," Theodora retorted, unafraid of him or his anger. Her eyes flashed with an answering passion. "You should believe in the concrete, not some dreamy illusion of celestial life. You should believe in what you can see and feel, what's a part of this world, what you can change and what you can't."

"I do," Armand said with resolve.

"Angels?" Her skepticism was tangible and it rankled.

"Yes, *angels*." Armand let his voice drop low. He saw her eyes widen and knew she was as aware of him as he was of her. There was a charge in the air between them, one that couldn't be attributed to exhaustion or strain. The argument sparked it, gave it life and dimension, made it harder to think of anything other than Theodora.

And how the soft heat of her kisses contrasted with the

cold logic of her appearance. She would give everything to complete a mission.

But really, she would give everything to protect the lost children she claimed as her siblings.

He was keenly aware of her femininity, of the fact that he had nearly lost her, of the reality that if he was doomed to remain in this sphere, then he wanted very much to stay with Theodora.

He just had to persuade her of that.

He knew with sudden clarity how to do it. He had precisely nothing to lose and everything to gain.

Armand dropped his voice to a growl and stepped slowly toward her. "Let me give you something to believe in, Theodora," he said, keeping his words low and hot. He saw her eyes widen, saw her catch her breath, and the sight inflamed him. "Let me show you something more compelling than cred."

As Armand closed the distance between them, he unfastened his pseudoskin with slow deliberation.

XIV

IT WAS the moment Theodora had been waiting for.

She couldn't move, couldn't breathe, couldn't tear her gaze away from Armand. His eyes were vivid green, glittering like cut glass.

Or maybe like gems. His lips were set into a firm line, and he moved with both strength and resolve. Theodora watched him stride closer and her determination to resist him dissolved a little bit more with every step he took.

He unfastened his pseudoskin and cast aside his gloves. He pushed the dark polymer over his shoulders and tugged the sleeves over his wrists. Theodora looked. His skin was tanned, firm, healthy, the auburn hair on his chest curly. There was dried blood on the bandage on his shoulder, but the flow seemed to have stopped—and the injury didn't seem to trouble him. She watched his muscles flex as he moved, and savored the sight of his vitality.

There weren't many men like him.

Theodora had the fleeting thought that he had been worth the wait.

Armand unfastened his belt when he was only a step away from her and flung it onto a bag of corn. He watched her with that small seductive smile, then rested his hands on his hips. Theodora felt herself flushing, her gaze alternating between his eyes and his waist. She was sure he was going to push the pseudoskin down to his thighs, to show her the rest of his strength, and that things would get interesting.

Instead he pivoted with the grace of an athlete and held out his arms at his sides. He was gracefully built, elegant and strong, but she gasped at his back.

Things *had* become interesting.

There were two diagonal scars on Armand's back, exactly the same as those on Baruch's back. They were healed, but still red ridges in his flesh. They looked as if the wounds had been deep and painful—it was hard to look at the marks on his flesh even now without flinching.

What had caused them?

"I know that the angels exist for a simple reason," he said, his low words filled with conviction. "I was one, just months ago."

He glanced over his shoulder and Theodora knew he believed what he was telling her. Her own mouth was completely dry. Could this be true?

"I volunteered to shed my wings to help to save humanity, but in killing that shade, I surrendered my opportunity to return to what I've known for eons. I will die in this realm, in mortal form." Armand turned and took her left hand in his. "I need your help, Theodora. Just like the children you shelter, I need to disappear into the shadows or risk being harvested."

Theodora felt her mouth open, then close, then open again. "Angels?" she echoed, but there was less question in her tone than there had once been. She was thinking of the vitality of Armand, of Baruch, of the Oracle's consort Rafe. All three men were unusual in that they were so strong and healthy.

And all three were said to be fallen angels.

Could this be the truth? Armand certainly was convinced, and if this was a mark of insanity, it was his only indication. He also was incapable of lying to her. Theodora found the evidence of the physical health of these men more compelling than that of their scars. There was something more than human about them.

Angels.

"We are Armand and Baruch, formerly Armaros and Baraqiel." He spoke quietly, that smile touching his lips again. "We were at the Nouveau Mont Royal Circus before we made the sacrifice.".

Theodora eyed him for a moment, the pieces falling into place. His smile *had* reminded her of something before. Its serenity and confidence were uncommon. She guessed what it was. Theodora tapped her palm furiously, pulling up the news articles on the angels at the circus, then following the hotlink to their image.

She was right. She could see the resemblance immediately. Once she looked past the pearly brilliance that whitened the image, once she ignored the large luminescent wings, she could see the resemblance.

In that smile.

Armand.

Armaros.

It *was* true.

"This one was you," she said quietly, knowing it to be so. She considered the image, seeing now the similarity between the other angel's features and those of Baruch. She thought of the pair's silent bond in Cosmopoulos's lab and was convinced. "What happened to Baruch, then?"

"The others must have come for him, because Blackstone is dead."

"But they left you behind."

Armand nodded once. Theodora had a glimpse of how much the loss troubled him, then he hid his thoughts away. The pain lingered in his eyes, though, filling them with shadows.

"Would you have gotten your wings back?"

He nodded once, disconsolate, then visibly dismissed his pain.

"Is it that much better?" She had to ask.

He smiled then, the expression lighting his face. "I wish I could show you." He sobered as he gestured with one hand, seeking the words to explain. "I wish I could show you the sense of unity we have with all living beings, as if all of life is one great unit and we are each a part of the whole. It is impossible to hate when we hear each other's thoughts and feel each other's emotions as keenly as our own."

"Do you still have that power?"

"No." His lips tightened. "It was surrendered with my wings."

Theodora watched him closely. "And what's the worst part?"

He flicked a glance around the storeroom, a quick one that communicated his feelings about her world eloquently all the same. It must be a rude awakening, to go from heaven to this place.

Theodora reached out and touched him. He was warm, flesh and blood, not an angel anymore. Her throat tightened that he never would be again, that his dream had been sacrificed in saving her, and that there was nothing she could ever do to redress the imbalance or pay that debt. "The worst part," she prompted.

He sighed. "The loneliness of hearing only one's own

thoughts. I have never known such solitude as this. And it dismays me that the lack of connection makes me think of myself first, instead of the whole of creation as one."

"It makes you understand us better, maybe."

"It makes me think like a mortal. It gives me a self-motivation I have never known, and one that I believe is the root of all evil in this sphere." He clenched his fists and would have paced the room once more, but Theodora caught at his hand.

She knew what she had to do.

She understood his frustration, understood how it felt to be compelled to take a role you didn't desire. She knew how it was to be shaped into something you would never have chosen to be, to have a transformation inflicted upon you.

She knew what it meant to be alone.

And she knew the one act that gave solace. It was a seductive solace, a temporary union, sometimes a false luxury and one she avoided because of that, but it was the best a human could have.

She reached for Armand, sliding her hand over his shoulder. "Now, let me give you something to believe in," she whispered, smiling slightly as she stretched to touch her lips to his. "Let me show you where we find magic in this world," she whispered against his mouth.

Then she kissed him.

ARMAND WAS seduced by Theodora's kiss. She touched him so gently at first, so tentatively, as if she imagined he might reject her advance.

There was no possibility of that. He slid his fingers into

her hair, drawing her closer, desire making his heart pound. He knew that she wasn't the mercenary she pretended to be. He knew that she was troubled by her choices, but felt there was no other option. He noted her chopped hair, the wound on her temple, the ferocity of her determination and his chest squeezed tightly.

Armand was filled with tenderness, with a potent echo of the love that had once governed his every move. That, too, he had believed to be lost, for he had thought such compassion had no place in this sphere.

He had been wrong.

He had only to look at what she did for these lost children to see how he was wrong. Her kiss was a heady promise of the union they could make.

Of the promise in neither ever being alone again.

Armand lifted his right hand and cupped her jaw in his hand. She was so soft, her skin smooth beneath his hand, her softness in contrast to the rough life she led. As their kiss turned demanding, a sense of purpose filled him, a conviction that he would help her find alternative solutions.

He dared to believe in a new partnership, a new team. One fueled by kisses like this one, kisses that began sweet and turned hot. Kisses that made a person forget the cruelty of the world, the immorality of this sphere; kisses that reminded him of the existence he'd left behind.

They would create magic together in this place. He caught her close and deepened his kiss, sampling her, exploring her, almost fusing their flesh together. Theodora clutched him tightly, slid her tongue between his teeth, locked her fingers into his hair. He felt his body harden and tighten, smelled the heat of her desire and *wanted*. His heart pumped and his skin flushed, every increment of his skin coming gloriously to life. He was alive, vibrantly so, and he reveled in the reaction of his body.

She caught her breath when he lifted his head, her gaze flicking to his lips. Armand felt himself smile, that old confidence filling his heart once more. He knew who had given him the purpose he needed to continue in this earthly sphere, knew who would ensure that his mortal life wasn't wasted, and he knew it was time to celebrate the gifts they had both been given.

He kissed Theodora again, cautious no longer. Heat flared through him, desire flooding through him. Theodora immediately twined her free hand around his neck, pulling him closer. Her reaction made his heart skip a beat, made his optimism soar. Armand deepened his kiss and savored. He swept his hands over her curves, loving the differences in the shape of their bodies, exploring which curves best fit his hands.

It didn't matter where they had to go or what they had to do, what might come against them or how matters might turn for the worse. There was only this moment of perfect communion, this unison of purpose.

Together, they could make a difference.

They already had.

But for the moment, there was only the pleasure that could be found in sensation. There was only Armand's need to explore every facet of it, to give and to receive. It wasn't just sensation anymore, wasn't just illusory and forgettable. No, this would mark far more than a physical union, a purpose that would endure beyond the years of both of them. They would defend the children together, as a team.

Their thoughts truly were as one.

* * *

THE MAN was irresistible.

When Theodora had realized he was watching her, she had looked up into the endless sparkle of his eyes. Armand had amazing eyes, more filled with color and light than any Theodora had ever seen. His feelings were clearly illuminated in his eyes, his passion, his frustration, his pain, his joy. The secret of his soul was there, free for the looking. She could have stared into his gaze for the rest of her life without regret, just to watch the shift in his moods and temper.

But in this moment, they were dark with intent, smoky with passion and desire. Desire for her. Theodora responded immediately, every pore of her body answering that summons, her heart skipping and her breath catching. She felt warm and shivery at the same time, edgy with a desire more potent than any she'd ever felt before.

When he slid his hand along her jaw—so gentle, so powerful—then into her hair, she felt claimed. She loved that he tempered his strength, that he was determined to avoid injuring any other being.

She particularly liked that he treated her like a rare gem. She hadn't felt special very often in her life, except for her carefully honed talents. It was intoxicating to be valued for herself alone.

Simply because she existed.

Armand's firm lips curved in that slow smile, the one that made his eyes dance and her blood boil, the one that was reminiscent of angelic serenity. It was easy to believe in angels when Armand looked at her in that way, exciting to know that such a man was intrigued with her.

And when he kissed her, Theodora forgot everything except the powerful heat of his kiss. She had run too far on adrenaline, had too many close calls, had tasted death a bit too often in the last day to show any restraint.

She was alive.

She was in the company of the most attractive man she'd ever met.

And he wanted her.

Theodora wasn't going to argue. In fact, she would meet him halfway. Her free hand was locked in his hair within a heartbeat, her fingers gripping the thick curl of it. He was so healthy, so virile, so strong that Theodora wanted to explore every inch of him.

She wanted him inside her.

His kiss deepened, his tongue easing between her teeth. Theodora opened her mouth to him, letting her tongue dance with his, loving the graze of his teeth across her lips. Their kiss turned hungry, more demanding than sweet, and that passion was precisely what she wanted. She would have eaten him whole if possible, consumed him and made him her own.

Forever.

She locked her hands around his neck. He pulled her onto his lap, never breaking his kiss. Theodora spread her hands wide, sliding them down his neck and over his shoulders, marveling at the corded strength of him.

He was exploring her as well, his touch lighting a fire in her veins. His hands were on her buttocks, her hips, her waist. They slid to her shoulders, then he reached for the fastening of her pseudoskin.

Theodora was breathing quickly when he broke his kiss. She felt flushed and anxious, wanting him immediately yet wishing to take it slow. Their gazes locked and held, his breath coming as quickly as her own. Theodora saw the leap of his pulse at his throat and smiled at the sign of his arousal. She put her fingertips on it and the way he swallowed made her smile.

His own smile broadened, his fingertip touching the corner of her mouth. Theodora realized that she hadn't really smiled in his presence before.

She wasn't much for smiling. There was seldom much to smile about in her world, but as she looked at Armand, his hair tousled and his eyes filled with stars, she felt her smile broaden.

"Maybe joy has to be cultivated," he murmured, seeming to read her thoughts.

"Maybe. Let's create some now."

Armand chuckled.

Theodora unfastened her pseudoskin, watching his eyes light as her skin was revealed. His fingertips slid over her throat and shoulder, caressing her gently as if he was afraid she'd disappear. Theodora arched her neck, moaning when he touched her breasts. She felt precious and beautiful, and she gasped with pleasure when he slid the edge of his thumb over her erect nipple. He bent to take that nipple in his mouth, his caress making her back arch and her pulse leap. His tongue flicked, his teeth grazed, and she squirmed in his embrace.

Theodora didn't know how the rest of her pseudoskin was removed. She was lost in sensation, in the pleasure that Armand deliberately cultivated. There was nothing in her world but the warmth of his skin and the heat of his fingertips, the sure touch of his lips and fingers.

She closed her eyes and surrendered to sensation, every

inch of her skin alive with pleasure. She was vaguely aware of the sacks beneath her, of her own nudity, of Armand's fingers sliding down the length of her. Then he was over her, running kisses down her body, his hands exploring as quickly as his mouth.

When his mouth closed over hers, she nearly cried out in pleasure. His tongue and teeth teased her in an intimate kiss, one that left her writhing. She imagined that they were in a finer setting, that this was just the first of many such moments together, and dared—for the first time in all her life—to hope for a future.

A future with Armand.

The tumult rose within her, making her skin tingle, making her yearn and burn for more than his tongue. Theodora twisted, but Armand held fast, his grip on her hips keeping her captive to the pleasure he was determined to give. She felt her hips begin to buck, knew the climax was close, and knew that she didn't want to reach her pleasure alone.

She caught his wrists in her hands and met his gaze, knowing that she was flushed. "Not alone," she said, hearing a ferocity in her tone. "Never alone again."

She saw understanding light his eyes and he let her push him back. Jangled and tousled, she slid to her feet, that dizziness because of his sure touch. She removed his boots and pseudoskin, marveling at the magnificence of his healthy and strong body.

Then she touched him.

She caressed him and explored him from head to toe, the feel of his skin beneath her hands taking her arousal to a fever pitch. She slid her hands over the length of his erection and he bared his teeth, closing his eyes against her touch.

Theodora felt powerful and strong herself, able to evoke

such a strong reaction from this remarkable man. She touched him with increasing boldness, feeling him grow harder and thicker between her hands. His entire body went taut and one hand locked into a fist.

But he didn't stop her.

Theodora bent and closed her mouth over him. She loved how Armand moaned, how she could affect him. She teased and touched him, just as he had teased her, coaxing his response just as he had fed her own.

"Theodora!" he gasped suddenly and seized her shoulders. He moved with that lightning speed, rolling her beneath him in one smooth gesture. His eyes were glittering like jewels and it seemed that sparks flew from him.

Theodora smiled up at him, content as she had seldom been. She parted her thighs and put her legs around his waist, welcoming him inside her. She slid her hands across his shoulders, enjoying this moment, then gasped at the size of him as he slid into her heat.

Their gazes locked again for a potent moment, and she felt that communion again. She saw her own awe echoed in his expression, then she reached to touch her lips to his again.

Armand caught her mouth with his. His kiss was hungry and demanding, and she knew that neither would have enough of the other soon. Their kiss was devouring, bruising in its intensity, filled with fire and passion.

They were two of a kind.

She drew him even closer, clutching at his shoulders, wanting to feel his skin against every inch of her own. He kissed her roughly, forgetting himself in the heat of the moment, and Theodora reveled in his touch.

Armand moved with confidence and power, each stroke

taking Theodora closer to the crescendo again. He whispered to her and kissed her, his hands roving as they tempted each other. Her pulse pounded, her breath raced, her skin was flushed, her desire climbed to a fever pitch.

She felt the heat rise again and stared into the ferocious glitter of his eyes. She dug her nails into his shoulders, saw the bead of sweat on his brow, watched him clench his teeth. They moved together as if they had been lovers a thousand times before, each anticipating the other, each urging the other higher, each holding on as long as possible.

When the climax finally rolled through her, it was worth every effort. It soared through her body, eliminating every barrier, making her heart leap and her blood surge. Theodora heard herself cry out in pleasure and didn't care.

In the same moment, she felt Armand's hot seed spill inside her, even as his entire body clenched with his release. He roared into her shoulder, lifting her high in the air as his release claimed him.

Then he collapsed onto the sacks of corn, carefully bracing his weight above her. He rolled to his back and gathered her against his chest, almost purring with contentment.

Theodora heard a strange sound and realized that she was laughing. She felt lighter and happier and she pulled him closer, never wanting to let him go.

"Theodora," Armand whispered in her ear, his voice uneven and filled with awe. He looked at her with shining eyes as he caught his breath.

And he smiled, not his bemused and secretive smile, but a broad smile that revealed his teeth and left his eyes sparkling. He looked like a man, a man enamored of the world and its pleasures, maybe one enamored of her. She had time to think he looked mischievous before his hand slid between them and his finger touched her clitoris.

Theodora gasped and arched her back, her body raging for release once more.

"Again," Armand murmured with purpose, his sure touch stealing her words away.

Not that she intended to argue with him over that.

THEODORA AWAKENED in darkness, the hairs on the back of her neck prickling. She didn't move, even as she strained her ears.

Something had awakened her.

She remained still, listening.

Armand slept beside her, the rhythm of his breathing deep and soothing. They had made love three times, exhausting each other completely, then cleaned up and put on their pseudoskins again to sleep. If nothing else, the polymer was warmer than being nude in the netherzones.

A slight click echoed in the darkened storeroom.

It came from the door to the netherzones, the one that Theodora had locked. This was what she had heard.

Someone, she was certain, was picking the lock.

She had a pretty good idea who it might be.

She silently rolled away from Armand, glad that he had listened to her advice that they sleep on a pile of sacks that were out of sight of both doors. He wouldn't be visible to the attacker—or attackers—even after the door was open.

Theodora thought quickly. One of the mercenary shades employed by Maximilian Blackstone must have come to take vengeance for that man's death. If so, they'd be lucky to get away alive—and even if she evaded a mercenary shade, it wouldn't be for long. They kept coming, and sooner or later, they would get her and Armand.

Unless she and Armand separated. She could ensure his survival by leading the mercenary shade away.

She swallowed at the realization. This was the gift she could give Armand, the payback she could make for his sacrifice. This was how she could repay him for choosing her life over his own dream.

She could ensure that Armand survived.

The mercenary shades would be primarily after her, after all, because she had been the one to kill Blackstone. If Armand was lost in the shuffle, they wouldn't backtrack to him.

And if they did, maybe he'd get far enough away that they wouldn't find him.

She was tempted to kiss Armand farewell, to share a last word, but she was terrified to awaken him. That would only put him in danger. His best defense was to remain asleep and unnoticed for as long as possible.

If her plan worked, that wouldn't have to be long.

Theodora pulled her laze. Her heart was pounding and her mouth was dry. She knew what she had to do, but she didn't want to do it. She didn't want to leave him. She didn't want to part without a farewell.

Even if it was safer.

Even if it was smarter.

This was no time to get sloppy and sentimental. Armand's life hung in the balance.

All the same, there were tears in Theodora's eyes when she checked the charge of her laze. It needed a big hit of juice, but there should be enough to get her out of this situation.

Once she was away from Armand, she didn't care when

or where they took her down. In a real sense, she was living on borrowed time already. She should have died in Blackstone's suite, would have died without Armand's intervention. Instead, she'd experienced the glory of making love, not just again, not just wondrously, but with Armand. Instead, she'd had her faith restored. She owed him so much.

And it wouldn't be such a loss to the world for a wraith assassin to die. Officially, she'd been born dead. She'd been living on borrowed time her entire life. She liked the idea of sacrificing herself to save an angel, the potential of making a difference in the world.

All Theodora wanted to ensure was that she wasn't harvested.

Which meant she had to fire first and as much as possible. They would shoot a violent victim rather than try for a capture. She left her hood off, wanting to be sure the mercenary shade had no doubt as to her identity.

She quietly climbed the stairs to the entry to the shop overhead and moved the sacks of corn aside. One fell heavily to the floor and she was sure the mercenary shade was too silent.

Listening.

Armand's breathing didn't change.

There was another click from the netherzone door, a more aggressive one. Theodora opened the door to the shop and hoped that there was an easy path to the street. She shone her palm's flashlight into the room beyond, and saw that the stairs opened at the back of a large space. There seemed to be few obstacles between her and the barricaded shop window at the opposite end. There was a door beside that window, one that looked to have a single old lock securing it.

She refused to consider that she might die, right there on that vinyl floor. She hoped she would get farther than that.

She *had* to get farther than that, for Armand's sake.

The door to the netherzones rattled again.

It was time.

Theodora fired down the length of the shop, aiming for the lock on the shop door. It shattered and fell, then a shrill alarm began to sound.

A silvery fog slid through the opening doorway, gliding along the floor toward her. Theodora blinked. The fog seemed to have purpose. It moved as if it was targeting her.

Like a poisonous snake.

"What . . . ?" Armand began to ask.

"Silent and hidden!" Theodora hissed, hoping he would listen to her.

He didn't say anything more, and she didn't have time to check that he was following instructions.

Because at the sound of the alarm, the mercenary shade abandoned all pretense. He shot at the lock of the door to the netherzones and kicked it open. The metal door banged against the concrete wall and the race was on.

Theodora pivoted just as the mercenary shade stepped into the storeroom. He was dressed precisely the same as the one who had admitted them to Blackstone's suite, which was all Theodora needed to know. She gave him time to see her, then fired at him. She deliberately singed him. She prayed that Armand would stay down, and was glad to not see any sign of him.

The mercenary shade ducked back into the netherzones to evade the shot. Theodora ran, confident that he would follow. She was racing down the length of the shop when she heard his footfalls on the metal stairs.

At least she hoped it was him, not Armand.

She kicked the door to the street wide open and a shot grazed past her shoulder. Not Armand then, but the mercenary shade. At least something was going as planned.

The fog poured past her, moving toward the storeroom. The street was full of its strange luminescence, and it glimmered around her hips. The sky was becoming dark.

But she couldn't see far because of the fog.

Theodora had no time to consider the strange weather. She spun in the doorway and fired a shot back at the mercenary shade. He barely got out of the way, then raised his laze once more.

She fired again, then leapt into Chicago's fog-filled streets. She ran with all her might, ducking into an alley when his laze shot fired past her.

It was her versus the mercenary shade.

She knew this game and played it well. As a bonus, the fog would make it easier for her to be evasive.

But this time, she wasn't playing for her own survival but for Armand's. Her main goal was to lead the mercenary as far as possible from that storeroom. Armand was safe and that was all that mattered.

Yet strangely enough, even though her demise would be the neatest end to the game, Theodora didn't want to die.

She got her bearings, checked her palm, and ran the most evasive course she could devise. The farther she could lead the shade from Armand, the better. If she could manage to escape and return to him, that would be even better.

Odds were long against her, but Theodora was honest enough to admit that it wasn't about the children anymore.

XV

ARMAND AWAKENED with a start, disoriented in the darkness. Theodora was gone from his side when he reached for her. He heard her hissed command from somewhere in the storeroom and stayed low, instinctively following her instruction. A chill pricked at his skin despite his pseudoskin, a strange chill that sent shivers over his body yet fed his desire once more.

But again, chaos erupted in a hurry.

There was a shot, then an alarm began to ring with shrill insistence. Someone kicked in the door to the netherzones, rapid fire was exchanged. Armand saw Theodora silhouetted at the top of the stairs, then she fled. He saw the assailant race after her and recognized his uniform as those worn by Blackstone's bodyguards. Shots were fired again, then there was only silence and the dampness of the air seeping in from the street.

And the fog. An oddly glimmering fog, it slithered over the threshold and tumbled down the stairs. Armand had the strange sense that it was targeting him, a sense only amplified when it swirled around him. ·

It seemed to caress his skin, roiling against his genitals as if it would stroke him, and it repulsed him. He was glad to be dressed, because the possibility of this fog touching his skin filled him with dread. He strode through the fog, wanting only to be away from it.

Armand climbed to the top of the stairs and looked down the length of the shop. There was no sign of either Theodora or the attacker. The door at the far end of the shop hung open, fog tumbling over the threshold. He was hesitant to follow her, given her instruction.

He went back down the stairs, grimacing as the fog closed around his hips, and made for the damaged door that led to the netherzones. A few wisps of fog coiled into the shadows, but it seemed to gather around him, swirling around his body in a disconcerting way.

Armand ignored it and its provocative touch. He peered out into the darkness of the netherzones and listened. He considered his options. He didn't want to abandon Theodora, although he suspected that following her directly would only create trouble.

The mercenary shade was one of Blackstone's bodyguards. He must have pursued Armand and Theodora to retaliate for Blackstone's death. That meant that Theodora was trying to lead the shade away from Armand.

It made sense, especially as she was the better strategist in these matters and also more likely to shoot to kill. He recognized that she had understood the likelihood of this occurring, and that that was why she had confided in him about the lost children. Once again, he felt left in her dust, so to speak, when it came to understanding her world.

Where were those children she safeguarded? How could he find them and defend them in her stead?

If she'd intended for him to do that, Theodora would have given him more information.

Maybe she didn't trust him, after all.

Maybe sharing her body was as intimate as she could be. The prospect sent disappointment through him and Armand hoped that he had the chance to persuade her otherwise. He had finally found something of merit in this world, something to believe in, and he could not believe that Theodora would have abandoned either him or the promise of their dawning relationship.

He would trust her.

He would have faith that she would find him once she believed herself to be safe. He had a sense that Theodora wasn't accustomed to being trusted and that his trust in her could be the key to winning even more of her confidence.

If not more.

And Armand wanted that perfect union with a vigor that shook him. He knew though that defying Theodora, who knew so much more about the workings of the mortal world, could lead to failure.

Waiting here would only be an invitation to disaster. What he should do was trust her and prove himself worthy of her trust by finding those children. He was sure she must have told him what he needed to know—while he figured it out, he would leave the danger of this place behind.

Armand stepped into the darkness and let the shadows embrace him, walking even as he was uncertain where he should go. The fog trailed behind him, matching his pace, the silvery tendrils stark against the darkness. He glanced at his palm, wondering whether Theodora had given him directions to the location of the lost children.

Its chime nearly made him jump out of his pseudoskin.

He had an incoming message.

And its content completely shook his world.

Announcement to All Students of the Institute for Radiation
Studies
September 20, 2100; 08:00

You are summoned to witness the first surgery in the current
laboratory experiment of Dr. Paul Cosmopoulos upon the
captured shade formerly known as Baruch Harding.

The surgery will commence at 09:00 Thursday, September
23, 2100 in the Main Observatory Lab, level 1, sector 7. Please
come prepared–questions on this procedure will form a
significant portion of your final exam in the relevant level of
Dissection & Vivisection. Those of you who still have the
outstanding exercises in Laboratory Protocol are welcome to
help in the lab between now and the commencement of the
surgery in taking tests and preparing files.

Ref: <u>Research Proposal 17243</u>

"Oh, that does look dire," a man said softly from behind Armand. "It would seem to be a logical impossibility, unless of course, our fellow angels lied to you."

Armand spun in shock. A man stood behind him, a man all in black. No, he wasn't just dressed in black—he *was* black. Every increment of him was the color of midnight. It could have been another mortal in a pseudoskin, but Armand knew better.

The large leathery wings and the malice glinting in those eyes told him all he needed to know.

"Lucifer," he hissed and took a wary step back.

Lucifer smiled. "How lovely to be recognized. I have to admit that there have been times when I have despaired of my influence upon the hearts of men." His smile broadened. "This, fortunately, is not one of those times."

"I wouldn't expect as much," Armand said with disgust. "This realm is a wasteland."

"It's all a matter of perspective, isn't it? I think things are coming together quite well. Hell on earth and all that. Or maybe earth has gone to hell in a handbasket. Suits me either way." His dark eyes glinted as he considered Armand. "You actually imagine that you can still win?"

"Good must triumph—"

"Really? Even when the angels abandon you?" Lucifer interrupted him, his tone mocking. "Maybe you're seeing now what I've known for millennia. They simply can't be trusted."

The very suggestion infuriated Armand. "You lie! The angels are above rebuke."

"Oh? And why then did they leave both of you behind?"

"There must be another reason for this," Armand insisted, although he couldn't think of one.

Lucifer sidled closer, his voice falling low. "Have you not read the great book for yourself? Is it not prophesied that the angels themselves will destroy the earth?"

"No!"

"Yes! Revelation Eight, in which the angels blow their trumpets." Lucifer cleared his throat and struck a pose to recite the verses. " *'The first angel sounded, and there followed hail and fire mingled with blood, and they were cast upon the earth; and a third of the earth was burned up, and the third part of trees was burned up, and all green grass was burned up. The second angel blew his trumpet and as it were a great mountain burning with fire was cast into the sea. A third of the sea became blood, and the third part of the creatures which were in the sea died and a third of the ships were destroyed.'* "

He paused to wink at Armand. "Here's my favorite part. *'The third angel blew his trumpet and a great star fell from heaven, blazing like a torch, and it fell on a third of the rivers and on the springs of water. And the name of the star was called Wormwood, and a third part of the waters became wormwood, and many men died of the waters because they were made bitter.'* "

The words seemed to linger in the darkness, long after he had fallen silent.

"It's nonsense," Armand began to argue. "Garbled in translation from the original source."

Lucifer eyed him, his expression mocking. "Nonsense? You do know, of course, that the word Chernobyl translates to wormwood." He raised his brows and continued. " *'And the fourth angel sounded, and the third part of the sun was smitten, and the third part of the moon, and the third part of the stars, so as the third part of them was darkened, and the*

day shone not for a third part of it and the night likewise.'"
He shook his head. "What a troublesome bunch these angels
are. But it grows worse. *'And the fifth angel blew his trum-*
pet, and I saw a star that had fallen from heaven to earth,
and he was given the key to the shaft of the bottomless pit;
he opened the shaft of the bottomless pit, and from the shaft
rose smoke like the smoke of a great furnace, and the sun
and the air were darkened with the smoke from the shaft.'
Would that be you or me? Or one of the other volunteers
who have shed their wings to become flesh?"

"You twist the words to suit your purposes," Armand
argued. "Is it not said that the devil can quote scripture?"

Lucifer laughed. " *'Then the sixth angel blew his trum-*
pet . . . so the four angels were released, who had been
held ready for the hour, the day, the month, and the year,
to kill a third of humankind.'"

"It is our intent to *defend* humankind . . ."

"Truly? Then where are your fellows? The state of this
world isn't new. Why have they abandoned you? Why have
they broken their pledge to you?" Lucifer's eyes brightened. "Seems to me that the end times are present and
accounted for, when the angels themselves sin." Before
Armand could argue with that, he lifted a dark finger. "As
you did yourself, with such gusto."

Armand froze at that assertion and stared at the adversary of all he knew. Lucifer was manifest, which explained
so much about the state of the physical world, why it had
detoured so far from divine creation.

But was he not becoming what he despised?

"Did you think I hadn't noticed? I do keep track of such
things, especially among the angelic volunteers. We have
so much in common, after all."

"We have nothing in common!"

"Really?" Lucifer's eyes glimmered in the darkness and he held up one hand, his nails long on his fingers. The fog swirled around them, enclosing the pair and blocking the rest of the corridor from view. "Let's review the seven deadly sins, shall we? Sloth? A challenge for many, I've noticed, but not for you."

Armand was outraged at the idea that he had anything in common with the Prince of Darkness. "I am not lazy . . ."

"Oh? What precisely have you achieved in the time since your arrival? You were at the circus for months and did nothing but watch. You shed your wings in February and did nothing until this past week. You could have been an active force for change in the Republic, and to be sure, I had my concerns. They were undeserved." Lucifer smiled as Armand fought his own doubts.

"I did as I was instructed to do . . ."

"Always the excuse, isn't it? *'No one told me to be proactive.'*" Lucifer shrugged and stifled a yawn. "I believe we can make a case for sloth." He ticked off one finger, then tapped the next. "Anger?" He chuckled. "You are the most furious angel I have ever met."

"It is only right to outraged by injustice . . ."

"So right that you kill for it?"

Armand couldn't argue that point. He tried to step away but the fog seemed to have become a restrictive barrier, one that held him captive to Lucifer's beguiling words.

Lucifer nodded with an engaging confidence. "Anger, then, is covered. Pride." His voice dropped to a confidential tone. "You know, I have never understood the concern over pride. It's only decent for an individual to challenge the status quo, to be ambitious, to protect oneself, even if at the expense of others. You have no lack of pride in your intellect and your appearance." He winked. "I think we have that in common."

"I have already said that we have nothing in common!"

"*Au contraire.* We are two of a kind, fallen from on high, you by choice and me by command, but still. The details are irrelevant. We have so much common ground. Imagine what an effective team we could be . . ."

Armand tried to back away again, appalled by the suggestion. "I will never join you. Never!"

Lucifer's smile turned sly. "But maybe you already have. We're moving through the list quite rapidly, aren't we? How about lust? A personal favorite of mine, I must say. Among the big seven, it's the most fun."

Something touched Armand between his legs and he jumped back, startled to find Lucifer's tail rapping against his codpiece. He also had an erection, his thoughts filling unexpectedly with the glory of Theodora and what they had done together. The fog seemed to have slithered into his ears, diverting his thoughts, and under his codpiece, caressing him with an intimacy that he found shocking.

"Maybe she is a gift from the divine," Lucifer whispered. "A little bit of destiny intended to drive you directly toward me."

"No!" Armand shouted and struck at Lucifer with his fist. He encountered a slight obstacle, then his hand moved as if through the air. Lucifer wavered but didn't disappear.

Then he laughed. "Covetousness," he whispered, eyes shining. "A wonderful old word for greed. What do you covet, Armaros? Oh, I think I know. She's blond and tiny . . ."

"That's not covetousness!" Armand argued. "You know nothing of love." As soon as he said the word, he recognized the truth in it. He had come to admire Theodora and to love her. This demon was trying to twist all of that into some ugliness that served him better. Armand pointed at his adversary. "You know nothing of respect and decency and admiration. A woman is not an object of desire, even if a man is so lucky as to make her his partner."

"Really? What about those lost children of hers? Do you think she loves any of them better than she loves you? Do you think any of them are particular *beneficiaries* of her affection?"

Lucifer's words sowed a dark seed in Armand's thoughts, one that he fought against. It was a lie, and he knew it.

"Do you imagine that she came to you untouched?" Lucifer hissed. "Who was first? Who was last? Who is next?"

Armand fought the barrier of the fog again, fed up with such manipulation of the truth. "You are evil in your insinuations . . ."

"That, my dear friend, is the point." Lucifer smiled, then whispered again. "Will you be envious when she chooses another over you? Envy, as we know, is number six."

"You would misguide me for your own purposes . . ."

"And why not? I would like an ally in this great lonely world, someone who truly understands me, someone who thinks as I do." Lucifer leaned closer, sliding his arm across Armand's shoulders. "Just between you and me, I think gluttony is a detail. I can finesse it, if you take care of the other six. I can make you an offer, maybe even the proverbial one that you can't refuse."

Armand recoiled and tried to pull away. A horrific thought swirled in his mind. Could Lucifer save Baruch? What would he pay to end his friend's torment?

Lucifer smiled.

It was a trick! "You have nothing to offer me," Armand said with force.

"No? Don't underestimate my influence. What about a confirmed sanctuary for Theodora's lost children? What about survival for Theodora herself? What about Baruch's release?" They were all tempting possibilities, but Armand knew they would come with hidden conditions.

Conditions that would condemn him. It was one thing to be surrendered to a mortal existence, quite another to volunteer for an eternity of hellfire. No, so long as he was in this sphere, unfettered to Lucifer, he could make a difference.

He could undermine Lucifer's efforts, and perhaps take the world closer to the original divine intent. Hadn't he made a change in Theodora?

Lucifer leaned closer, fire and brimstone on his breath. "What about an assured place for you in the new order?"

"There will be no new order, unless it excludes you." Armand shrugged loose of the dark angel's grip and stepped away, his resolve redoubled. "That's why I volunteered, to help to stop your domination of the physical plane."

"That's nonsense! My time is close enough to taste." Lucifer laughed. "Surely you're smart enough to know that the game is already lost. Surely you're smart enough to play for your own advantage."

"Surely I'm smart enough to recognize a snake, no matter how he chooses to appear."

"Oh, let's not bring the past into this . . ."

Armand had heard enough. He pulled his laze and fired directly at Lucifer's heart. The dark angel made a choking sound, his eyes flashed, then he disappeared. There was a darker shadow where he had been, a space from which even the fog seemed to recoil.

"Your choice is made, then," Lucifer said, his low voice coming from everywhere and nowhere. "May the best angel win."

It was suddenly cold, a damp wind rolling through the netherzones and dispersing the fog.

Armand reviewed the data Theodora had installed on his palm. He had no information about the children at all, let alone their lost sanctuary. He could hunt it and maybe find it, but that would take time. Precious time.

He had to assume that they were safe for the moment—because Theodora wouldn't have left them any other way—and help Baruch first.

He had to go back to the Institute.

Alone. Then they'd go together to the children.

Armand headed back in that direction, ignored the last tendrils of fog and his sense of foreboding. He didn't know how he'd save Baruch but there had to be a way. He strode quickly through the darkness, his thoughts spinning, turned a corner, and came face-to-face with a man in a patched pseudoskin.

"Turn around, hunter," the man said, his voice vibrating oddly. He had a voice-box modifier mounted on the side of his throat, similar to the one Theodora had worn when Armand had first met her.

Armand took a step back and halted when he collided with the snout of a laze. A glance over his shoulder revealed that another man, more slight than the first, stood behind him.

He was trapped.

Captive.

Condemned by his own disguise.

Maybe he would never even get to Baruch.

* * *

ANTHONY CAME into Ernestine's room and shook her gently awake. It was late evening, she could tell by the color of the light seeping into the room. Ernestine, though, had been late coming back to bed, consumed as she had been in examining her father's file.

"Not now, Anthony," she said with some impatience, rolling over and pulling up the covers.

"But Maximilian Blackstone is here." Consternation marred Anthony's handsome features. "I told him that you were unavailable, but he insisted."

Ernestine pulled back the covers. "Max is here? At this hour?"

"Yes, my lady. And most emphatic about seeing you." Anthony blinked. "Immediately, he said. He seems somewhat agitated."

Ernestine was surprised. Why had Max come to her? He had explicitly said that she had until the next panel discussion to decide upon his offer. Why would he be agitated?

Did he know that she had found her father's file?

How could he know such a thing? No, no, she was worrying unnecessarily. There was no reason for him to have suspicions.

If nothing else, the news of his presence awakened her completely. She turned to dress, then knew that was a mistake.

No. Max wanted her. He had come at this hour of the night in order to pursue a union of the most intimate kind.

And if he hadn't, it was possible that she would be able to distract him with the prospect of sex.

Ernestine sprayed perfume over her body and donned a thin nightgown that left little to the imagination. She combed her hair and painted her lips, assumed a sensual pout and went to beguile her unexpected guest.

THIS WAS the chance Max's fetch had been waiting for.

He stood at the window of Ernestine's unit, looking over the grounds of the Institute for Radiation Studies. The campus was secured, cordoned off from the rest of Chicago by high gates, and the contrast between the two zones was striking.

There were trees planted on the grounds of the Institute— even in the shadows of the night, he could see that their leaves had turned hue in the autumn chill. The fetch tried to recall when he had last seen trees of such size and health. There was no vegetation in the city proper—just concrete, asphalt, and desolation.

There were also students on the pathways of the Institute, students he assumed at this hour were moving between parties. They stopped to chat, some in pseudoskins, some in lab coats, others in street wear. They laughed together, clearly feeling safe.

Beyond the protective walls of the Institute, the fetch could see the deserted streets of Chicago's downtown. No one walked on the streets and only security vehicles patrolled the roads. If he narrowed his eyes, he thought he could glimpse movement in the shadows.

But it could have just been a trick of the light.

Windows were broken in some shop fronts while others were barricaded with metal shutters. The taller buildings stood empty, their windows like vacant eyes. Even the stray dogs seemed furtive, figments of his imagination that disappeared before he could look twice.

In the distance, he could see the tall silhouette of the Intercontinental Hotel. He wondered whether Max himself was looking back at this residential tower of the Institute, peering into the night in an attempt to see the results of his plan.

He wondered whether Max would be surprised when he learned of his fetch's ambitions. The fetch liked to think that he was inscrutable, that he hadn't revealed his hand, but Maximilian Blackstone had a way of knowing more than he should.

The fetch took a deep breath and glared at the distant hotel, knowing that this would be his only chance to truly replace the ambitious politician with himself.

"What a surprise, Max," a woman said and the fetch turned to find Ernestine entering the main room of the unit. He was startled by the change in her appearance from the night before.

The light was harsh in her apartment, less flattering than that of the suite at the hotel. He could see the fine lines around her eyes and mouth, the wariness in her expression, the silver-touched roots of her red hair. She was slender and fit, but the tendons on her hands were more markedly apparent than they would have been in her younger days.

Still, she was attractive.

Especially in a filmy black robe, her feet bare. He liked that she came to him this way, as if she was amenable to the idea he hadn't even expressed. He could see the shadow of her breasts through the sheer fabric and his body responded with predictable enthusiasm. Her red hair flowed loose over her shoulders and she smelled of a sweet perfume.

Oh yes, he could make an alliance with her.

"I must apologize for my appearance," she began, making a gesture with one hand that wasn't apologetic in the least. There was a cunning in her eyes, and he understood that she had planned to distract him with her body. He should have been more worried by how well it worked. "I'm afraid I overslept today and am still exhausted." She let her voice rise, as if she were a foolish woman. "My thoughts were just spinning with all you suggested. It's so exciting!"

The fetch didn't believe for a minute that a woman like Ernestine would be overwhelmed by a plan that proposed more power for her.

No. She had been doing something else.

He eyed her sex slave, a handsome young man who stood by the door and immediately averted his gaze. The image of her father, Ernest Sinclair, which dominated the room, did not avert its gaze. The fetch felt as if the portrait was watching him, judging him, which was absurd.

He turned his best smile on the lady.

"No, no, I'm the one who must apologize." The fetch went directly to her side, summoning every vestige of his charm. "I didn't know where else to turn, who else to go to, especially at this hour. And I didn't dare ping you, given what has happened."

"Why? What has happened?" Her surprise seemed to be complete. If she was responsible for the attack on Max, she hid it well. The fetch admired that.

He considered the sex slave. "Can we be alone?"

"We are," she insisted with a smile. "Anthony isn't

important." There was a hitch of fear in her tone then, an uncertainty.

She was guilty.

The realization made him jubilant, confident of success.

"Alone," the fetch insisted, summoning Max's firm tone.

Ernestine looked between the two of them, then at the mercenary shade who was his bodyguard. "If one goes, they both go," she insisted, smiling. "Then we'll truly be alone."

"Agreed." The fetch turned to his bodyguard. "You will wait outside the unit, with the lady's shade." The bodyguard clicked his heels together and moved immediately to do as he was bidden. Anthony hesitated only a moment, then at Ernestine's minute nod, followed suit.

The fetch secured the door from the inside, knowing it would provide no barrier to the mercenary shade.

Had Ernestine paled?

If so, she moved quickly to disguise her discomfiture. She smiled a sensual welcome, pushing the robe from one shoulder as she strolled toward the fetch. "I suppose you are one who doesn't like witnesses," she purred.

She wanted to distract him.

She realized that he knew her guilt.

This would be his only chance to make an alliance. Anyone who had tried to kill Max was halfway persuaded to his cause, after all.

The fetch was filled with urgency, but not for exchanging confidences. Not even for intimacy. He went to Ernestine's side and took her cold hand in his. He leaned close, caught the scent of her perfume and let her see his desire. She parted her lips and reached for him, all sensuality and compliance.

"I am not Max," he whispered, when her lips touched his throat.

Ernestine froze, her gaze flicking over him, confirming what she must have suspected.

"His fetch," she breathed and he liked that she was a smart woman. "The eyes of the Republic are everywhere," she warned in a whisper and reached to kiss him.

The fetch kissed her thoroughly in return, letting her come to terms with her conclusions. He grazed her earlobe with his teeth, murmuring quickly. "Someone tried to kill Max, the assassin came to the suite and got past the guards. The first fetch died. Max blames you and sent me here to kill you." Continuing the charade of seduction, he pushed back the front of her robe and caressed her breasts, closing his hands over their fullness.

Ernestine caught her breath, her gaze wary even as she leaned back in apparent pleasure. "Who were they?" she asked without moving her lips.

"They were killed before they could be interrogated," he lied. They would be dead by now. He bent and kissed her breast, easing her back onto the low couch. The scent of her was distracting, but he was determined to succeed.

If he did, there would be lots of time for this pleasure.

"Their identification was faked," he confided against her skin. "Their palms were wiped and their identification beads overwritten with false identities. That's why he blamed you."

Ernestine caught her breath, then framed his face in her hands. She held his gaze with resolve. "Why are you telling me this?"

"Because Max has to be stopped." He brushed his lips across hers, pinning her down with his weight. She writhed beneath him and he unfastened his trousers, wanting what she was offering. It was exciting to plan a conspiracy while engaging in a seduction, the combination making his pulse pound.

He could get used to scheming with Ernestine.

"His plan for war is wrong. I could replace him, with your help . . ." He saw a flicker in her eyes, and understood intuitively that Ernestine wouldn't agree with him.

So, Max's plan had appealed to her ambitions.

The fetch would have to kill her, after all.

But first, it couldn't hurt to extend the charade.

"I didn't send them," Ernestine said quickly, speaking so loudly that he wondered whether the walls had ears. "I wonder who they might have been . . ." She reached for her palm, but the fetch snatched at her wrists, holding them captive above her head. He leaned his full weight upon her, liking how she was immobilized beneath him. He liked the way she caught her breath in fear.

"I'm offering you a chance to survive," he said, his words tight. She struggled against his grip and he quickly tugged the tie from her robe, knotting it around her wrists so he could hold them down with one hand.

Ernestine glared at him, her eyes cold. "You have no such guarantee to offer," she said softly.

"We could do it . . ."

She laughed then. "Idiot," was all she said before she rolled abruptly.

The fetch fell to the floor, launched from the couch by her sudden move. Before he could stand, Ernestine smashed both fists into his head. He reeled, dizzy with the force of her blow, then stumbled to his knees. Ernestine kicked him in the crotch.

He fell backward, stunned by the pain. She ripped the

tie that bound her wrists loose with her teeth and cast it aside. He lunged for her, but she punched him in the face. Her faceted ring caught him across the cheek, and he grimaced as it cut the skin.

"Only one of us will leave here alive," Ernestine said, looking as if she was enjoying herself. "Traitor!" She was nude, her muscles flexing as she circled him like the warrior she was. Her eyes shone with determination and he recognized that she was also a predator. "I know who I'd bet on."

The fetch roared and launched himself toward her. There was no pretense now, no cause to be gentle. They fought hard. He backhanded Ernestine, sending her into the wall with a crash.

Her lip was cut and she was bleeding, but Ernestine didn't seem to notice. She came directly for him, but he caught her around the waist and made to fling her weight over his shoulder.

She tripped him en route, hooking her ankle behind his knee, and they fell together, landing heavily on the floor. He punched her in the gut, then in the face again. She bit and kicked, driving her elbow into his chest as she tried to evade him. She drove her heel up at his crotch and barely missed.

Meanwhile, he snatched the discarded belt from the floor and looped it around her neck from behind. He hauled Ernestine to a halt, then knotted it tightly.

She squirmed.

She fought.

She flailed. She gurgled and scratched, but he held fast. She kicked, she turned red, she drove elbows and knees into him.

It made no difference. He knew he just had to wait.

It seemed to take an eternity but finally, a flailing

Ernestine fell to her knees. She coughed and dropped to the floor. He didn't trust her a bit, and waited until the breath faded from her.

She was finally still.

She had no pulse and she wasn't breathing. The light of her palm flickered and died. He had a moment to recognize his success, to know that although this part of his plan had failed, he could still win over Blackstone.

No sooner had he confirmed that she had no vital signs, than the worst happened. To the fetch's shock and dismay, Ernestine's palm illuminated. It had no business being activated. It had no spark of power to draw upon, because Ernestine was dead.

Nonetheless, the palm began a countdown from one minute, the seconds counting down steadily.

How could this be?

The palm must have had auxiliary power. The fetch tried to turn it off, tried to smash it, tried to stop it from doing whatever it was doing. The countdown on the palm was relentless. He smashed her hand against the coffee table, but the display didn't even crack. He was desperate to stop whatever subroutine it was running, but nothing made any difference.

He was in a cold sweat by the time the countdown got to thirty seconds and the display abruptly changed. He heard a crash and knew the mercenary shade had kicked in the door. He sensed the mercenary shade behind him, but didn't dare look away. The sex slave mewed in anguish and the fetch heard a scuffle.

He didn't dare blink or avert his gaze. Ernestine's palm sent five messages in rapid succession.

Five messages to persons unknown, at five second intervals.

They must have been preprogrammed, to be sent upon her demise.

Then it played a tune that was all too familiar to him, the tune that always accompanied a display of the logo of the Society of Nuclear Darwinists. A golden orb appeared, split in half and opened to display the Society's logo. Then the logo spun, faded, and disappeared until it was a single small gold dot.

The dot faded to black when the countdown reached 00:00.

Ernestine's palm did nothing more. Who had she sent those messages to? What had been the content? How could he fix his mistake? What kind of worm would he catch if he datashared?

Would it be worth it?

Could he do it in time to save what was left of his own hide?

The fetch stood carefully, backing away from Ernestine's body as his thoughts spun. The mercenary shade threw the corpse of the dead sex slave beside his former mistress, the impact making the fetch jump.

"Five messages too many," that shade said tonelessly.

The fetch realized that he had already been condemned.

Before the fetch could defend himself, he was grabbed and flung through the plate glass window. It shattered all around him, providing no barrier to the strength of the mercenary shade.

It was fifteen stories to the ground, just enough time to see the body of the sex slave being flung after him.

Just enough time to regret his choices.

Just enough time to wish Maximilian Blackstone a long sojourn in hell.

from *The Republican Record*
Monday, September 20, 2100
23:35
download v. 4.6
Special Supplementary Edition

Maximilian Blackstone Found Dead

CHICAGO—In a shocking development, presidential candidate Maximilian Blackstone was found dead this evening. Police have secured the area, but it appears that Mr. Blackstone fell to his death from a fifteenth-story unit in the residential tower upon the grounds of the Institute for Radiation Studies. Another body was recovered from the scene, although officials are not releasing any names.

It is unclear why Mr. Blackstone might have been at this location. He was in Chicago to attend a debate at the Institute, originally planned for Saturday night, but interrupted by the arrest of an armed individual in the auditorium. Police have not confirmed the intended target of that individual, but declare that their investigation will cover all angles. That debate was rescheduled for Thursday, and it appears that Mr. Blackstone chose to remain in town until that point in time. Why he should be at this building when he was a guest at the Intercontinental Hotel is unclear.

The unit with the broken window is the residence of Ernestine Sinclair, past president of the Society of Nuclear Darwinists and daughter of Ernest Sinclair, founder of both the Society and the Institute. In a press conference earlier this evening, police confirmed that Ms. Sinclair had been found dead in her unit, although no further details were provided.

Witnesses at the scene testify that the second victim had

a shade tattoo on his left forearm, and several insisted that they recognized the shade as having been in the employ of Ernestine Sinclair. Students from the Institute speculated openly about the prospect of shades taking vengeance for their situation upon the daughter of the man who created the S.H.A.D.E.

President Van Buren elevated the existing State of Emergency in Chicago to Code Red, urging citizens to be vigilant and to report any suspicious persons to the authorities. He confirmed that this does include shades, especially those apparently unsupervised or unsecured.

Mayor Mike McGuire of Chicago was more forthright, declaring in a press conference that this was the culmination of his fears. "I knew it was only a matter of time before they turned on norms," he said, in response to questions from reporters. "I knew that the citizens in Chicago weren't safe, and that at any moment, even our domestic shades could turn on us. It's clear to me that Ms. Sinclair was killed by her own shade, who was in a jealous rage, and equally clear that none of us can take our own security for granted." He called for residents of Chicago to imprison their domestic shades and defend themselves against the shades that wander the city's streets at night. "There's only one way for this to end," he forecast. "With all of them either dead or back where they belong."

Residents of the city appear to agree with their mayor—sales of weapons, ammunition, and locks have increased dramatically within hours, many stores reporting exhausted inventories.

Maximilian Blackstone was the front-running candidate in the race for the presidency. He served a long and distinguished political career, and was well-respected in New D.C.

President Van Buren has called for two minutes of silence at 11:00 Monday morning to mark the passing of a "noble adversary." Mr. Blackstone's running mate, Thomas O'Donohue, will assume Mr. Blackstone's candidacy and all of his prior commitments for public appearances. Mr. O'Donohue gave his assurance that a new vice-presidential candidate would be added to his party's ticket by Tuesday.

Funeral arrangements for Mr. Blackstone have yet to be confirmed but services are expected to be held this week.

Related Articles in Today's Download:
- Maximilian Blackstone—Obituary of a Visionary
- Thomas O'Donohue—A Dark Horse Takes the Lead
- Tide of Muggings Blamed on Chicago Shades
- What the State of Emergency Means to You
- At the Polls—O'Donohue Rides a New High

Archived Articles of Relevance:
- Violence Interrupts Panel Discussion—Sept. 18, 2100
- Oracle Unlocks Chicago's Netherzones—Feb. 15, 2100

Society of Nuclear Darwinists
Notice to All Shade Hunters
Chicago Vicinity
September 21, 2100; 02:00

Alert—All Shades Considered Dangerous

Please note that all shade hunters, all members of the Society of Nuclear Darwinists, and all students and faculty of the Institute for Radiation Studies are now authorized to shoot to kill any shade within the Chicago area. This is by direct request of the president.

The murder of Ernestine Sinclair, past president of the Society and Nuclear Darwinists of the Seventh Degree, by her companion shade in the security of her residential unit, makes the threat to all of us clear. Chicago's streets must be immediately cleared of unauthorized individuals for the safety and well-being of all citizens of the Republic, and the task of so doing falls to us.

Please review the laze safety protocols if you have not hunted in the past year, and ensure that your weapon has been serviced properly. It is strongly suggested that no hunter travel alone because of the sheer number of shades loose in Chicago—see below to join a nocturnal expedition into the city.

The Society and Institute remind all members that discussing any matter of Society or Institute business with the news media—including this dictate—is expressly forbidden. Defying the code of ethics can lead to the suspension of membership, the confiscation of all items issued by the Institute, including lazes and pseudoskins, and the removal of such individuals from Society property.

Please remember to hunt safely.

- <u>Boundaries of hunting ground defined by regional map</u>
- <u>Laze maintenance and upgrade application</u>
- Join a shade hunter's expedition <u>here</u>

XVI

THEODORA STRAIGHTENED with care. She was in an alley, a space abandoned to trash and debris, a place perfectly suited to the decomposition of the mercenary shade. His fallen body was still smoking from the hit from her laze and her heart was pounding.

He'd come dangerously close to finishing her off, but she'd managed to get him first.

Theodora recognized that she had gotten lucky. She exhaled slowly. It had been a long and convoluted chase, and now it was dark. She checked the charge on her laze and grimaced. She really needed some downtime and some juice. Her temple was still raw and she had a massive headache.

She dumped a bin of trash over the corpse of the mercenary shade, knowing that scavengers would find his body anyway. It was tempting to take his laze, but she knew that possession of it would only condemn her.

Let another volunteer for that fate.

In fact, she didn't even want to touch him. There was something creepy about mercenary shades, with their glazed determination and lack of moral code. He probably had his body booby-trapped so that it would explode if anyone touched it.

But then, hadn't Theodora insisted that she didn't have a

moral code either? Her discussions with Armand made her realize that she had chosen her course.

And that she could chose a different one.

She wanted very much to believe, as he did, in something that trumped cred. Was it possible that she already believed as much? That beneath all of her talk of cred was the truth, the truth that she would do anything for the lost children, independent of how cred figured into the equation?

She checked her palm, and found a suite of new messages, received while she was playing cat-and-mouse with the mercenary shade.

The first was a summons to students of the Institute, forwarded by Shadow.net, announcing the public exhibition of Baruch's surgery.

She considered the news about Baruch and wished there was a way she could intervene. She knew what Armand would do. He would charge back into the Institute, even knowing that the stakes were against him, and try to save his friend.

He would be harvested.

The prospect made Theodora's heart clench and her knees weaken. He would be placed beside Baruch, the size of the sample group doubled by his presence, and be dissected in front of the students of the Institute.

Theodora thought she would be sick.

Then she realized something. Baruch was still captive in the Institute, which meant that the angels hadn't come for him either.

Why not? They were real, Theodora had Armand's pledge of that and the proof of his own scars—never mind his smile and how it resembled that of Armaros, who had disappeared—and she had to believe that they were as ethical as he was.

So, why hadn't they come for their fellows?

The next message initially confused her even more. The obituary for Maximilian Blackstone declared that his body had been discovered in the wrong place. How had his corpse gotten from the Intercontinental Hotel to the residence in the Institute? It was impossible.

Then Theodora remembered a horrible rumor she'd once heard, another way that people could disappear in the Republic. No one talked about it much, but there were wraiths who specialized in finding fetches for famous people. A person who resembled a famous individual in need of a body double could be compensated for the sacrifice of his or her identity. There would be plastic surgery and training, all expenses paid, and every luxury provided.

In exchange for one's own life.

A fetch was a body double, frequently one who wished to obliterate his or her past. Criminals had been known to take on the role of a fetch, and sometimes their buyers insisted upon memory wipes.

Did Blackstone have a fetch?

Maybe more than one?

It would explain his corpse being in the wrong place.

It would also explain why the angels hadn't come for Baruch and Armand. It hadn't been because Armand had defended her. It had been because Baruch and Armand's mission was as yet incomplete—their quest had yet to be fulfilled.

Should she tell Armand about her suspicions? She knew he wouldn't think twice about heading back into the Institute, even if he realized he could be recognized and harvested. Theodora knew better than to anticipate that any effort to save Baruch would go well. She wasn't inclined to let Dr. Cosmopoulos add to his sample group that easily and found herself wanting to defend him as determinedly as she protected the children.

He was probably already on his way to the Institute to save Baruch. If willpower was all a person needed to succeed, she knew that Armand would succeed.

Unfortunately, it wasn't enough.

She had to get to him first. She headed toward the storeroom with purpose, uncharacteristically careless in her haste.

That must have been why she didn't even sense a presence behind her before she was jumped and thrown to the ground.

ARMAND ASSUMED that his captors were shades, although he had little upon which to base that conclusion. Both wore helms with their dark filters down, so he could never have identified them. He simply assumed that any citizen or member of the Society or Institute would have no cause for objection with a shade hunter.

A shade, however, would have a very different perspective.

And the shades of Chicago had been released from the netherzones by the Oracle. At night, they milled in the streets, foraging for food. In the daytime, they disappeared. It made perfect sense to Armand that they would frequent the netherzones of the city, which they must collectively know well.

Armand became aware that there were a number of

figures moving out of the shadows, stepping forward to cluster around him.

"I'm not a hunter," Armand said with care. He was officially a student of the Institute, which likely wouldn't do him any favors in this situation.

"Liar!" hissed a woman from the crowd. Their eyes gleamed as they came closer, their short stature and misshapen figures revealing that they were shades.

The shades who lived in the netherzones of Chicago had found him.

"We saw you with that shade," the man who had challenged Armand said. "What did you do with her, hunter? Did you leave her dead?"

The man behind him poked Armand with the laze. "Did you use her for your pleasure and cast her aside?" he sneered.

"I am not a hunter," Armand said with confidence, looking at each and every one of them. "And she is not a shade but a wraith."

The man before Armand didn't budge, even as his companions stirred at this news. It was clear they knew about the wraiths. "Prove it," he challenged.

Armand considered his opponent. He felt the steady pressure of the laze against his back. He could easily die here, in the shadowed netherzones below the city of Chicago. He had been abandoned by his angelic fellows for his sins, he might never find Theodora again, and he had just about nothing left to lose.

No, he was going to make a difference with his presence. His angelic gift was the ability to see through enchantment— that was how he'd guessed Theodora's truth. He decided to try to lift the scales from the eyes of these shades who had been treated so poorly for so long.

He decided to trust them, to trust that there was yet good within the hearts of men.

He decided to rouse them.

Maybe they could help him to save Baruch.

"I am an angel of the Lord," he said, letting his voice fill with the resonance of conviction. His captor stepped back warily as Armand's voice rose. "I have voluntarily shed my wings to bring light into the darkness, to try to save the world from evil. I was Armaros before my wings were lost, and these are my scars." He peeled off his pseudoskin with a grand gesture, pushing aside the muzzle of the laze.

As he had anticipated, the shade behind him did not have the force of will to fire it. They had been downtrodden for so long, cheated of any inherent initiative, that he guessed they were more likely to follow than to lead.

They could follow him.

"You're one of us," the man behind whispered in amazement. "You've failed the S.H.A.D.E."

"No," Armand said. "Because I've never been evaluated. You all know my secret now. Any one of you could reveal me."

They backed away, cautious and watchful.

"But I don't think you will," Armand said. "I don't think you will because each and every one of you knows what would happen to me."

One shade turned abruptly away, averting her face.

"Maybe the same thing that's happening to my friend, Baruch. He, too, was of the angelic host. Maybe you saw us together when we were at the Nouveau Mont Royal Circus."

"Armaros and Baraqiel," someone whispered and a ripple of excitement passed through the group.

"Why should we believe you?"

"Because I need your help. And in helping me, you will help yourselves. I suspect it is the will of the divine that I find myself amongst you, that the Oracle who set you free is inspired by the touch of angelfire, that here in the darkness is where we can change the future of the Republic."

"If there is a God, why hasn't He helped us?" demanded one short man.

"There is a God, but He helps those who help themselves," Armand said. "You have the power to make change. Come with me and bring down the Institute that shackled you."

"That's a lie," muttered a shade in the crowd.

"But how could we do that?" demanded the man who had initially stopped him.

"You give them the power that they have," Armand said. "Not willingly, but that's still the case."

"It's not up to us to change the rules of society," argued the spokesman. "We have no legal power in the Republic."

"No," Armand interrupted. "I mean a more literal kind of power. The electricity upon which the Institute depends is generated by shades. What if they were untethered? What if they were freed?"

He felt the ripple of surprise pass through the company, then a tentative whiff of hope. He dared to think he could persuade them. "We'd have to work together and coordinate our efforts . . ."

"We don't know the way in," argued one.

"We don't have a map of the interior," declared another and the tentative accord began to collapse.

"I know the way in," Armand argued, feeling success slip from his grasp. "I can find a map and lead you . . ." He felt their hesitation growing by leaps and bounds, then saw a number of them step away from him and his dangerous idea. He wondered how he could persuade them to be bold, they who had never been bold in all their lives. "Aren't you tired of the darkness? Aren't you tired of the hunger?"

"At least we're not dead," countered the spokesman. "At least we're not captured and sedated all over again. What you suggest is suicide. Not only will we be recaptured, but they'll punish us for daring to challenge them."

The other shades nodded and murmured agreement. "It's better this way, the best we can hope for," insisted one, and they all nodded again.

"You must rise up," Armand insisted, but he knew they had turned against him.

"He's dangerous," said the one behind him. "Let him go."

"No," the leader said with resolve. "He'll only betray us. He's one of them, after all." The muzzle of that laze prodded more deeply into Armand's back. "He stays with us."

He thought to fight them, to fight for his freedom, but didn't want to hurt them. He had a feeling they wouldn't strike back.

He still believed he could persuade them, still was convinced of the merit of his idea. And the best way to present his case was to remain in their company.

Armand went peacefully, his thoughts whirling with possibilities. Somehow, he would convince them.

He had to convince them.

He only hoped he could do it in time.

THEODORA STRUGGLED against her assailant, realizing quickly that he didn't intend to kill her.

He was furious and his every gesture showed as much, but he held his punches. She would have bruises, but nothing would be broken.

She had a moment to marvel at this, to wonder at the reason, then he made a familiar incoherent sound of frustration.

"Ferris!" she said with pleasure and squirmed from his grip.

He wore the patched pseudoskin she had found for him, and his hair had grown over his eyes again. He was taller than he had been just the previous February and was filling out through the shoulders. He had refused to let her replace the palm that had been destroyed before his becoming a wraith, and the skin on his left hand had healed into a scarred mess. The surgeon would have fixed that too.

If she'd earned the cred.

His eyes were flashing with anger and she was glad he couldn't speak. Whatever he might say wouldn't be gentle on the ears. He shook his finger at her and snarled.

"What did I do?"

He pursed his lips into a kiss and touched his forehead with one finger, his gaze filled with accusation. *Delilah,* he mouthed, as if she could have had any doubt.

Theodora exhaled. "I didn't do it, though."

Ferris snorted. It was clear he knew that hadn't been her choice. He lifted his hands, mouthed *why?* then folded his arms across his chest in anticipation of her response.

He wouldn't be easy to convince.

"I took the job for you," she admitted.

Ferris glared at her.

"For the surgeon's fee, to fix your throat."

Ferris spat into the dirt and shook his head.

"He wants a lot of cred, Ferris, and the bounty was high."

The explanation sounded thin, even to Theodora's ears. She had been listening to Armand too much. "Don't you understand? You would have been healed. You could have lived as a norm! They could never have taken you again!"

Ferris shook his head repeatedly, a small gesture filled with revulsion. He spread his hands in a cutting motion.

"I was trying to give you your dream!"

Ferris shook his head again, his expression changing to frustration. He reached for her palm, and tapped in the words.

Too high a price.

"Even for freedom? Even for life as a norm?"

He didn't hesitate. He nodded once, decisive, his fingertips touching his chest. His gaze then fixed upon her, searched hers. Whatever he saw seemed to disappoint him, but he reached for her palm again.

She let him explain himself. She owed him that.

Because I love her—the world is better with her alive.

Theodora read the words and felt an intuitive understanding of them. She saw her mother's choice in his logic. In fact, she saw her own choice to lead the shade away from Armand.

So this was love.

She met Ferris's gaze ruefully, understanding right to her marrow. "No matter what happens to you?"

Ferris nodded.

"And you would never choose your welfare over hers?"

He shook his head.

"But she loves Rafe, her consort. She's bearing his child. You can't really believe that you have a chance to be with her?"

Ferris shook his head sadly. He typed quickly again.

But she is happy. That's enough.

Theodora stared at the words and her vision blurred with tears. "I'm sorry, Ferris. I didn't really understand."

Not until Armand.

Ferris snorted, making a scoffing sound, then poked a finger at her patched pseudoskin. His gaze was challenging.

Okay, so she did understand something about personal sacrifice. She was going to argue with him that she'd never loved one individual enough to pay any price for that person's welfare, but the words stuck in her throat.

She would have saved her mother if she had ever had the chance.

She would have let herself be taken if it would ensure the safety of her children.

She knew with sudden vehemence that there was one person whose welfare she was determined to protect.

Armand.

She wanted him to have what he wanted. She wanted him to have the chance to return to the angels, which meant she would complete his mission for him.

Even without there being any cred involved.

Even though she already had her laze back.

She'd called it "loyalty" for years, "duty" and "integrity" even, but it was love that motivated her.

Perhaps it was what motivated everyone.

She looked at Ferris. "You have to know that the bounty

on the Oracle remains unclaimed. Someone may finish what I intended to do."

Ferris rolled his eyes. He crossed his arms, indicating diagonal lines on his back, then mimicked firing lazes with both hands simultaneously.

"Right. She has Rafe, the Consort, to defend her."

Ferris gave her a confident thumbs-up. He feigned a man pulling a laze very quickly and aiming it directly at Theodora. His eyes widened as he moved his finger, as if pulling the trigger.

Theodora put a hand on her hip, guessing his implication. "You think he would have finished me off, instead of me killing the Oracle."

Ferris shrugged.

Theodora had to admit that there was justification in his expectation. "You're right, he's fast." She scanned the street, intending to seek out Armand, but Ferris caught her elbow.

He seized her left hand, tapping quickly.

**I would miss you. Don't take such chances,
not for me. Not for any of us.**

Theodora stared at the words gleaming on her palm display and a lump rose in her throat. She glanced up—how had Ferris grown so tall so fast?—and found tears shining in his own eyes.

I love you too, he mouthed.

"Not so much as you love her," Theodora teased and he shook his head quickly, the back of his neck turning ruddy.

"More like a big sister," she guessed, and he nodded with enthusiasm. "Well, you're the brother I never had, Ferris. Don't you go taking foolish chances either."

He grinned and caught her close, awkward in hugging her although he was sincere. When they parted, he stared at the ground and shuffled his feet, even more uncomfortable with the warmth between them.

Theodora, in contrast, felt as if something had thawed within her. Not by Ferris, he had simply accelerated the process.

No, it was Armand who had changed her.

"There's someone I want you to meet," Theodora said impulsively, and reached out her hand to Ferris. "Come with me."

THEODORA AND Ferris moved quickly as the stars began to come out. That strange silvery fog was gathering in the streets again, and just the sight of it made her shiver. The city seemed both deserted and alive.

Theodora had decided to return to the shop with the storeroom, in the faint hope that Armand would still be there. If not, she might be able to follow his trail. If that failed, well, she would guess that he had headed toward the Institute.

She saw shadows moving in the destroyed gates of the netherzones, shadows that became more numerous as the sky became darker. She heard them whispering and tried not to look. She guessed that these were the released shades of the city, and assumed that they were coming out of their hiding places to forage.

Ferris stared openly, his brow furrowed, then hastened after Theodora.

Although she didn't believe they would hurt her, she didn't want to take a chance. She certainly didn't want to kill any of them, even in self-defense. She kept her head down and hurried, disliking that she would have to go all the way back to the shop with the storeroom. She simply couldn't risk a plunge into the netherzones when the shades were loitering at the portals.

She was a block from the shop when she heard the sound of motorcycles.

Six of them.

Racing toward her.

She heard laughter as well, the raucous laughter of a man, laughter that seemed to come from everywhere and nowhere. Laughter that made the hair stand up on the back of her neck. Ferris inhaled sharply.

They both jumped at the sudden fire of a laze shot.

They dove in unison into the shadows of a doorway, hunkering down behind a pair of trash cans. The door immediately behind them had a window in it, but curtains were hastily drawn across the glass. She heard a bolt sink home in the same moment that the motorcycles roared around the corner. Ferris kept his hand on her shoulder, as if fearing that she would leap out and challenge the riders.

The motorcycles were ridden by helmeted men in pseudo-skins, although Theodora didn't think they were police officers. They had no insignia, and their lazes were very high-end.

Theodora had a very bad feeling. She hunkered down in her hiding spot, and tried to be invisible. She felt Ferris begin to shake.

Meanwhile a shade peeked out of a netherzone portal on the opposite side of the street. That shade froze in alarm at the sight of the motorcycles.

The men shouted at the sight and convened on the poor creature, circling their bikes around it. Theodora tapped commands into her palm and raised it to make a vid. Ferris shook his head, but she ignored him. If these were troublemakers, sick norms who would torment the shade but leave it alive, then she would ensure that they were punished.

She never liked humans who found that amusing, and the vid would give her the chance to report them to the authorities.

But after they taunted the shade verbally, one fired his laze at the shade's leg. Theodora was shocked. The shade fell, screamed, and all six fired their lazes simultaneously.

Theodora was appalled. Ferris locked his hands on her shoulders and held her down, evidently guessing her inclination.

They fried the shade to dust in an instant, right before Theodora's eyes.

"It came out of there," one said, gesturing to the netherzone access.

"There'll be more," agreed another.

Then two left their bikes and dove into the darkness of the netherzone access. There was the sound and flash of laze fire, then they dragged four bodies back into the street, one shade pleading for clemency even as his arm bled.

One man shot the coherent shade in the head, silencing him forever. The others were executed in quick succession. There was blood all over the street, smoke in the air, and a terrible stench.

And a watchful silence. Theodora couldn't believe that anyone who had witnessed this violence wouldn't be appalled.

The men left the corpses smoking in the middle of the street and got back on their bikes, firing their lazes randomly at shadows. Then they roared down the street, leaving a bloody testament to their firepower and their viciousness.

Theodora found herself shaking, not just at the violence she'd witnessed but at the injustice of their executing unarmed shades.

Her left hand was trembling, but she had the whole sequence on vid. She tapped her palm, accessing Shadow.net, and tried to decide who best to receive this news.

The police might be corrupt.

The Society had issued the command to execute shades.

The president would probably be glad to have the shades eliminated.

The Oracle might not be able to do much to intervene.

Ferris reached over her shoulder, sought an index, then chose Reverend Billie Joe Estevez.

Theodora looked his way in surprise.

He nodded with conviction and pointed at the palm.

The reverend also bore the mark of the angels' kiss and had defended the Oracle before everyone. She made a vidcast every single day of the year. She was the most watched videvangelist in the Republic and Theodora chose to believe that this segment of vid would outrage the reverend.

As a bonus, the reverend was due in Chicago for the rescheduled debate. She might even be in Chicago now.

Theodora sent the vid, without any datatrail.

XVII

THE SHADES of Chicago had claimed an area of the netherzones that was reasonably easy to defend. There were tracks on the ground and low tunnels, tunnels in which Armand could barely stand upright.

Their leader called himself Dennis, defiance in his declaration. Armand called him by his chosen name without discussion, never asking after his number, and knew that the leader was pleased.

Dennis explained to Armand that there had once been a scaled-down train system beneath the city, one that delivered freight to businesses. The trains had been coal-operated, and though they were long gone, the tunnels still existed.

The only trains that still ran were those of the Society of Nuclear Darwinists, the freight trains that brought harvested shades to the Institute. The freed shades avoided those tracks and didn't speak of those trains, although Armand felt the vibration of one in the tracks in the middle of that first night.

The shades did, too. He could tell by their watchfulness and discomfiture.

He was cooperative and easygoing with his captors, preferring to win their trust than frighten them. When they brought their foraged food to share, he took only a small portion, telling them that he had no need of more.

The shades were ravenous, he could see as much. In the

flickering candlelight of their sanctuary, he could see their hollowed cheeks. They had become gaunt in exile, shadows of their former selves. He doubted that many of them had been that robust or well-nourished in the first place, and feared for their future, without enough food.

But there was determination in their eyes, and more than half of them sported a temporary tattoo on the forehead, one meant to replicate the port wine mark of the angelic kiss on the forehead of the Oracle. They were defiant and even those who were slow of intellect had a spark in their eyes.

They weren't sedated anymore, and they never wanted to be again.

Dennis kept a wary distance, perhaps sensing that Armand could win the support of his followers. Armand was careful to not challenge him or his edicts. Still Dennis lounged a good distance away, clearly monitoring Armand but not coming too close.

Maybe not close enough to be drawn into Armand's plan.

The shades' palms were primitive and not built to receive or send messages. Armand quickly learned that he could attract an avid group by using his own palm, particularly if he played vid of the Oracle. They watched the archive of her appearance in Chicago a dozen times and would have watched it a dozen more if Armand hadn't insisted upon moving on.

He showed them the images of himself and Baruch at the Nouveau Mont Royal Circus. He realized that many of them were not literate either, so he read them the news dispatches. The group clustered around him grew larger with every item Armand shared, and even those who didn't come close to him were listening.

Dennis eased closer, finally joining the perimeter of the group.

The laboratory protocol for Baruch sent a shudder of horror through them and Armand himself was shocked at the edict he received from the Institute.

"You're one of them," Dennis insisted. "You're associated with the Institute. That's why you received that." He pushed to his feet and drew the laze he'd confiscated from Armand. His voice rose. "Is that why you came to our sanctuary? To kill us here?"

The shades rose as one and moved away from Armand, their eyes wide with apprehension.

"I am not one of them," Armand explained again. "I joined the Institute in order to get inside. Baruch and I both did, in order to fulfill our mission. If I had ever been evaluated, I would be found a shade, like all of you."

"We could turn you in," Dennis said softly. "We could trade your freedom for ours. If they're looking for potential angels, for shades with those scars, we could make a deal."

"Do you really believe they will negotiate with you?" Armand asked. "This edict gives hunters the right to execute you in the streets."

"It's a lie," Dennis insisted, turning to pace the area. His paranoia was well-deserved, in Armand's opinion, and he wondered what deficit had prompted Dennis's assessment as a shade. "We've only heard about it from you. It's a trick, meant to disarm us. We'll know the truth when the others come back."

"We need to attack the Institute sooner rather than later," Armand argued.

"If the others don't come back, there will be fewer of us,"

a woman argued who had been sitting close by Armand's side.

"You don't know the truth!" Dennis cried in frustration.

"But I do," a woman said with confidence.

The leader spun and Armand looked up, recognizing that voice. He got to his feet in anticipation, smiling broadly in his relief, his heart thumping.

Theodora.

She'd found him.

His expression made the shades begin to whisper, and one bold woman reached to touch his lips. Had they never seen anyone smile? Armand was shaken by the prospect.

Theodora stepped out of the shadows then, her left hand held high. She looked as determined as ever and didn't appear to be injured.

Armand doubted that the same could be said for the mercenary shade who had pursued her. She'd won. He grinned openly, not caring how she had found him.

A tall, slender man followed her, a young boy really. His dark hair hung in his eyes and Armand recognized him from the image on Theodora's palm.

Ferris.

"The executions have begun," she said to Dennis. "Look."

He hesitated. "You're the captive shade he took to the Intercontinental. Tell me first how he betrayed you."

Theodora smiled. "I'm no shade, although I could have been. I'm a wraith. And Armand never betrayed me. On the contrary, he risked his own life to save mine." She stretched out her hand, the display vivid. "Look what just happened in the streets above."

Ferris pointed, making a distressed noise in his throat.

Their manner, or perhaps Ferris's obvious defect, persuaded Dennis to look. Whatever Theodora showed the leader of these shades horrified him completely. Dennis stepped back in shock, his throat working in dismay.

Theodora tapped her palm and Armand's palm pinged. He opened the message from her and played the vid on his own palm. The shades in his vicinity clustered closely around him.

The execution was horrific and he wished belatedly that he could have protected them from that truth.

The shades around him became flustered, murmuring to each other in agitation. One insisted that he show it again, and the others concurred. Armand complied, impressed by their fortitude. The vid was time-stamped just hours before and he knew that Theodora hadn't manipulated the images.

"I know that corner," Dennis said. "I recognize it."

"Lee and Louisa," one shade murmured.

"Hugh and Stephen," added another.

A female shade began to cry in ragged sobs, the others gathering close to console her.

Dennis looked from the shades to Theodora. His gaze lingered on Ferris, whose discomfiture seemed to add credence to the vid evidence. "What do we have to do to survive?" he asked.

"Send a runner and confirm the truth, if you must," Theodora said. "We'll stay here and await your decision."

"I believe you," Dennis said with resolve, then indicated Armand. "He says we need to invade the Institute."

Theodora's mouth rounded in surprise.

"I have a plan," Armand said, stepping forward to persuade her. "I thought we could invade the Institute and unshackle the shades who give it electricity. In the power failure, the live wire would fail. We could save Baruch and liberate the captive shades, while undermining the influence of the Institute and Society."

"Brilliant!" Theodora breathed.

And the light in her eyes was all the reward Armand needed.

ARMAND'S PLAN *was* brilliant.

Theodora had followed the trail from the storehouse easily, probably because the group of shades hadn't made any attempt to disguise it. The dust had been stirred with the passing of many people—at first, she'd thought that Armand's path had been disguised by a moving company. There was no possibility of discerning a single trail, and she had followed the group in the hope that they might know where Armand was.

Instead, she found him in the company of shades of the city of Chicago. She and Ferris had watched from the shadowed tunnel for a while, drinking in the sight of him. He was displaying vid on his palm for a fascinated group, and reading news items aloud to them. They were hungry for information, and gathered close.

She noted that they weren't afraid of him, and knew that their senses were keen in that regard. He was kind and gentle, as she had witnessed before, never condescending, and they responded to him readily. He earned trust from even these wounded souls.

All the same, they were a skittish bunch and she knew that revealing herself would frighten them. One man paced on the opposite side of the large room, the way he cast glances at Armand revealing his disapproval. Theodora guessed that he was the one in need of persuasion. Her gaze kept trailing

back to Armand, her heart swelling at his patience and kindness.

Ferris tapped her arm to get her attention. He indicated
Armand, then tapped Theodora's chest with a fingertip, his
gaze knowing.

He was right.

She did love Armand. Theodora nodded and blushed a
little.

Caught, she mouthed to Ferris and he grinned.

In that instant, she knew what she would do. She wasn't
one to have high expectations for herself or her own future.
She didn't believe that people would give much to her, for
her own sake, and she knew that Armand disagreed with
what had been her philosophy. He might have judged her
and found her wanting.

What truly mattered was for him to exist, as he wanted
to exist. Just knowing that he was happy and had achieved
his dream would give Theodora hope and strength.

She knew then that she would personally hunt down
Maximilian Blackstone. She would unravel the truth of his
fetches and his so-called death, and she would fulfill Armand's mission. She wouldn't tell him of her suspicions,
she wouldn't give him false hope, but she would do everything possible to ensure that he gained the result he wanted.

And maybe, just maybe, it would be enough.

Theodora chose her moment and revealed herself, de-
lighting in the way Armand's eyes lit at the sight of her.
The truth of his thoughts was in his eyes, once again. His
relief made her own heart skip a beat, but there was work
to be done before they could celebrate.

It was only after the leader had dispatched a runner to the
site of the slaughter that she dared to go to Armand's side.

"You saw it," he murmured, his eyes filled with concern.

"They really are going to hunt the shades to extinction," she said. "No game. It was vicious."

Shades hovering close looked between the two of them, following the conversation with dismay. Armand turned to one woman who had been sitting beside him.

"It's going to end soon, one way or the other," he told her gently and she shivered.

"But going into the Institute?" she asked, her voice tremulous. "No one ever comes back out of there."

"Maybe it's time for that to change," Armand suggested. "Maybe we're on the cusp of a new beginning, one that you can help to create." The shades murmured among themselves, moving restlessly in the darkness. Theodora could feel their anxiety rising.

By the time the runner returned, they were unable to remain still.

"It's true!" he cried. "And not just there. All over the city. I saw the motorcycles and I saw the bodies." He took a shuddering breath. "It'll be over in days." The shades fluttered in fear and Theodora worried they were incapable of rising to this challenge.

"You see, then? We have no real choice," said the leader, his voice echoing with resolve. "We'll be dead in days either way. I'm not going to die in a corner, stalked by hunters. I'm in."

"Rise up!" cried the runner. "The Oracle set us free for a reason."

"To the Institute!" shouted the leader. "To do as much damage as we can."

"Yes!" Armand agreed. "That's what we have to do. We can destroy it. We can make change in the world."

"To change," cried the leader, crossing the space to shake hands with Armand. Ferris applauded, his show of resolve seeming to infect the other shades.

"To the Institute," Armand said, clasping his hand and holding it high. The two stood together, their fists locked together, one tall and robust, the other smaller and sinewy. There was no difference in their determination, though, and Theodora thought she could see the force of Armand's will giving strength to the leader of the shades.

"To the Institute!" echoed the shades, their voices growing stronger as they repeated the chant. "To the Institute!"

Armand turned that glittering gaze on Theodora and smiled. "Theodora will create the plan."

That was something she could do.

THE REVEREND Billie Joe Estevez sat in her penthouse suite at the Intercontinental Hotel in Chicago and peered at her palm.

She was confounded by the file she had received, purportedly from Ernestine Sinclair. The file clearly illustrated that Maximilian Blackstone had consistently not only fathered illegitimate children, but had consigned those children to the netherzones.

With bought negative S.H.A.D.E. scores.

It was horrifying news, but irrelevant in a sense. After all, according to the news update, both Max and Ernestine were now dead. What had been Ernestine's point? There was nothing to be gained in making accusations against a dead man, and evidently no trail to follow in finding these falsely condemned children.

Just thinking about them and the lives they must have

lived made the reverend feel ill. She was not a woman to sit by—but what could she do?

She considered the message again, noting once more that it had been sent to both her and Lilia Desjardins. Her own subsequent messages to Lilia had been returned as undeliverable, which made no sense at all. Had Lilia died? It was impossible to imagine.

It was easy to imagine that Lilia, the most rebellious member (well, *former* member) of the Society of Nuclear Darwinists, would know what to do with this information.

As the reverend did not.

Her thoughts turned to the Oracle, who she expected to arrive in the next day or so, and she reviewed the plea she planned to make to Delilah. Only the Oracle could summon the loosed shades to order, although so far she had refused to do so.

The reverend froze suddenly, recalling a critical detail. Delilah was the daughter of Lilia Desjardins. She had been condemned as a shade at birth, and Lilia had never named the father of her child.

Could there be another—more personal—reason for Ernestine to send the file to Lilia?

The reverend remembered then the shock Max had shown the previous February, when Delilah had revealed herself, right here in Chicago. She pulled up the vid of that amazing night and replayed it, pausing and replaying a segment over and over again.

Yes. There it was. Max's exclamation when Delilah appeared.

He had called her "Lilia."

As if he had seen a ghost.

The reverend bent to her task, then, hunting the details

of Delilah's birth. She found the birth record for Lilia's only child, accessed the hospital records, pinged an employee, and asked a favor "for the sake of the Republic." She drummed her fingers while awaiting clearance to view the security vid from that fateful night.

In half an hour, she had grainy vid of a man who might have been Maximilian Blackstone arriving at the hospital.

With a man identified as a shade hunter.

It appeared that he'd decided the child's fate, even before he had seen her.

It fit the pattern of Ernestine's file.

It was dreadful to imagine that this man could have become president of the Republic, that he had dared to suggest that he was on the side of shades and arguing for their emancipation. The reverend was glad to know that it had all been a lie, and wondered what his true objectives had been.

And again, she wondered why Ernestine thought it mattered now.

"Excuse me, Reverend," said her aide from the doorway, and the reverend started from her thoughts.

She turned with a smile. "Yes, Michael?"

"I didn't mean to disturb you."

"It's fine. I was considering a problem that isn't easily solved."

"You will find the solution, Reverend. You always do."

"Thank you. I appreciate your confidence."

"There is a man who wishes to see you, Reverend."

The reverend sighed, for there were always enthusiasts seeking an audience with her.

"I tried to turn him away, but there is a desperation about him." Michael frowned and glanced back toward the foyer. He had good instincts about people, and the reverend was always interested in his impressions. He leaned closer, lowering his voice. "He says he's Maximilian Blackstone, that someone is trying to kill him."

"According to the news, that person has succeeded."

"He says not. He's asking for your protection."

The reverend considered her most astute aide. "You think he's telling the truth."

"I do. He says the dead man was his fetch, that he was the second fetch to be killed yesterday." Michael frowned as the reverend considered this information. "If he is telling the truth and we turn him away, it'll be his death sentence."

The reverend pushed to her feet and paced. "I appreciate your concern, Michael. He can stay until tomorrow night. He can accompany us to the debate and declare himself there. The Republic will defend him after such a public pronouncement."

"And maybe the death of the fetch will have been investigated by then," Michael agreed. "Although the rumor is that the domestic shade was responsible."

The reverend frowned. "Do you not think that unlikely, Michael? That one trained to be meek would rise up in violence?"

"Well, he might perceive her favor of another to be an injustice . . ."

"Michael, shades live with injustice every day of their lives. I cannot believe that one would finally turn, especially given the fact that domestics are often sedated."

Michael watched her, understanding dawning in his eyes. "I understand, Reverend. My experience of shades is limited to the Oracle, and she is not deferential."

The reverend smiled. "No, not in the least. But that is the angelfire that animates her. She is unique."

"Yes, Reverend."

"Tell Max that he can stay, as I've specified. I will not see him, though."

"Reverend?"

"That is all, Michael." The aide left immediately and the reverend heard voices from the foyer. She heard Max's expression of gratitude and closed her eyes against it, hearing now the tinge of insincerity in his voice.

The reverend knew that her disgust would show in a personal interview, and her opportunity to reveal Max in all his truth might be lost. No, it was important that Max have the chance to condemn himself publicly, before witnesses.

Because truly, if he had ever intended to defend shades, he would have started decades ago.

With his own children.

He was a liar.

But as Max had sowed, so should he reap.

Reverend Billie Joe Estevez would ensure as much. She knew exactly what to do with this file. She looked out at the city of Chicago and saw fires lit in the streets. Her eyes narrowed and she feared for the future.

But still she wondered what had happened to Max's children. Was there any chance they could be found and saved?

The reverend intended to try.

ARMAND TRUSTED Theodora, knew her instincts were more refined than his own. She spent hours reviewing her maps of the Institute and its schedules, then drilled the shades on her plan of attack. He was surprised, in fact, that she endorsed his plan at all, given her previous aversion to excessive risk.

And going into the Institute itself, again, could only be seen as risky. He decided that her compliance was a mark of her dawning trust in him, and their developing rhythm as a team.

Given that, he was prepared to proceed however she decreed. He instinctively liked Ferris, and respected that the boy had come after Theodora. There was an ease between them, as siblings often shared, and he saw the depth of their mutual affection. Something had softened in Theodora's manner, as well, and Armand wondered whether Ferris had challenged her plan.

She put him in charge of the shades and the debilitation of the power plant. Dennis had ceded to that instruction, perhaps sensing as Armand did that Ferris was accustomed to making choices on his feet. He evidently had some experience inside the Institute and that gave him another advantage.

Theodora insisted upon waiting until the next night. Although Armand chafed at the delay, he knew that a well-formed plan took time. He also knew that he needed some rest.

They all did.

Armand checked the news on his palm and saw that the president had visited the Oracle with a plea that she instruct the shades of Chicago to surrender to the authorities. The Oracle had refused, and was under house arrest.

The shades didn't take that news well.

Neither did the citizens of the Republic. Van Buren's popularity rankings had fallen even lower. It seemed that no one was happy, either with the status quo or a return to how things have been for decades in the Republic.

Armand's uncertainties multiplied as the night passed.

How was he going to survive in this place, now that the angels had abandoned him and Baruch? In what condition would he find Baruch? How would they make their way together? They would certainly be considered to be shades, but Armand no longer had any ability to link to Tupperman. Could they return to New Gotham and find that liaison? It seemed like a long and treacherous journey for them to undertake, especially as Baruch might be injured.

And what would they do after that? How would they earn money? How would they live in the mortal realm? His questions seemed overwhelming in his comparative solitude. He sat and tried to educate himself even more about the world that was destined to be his own.

Armand was following a link to a position paper by Thomas O'Donohue when Theodora suddenly dropped down beside him.

"Here," she said. She looked tired, but determined. She had been counseling shades for hours, instructing them on their role in the attack, and reviewing the details over and over again. As Armand might have expected, she was all brisk efficiency.

It occurred to him that this kind of strategic thinking was what she did best—and there was a gleam in her eye that revealed how much she enjoyed it.

What did he do well? He couldn't think of a thing.

All the same, he was pleased to be in her proximity again. He smiled at her, not troubling to hide his pleasure, and she flushed.

When she sat down beside him, he deliberately bumped her leg with his own. Theodora caught her breath but didn't move away. "Give me your palm and pick a name."

"I don't understand." Armand put his hand in hers just

the same. She flicked a glance at him, as if surprised by his trust, and he smiled.

She flushed more deeply and frowned, looking disheveled and sexy, but focused on his palm. "You can't cross the threshold of the Institute with your current identification," she said sternly. "It'll launch every alarm they've got."

"Do you think they're looking for me?"

She froze for a telling moment and didn't look up. "Guess," she said crisply and Armand sensed that she was hiding something from him.

"What do you know?"

"Nothing," she said and he guessed that she lied. "Pick a name."

He pulled his hand from hers and folded his arms across his chest. "Not until you tell me what you've learned."

"We don't have time for games!"

"It's not a game. The stakes are too high for that."

Theodora looked around the cavern of the shade's sanctuary. The shades went quietly about their business, murmuring to each other in corners, eating and sleeping.

"Look, I'll make you a deal," she said abruptly. "Pick a name, then I'll share a secret with you."

Armand sobered as he watched her. Something was wrong. Something so wrong that she was afraid to tell him about it. He respected her instincts and feared the root of them. "Can I pick which secret?" he said, trying to keep his tone light.

"I don't have that many."

Armand laughed. Theodora glanced at him in surprise and the shades started, their gazes fixed upon him. "You have enough secrets for all of us," he declared, then bent down so that their noses were almost touching. He liked the way her eyes widened, the evidence of her awareness of him that she couldn't hide. "Tell me where the children are."

Theodora paled. "I can't do that."

"Then I don't need to pick a name." Armand watched her struggle with this, her agitation more than enough evidence that the threat she perceived was dire.

"It would be a breach of their confidence," she said, her words falling fast. "I've protected them for years, I can't just risk their safety like that."

"Then why did you even tell me about them?" Armand asked.

"It was a mistake. . . ."

"You don't make those kinds of mistakes, Theodora," he insisted, noting how she avoided his gaze. "It was a choice, and I believe you would have told me more. What's changed?"

"Nothing!" She was flustered as he had never seen her, and that told Armand more than her words.

He decided to call her bluff.

"Then you don't trust me. And if you don't trust me, then I shouldn't trust you." Armand didn't believe that anymore. Whatever she wasn't telling him held the threat to the children. He continued though, deliberately provoking her. "I certainly shouldn't trust you to reprogram my palm in a way that I can't."

She stared at him for a long moment, then looked away, blinking rapidly. "Just let me make you safe."

"None of us are safe. You taught me that."

She swallowed, torn between her notions of what was right.

"Tell me, then, who they really are," Armand invited softly. "There's a pattern, isn't there? They have something in common."

"Not all of them. Initially, they did. Initially, I searched for the children who were like me." She looked up at him then, her eyes dark. "Originally, I looked for my brothers and sisters."

Armand didn't say anything. He just waited and listened.

"You wanted to know why I hated Maximilian Blackstone. You wanted to know what my mother had to do with it. Well, he was my father, and he bought a false S.H.A.D.E. to make me, his illegitimate child, disappear forever. My mother took me to the wraiths instead."

"And then she was killed."

"Right. But there was no datatrail of her involvement with my father, with his link to me or my existence. Just the way he wanted it." Theodora sighed. "The thing is, I wasn't the only one. Once I heard that rumor, I had to find out for sure. I used the networks of the wraiths and I found more. I started to track them down, break them free if necessary, and give them the sanctuary they deserve. Along the way, some others joined us, sometimes by choice, sometimes by necessity."

"And you take this work to care for them?"

"It pays well. In fact, it pays better than anything else I could possibly do." She looked up at him with a smile, her eyes filled with tears. "Once upon a time, I didn't have a lot to lose. I could afford to take the risk. Now, I'm good, maybe the best, and my pay is commensurate."

"But what is the *cost,* Theodora?"

She exhaled shakily and averted her gaze from his. "It's easier when the target isn't the most morally upstanding citizen who ever lived. I do search their histories, looking for some justification. Sometimes there isn't one."

"Who were you targeting on Saturday?"

"The Oracle. It was about the cred, Armand, but I don't

know." She looked up at him again. "I don't know whether I could have really done it, even for the children, if Baruch hadn't interrupted me."

Armand took her hand in his. "One of his titles is the lightning of God."

Theodora laughed, the first time Armand had ever heard her do so. "Maybe he was the proverbial bolt from the blue."

Armand kissed her knuckles. "Maybe he was calling you back to what you know is right."

She looked at their entwined hands, then up at him. She seemed shy to him then, cautious as she seldom was. "I'm glad, you know. I'm glad I was interrupted." She sighed and her gaze followed Ferris. "You were right about him, you know. He hunted me down to chew me out, once he figured out what I'd tried to do." Her voice softened. "I'd never understood that just knowing that someone was happy could be enough." She looked up at him, her eyes shining. "You were right and I was wrong."

It was a confession he'd never expected to hear from her, an acknowledgement that touched his heart. Maybe he did have a role to play in this sphere, if he could change the thinking of a woman like Theodora who had endured so much.

Maybe there was a reason for hope.

They smiled at each other for a long warm moment, then Armand bent to kiss Theodora. His mouth closed over hers and she reached to meet him halfway, her hand falling on his shoulder. His chest tightened with the conviction that their desire was as one, that they each wanted the same thing and weren't afraid to show it.

It was a connection far less than the one he had once known, but it was potent all the same. Armand deepened his kiss, pulling her closer, wanting as he hadn't wanted before.

XVIII

THEODORA WAS left dizzy by Armand's kiss, both by the passion and demand of his touch. Something had changed. She tasted urgency in his embrace as well as an unexpected joy. She could have let him seduce her again, but there were shades all around them.

And she still had preparations to make.

It was his gentleness, she decided, his compassion and understanding. It wound beneath her own armor, compromising her conviction that the world was devoid of good, awakening a part of her that had been slumbering for too long.

Armand challenged her surety that every man worked only for his own benefit. He compromised her conviction that people had to act that way. He made her believe that she could provide an impetus to change. She had a heady sense of what they two might accomplish together, one that was shattered by her surety that he would soon be gone.

Because she would ensure he had the choice.

The realization made her pull him closer. Fear that he could be claimed by a bounty hunter, that there was no guarantee of how much time he would be in her presence, had her tongue dancing with his and her fingers locked around his neck.

Someone gave a wolf whistle and Armand lifted his

head with obvious reluctance, that warm smile lighting his features. He didn't release her though, but pulled her into his lap. "I suppose we should be more subtle," he said, then ran his fingers through the chopped remains of her hair.

Theodora shivered with delight, but claimed his left hand. "Pick a name," she said sternly, his grin undermining her attempt to focus on what remained to be done.

"I can't," he said, his eyes dancing. "Any name I pick will give us away." He shrugged and smiled. "Baruch Harding. Theodore Darkson. Maximilian Blackstone the second."

"Make that the fourth," Theodora muttered and shook her head when he gave her a puzzled glance. She wasn't going to tell him about her theory of Max's survival, not until she had proof. She might be wrong, and she didn't want to give him false hope of his possible return to the company of the angels. "All right, I'll pick a name for you. Henry Mac-Dougall."

"I don't like it."

"You had your chance to pick another. You can ditch it once we get out of there," Theodora said. "Just let me make you safe."

Armand touched her chin with a fingertip, compelling her to meet his gaze. "You can't make me safe," he said softly. "Just as I can't make you safe." The low thrum of his voice brought a lump to Theodora's throat. "I thought that was part of what you thrived on—risk. I thought that made you feel more alive."

"It does," she said briskly, realizing that her perspective had clarified. She was fine with taking risks herself, not with seeing those she cared about take risks. "Safer will have to do, then."

"Theodora," he said quietly, his gaze piercing. "What's the matter? What did you learn?"

"Nothing," she lied again. "I just don't like that you'll be back in the Institute."

It was only half of the truth and she guessed that Armand saw as much. He seemed to also understand that she wouldn't confide in him any more, even if he pressured her. "I don't like that you'll be there, either."

She swallowed and tapped at his palm. Then she squared her shoulders and reached for his neck. "Bend down. I need to reprogram your identification bead."

He let her concentrate on her task, but didn't disguise the fact that he was watching her. She didn't look him in the eye, but she slowly began to blush, the tinge of red rising from her throat over her cheeks.

"Don't do that," she whispered.

Armand slid his hand around her waist. "Do what?"

"Watch me like that," she said.

Armand only smiled, a slow sensuous smile that dismissed Theodora's reservations. It was a smile that made her remember what they had done together in the storeroom, how powerful and seductive it had been. She stared at the curve of his lips and knew that a kiss wouldn't suffice.

It would be good to feel his caress again.

Maybe one last time.

Maybe as a memento of their time together.

"It's the one good thing," he murmured and Theodora was startled by his words. "It's the one good thing about this world that I don't regret."

"What do you mean?"

"You. Sensation." His eyes almost glowed. "What we

did together. I had no idea that such pleasure existed." His smile left her blushing, again.

"Neither did I," she admitted, letting herself smile. "It was pretty special."

To her surprise, he sobered. His gaze danced over the company of shades, his consternation clear. "Theodora, may I confide in you?"

"Of course."

"I am trapped in this realm, abandoned by the angels. I have no idea what I shall do here, in what state we will find Baruch, how I will care for him afterward. You are the one who urged me to make a difference, to find purpose in what I can do. But I see no purpose for myself in this realm. I see no future and no prospects. I don't know what to do, without the angelic purpose that has driven me for so long."

It tore at Theodora's heart to see his uncertainty, to see how it troubled him to be without a mission. She sensed that he was deeply troubled by the choice that he believed had condemned him to the physical sphere.

Still, she didn't want to give him false hope.

She gave him another kind of hope.

She wasn't at all certain that she'd return from a mission to eliminate Maximilian Blackstone. She knew that her determination to aid Armand might persuade her to take greater chances than would be her usual habit.

But she had responsibilities. She could have charged Ferris with ensuring the welfare of the other children, but she saw in Armand an opportunity to achieve two ends in one.

She could ensure the safety of the children, regardless of her own fate, by giving them a new guardian.

And in so doing, she could give Armand the purpose he craved.

She didn't truly believe that Armand would be left in this sphere, not if she succeeded. But if she failed and failed before her task was completed, the children would need him.

They would need his tenderness.

She guessed that he yearned for trust, longed to feel again the connection with others that he'd had amongst his own kind.

Theodora suspected that she could give him that again. The union she'd propose would be more than physical. It would show her complete trust in him. It would bare her heart and soul to him.

Because Theodora couldn't just tell Armand about the children's refuge. She had to show him. She knew she had to remove all of the barriers between them to fulfill his desire.

And there was only one way to do that. As for risk, well, her plan would redouble the need for her to ensure Armand's survival. She would have to get him out of the Institute, no matter what the cost.

She dared to meet his gaze. "Armand, I don't have your conviction in divine will. But I've learned a lot about survival, about turning challenge into opportunity."

"What do you mean?" The warmth in his eyes, the intensity of his attention, the sheer appeal of him made Theodora dizzy. She'd never wanted a man in all the ways she wanted to be with Armand, and she doubted she would ever feel this way about another.

"Share my thoughts." She met his gaze, knowing her feelings showed in her own. He had sobered, his attention completely fixed upon her, his eyes cat-bright. "Help me protect the children."

Before Armand could speak, Theodora took the probe from his palm and pushed it into the port on her own.

It was the first time Theodora had willingly datashared. It was the first time that she had opened her portals and dismantled her firewalls. It was the first time that she had let anyone, living or dead, into the inner sanctuary of her palm. A tiny voice in the back of her mind insisted that she was making a mistake, exposing her vulnerabilities and doing it out of lust or exhaustion.

But a much louder voice declared that it was past time. In her heart, Theodora knew she was making the right choice.

Maybe even the destined choice.

THEODORA WAS sharing her secrets in the most intimate way possible.

Armand was astounded.

He watched the data scroll, appearing on her palm's display and then on his own. Their left hands were entwined, the space between the middle finger and the ring finger touching where the probe sank into the port. Both had their palms up, so the displays were visible. Theodora's index finger and middle finger were on top of Armand's palm and his index finger and middle finger lay over hers. Only a small portion of each display was obscured.

He was struck by the contrast between their hands—his larger and more golden; hers delicate and fair. She seemed fragile to him again, small and in need of protection.

Although she was the one who had defended him first.

He watched her tap in passwords and commands, systematically eliminating the barriers between them. He kept thinking she would stop, that they would reach some level and she would stop the datasharing.

But she didn't.

She opened the doors to one level after another, doing so with a conviction that amazed him. She trusted him! When she was done, their palms would be in complete union, each filled with data that mirrored the content of the other. He saw images and files move from her palm to his and knew that she was confiding the deepest of her secrets.

To him.

He saw maps and medical protocols, he saw images of children, their histories, and the location of those whose services could be bought to help the lost children. His heart swelled that she undertook such risk to help others, that she was willing to sacrifice anything to ensure that others survived.

And thrived.

Armand's own palm knew little of his secrets, although he realized it didn't matter. There was nothing of interest to be found on his electronic memory, but that was irrelevant. He had similarly confided his truth to Theodora, by telling her the secret of his origin. They were in communion, no barriers or lies between them, their purpose as one. Their palms shared the same data—in a real sense, their thoughts were as one.

Against all expectation, Armand had found the union that he had thought lost forever with his wings. He knew precisely how he wanted to celebrate.

But first he had one question for her. "This isn't about the cred," he said quietly.

Theodora swallowed, then met his gaze steadily. "I wish we had met in another time and place," she said softly, her heart in her words. "I wish I wasn't what I am, and that this world wasn't what it is. But wishes don't change anything."

Armand would have spoken but she raised her hand, silencing him with a gesture. "I don't know how this will work out. So, I will tell you now, while I have the chance, that you have changed the way I see the world. I've always wished it could be different, but now, now I'm ready to do whatever is necessary to make it different. You've made me reconsider my assumptions."

"It's not just about the cred?" he asked lightly and she smiled.

"I think you were right. I don't think it ever really was." She shrugged and pulled her palm free of his, made to return to her preparations for the night's assault.

But Armand couldn't let her walk away. He caught her in his arms, hauling her into his embrace and capturing her lips with his. He kissed her thoroughly and she kissed him back, the heat of their embrace making his heart leap.

"Let it wait," he urged, his lips against her throat. He felt her tremble, felt her fingers tighten in his hair. "Let us take this for ourselves."

Theodora didn't answer him. She simply framed his face in her hands and kissed him with such ardor that his heart thundered in response.

It didn't take Armand long to find a corner where they could have some privacy.

It did take much of the day to celebrate their new union. She left at one point, finishing her preparations, then returning to him. He found a purpose in the shine of her eyes, in each gasp of pleasure, in every caress.

There was a thrill in living that came from something other than risk—it came from partnership like this one.

Armand realized that he had a reason to live now, one he hadn't had just a day before. He had condemned himself to remain flesh but he was less troubled than he had been. There was light in this darkness, a light he could kindle himself. He could make a difference, by looking beyond his own destiny to the ways in which he could influence the lives of others.

He had to succeed and survive.

For the sake of the children.

Armand was dozing when her palm chimed, but Theodora was immediately on her feet. "Midnight," she said as she hauled on her pseudoskin. "Time to go, Henry."

It took Armand a moment to realize that she was talking to him.

THEODORA LED the shades into the Institute through the hidden tunnels on the lowest level.

Her idea was to enter as close as possible to both Cosmopoulos's lab and the power generation zone. She and Armand would leave the others to follow Ferris—they would storm the power generation zone and release the captive shades. Theodora had located the backup generators, as well, and Dennis was going to lead a group to damage them. As soon as the juice was cut off, Theodora and Armand would be near Baruch. They'd free him, and all would flee as quickly as possible.

It wasn't a fancy plan, but the sheer numbers of shades made Theodora believe that most of them would escape the Institute.

Even so, with every step they took closer, she worried.

There were so many things that could go wrong.

And she was unaccustomed to working with so many people. Theodora couldn't anticipate how the shades would respond under stress, whether they would freeze or fight back. They were determined to undertake this task, but she was fearful that some of them would never return.

The netherzones in the proximity of the Institute were eerily quiet. There was that silvery fog, about knee-deep, in the dark corridors, and it swirled slowly.

Otherwise, there was no sign of life.

Armand took her hand in his and Theodora was glad of the contact. She kept her laze raised with the other hand, making steady progress toward a portal they hadn't used.

Where were the sentries? There was no sign of anyone guarding the entrance to the Institute, nothing but a solid red light on the lock.

Theodora wondered then why no hunters from the Institute had followed her and Armand into the city's netherzones. It would have been easy to track them—she had tracked Armand without a great deal of trouble—but there had been no hint of pursuit. It seemed unlikely to her that Dr. Cosmopoulos, at least, wouldn't be interested in vengeance for his injuries.

Were they that sure that Armand would return again for Baruch?

She thought of the bounty on Armand and wondered how many wraiths were tracking their progress, unseen and undeclared. Were those wraiths just letting the small party get close enough to make Armand's capture easy?

She dismissed her thoughts, as they were doing nothing to fortify her confidence.

"Stay close," Theodora said to him, having no intention of losing him to the same fate as Baruch. She'd surrender him to the angels, but no one else. Armand squeezed her fingers tightly and drew the laze he'd confiscated from the guard.

They lingered one last potent moment in the shadows, the shades clustered behind them.

"Last chance," Theodora whispered, but the shades didn't break rank. If anything, they looked more determined. They were armed with weapons pilfered from beneath the city, old lazes, knives, and lengths of pipe. Several had wire cutters and shears, intending as they did to cut the shackled shades free. Their expressions were filled with resolve.

They knew the risks, perhaps better than Theodora did.

She scanned them once more, then released Armand's hand. She braced her laze with her other hand, sighted it, and fired at the security lock. She held the burn until the lock shorted in a flurry of sparks.

A gap appeared between the two doors, and Ferris lunged forward to shove the metal panels back. Dennis was right behind him, pushing back the other door. Theodora took out the pair of sleeping guards, one at a time. Armand injured the second to keep him busy until she could finish him off.

The silent tiled corridors of the Institute stretched in either direction. An alarm began to sound as the shades flowed over the threshold with purpose.

They were in.

Theodora couldn't stifle her sense that it had been too easy.

Much less that the Institute was too quiet. They were in the hidden labyrinth, after all, a zone that didn't see much traffic. She attributed her observations to nerves and focused on the task at hand.

Armand grinned and gave her a thumbs-up.

The shades left them immediately, sprinting after Ferris and Dennis. Theodora and Armand headed toward the hidden lab, easing along the walls with their lazes high. All they had to do was be in position when the power failed. Armand eliminated image-snatchers as they went, erasing any potential evidence of their passage.

On the other hand, the trail of destroyed image-snatchers would also give them away. It was even money which was worse.

Theodora guessed that whoever was watching the security vid of the Institute already knew where they were going.

Any decision about advising Armand was made for her when the corridor was plunged into sudden darkness. She heard the thrum of generators and the light flickered for several moments.

Then a trio of explosions shook the building to its foundations.

Alarms began to sound in earnest.

Theodora and Armand ran. They leapt down the narrow corridor they had taken to escape the lab. Within moments they came to the portal hidden at the back of the lab. Theodora's bad feeling got stronger, but Armand bumped her fist with his, then kicked open the door.

There was only blackness beyond, but they knew the way. Theodora had a moment to fear that Baruch had been moved, or that he had been killed already, but Armand was through the door before she could stop him.

She followed him, sensing immediately the presence of others in the lab.

But there was no time to respond, much less retreat. She felt the panel slide home behind her and heard the click of a lock.

In the same second, a dozen upheld palms lit simultaneously, blinding her with their blue light. Theodora's laze was seized from behind.

It was going wrong!

THEODORA WOULD have fought for her laze, but she saw Armand stumble ahead of her. She went after him instead. A figure was bent over him and there was the glimmer of glass.

Theodora cried out, guessing what was happening.

She managed one step before two men seized her from behind, lifting her feet off the ground.

And Armand fell.

Theodora knew why. The way his feet slid out from beneath him, his apparent inability to get up, the lethargy that stole over his body. It was all too familiar.

Dr. Cosmopoulos straightened from emptying the syringe into Armand's buttock and held up another. "Sure you don't want any Ivanofor yourself?" he asked lightly. "I know how you wraiths dislike it and the inconvenience it causes."

Theodora saw the faces of avid students behind him and Armand's fallen form. "Thank you for delivering," the doctor said smoothly. "I always like a larger sample for any experiment."

He gestured to a fair man standing behind him. "Blake? Will you do the honors? We wouldn't want it to be rumored that the Institute doesn't honor its debts."

Blake Patterson stepped forward, his expression carefully composed. He didn't look into Theodora's eyes and she saw the strain in his expression. He pushed the dataprobe from his palm into the portal of Theodora's, flicking a glance at her before his lips tightened. She watched the display as 50,000 units of cred were transferred to her possession.

Fifty thousand units that she didn't want.

Fifty thousand units that had cost too much.

Theodora watched Blake closely in the light of their illuminated palms. She had the impression that he was a moral individual, that he was trying to make change within the Society—against formidable odds. She thought she might be able to make a connection with him, earn his support, find a way free, but he studiously avoided his gaze.

He was aware of her watching him, though. His color rose steadily as the transfer was made. His being so fair in coloring meant that there was no disguising his response, even in the bad light.

Blake's discomfiture told Theodora all she wanted to know.

The bounty came with strings attached. The Society had no intention of seeing her live to spend the cred. Undoubtedly, they would keep her from leaving the Institute.

And even if they didn't, there would be a new electronic tether installed on her palm, one that would let them track her wherever she went.

There was probably an invasive worm, as well, one intended to gnaw through her firewalls and surrender her secrets to the Society.

Theodora wasn't going to let that happen.

Which meant she had to act fast. She'd never be able to stop the worm, not without knowing its code.

She'd have to kill it instead.

By the time Blake stepped back, Armand had been stripped and flung onto a gurney. His eyes were open and he was facing her direction. Theodora wanted him to know that she hadn't betrayed him.

But any such declaration would risk them both.

It would also eliminate any chance she had of saving him from a gruesome fate. No, she would prove her commitment to him through deeds not words.

Theodora feigned satisfaction. At Blake's nod, the two men let her go. They stayed close though, not entirely trusting her impulses. She tapped her palm, as if happily confirming the transfer of cred, and saw the worm's path instantly.

It was working fast.

Attention was fixed on Armand and she took the opportunity to scan the lab. There were drawers all around the perimeter and she knew that one of them must contain what she needed.

She just had to pick the right drawer, as she wouldn't have many chances to explore. She noticed the radiation emergency alarm and scanned the ceiling for clues as to the kind of response that alarm would generate. Of course, it made sense that this deeper and more secretive lab would be used for more risky experiments, maybe those the Institute didn't want the citizens of Chicago to know about. It was the Institute for Radiation Studies, after all.

How did they contain a radiation leak? With lead, she'd bet. Theodora spied the receptacles in the ceiling for the steel walls immediately, noting then the subtle indents in the floor where they would lock down. She would guess that they were on a timer once locked down.

And even in a power failure, gravity would help them

sink home. All that would be needed would be a small backup battery to open the locks. She'd bet it was protocol to keep that battery charged.

Theodora knew then exactly where she wanted Armand to be, until the Ivanofor wore off.

She would use the Institute's equipment against them.

She chose a drawer close to the alarm button and eased closer. She put her hands behind her back and moved slowly. Her heart was pounding and she yearned to make a leap for it, but she knew she had to stay in control.

She was sure she could feel that software worm, nibbling into her secrets. Chewing, digesting, transmitting. How deep would it get before she managed to kill it? A trickle of sweat ran down her back, leaving her uncomfortable in her pseudoskin.

Two more steps and she'd be there.

Theodora could hear alarms ringing throughout the Institute. She smelled smoke and heard laze fire, and prayed that the shades managed to survive this assault.

The power didn't come back on, which she took as a good sign. Ferris was fulfilling his part of the plan.

"I want to make the first cut," a woman said, sliding her fingertip along Armand's thigh.

It was Philippa and her eyes were filled with malice. Theodora took another step.

Dr. Cosmopoulos turned suddenly to smile at Theodora. She froze in her tracks, her triumphant expression still in place. "You, of course, will remain our guest until the protocol is completed."

"I wouldn't dream of missing it," Theodora lied.

Dr. Cosmopoulos's eyes narrowed slightly. "I am certain you can understand the necessity of such caution."

"Of course." Theodora kept her tone light and conversational with an effort. "What about my laze?"

Cosmopoulos tut-tutted, his gaze cold. "It is our policy that only security staff possess weapons within the Institute. We shall see whether it can be returned to you upon your departure."

"I would appreciate that. It's a significant investment." Theodora spoke with apparent ease, seething inwardly at the evil of this bunch. Blake glanced between the two, his uncertainty clear. The pair smiled at each other, neither trusting the other, each assessing their relative strength.

Then the good doctor smiled more broadly, as if aware that he held all the proverbial cards. It seemed to Theodora that he called her bluff as he turned back to gloat over his prize.

Theodora accepted the dare.

She leapt for the button and slammed it with her fist.

IT COULD have been seen as the final betrayal, the indication that the mortal realm was truly as wicked as Armand had believed.

But Armand could not believe that Theodora had deceived him in order to collect a bounty posted on him.

He didn't want to believe she had done it.

Even though such a choice would have been perfectly consistent with everything she had told him, his heart cried false.

He could believe that she had known about the bounty. That had been what she'd been hiding from him, he was sure of it, the bad news she'd refused to share.

But he knew she hadn't intended to collect it. Why would she have told him about the children, if she'd intended to surrender him to the Institute?

Theodora wouldn't have taken the risk.

It was that simple.

It was only a matter of time until someone interrogated Armand's palm and emptied its data. If Theodora had intended to collect the bounty, she would never have confided that data.

He appreciated now the full magnitude of the gift she had given him. In offering him a purpose for his future on earth, she had put those she defended at risk. She had trusted him, and he was determined that his captivity wouldn't put them in peril.

Except the Ivanofor made it impossible for him to do anything. He supposed he should be glad that the bounty she'd earned on delivering him to the Institute would be used for the surgery Ferris needed. And there was an irony in the Institute's cred ultimately being used to save someone from ever being harvested by them.

But that assumed that Theodora herself would leave the Institute. Armand was certain that the Society didn't plan to release either of them alive.

The use of Ivanofor made him livid, which probably only made it metabolize more quickly. His thoughts flew as he sought some way to make a difference, some way to save Theodora and those she protected.

But as he should have known to expect, Theodora didn't wait to be saved.

As soon as she was released by the guards, she began to move slowly toward the outside of the lab. Armand only noticed her steady progress because he was watching her, because he couldn't do anything else. She moved stealthily and steadily, making him wonder at her plan.

He didn't have to wonder long.

No sooner had Cosmopoulos turned his back on Theodora than she leapt for the red emergency button on the wall. It was labeled as being for radiation leaks, but she slammed her hand into it anyway.

"Hold your fire!" Blake commanded the guards and they froze with reluctance. "The bloodshed must stop!"

The response to the alarm was immediate. Red lights lit all around the perimeter of the lab, flashing steadily. Armand supposed they must be on battery power or alternative generators. The light was the color of blood, brilliant and disorienting.

At the same time, horns began to sound. They were different from the incessantly shrill alarms that were already ringing throughout the Institute. These sounded like foghorns and he supposed that a radiation leak called for more serious and distinctive response.

The students in the lab panicked, racing toward the doors.

"Stop!" cried Dr. Cosmopoulos. "Remain calm!"

"Exit in an orderly fashion," shouted Blake Patterson, but no one listened to him.

Metal plates were sliding out of the ceiling to contain the core of the lab. They fell steadily toward the ground, looking like guillotines in the flashing light. Armand saw that they would secure the central surgical area from the rest of the lab.

One was going to cut him in half. All he could do was watch.

Philippa screamed and bolted for the door, shoving her

fellows aside. One tripped her and she lashed out, a scuffle erupting between them and halting the evacuation.

Theodora, meanwhile, was flinging open drawers along the perimeter of the lab. She threw gauze on the floor from one, dislodged a number of rolls of adhesive tape from the next, then grinned at the contents of the third. Armand saw her snatch up something small and shiny, slipping it into the sleeve of her pseudoskin.

Then she ran for him. She shoved the gurney right into the middle of the the descending steel walls, ensuring that Armand was inside of the secured area. She locked down the wheels as the walls closed around him. He thought they would be enclosed together, but she winked at him.

Later, she mouthed, then blew him a kiss. She dropped and rolled beneath the dropping steel. The walls fell home with a clang, sealing Armand inside a cylinder of metal.

Alone.

He was trapped.

No. Armand realized belatedly that no one could hurt him here. No one could give him more Ivanofor. No one could dissect him. No one could interrogate his palm against his will.

He closed his eyes with relief. Theodora had made a brilliant choice.

"This zone will be secured for twenty-four hours as a matter of protocol," declared a toneless female voice. "Please remain calm. Agitation will only compromise your oxygen supply. This area will only be unsealed when the contained radiation level drops to acceptable standards. Please refer to the radiation guidelines for a full explanation. Twenty-three hours, fifty-nine minutes until the first automatic atmospheric test."

Armand wanted to laugh out loud. Theodora had given him a sanctuary, a safe place to wait out the drug's effects. He wouldn't let her down. When the steel walls lifted, he'd be ready.

For anything.

•

THEODORA RAN. She didn't care why Blake didn't want her shot—she wasn't going to argue with him. While the students ran for the door to the corridor, she headed for the netherzone access.

Armand was safe. She didn't care about the rest of them.

She heard the doors to the lab crash open, heard the exchange of laze fire. She heard Cosmopoulos demand the execution of the invading shades and heard Blake insist again upon no violence. She didn't doubt that the shades would take advantage of the uncertainty.

Chaos erupted behind her. There was smoke and there was fire, and there was the sound of shattering glass.

All good as far as she was concerned.

She ducked into the netherzones and ran with all her might. She knew they could follow her, knew they'd find her.

There was one thing she had to do first.

The minutes ticked away.

At least she had memorized the layout. Calling it up on her palm would only reveal her destination to them.

Precious moments later, Theodora came to the power generation plant for the Institute. The doors were secured, even those that led to the netherzones.

While she was glad the shades had succeeded, she needed to get to Ferris.

Soon.

She backtracked and emerged in a corridor that led to the power plant. She saw fallen shades in the hall, as well as others being carried by their fellows into the power plant. They might have been injured or sedated or simply exhausted. Three lazes pivoted to lock on her when she strode toward the door.

She ripped off her hood, having no further need of disguise. She couldn't see the shades guarding the door, couldn't identify them, so she simply had to hope.

She heard pursuit in the corridor behind her and knew the Society was coming for her.

"Incinerate my palm!" she cried, stretching out her left hand as far as she could.

It was Ferris who stepped forward to fire. She recognized his silhouette. Theodora's knees weakened in her relief. Ferris would understand. After all, she had done the same for him once.

The fire from his laze was so brilliant that she had to close her eyes against its white light. It hit her palm and sparks flew as the unit shorted out.

Ferris wasn't fooled. He held the burn, just as she had done once for him. He remembered. His expression was grim as he walked closer and cooked the computer unit. Theodora closed her eyes against the searing pain, her nostrils filled with the scent of burned flesh and melted plastic. She wanted to writhe and scream, but didn't want the damage to be more extensive than necessary.

She wanted that bastard worm dead.

The approaching guards shouted and fired at Ferris.

"Go!" Theodora commanded. She pulled out the scalpel

she'd stolen, gritted her teeth against the pain, and dug beneath the smoking palm.

Ferris fired at the attackers instead, standing over her.

"They'll take you again, Ferris. Don't do it." She grimaced as she worked the palm free, her tears falling. The pain was excruciating, but it would be temporary. There was only one way to make sure a palm couldn't tell any tales, after all.

In contrast, even if she died, her palm could be persuaded to talk. She had to ensure its silence.

Ferris made a sound that she recognized as a protest. The laze fire became heavier, just as Theodora worked the palm free of her flesh. She was breathing fast, her heart hammering and her body shaking with the pain.

But it wasn't done. She dug into her own flesh for the two fine cables that wired the palm into her nervous system.

"They can have me," she whispered as she cut the connection. "Don't lose what we've gained."

Then she flicked the worthless palm onto the ground. It rattled across the tiled floor, its power destroyed in every way. Theodora saw Ferris grind it beneath his heel, then she thought her pain might make her sick.

"Run," she whispered. She heard his protest, heard the others calling him from the power plant, heard the sentries running closer. "I'm begging, Ferris!" she cried.

She heard his incoherent moan of regret.

She heard him retreat.

She heard the doors lock down.

Theodora knew they were all safe, at least for the moment, and that was when she let unconsciousness claim her.

She didn't even feel the guards scoop up her body and take her into the Institute's captivity.

from *The Republican Record*
September 22, 2100
Afternoon Edition
download v. 1.45

Chicago in Crisis

NEW D.C.—President Van Buren upgraded the State of Emergency in Chicago to a Code Red at 14:00 today.

Chicago has been plagued by loose shades in the streets since the Oracle unlocked the netherzones in that city last February. Until this week, the shades have been peaceful and there was no local will to see them injured or restrained. This week, however, matters took a turn for the worse with the dramatic deaths of both presidential candidate Maximilian Blackstone and Nuclear Darwinist, Seventh Degree, Ernestine Sinclair. Their deaths appear to have been murders, perpetuated by Ms. Sinclair's domestic shade, which also died in an apparent suicide. Citizens feared immediately for their personal safety, many arming themselves and others exiling their own domestic shades.

The Chicago police began working alongside with shade hunters from the Society of Nuclear Darwinists to reclaim Chicago's streets from these rogue shades. Perhaps in retaliation for many deaths, shades invaded the Institute for Radiation Studies in Chicago last night, in a further escalation of hostilities. The Institute also houses the offices of the Society of Nuclear Darwinists, and many senior Nuclear Darwinists reside within the complex. Although information is scanty, it appears at this point in time that the shades are in control of the Institute's campus, and that the core of citizens remaining on the site have secured themselves within the Institute's auditorium.

Ironically, that same auditorium was scheduled to be the site of a debate upon the future of shades within the Republic, this evening at 20:00, to be attended by such luminaries as Mr. Blackstone, Ms. Sinclair, Reverend Billie Joe Estevez, the Oracle, and President Van Buren. The president has extended his regrets as of this afternoon. The reverend is unavailable for comment at press time, while the Oracle is said to be in transit.

Presidential candidate Thomas O'Donohue has confirmed his intention to attend, in the place of his former running mate. "Surely, this is an opportunity to strike at the heart of the most pressing challenge confronting the Republic and its citizens," he said at a press conference. "Surely, now, in Chicago, is the moment to chart a new future for the Republic." Mr. O'Donohue declared that he would unveil his own plan for the future of shades at this evening's debate.

Related Links:
- O'Donohue riding a tide of popularity
- Chronology of the crisis in Chicago
- History of the Society of Nuclear Darwinists
- Maximilian Blackstone laid to rest today

XIX

~~~~~

REVEREND BILLIE Joe Estevez was afraid.

She stood on the roof of the Intercontinental Hotel, fearful of what the evening would hold. She could see the residence of the Institute for Radiation Studies burning like a torch in the night. She could see the office tower of the Institute for Radiation Studies, gutted and dark. The fire there had extinguished itself, after burning the whole day. The building was a dark skeleton now, blank and vacant against the night. The compound that contained both it and the campus of the Institute were dark and still.

A wasteland.

In the middle of that desolation was the rounded dome of the auditorium. It seemed serene and still in the night, if dark. The reverend eyed the auditorium and her determination wavered.

Would any of them survive a journey to that place?

In contrast to most nights in the Republic, the sky was clear. She could see the glitter of stars high overhead. It was cold and the wind was brisk—it seemed to penetrate to her bones and the reverend wished she were somewhere sunny and warm.

Somewhere far away from Chicago.

Blackstone huddled in the middle of her company of aides,

his bravado lost with his apparent murder. She didn't doubt that he would recover his former boldness, especially once he had an audience. He was already seething over O'Donohue's quite reasonable assumption of his role as leading presidential candidate.

She heard the chop of helicopter blades and wasn't sure whether to be relieved or not. In a way, she'd hoped that the Oracle would cancel, because then the reverend would have the opportunity to cancel her own appearance without losing face.

But the small white helicopter that was reserved for the Oracle's use came steadily closer, the beat of its turbine loud against the night. The reverend watched it approach, and knew she couldn't just follow.

She tapped a message on her palm, dispatching it to the Oracle herself.

Are you certain this is wise?

The reply was immediate.

Surely you, of all citizens, trust in the divine purpose?

The reverend's lips tightened, sensing as she did a thread of mockery in the Oracle's tone.

It can't be safe. Not for either of us.

The Oracle was quick in her response.

Where is there safety in the mortal realm? Are you afraid to face your destiny, Reverend? Are you

**afraid of judgment? Or is the issue simply that the
vidfeed will be inadequate to build your ratings?**

The reverend inhaled sharply and typed quickly.

**You cannot be irresponsible! You have a duty
to the citizens of the Republic . . .**

She was interrupted by the brisk reply.

I have one duty only, and that is to truth.

There was a conviction in the Oracle these days, and the
reverend wondered suddenly if there might be a cause. She
typed a query quickly.

Have you had a vision?

The reply was both direct and obtuse. The Oracle was
learning more from her mother by the day.

**I dream of a new dawn for the Republic, a future of
justice and equality. I envision the New Jerusalem, in
your terms, becoming real in our own time. Do you truly
intend to miss that, Reverend? Is it worth mere physical
safety to not stand witness to that transformation?**

The reverend had been challenged and she knew it. She
watched the white helicopter draw closer to the auditorium,
saw it begin to descend to the helipad on the roof. She
thought she heard a roar in the distance, although it could
not have been possible.

The Oracle had nothing to fear from the shades. The reverend was not at all certain that any other norm in the Republic could share that confidence and security.

Another helicopter appeared just then, the sight of it making Blackstone inhale sharply.

O'Donohue was arriving.

That left the reverend with no choice. She might be entering the company of fools, she might not return alive, but she supposed it would make good vid. If she was going to die, she wanted to die on live vidcast. She summoned her image-snatchers and her aides, snapped her fingers at her pilot, and climbed into her helicopter.

And if Billie Joe said a silent prayer on the flight across the city, no one was the wiser.

ARMAND WATCHED the minutes tick down. He was fully in command of his body again and ready, his booted foot tapping with impatience.

He listened as the automatic atmospheric test was performed.

He waited as the results were tabulated.

He grinned as the voice announced the results to be satisfactory.

He heard the locks release but the doors didn't rise as he'd expected.

The power was still out. He struggled to get his fingers beneath one metal wall. He coaxed it up with his fingertips, its significant weight the main obstacle to his progress.

Just when he thought he'd have to let it slip down again, someone wedged a length of metal into the gap.

It was a length of copper pipe.

Armand knew who had wielded such a weapon when they had invaded the Institute.

"We've got to lift it together," Dennis said from the other side. "Ready, Ferris? Armand, roll beneath it as soon as you can."

THEODORA WAS escorted to the festivities in the auditorium on Wednesday night. She hadn't died of the trauma from destroying her palm, so she guessed that the Society had kept her alive on purpose. She didn't really want to think about why.

Maybe it had to do with the only record of what had been on her palm remaining between her ears. They couldn't get it by dissection of her brain, but Theodora wasn't interested in being persuaded or cajoled to part with any data.

She'd ensure Armand's departure, if she could, and if that was her last deed in this world, well, so be it. Ferris would take care of the others.

She knew that her presence in the auditorium wasn't because the students and faculty of the Institute were so anxious to share her company. The students, faculty, and administration had taken refuge there, and to have put her anywhere else would have put one of them at risk in guarding her. They weren't so confident that they were anxious to let the shades claim her either.

The auditorium was secured against the shades, who evidently otherwise had the run of the place.

Theodora enjoyed that Ferris hadn't chosen to retreat. She liked that he and Dennis had simply laid claim to the Institute, a gesture of defiance and significance.

She felt terrible, much weaker than she would have liked. She wasn't fond of either the street clothes she'd been given or the absence of her laze.

But she was alive.

And she was curious as to what would happen. Theodora itched to have matters come to a resolution, so she could descend to that lab and free Armand. He should be coming out from the spell of the Ivanofor. Theodora was wondering how she could help him, when she spied a familiar figure in the milling groups of students and faculty.

A heavyset man dressed in black moved through the crowd, ducking and weaving in a way that should have made him easy to overlook. The furtiveness of his manner, though, caught at Theodora's attention, she who had learned a long time ago to look where others didn't.

Once she started to watch him, she couldn't stop.

Because it was Big Ted.

And he was not where he'd said he'd be. He was dressed differently than his custom, and he was trying to hide his presence, but it was unmistakably Big Ted. He moved with the same light step, the one that belied his size.

What was he doing here? He had told Theodora that he was leaving the Institute, that he was off to serve the Oracle. But the Oracle lived in New D.C., and her party hadn't arrived yet.

Theodora watched Big Ted and wondered at his motives.

There was one obvious possibility. No one had collected the bounty that Theodora herself had intended to claim a few days before in this very hall.

* * *

ARMAND ROLLED beneath the metal wall and spun immediately to his feet. Dennis and Ferris let the wall sink home, and the trio turned as one to flee the lab.

"I've got to get to Baruch," Armand said, and Ferris showed him the way.

The mute boy made a gesture to Dennis, who nodded agreement. "I'm heading back to the others." Then he smiled unexpectedly. "We did it, you know, and it was because of you. We're in control of the Institute!"

"You should tell the press," Armand urged. "Tell them who you are and what you want."

Dennis's eyes lit, then he turned and strode into the darkness, a new confidence in his step. Ferris tapped Armand on the shoulder and indicated the other direction.

The pair quickly reached the lab. It was locked, which Ferris solved quickly, but otherwise abandoned.

Except for one figure. Armand lifted his hand and illuminated the space. The windows of the observational surgery glinted all around him, reflecting the palm's light. Baruch looked very small and frail, alone as he was in the middle of the room.

He seemed more pale to Armand, as if he had faded. The monitors around him were silent and dark, testament to the lack of power.

Armand went directly to him, pulling sensors and wires from his friend's body with impatience. He pulled out the intravenous needle with its incessant drip of Ivanofor and cast it on the floor. The bag was empty but he couldn't tell when his comrade had ingested the last of it.

Baruch moaned.

Ferris' expression was concerned. He caught his breath when Armand picked up his oldest friend and Baruch's back was exposed to view.

And Ferris eyed Armand with new understanding.

"We have to get out of here. We have to take him somewhere safe," Armand said to Ferris. "Where is Theodora?"

Ferris frowned and his mouth worked in silence. His frustration was clear, but it was Baruch who provided the answer.

"The auditorium," he whispered.

Armand lowered his friend to the gurney so he could look into his eyes. "No, no. We must leave this place . . ."

Baruch shook his head, raising one weary hand to Armand's shoulder. "It will end where it began, Armaros." He met Armand's gaze, his own filled with conviction. "I saw it in the stars."

Armand smiled. "To the auditorium," he said to Ferris, who nodded and indicated the way. Armand wrapped Baruch in a sheet and shouldered his weight, determined to carry him as far as necessary.

Whatever the ending might be.

THEODORA WAS standing in the wings of the auditorium stage, seething at her own inability to make a difference, when the Oracle herself arrived. Blake Patterson stepped forward to greet her, his admiration apparently heartfelt. Two of his bodyguards flanked Theodora, but she knew what she had to do. She was pretty certain what Big Ted had planned.

She had to defend the Oracle.

And since she couldn't do it herself, she knew who could.

The Oracle's Consort, Raphael Gerritson.

Just as Ferris had said.

The Oracle scanned the group assembled in the dim light of palms and battery-powered lights. Her glance swept over Theodora, then she froze in recognition. Her Consort stiffened, his hand going to his partner's elbow. His other hand went to his holster.

"I am glad to see you again," the Oracle said, smiling with genuine pleasure. Blake looked between the two of them with surprise. "I trust that everyone of our mutual acquaintance is well."

She was asking after Ferris. Theodora found herself smiling in response, because she knew the inquiry would please Ferris. "Everyone, my lady."

"Enough cred?" Rafe asked, a measure of suspicion in his tone.

Theodora held his gaze and let her fingertips rise to her throat. "I had to sell a few treasures, but what's the point of material goods when someone is in need?"

They both smiled, then Theodora cleared her throat. "Which reminds me—how is your new cook working out?"

The Oracle blinked in surprise.

"I'm not sure who you mean," Rafe said.

"I saw an old friend a week or so ago," Theodora said. "I must have misunderstood him, because I thought he said he was going to work for you."

"Who was that?" Rafe asked tightly.

"I don't know his real name," Theodora said with a shrug. "We always called him Big Ted."

The Oracle caught her breath and averted her gaze. So, she did know Big Ted. Maybe they both did. Rafe scanned the crowd with purpose and Theodora knew the moment that he spied Big Ted.

She did respect observant men.

She hoped Rafe was fast enough.

The presidential candidate Thomas O'Donohue arrived then, the sight of him shocking Theodora to silence. He was tall and muscular, his smile filled with confidence and a ready charm. There was a touch of silver at his temples, an intelligence in his eyes. He seemed sincere, as well, quite a feat for a politician.

Perhaps he truly was genuine. Theodora found herself responding when he insisted on shaking her hand—along with those of everyone else backstage. "I hope to count on your vote," he said with a smile that made Theodora want to vote immediately.

She hid her left hand behind her back, not wanting him to realize that she was a wraith and thus an unregistered voter.

"I intend to earn the continued support of the electorate," he said and she marveled that he seemed to be untainted. She looked into his eyes, tempted to challenge him, and saw a sparkle there that reminded her of someone.

There was a light in him, in his eyes, that one didn't often see. Theodora struggled with her tentative thought, not wanting to be hasty.

O'Donohue stepped away, making his rounds, and Theodora noted that both he and Rafe were the two most physically remarkable men in the area. She saw the barest smile exchanged between them.

Was that an acknowledgement?

Was she imagining things?

Then the Oracle turned her smile on Blake. "You should

unlock the doors to the auditorium," she said, her soft words filled with challenge.

Blake's shock was clear, given that he choked on his response.

"Are the shades not in possession of the Institute?" she asked and Blake nodded. "We are discussing their future," the Oracle chided, her tone turning imperative. "Open the doors."

The presidential candidate glanced over his shoulder and nodded agreement. "An excellent idea," he said, and Blake sputtered.

"But the security risk . . ."

"I do not fear my own kind, nor do I fear retribution for whatever I have done," the Oracle said smoothly. She smiled, a dare in her blue eyes. "Don't tell me that norms will cower in the shadows from this point onward?"

Blake shook his head. "It cannot be done. The security hazard is too great."

"On the contrary," the Oracle said, "the only hazard lies in excluding them." She held his gaze, her shoulders squared and her chin high, so confident in her claim that Theodora wanted to applaud. Her eyes seemed to snap and there was a tingle of electricity in the air.

Blake's inevitable protest was interrupted by the arrival of Reverend Billie Joe Estevez and her party. Theodora knew she didn't imagine his relief.

There were an astonishing number of people in her party, aides and bodyguards and various hangers-on. Of course, there were the inevitable image-snatchers. They powered up the batteries in their backpacks and turned their bright lights on the interior of the auditorium.

One of her aides paused to glare at O'Donohue, his dis-
taste so tangible that Theodora found herself noting his
response. He was oddly dressed, once she looked, his hat
old-fashioned and pulled low over his forehead. All she
could see of his face was an enormous moustache, one so
bushy that she doubted it could be real.

The reverend wasted little time on formalities, simply
strode onto the stage and usurped Blake Patterson's role.
"Here we are, live, at the auditorium of the besieged Institute
for Radiation Studies," she informed one image-snatcher, and
Theodora sensed that she was anxious to be gone. The students and faculty of the Institute and Society took their seats,
their expressions forbidding. "There is peril in the streets of
Chicago tonight . . ."

But there was more in the auditorium itself.

Theodora scanned the crowd once more. She found Big
Ted in the shadows by the stairs, just barely discernible
and only visible at all because of the powerful lights of the
image-snatchers.

"And history will be written as a result of this evening's
events. Let us pray together in these uncertain times." The
reverend raised her hands and closed her eyes, her voice
booming over the assembly. "*The Lord is my shepherd, I
shall not want. He makes me lie down in green pastures;
he leads me beside still waters; he restores my soul. He
leads me in paths of righteousness, for his name's sake.*"

The reverend's voice rose to a crescendo. "*Even though
I walk through that valley of the shadow of death, I fear no
evil; for you are with me; your rod and your staff—they
comfort me. You prepare a table before me, in the presence
of my enemies; you anoint my head with oil; my cup over-
flows. Only goodness and mercy shall follow me all the

*days of my life, and I shall dwell in the house of the Lord
my whole life long.'* Amen!"

Theodora recognized that the reverend was afraid.

The reverend pivoted crisply to introduce those who had
come, speaking primarily for the benefit of the vid audience. "The Oracle of the Republic joins us here tonight for
this important discussion," she said, beckoning to the Oracle. There was no applause on this night. "And the presidential candidate Thomas O'Donohue."

O'Donohue waved and smiled, seemingly untroubled by
the lack of enthusiasm for his presence.

The unhappy aide came to Theodora's side, his attention
fixed on O'Donohue. "Filthy opportunist," he muttered and
flung his hat aside.

He peeled off the moustache and threw it down, revealing himself even as he strode onto the stage.

He raised his arms, addressing the crowd with apparent
pleasure. "I am Maximilian Blackstone," he said. "Rumors
of my death have been greatly exaggerated."

There was a smattering of applause and a few gasps of
shock. The Oracle watched Blackstone, her eyes narrowed
with uncertainty and her hand curving around her stomach.
O'Donohue appeared to be more amused than dismayed,
and stepped forward to shake his former associate's hand.

Theodora saw Max hesitate before he put out his own
hand.

She saw anger light the eyes of Reverend Billie Joe Estevez. "Maximilian Blackstone," she said. "Do you stand by
your earlier scheme to liberate the shades?"

"Of course!"

"To what purpose?"

Max smiled and warmed to his theme. "It is past time

for the Republic to acknowledge that shades should have rights and opportunities . . ."

"Those would be the same rights and opportunities you denied to your own children," the reverend said. "The same rights and opportunities you denied to thirty-four children, born of your seed and condemned as shades, even though the majority of them had falsified S.H.A.D.E. evaluations."

Max paled.

He sputtered.

Theodora was amazed. The reverend knew the truth and was putting it on national vid! She glanced over the crowd to gauge reaction, just in time to see Big Ted lift his left arm. She knew he was disguising his laze in the shadow of his sleeve.

Her kingdom for a laze. She looked at Rafe in silent terror.

The reverend held up her palm. "I have documentation, evidence, links, images." She tapped her palm. "I am forwarding it to five members of the press right now."

"No! It's a lie!" Max shouted and leapt at the reverend.

Theodora saw the faint red glimmer of Big Ted's sight.

"No!" she cried. She lunged out of the shadows, tripped in her efforts to evade the guards, and shoved Blackstone hard. He fell toward the Oracle, shouting with outrage, just as the laze fired.

The shot caught Blackstone in the back of the head. He was killed instantly, his blood spurting high and wide. The Oracle cried out as his weight landed upon her.

Rafe fired twice in immediate retaliation, his first shot sounding in the same instant that Max was struck. There was screaming and confusion, the image-snatchers turning this way and that in their effort to record events.

An uneasy silence fell over the hall. One image-snatcher

leapt into the crowd and confirmed that Big Ted was dead, as well. There was a hammering on the doors to the auditorium, a chant from the corridors outside.

"Oracle, Oracle."

Theodora caught her breath at the familiarity of one voice, one raised louder than all the rest.

One as low and seductive as that same man's touch.

Rafe spared a look at Blake, then lifted his laze and shot off the lock securing one pair of doors. He repeated that on the second pair of doors. Faculty and students retreated in horror as the shades streamed over the threshold, pouring down the aisles toward the stage.

Armand led one group and Theodora found herself smiling at the sight of him. He had his arm wrapped around Baruch, who leaned on his friend for support as he limped along.

Ferris and Dennis led the group that surged down the other aisle, their determination making her heart clench. She saw the shades from the netherzones following behind, saw some of the wraiths with whom she'd worked.

The Oracle stepped forward and raised her hands in greeting, as radiant as the sun despite the spattering of blood on her clothing.

"Welcome to those who have been hidden too long!" Her joy at seeing the shades was tangible, and they fell on their knees before her.

Theodora found her cheeks wet with tears. Armand grinned at her and she laughed, then he pointed upward and her joy evaporated.

Then her heart stopped cold.

She saw the shimmer of brilliant white light. She felt the heat of a hundred suns.

The angels were coming.

Which only meant that Armand would leave forever, his assignment complete.

IN THE far north of the Republic, well beyond the old Frontier, a little girl left the warmth of a cabin to venture into the night. She skipped across the tundra, without her coat, staring up at the sky. Two women ran after he as the northern lights danced in shades of green above them. The little girl barely noticed them, her gaze locked on the sky above.

The younger of the pair snatched up the little girl.

"Micheline, what are you thinking, running out in the cold like this?" chided Eva, the older one. She shivered and made to head back to the cabin, rubbing her upper arms with her hands.

"What do you see, child?" murmured Lillian, who held Micheline close. She knew that Micheline's third eye sometimes gave the child visions, also knew that Micheline didn't always have the ability to express the truths she saw.

Micheline raised one hand to the sky, her fingers outspread and her expression rapturous. "Angels," she whispered with awe. "Angels."

"I see no angels," Eva complained, pragmatic as always. "I'd like to see a hot cup of tea, though." She headed back for the cabin, her impatience showing with every step.

But Lillian followed the child's gaze, and looked up into the sky. She felt a little frisson of electricity, one that made the hairs on her skin stand up. She had time to fear that the child was right before the white brilliance of angelfire slid across the rock.

Eva cried out and fell to her knees, hands outstretched.

"Angels," Micheline whispered and reached both hands toward the glowing radiance.

"Angels," Lillian agreed. They were coming, here and now. How could a person ever be prepared for such an encounter?

What did they want?

She knew from her daughter, Lilia, that Micheline had been taken into the custody of the angels once before. As much as she knew that might be right for the child, she had grown so fond of the little girl. She couldn't imagine her life without Micheline.

Lillian held fast to the child entrusted to her custody. She stood on the rock and watched the light grow ever brighter, her heart in her throat.

They would come, independent of her desires, and they would take what they wished. She only hoped they were compassionate.

THEODORA HEARD the roar of the angelic chorus. They sang a hymn of praise, but sang it at such volume that the auditorium building began to vibrate. She heard the cracks open in the roof and felt the floor bounce beneath her feet. The song grew only louder, and people began to panic. The reverend called for order, as did Blake Patterson, but when the roof cracked wide open, no one was listening.

The light that poured through the broken roof was searing in its intensity. Theodora closed her eyes against it, felt its heat upon her face and thought her eardrums would break with the sound of the angels' song.

The Oracle stretched her hands out in supplication.

"Hallelujah!" she shouted, and the shades echoed her ec-static cry.

The reverend fell to her knees in prayer.

And the angels came.

Theodora had never thought of angels as warriors before, but her glimpse of them made her think of angelic knights. Their eyes shone with the fury of righteousness. They were large and white and powerful, and they invaded the audito-rium as if it was their right to do so.

She saw that some people fell before the angels and did not rise. She heard cries of anguish mingled with those of joy. She saw the blaze of laze fire and saw the angels smile as they deflected the light that dimmed against their own.

She saw some dare to look openly upon the angels' glory, then recoil in pain as their faces were burned. And she heard the angelic hymn, a rhythmic potent call to arms, an invocation to those who would dare to fight for justice.

She saw people in the crowd respond to the angels' sum-mons. Not just the shades, whose faces lit with hope and possibility. She saw hunters put down their lazes. She saw students cast aside their books.

The angels sang louder as one descended faster. He opened his arms to Armand, who urged Baruch toward the angel. The hymn was magnificent and powerful, making the floor resonate. There was gentleness in that angel's every gesture as he accepted the burden of their fallen one. He raised Baruch up into their company again, lifting him in his embrace and carrying him high, apparently without effort.

A second angel cupped Baruch's face in his hands and kissed Baruch, on one cheek and then the other. Theodora could see even through the white light that the pain had left Baruch's expression. She saw that affection in Armand's expression again, the satisfaction that he had brought his comrade back, and her heart pounded for him.

The light became impossibly brighter, and when next she could see their figures, she thought there was another in the luminous company.

And the human form of Baruch was gone.

Armand had been right. There were angels and they hadn't broken their word to him. They had come to collect him and Baruch.

A promise kept.

She watched Armand, saw him smile at one member of the angelic company, and fought her tears over what she knew would come.

Her own happiness was nothing compared to the reshaping of the world, though. She loved Armand and that had changed her.

She would be part of the new order, the new order delivered by the angels.

She knew better than to hope for more. She watched and marveled, feeling lucky to be a witness to this event.

Armand turned to Ferris, extending his hand to the boy. Ferris looked from Armand to the angels, then he looked at Rafe. At Rafe's encouragement, he came forward, swallowing as an angel descended toward him. The hymn was furious and powerful, the light cleansing in its brilliance.

The angel smiled as he touched one hand to Ferris's throat. Ferris closed his eyes, his fists clenched at his sides. A moment later the angel kissed his cheeks, just as the other had kissed Baruch, then slid a luminous fingertip across Ferris' mouth.

"I can't," Ferris said, his eyes widening when he realized he had made a sound. The Oracle clapped her hands and laughed in pleasure, her tears cascading down her cheeks. "I can speak!" Ferris said, then shouted. "I can speak!"

The reverend seemed to recover herself. She strode to Ferris's side and lifted his hand in hers. "Is it not writ, *'Though I speak in the tongues of men and of angels, but do not have love, I am but a noisy gong or a clanging symbol'*?" she cried to the crowd. They applauded, their gazes rising to the angelic host.

The angels sang of love, and the reverend could not compete with the chorus.

The angel who had healed Ferris turned the boy to survey the crowd as well as those who were on the stage. He touched Ferris's lips again, as if to urge him.

"Speak of righteousness and of evil," Armand said to Ferris. "That justice might be done."

The boy turned, seeking faces he knew. He pointed at Dr. Cosmopoulos, who quailed. "He was merciless," he said to the angel. The angels' song became emphatic and rhythmic, a summons to war. Three descended in unison, their marvelous wings arching high and bright behind them. As they came lower, they seemed to become brighter.

Theodora realized it was no illusion. They were becoming brighter, and brighter again. She averted her face, shielding her eyes. She smelled garments burning and heard Dr. Cosmopoulos scream in agony. His death was quick, his body incinerated on the auditorium stage.

There was an awed silence from the audience. Even the reverend couldn't summon a verse. She was pale when the angel turned back to Ferris, inviting his judgment.

Ferris pointed to Blake Patterson. "He was kind."

Blake's relief was tangible, although his uncertainty was still clear as one angel came to stand before him. That angel caught Blake's face in his hands, bent and kissed his brow.

When the angel moved away, a port wine kiss glowed red on Blake's forehead, one much like the mark on the Oracle's brow. He smiled in obvious relief, and touched it with a tentative finger.

Then the angels got down to business. Theodora watched them urge the reverend aside. Truly, they were the main event on this night. She saw them reach down to the shades from the netherzones, pull them into the light, and kiss their cheeks. She saw them draw the gathered shades onto the stage.

Each shade walked straighter when he or she left the angelic embrace, each stood taller, the eyes of each shone with a new bright sparkle. It took Theodora a moment to realize that each and every one had been healed with the angelic touch.

A circle of angels formed on the stage, six or eight of the celestial host laying their hands upon everyone who came to them in joy and supplication. It was hard to be sure of their numbers because of the blindingly white light. She could barely discern Armand in the midst of the luminous company.

The rest of the angels faced outward, turning their power upon the building itself. Theodora enjoyed hearing its supports crack. She was glad to see the Institute destroyed due to the angels' presence. There was a lump in her throat, but she couldn't just stand aside.

No, she had to be a part of this goodness.

Theodora reached down to help the shades climb to the stage. "Hurry," she said to each shade as she took his or her hand. "You don't know how long they'll stay. Give me your hand."

XX

Tupperman and Joachim were south of Gotham with their party of shades and former circus employees when the sky lit with astonishing brilliance. The light was white, blinding in its intensity, illuminating the decrepit rail yard and abandoned tracks with painful clarity.

But the light didn't come from the sun. Not even from the moon. It wasn't from some man-made source either.

No, it was the light of the angels.

The light of merciless truth.

The light of redemption.

It touched the edges of the broken buildings, it ran along the rail tracks. It turned the deadened trees to silver, and heated the top of Tupperman's head. He looked up and had to squint at the ferocious white of the angelic glory. The light fell, like so many fireworks, white lights descending in numbers beyond count.

The entire host, then.

"Sweet Jesus," Joachim whispered beside him. The shorter man crossed himself and fell to his knees.

Tupperman glanced back at the shades who followed them. Some stared upward, rapt. Others covered their faces. Many were on their knees and more than a few were praying, their lips moving but little sound coming forth. No matter what they had borne, they recognized a fundamental truth of the universe.

Tupperman's heart was pounding, his palms sweating. His body seemed to recognize that he would soon have no use for it. He'd waited for this moment for so long, ever since he had shed his own wings. He'd had moments when he'd believed it would never come. He'd had doubt, but mostly he'd had faith. And a measure of impatience, not unlike Armand's.

But the time had come. And though it came to him in the last place he'd expected, he was ready.

He didn't want the angels to descend anywhere. He wanted to summon them to this very spot, to do their work with this very group of people. Tupperman could think of none more deserving.

He stepped forward proudly, ready to reclaim his rightful place in the chorus, ready to ensure that the righteous were rewarded. He squared his shoulders and threw his head back, closing his eyes against the angels' glory, and he sang.

Tupperman sang, a hoarse approximation of the splendor with which he had once sung, but his heart was in every syllable. He could see the veins in his eyelids, brilliant red suffusing his vision, a keen reminder of the flesh and blood he had volunteered to don.

Tupperman sang an ancient hymn of praise, the hymn of the angels, its words long lost to humanity. The sound of it on his own lips was sweet beyond measure.

He tasted the words. He breathed the blessing. He tasted the exultation of the divine. His body responded to the music of his own voice, his blood pumping in rhythm, every sinew and synapse leaping in time. Tupperman raised his hands and sang with all his heart and soul.

And the angels came to him. He heard the rustle of their feathers. He heard the wind in their wings. Mostly he heard their glorious rich voices, joining his song. He felt a joy he had almost forgotten and welcomed the company of his fellows once again.

ON THE tundra, far to the north, an angel bent to embrace a small girl, a small girl who extended her hands to him in complete trust. He kissed her cheeks, one after the other, then her brow. His radiance flooded the empty land, illuminated the trepidation in the features of the older woman who held fast to the child.

The angel smiled, slid his fingers down the child's left arm. He kissed the forehead of the child, then of the woman who began to weep silently.

When he left to rejoin the chorus, the little girl had no deformity, no tattoo. But both woman and child had a burning kiss upon their brow, a mark of angelic favor.

And their hearts were singing.

IN THE plains far from Chicago, a dozen angels descended upon an area that looked to be unoccupied. Their light coaxed first one child, then an entire group of children and young adults from the darkness. A former missile silo was their abode, hidden from the eyes of the Republic but not from the eyes of the divine.

Here again, the angels set to the business of healing,

their song creating an answering rhythm in the blood of the astonished recipients.

TUPPERMAN SANG as the white glory of the host surrounded him and he wept. The angels landed all around him, their feet barely touching the earth. Their wings arched high overhead and they dimmed their light slightly. He opened his eyes to see one bend over Marianna, a trapeze artist with extra toes. Her eyes were wide with astonishment as the angel reached for her. She seemed to be too awed to move.

Tupperman sang as the angel caught Marianna's face in his hands, as he kissed her cheeks in turn. Tupperman sang and he watched as the angel moved with that leisurely grace he recalled, that ease of movement that seemed in defiance of gravity and all mortal restraints.

The angel lifted Marianna's foot with consummate care. He slid his hand across her toes, his smile filled with gentle kindness. And when his hand was passed, the foot was normal.

Marianna gasped, then felt her foot with both hands, astounded. When she stammered her thanks, the angel only extended his hand.

Trembling, she entrusted her other foot to his touch.

By the time the angel reached for her tattoo, Marianna was praying and crying. She kissed his feet when he was done and he bent to kiss the back of her head.

When she stood, she came to Tupperman's side, still quivering, and lifted her voice to join his song of praise. Tupperman watched the angels heal on all sides, he heard the chorus grow ever stronger. Although each angelic gesture seemed to occur with consummate slowness, the healing of the shades in Joachim's company passed in a blur of triumphant faces. The shades took on a radiance of their own, although it couldn't rival that of the angels.

Tupperman wasn't sure how much time had passed when a pair of angels turned to him. They smiled their smiles of knowing compassion and each offered a hand to him.

"Come, brother."

He heard the words in his thoughts, just as once he had heard the words and thoughts of all his fellows.

"You're going, aren't you?" Joachim said beside him. "Doesn't that just figure? Give us a break, then bail before the hard work is done. Change doesn't come easy, you know."

Tupperman turned to the smaller man, intending to argue his own case, but the desolation in Joachim's eyes silenced him.

"If you go, it will just happen again," Joachim said bitterly. "If you abandon us now, there will be nothing gained over the long term. This will just be an interlude, not a change."

"You're too cynical," Tupperman said gently, but his heart recognized the truth in Joachim's words. Could he leave the task half-done, even if his own quest was complete?

Joachim scoffed and turned away. "I know men. I know how it will be." Disappointment rang in his words. He waved dismissively. "But go. We'll do what we have to. We'll survive. Somehow." He swallowed and took the hand of one of the former shades, then forced a smile. "At least, we're in better shape than we were before. Thanks for that."

The angels eased closer and Tupperman saw the ex-

.tended hand of one. He couldn't look away from Joachim, though, because he knew the other man spoke out of fear.

And that he was probably right.

"Come, Turiel. Your labor is done."

Turiel. It was Tupperman's angelic name, one he hadn't heard in decades. It meant "rock of God."

"The task is not done," Tupperman said to the angels.

"But the mission you chose to accept is complete."

"We can't go," Tupperman said, his gaze fixed on Joachim. "We have to finish the whole job. Joachim's right."

"You cannot know the mind of the divine. In the fullness of time, there is a plan."

"And who's to say that my decision isn't part of that plan?" Tupperman challenged.

The angels stirred in agitation, but the one on Tupperman's right watched him with avid interest. He couldn't hear the thoughts that flew between them anymore, but he could almost see the crackle of electricity. He knew they were debating his idea, weighing it, deciding for or against. The choice would be made in the blink of an eye, all possibilities explored.

"You cannot accomplish this alone, Turiel," said the one on the left.

"No." Tupperman challenged the angels, his decision made. "No, I can't. But that doesn't change that Joachim is right. It won't be easy to turn the Republic around, to make a change for the better. He knows more of men than we do. You should volunteer, as well." Tupperman raised his voice. "All of you should volunteer! We need every angel we can get in this sphere. Choose!"

There was a silence then, a silence so profound that Tupperman feared they would reject his suggestion. The air snapped with blue electricity, indicative of the debate. Tupperman feared his fellows would leave and abandon him in this sphere forever.

Well, if they did, he'd try to do it alone. He knew where there were others, and he guessed that all of them wouldn't choose to depart on this night. He'd pull it together somehow, and make a difference that would last the duration.

He'd stay.

He sensed that the angels were aware of his decision for something changed in the moment that he chose. The rail yard seemed to reverberate in silence, as if time itself had stopped. Tupperman saw Joachim swallow, saw Marianna lift her hands to her lips. The entire group watched and waited.

Then the angel on Tupperman's right smiled. He knelt before his partner and bowed his head. Not a sound was uttered, not a word, the company fully aware of the choice made.

Tupperman held his breath as the left angel lifted his hand, one finger extended. That angel hesitated only a fraction of a second, then he touched his finger to the root of the other angel's wing.

No matter how many times Tupperman witnessed the surgery, it still shook him to his marrow. He forced himself to watch every time, willed himself not to blink. He caught Joachim's shoulder in his hand, hoping to give that man strength to watch.

Light spilled as the wing was cut free and the wounded angel wailed in pain, the first pain he had ever endured. The entire company of angels vibrated at that cry, as if they all had felt the severing.

They then briskly separated into pairs, one dropping before the other. The air was filled with shouts of pain, falling feathers, and spilling light. The feathers shone for a few moments where they fell on the ground, gleaming and bright until they gradually faded and disappeared. Tupperman could have been standing knee-deep in stardust. There was the smell of searing flesh as the wounds were closed, then the angels regrouped for the next volunteers.

They were *all* shedding their wings. Tupperman's heart thundered at the generosity of their gift, of the power they would have collectively.

The dream of a heaven on earth could be realized.

Simply because he had asked for their aid.

It was a miracle.

"Sweet Jesus," Joachim whispered, horror and wonder mingled in his tone. He was shaking beneath Tupperman's grip, but his eyes were wide open.

"Look up," Tupperman instructed, his own throat tight with emotion. "Look up at what we have wrought."

The sky was thick with falling stars.

ARMAND WATCHED Baraqiel ascend to the heavens, relief flooding through him that his old comrade would be healed and would survive. The surgeon came to him next, surrounding him in a halo of luminescence, but Armand looked back.

He saw Theodora, her heart in her eyes, and he knew where he wanted to be.

He knew that she had pushed Max, that she had ensured the success of his mission and his ability to return heavenward. He knew she had done it without any prospect of reward.

And he knew then just what he wanted to do with the rest of his existence.

He wanted to do something to make a difference.

He wanted to do something he believed in.

The surgeon embraced him, and drew him up, but Armand resisted. "I would remain," he said and felt the surgeon's surprise.

"You do not have to do so. You do not need to make such a sacrifice. Your task is fulfilled."

"But I would choose it. I would stay. The work of rebuilding this world has only just begun. I would be a part of it."

The surgeon paused and Armand felt as if his reason was being explored. He sensed also that something else had occurred, that the angel had been distracted by some tidings.

Then the surgeon smiled at him. *"You are not the first to make this choice, nor will you be the last,"* ceded the surgeon. *"If you stay, you may have the confidence of knowing that many of our kind will join you."*

"This realm has need of all the help we can supply."

"There is no recourse, Armaros. What you choose now will be your choice for the duration."

"I know. I beg of you to give me permission to stay."

He felt his cheeks burn with light and his heart surged with the conviction that his request had been fulfilled.

It was not within the power of the angels to stand in the course of love. Love governed all they did, and they stood aside rather than block its path.

And love was the reason Armand would stay with Theodora.

* * *

THE ORACLE was a conduit. She stood in the middle of the
stage with her arms held high, her raiment luminous white
and her body shooting sparks. There was electricity in the
air, a thrum of power that made the hair stand up all over
Theodora's body. She didn't want to blink lest she miss
something.

Because she knew she would remember this moment for
the rest of her life.

Her ears were ringing from the triumphant chorus. The
shades took up the hymn of the angels, adding their voices
to the sound. The building was crumbling on all sides. The
night sky above was thick with stars, although their light
was dimmed as the angels began to ascend. They rose like
a sun leaving the earth behind, the shadows seeming deeper
in their absence.

It was when she scanned the darkness on the stage that
Theodora saw that one figure remained behind.

Armand turned and offered his hand to her. She ran across
the stage, jubilant as he swung her high into his arms.

"But why?" she whispered, unable to believe that he had
stayed.

He smiled slowly, his eyes dancing as he surveyed her.
"Because I love you, and because I intend to act upon my
determination to make a difference."

The angels sang more loudly then, and their light became
even brighter. Armand held Theodora tightly and pointed
upward, up to the center of their luminosity.

She saw one angel separate from the rest, one who looked
familiar.

"Baraqiel," Armand whispered as the angel raised his

hands. He spread his fingers and threw out his hands, a thousand blue sparks erupting from his fingertips.

Theodora jumped as the identification bead in the back of her neck popped. Armand's broke as well, bursting from the skin and exploding as it fell to the ground. There was a tiny bit of blood on his neck and on hers, and only a twinge of pain.

Then lightning bolts flashed all around them. Armand's palm shorted and blew, the crack of its destruction echoing hundreds of times throughout the auditorium. She saw the reverend's palm light briefly in flames, O'Donohue's erupt blue, the Oracle's palm crackle and burn. Glass identification beads bounced across the floor and exploded, the shards disappearing into oblivion.

And with one last jubilant chorus, the angels rose to the heavens.

"We're all free," Theodora whispered in amazement.

Through the broken roof, the clear night sky was visible. It was abruptly filled with falling stars, their streams of light cascading toward the earth. There were so many falling stars that their brightness hid the night sky itself.

"A miracle," the reverend declared and Armand chuckled.

"They're staying," he whispered to Theodora, triumph in his voice. "Each falling star is an angel who has chosen to make the sacrifice of his wings."

"That many?" Theodora hung on to Armand.

"We'll have an army to save the world," O'Donohue said with satisfaction from close proximity. "It's all we need, and so much more."

He and Armand exchanged one of those knowing smiles, one that confirmed Theodora's suspicions and gave her even greater hope.

"Your children are healed," O'Donohue murmured to Theodora. "The angels told me so."

Before Theodora could respond, she heard the Oracle gasp. The three of them pivoted as one. Delilah's water had broken, and it spread across the stage. O'Donohue strode to her side to help her, as did Blake Patterson. Rafe caught her up in his arms as the shades in the auditorium began to cheer.

"A new beginning," Armand whispered to Theodora, then bent to kiss her once more.

She couldn't argue with that.

"Look over yonder, the sun blowed up."
—Anonymous civilian observer of Trinity Test
New Mexico, July 16, 1945, 05:30

"We didn't know what to expect, except that we were to wear the sunglasses issued to us. At 05:29, a light streaked across the sky. Later I learned that this was a rocket, indicating the beginning of the one minute countdown—at the time, I thought it was a falling star. Then suddenly, the entire world was illuminated with a brilliant light, whiter and brighter than anything I had ever seen before. Later, there was the sound of the explosion and the mushroom cloud, but I never forgot that blinding white light. It was as if the sun had fallen to earth—no, it was as if earth had been touched with the fire of the angels."
—Anonymous serviceman and observer
of Trinity Test
New Mexico, July 16, 1945

How art thou fallen from heaven, O Lucifer, son of the morning! How are thou cut down to the ground, which didst weaken the nations!

For thou has said in thine heart: "I will ascend to heaven, I will exalt my throne above the stars of God: I will sit also upon the mount of the congregation, in the sides of the north; I will ascend above the heights of the clouds, I will be like the most High."

Yet thou shalt be brought down to hell, to the sides of the pit.

They that see thee shall narrowly look upon thee, and consider thee, saying, "Is this the man that made

*the earth to tremble, that did shake kingdoms; that
made the world as a wilderness and destroyed the cities thereof; that opened not the house of prisoners?"*
                                    —Isaiah 14:12–17

Lilia and Montgomery reached Gotham without incident. It was midnight on Wednesday when they rode into the city in silence. There were only the stars above and the headlight on the bike lighting their path.

Montgomery shivered at the howls of the wolves.

"Wolf telegraph," Lil muttered. "Dinner is served."

They both had a sense of urgency, and Lilia was surprised to find herself missing the information fix from her palm. She had no idea what had happened in the world since their departure from Nouveau Mont Royal, but she had a feeling they were missing something big.

She was sure of it when Montgomery turned into Rockefeller Plaza. She'd first come to this place almost exactly a year before and it wasn't one of her favorite places in the world. She turned up the audio on her helm, but heard only the bike, the wolves, and the silence of the city.

It still seemed to be sentient.

She shivered. "Why here?" she asked Montgomery, holding tightly to him.

"Instinct," he said, and she guessed that he wasn't telling her everything.

Again.

But he would, in time. She trusted him.

She caught her breath at the glimpse of a shadow beneath that golden statue at the far end of the plaza. It was a statue of Prometheus, she remembered that, depicting his flight from the heavens as he stole the gift of fire to bring it to mortals.

Montgomery raced the bike toward the statue, more cavalier than was his usual style. He skidded the tires as he halted at the top of the steps. A patch of silvery fog swirled above the hollow that had been a pool, its movement desultory. Lilia caught her breath as the figure standing on the lip of the pool turned to look at them.

He was naked, black, his large wings arching high over his back. He wasn't insubstantial, though, but looked both solid and real. His eyes shone with hatred, gleaming like obsidian as he glared at them.

"So close," he hissed, his words slithering through the filters on Lilia's helm. He held up one hand, his finger and thumb an increment apart. "So close."

"But not close enough," Montgomery said. "Thank God."

Lucifer spat in their direction, then his manifestation faded abruptly. He was there, exuding antagonism. A blink of an eye later, he was fading into an insubstantial and dark mist.

And then he was gone, the silvery fog gone with him.

Lilia had time to read the inscription again.

PROMETHEUS, TEACHER IN EVERY ART, BROUGHT THE FIRE TO EARTH THAT HATH PROVEN TO MORTALS A MEANS TO MIGHTY ENDS.

There was a rumble in the earth, like a passing subway train. Lilia looked around, seeking its source but couldn't see it. The statue itself seemed to tremble, then all of the gilt that adorned it cracked. The gold crumbled from the statue of Prometheus, spreading like gold dust on the ground.

The wolves howled.

The wind swirled and cast the golden flakes away.

And the night sky lit as thousands of stars began to fall.

Montgomery stared upward and Lilia had to know what he was thinking. She reached and opened the dark filter on his helm, then saw his rare smile.

"More angels taking flesh?"

"A veritable host," he agreed with satisfaction, his gaze scanning the sky. "We need to rebuild the gene pool."

"Why now?"

"Because it's a new dawn for the Republic, Lil."

"How so?"

"The angels are descending in force, healing shades, opening netherzones, destroying palms and identification beads."

"You knew!"

"I hoped."

Lilia sighed. "And we missed the big finish. Here we were in Gotham when all this was going down."

"We didn't miss the show." He pointed back to the statue. "We stood witness to the most important part."

She saw the conviction in his eyes, the joy that he couldn't contain, and found herself smiling. "This is a pretty crummy place for a celebration, Montgomery, given that we can't get naked without dying in the act."

He laughed then, the sound making her own heart leap. "You're right, Lil. Let's get out of here. The show's over, anyway."

from *The Republican Record*
Tuesday, November 2, 2100
Evening Edition

Landslide Victory for O'Donohue

NEW D.C.—Presidential candidate Thomas O'Donohue accepted congratulations on his election as president tonight, as polls across the nation reported overwhelming support for the candidate. Even early results indicate that O'Donohue will carry most of the popular vote, as well as a majority in the electoral college.

Mr. O'Donohue was clearly pleased at his victory party this evening, which began earlier than anyone might have anticipated. "It's a great day for the Republic," he said. "And a wonderful endorsement. I'm thrilled to have such a vote of confidence from the citizens of the Republic, and am excited to have such support as we move to integrate those who have been called shades into the general population. This is the beginning of a bright new future for everyone in the Republic."

Mr. O'Donohue confirmed his intent to present a bill to the house and the congress immediately to eliminate the Institute for Radiation Studies and the Society of Nuclear Darwinists. The drug patents held by both will become the property of the citizens of the Republic, and the files of both will be incorporated into the Library of Congress and made available for public examination as soon as possible. Mr. O'Donohue has declared that confronting the past is the first step to accepting it, and making change.

Reverend Billie Joe Estevez, also in attendance at the celebration for the candidate she endorsed, was similarly pleased. "*'And it shall come to pass in the day that the Lord shall give rest from thy sorrow, and from thy fear, and from the hard bondage wherein thou wast made to serve,'*" said the reverend, choosing a biblical quote for the moment even as she strained to be heard over the celebration. "*'The whole earth is at rest, and is quiet; they break forth into singing.'*"

The Oracle also extended her congratulations to Mr. O'Donohue, arriving in person at his celebration with her Consort and their recently born son. Mr. O'Donohue expressed delight when told that the child had been named Thomas in his honor, and agreed to be a godfather to the child.

The streets of New D.C. are filled with jubilant shades on this night and there is a party atmosphere in this city. Citizens and norms are embracing openly with this news, and there is indeed singing in many areas of the capital.

Other articles in this edition:

- <u>Resource-sharing Treaty</u> in final negotiation with Middle East
- <u>Scientists Point to Quality Control Issue</u>—Attempts to explain mass simultaneous malfunction of palms and identification beads continue
- <u>The Blackstone Legacy</u>—his illegitimate children identified, found, and reunited

AUTHOR'S NOTE

If you are interested in the history of nuclear weapons and research, I recommend these two very readable volumes: *Before the Fallout: From Marie Curie to Hiroshima* by Diana Preston (Walker & Co., 2005) and *The Plutonium Files: America's Secret Medical Experiments in the Cold War* by Eileen Welsome (The Dial Press, 1999).

Truth is indeed stranger than fiction.

TOR
ROMANCE

Believe that love is magic.